DAWN OF THE AFTER DAYS

HEAVEN'S DARK SOLDIERS
BOOK FOUR

STEVE GILMORE

LIQUID MIND PUBLISHING

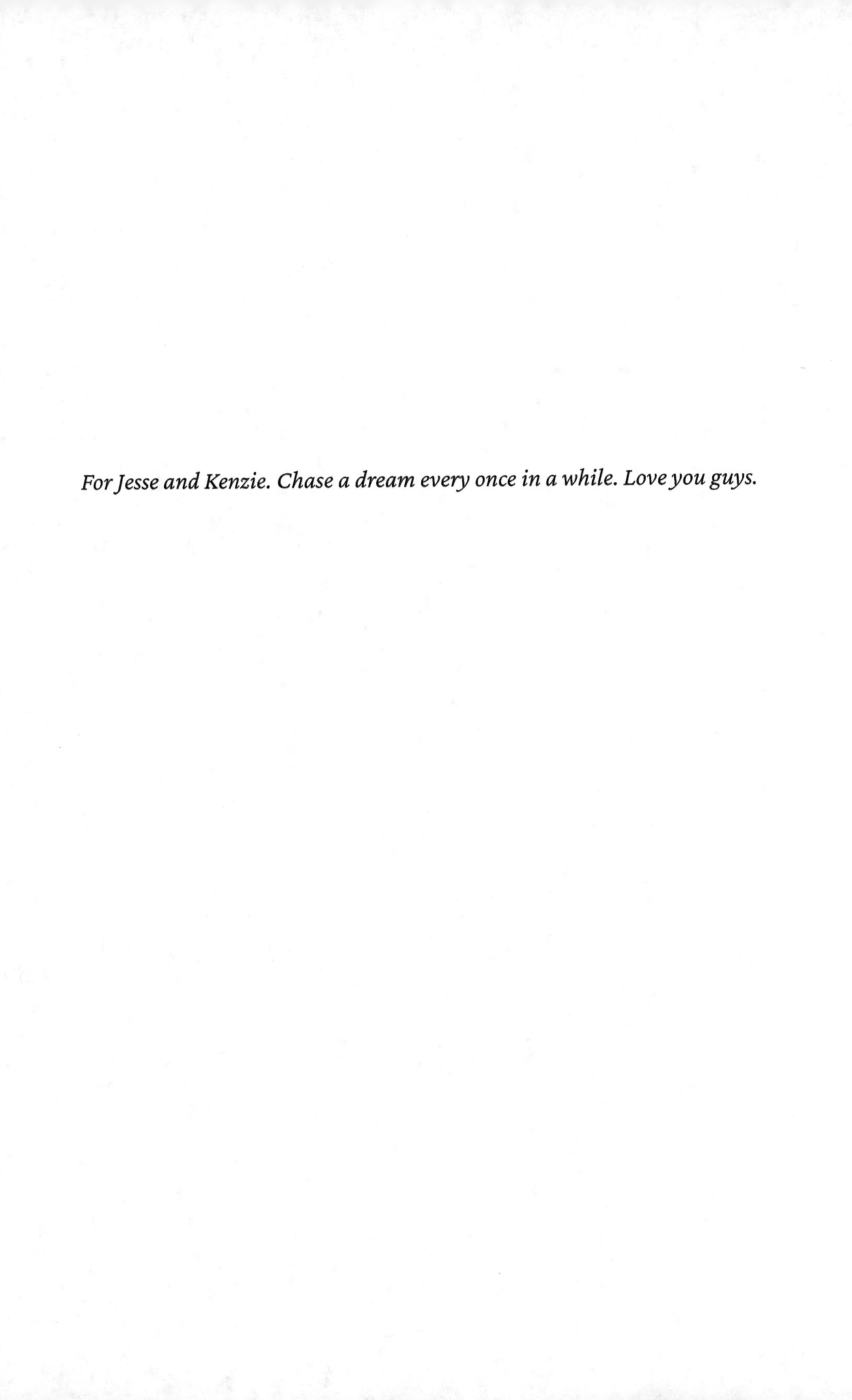

For Jesse and Kenzie. Chase a dream every once in a while. Love you guys.

MORE FROM STEVE GILMORE

Heaven's Dark Soldiers

Rise of the Giants

Wrath of the Fallen

Rage of the Heavens

Dawn of the After Days

Ride of the Horseman

Sign up for Steve's newsletter for updates on deals and new releases!

https://liquidmind.media/steve-gilmore-newsletter-sign-up-1

And when it fell upon the Earth, I saw how the Earth was swallowed up in a great abyss, and mountains were suspended on mountains, and hills sank down upon hills, and tall trees were torn up by their roots, and were thrown down, and sank into the abyss.

- The Lost Book of Enoch

PROLOGUE

IT IS SAID that life is the sum total of all our choices.

But that can't be true. Can it?

Does every single choice we ever make *really* count in the grander scheme? If so, I'd like a couple of do-overs. Maybe a couple, couple depending on the decade.

It is also said that the decision *not* to make a choice is a choice in and of itself.

Now that can't be right.

How can anyone be held accountable for the consequences of a particular choice they consciously decided not to make?

It's not fair.

Total crap.

Paradoxical, even.

I'd go so far to say that choices *not* made are the metaphorical equivalent of light beer. They're kind of like the real thing, but watered down to where they don't actually count. And they taste like bottled piss.

Maybe it's the same with choices.

Not the tasting like piss part, but the part about them not really counting if you don't make them.

Or maybe it's the complete opposite. Maybe every time you consciously decide *not* to make a choice, you unconsciously detract from your cosmic ability to make choices in the first place. Is there somebody out there keeping track? That's a horrible thought. Almost as horrible as the combined concepts of light beer and bottled piss.

But I digress.

The world was about to become exceptionally complicated. And unlike the days when the toughest choice to make was what to cook for dinner or where to stop for gas on the way home from work, there were now other factors at play.

Factors that challenged the status quo.

Things like angels.

And giants.

And unnatural half-bred beasties.

And although mankind didn't know it yet, everything was about to change. The esoteric veil separating humans from all the things that go bump in the night was about to be lifted in the most fantastical and terrifying of ways.

The arcane was about to become mainstream.

The hidden revealed.

For mankind no longer enjoyed the divine protection afforded by their great creator. They were about to experience some tough love on a global scale as God decreed that angel, human, and all things in between would learn to coexist on Earth. Or die trying.

A new world order was about to take shape, and for the first time in history, humans might not find themselves at the top of the pecking order. Or maybe they would. Either way, choosing or not choosing one's own destiny was not so much a luxury anymore. It was more of a survival strategy.

Because before you can learn how to live in an evolving landscape dominated by gods and monsters, you must first learn a more fundamental lesson. How to survive.

In life, I was a soldier. An elite product of the U.S. military. Upon death, I became something else. No longer human but not quite an angel. Conceived of mankind, but no longer part of it. Something blessed and cursed with the power of God's wrath. A warrior of the light that existed in the shadows.

My name is Dean Robinson.

I am — to maintain the Balance.

If such a thing existed anymore.

I

I WAS ENJOYING MY BEER.

It was perfect in every way.

The perfect ratio of grain, hops, yeast, and water.

Perfectly hand crafted to form a delectable, perfect golden ale.

Served at the perfect chilly temperature in a pint glass with the perfect frothy head on top.

And as the first sip graced my lips, it provided the perfect euphoric buzz.

Although everything else was a bit of a disaster, my beer was perfect.

And I was enjoying it. Very much so.

Right up until a chubby eight-foot oaf with a man bun and a god-awful Hawaiian shirt slammed into my back, and my coveted cup of liquid happiness sprayed all over the goddamn bar. It must have been something about the look on my face because before I could yell, 'Son of a bitch!' at the top of my lungs, the mini-giant we fondly referred to as Cosmic Charlie had already put several feet between us and showed no sign of stopping as he scampered toward the Reliquary with a massive rectangular crate propped on his shoulder.

"My bad, Deano!" the big galoot called out as I was snapped from my daydream of beer-induced nirvana and was back in the Quartermaster trying my best to ignore the general calamity that bustled around me. "Put it on my tab, dude!"

I grumbled something snide under my breath as Cooper Rayfield chuckled and slid another beer across the bar, quickly wiping up the mess. "Don't mind, Charlie, hoss," said the uncanny redneck archer with a thick Southern drawl. "He's just trying to be helpful is all."

Helpful. Right. As if anybody could be *helpful* right now, given the state of things.

I mean, hell, it was only a few short hours ago when *God*, also known as Ethan Roy, stepped into the middle of our apocalyptic spat with Lucifer and saved mankind from certain demise. Life was good for a solid couple of minutes. Then everything got complicated.

Astoundingly complicated.

So complicated that it would fry your brain if you tried to make sense out of it.

How, you ask?

Well, in the process of snuffing out Lew's misguided angel rebellion, Ethan concluded that a draconian change to his parenting style was in order. He summarily deported all the angels to Earth in one fell swoop. And shortly thereafter, he disbanded the Deacons, hence removing the arcane barrier between humans and their unnatural cousins, the nephilim.

In Ethan's mind, it was time for all his kids, regardless of species or bloodline, to get their shit together. And what better way to do that than to stick everybody on the same playground and force them to get along? Or take each other's lunch money. Or engage in a spirited game of dodgeball that had the potential to cause global genocide. You know, kid stuff.

And the best part of this grand experiment in cohabitation was that although he retired *most* of the Deacons from active duty, Ethan apparently still had plans for me, Stephen, and Abernethy. What those plans were was yet to be revealed.

At any rate, as we waited with bated breath for the almighty Apothecary to convene the first and only clandestine interdimensional peace conference before he rang the recess bell, a collective feeling of impending doom seemed to hang over the globe like the sword of Damocles.

As all that played through my mind on a recurring loop, I shook my head as Charlie vanished through the Reliquary doors, holding a crate the size of a small car. "What the hell is he carrying, anyway?"

"Plutonium," Roy MacCawill muttered, grabbing the beer Coop just poured for me and draining it in a single gulp.

"That was my beer," I protested.

The six-foot-three unnatural bounty hunter grinned a wolfish grin as he ran a hand through his salt and pepper goatee. "I know."

Shaking my head again, I called him an asshole a couple times for good measure as Coop turned up the volume on one of the countless tVs lining the wall above the bar displaying various images of pyramids floating over major cities.

"Aliens and *unnatural* disasters!" the newscaster yelled in a feverish tone. "Buzz Shea here, folks. And today's *buzz*? Flying pyramids! What the hell are they? And what are they doing hovering over every major city across the entire planet? The White House is telling us not to panic as these so-called *space pyramids* are *not* extraterrestrial and we are *not* being invaded. Instead, they're part of an elaborate weather monitoring system."

I chuckled. "A *weather monitoring system*. Seriously?"

"Yes, seriously," the reporter said as he flailed his arms around. "And what's with all the earthquakes rumbling through the country? Is everything OK? Are we seeing the beginning of the *end times*? Can somebody get me a goddamn drink? Stay tuned for a live interview with renowned Ancient Astronaut theorist, Georgio..."

"Turn it off," I grumbled. "I can't take any more of that guy. And I always feel like he's listening to me somehow. It's creepy."

"I hear ya, hoss," Coop said as he slid a fresh beer in front of me and all the tV screens went blank with a wave of his hand. "Sometimes I think that Buzz Shea character could talk the legs off a chair. And you know what's really funny?"

"What's that, Coop?"

"I bet that jack wagon doesn't know a widget from a whangdoodle."

Thinking that was the best Cooperism I'd ever heard, I turned to MacCawill. "Did you say Charlie was carrying *plutonium*?"

He nodded. "Yup. That's all that's left of the stuff I had stashed at my summer place on the moon."

"You have a summer place on the moon?"

"Of course."

"The one in space."

Pulling a fresh stogie from somewhere within his worn leather duster, he grinned again. "Doesn't everybody?"

Making the mental note that I wasn't in the mood for his bullshit at the moment, I said, "What's the plutonium for?"

"Rooster needed it. He said something about boosting the output of the Contraption. He's added a whole new wing of tech to the Reliquary to try to figure out the extent of the damage to the Earth's core."

"Wait, are you saying Rooster has a nuclear reactor? When did that happen? And who the hell thought that was a good idea?"

"Boys and their toys," Billy said with her goofy Nordic accent as she pulled up next to me and blew a puff of smoke in my face before grabbing my new beer and shot-gunning it. Turning the empty pint glass upside down, she placed in on the bar and winked at Coop. "Thanks, handsome. That hit the spot."

Muttering something else of a snide nature under my breath, I was about to tell our resident ivory-haired she-dragon to piss off when Doc Kelly pulled up. "Hey, guys," she said. "Anything new?"

"No," I grumbled. "Nothing's new. *Space pyramids* are popping up everywhere. The government's telling everybody that everything's fine, so naturally, people are completely losing their shit. And we're sitting here with our thumb up our collective ass."

"Steady now, laddie boy," Abernethy said, appearing from the Reliquary door just in time to hear me whining. "There's a plan in motion. We just need to exercise some wee patience."

I groaned. "Patience. And what happens when the angels inside those pyramids decide to come out and play? Or the military gets antsy and starts lobbing nukes at them. Or the giants start eating their way up the west coast again."

"They won't."

"And why not?"

"Because Ethan's directed it. There's a truce in place. Nothing happens until the parley."

"Right, the parley. And when is God's interdimensional peace summit supposed to happen?"

"Soon."

"Soon, huh?"

"Aye, soon."

"You don't know, do you?"

He scowled. "Nae, I do not. But, in the meantime—"

"In the meantime," I said before chugging my latest beer and placing the empty pint on the bar. "I'm gonna take a walk."

Jumping to my feet, I headed toward the Quartermaster's mighty front door as Erin joined me. "Want some company?"

"Sure. As long as it's not MacCawill, Charlie, Billy, Coop, Rooster, Bobby, Caveman, Duncan, Owen, Stephen, or Abernethy. *Especially* Abernethy."

"Anyone else?"

"*Everyone* else, actually. Except for you. And maybe Ziggy. I like Ziggy. Feel like we have a real connection."

She smiled. "So, my competition is a robot made from a beer keg. You really know how to make a girl feel good."

I smiled back. "It's a full-time job, Doc."

Pulling open the ginormous wooden door and crossing the threshold, we pierced the warm veil of primal energy that separated the QM from the outside world, and within a single second, we were standing on Westland Avenue in Boston's Back Bay. There was an uncharacteristic chill to the summer day, but it was still gorgeous as the mid-morning sun seemed to dance on Erin's olive skin and auburn hair. Pulling a windbreaker over her royal blue tank top, she carefully tucked one of her signature Heckler & Koch pistols into the waist of her jeans as I gazed into her dark brown eyes for a long moment.

"Beautiful day," she said as we both looked up to find a pristine blue sky without a cloud in it. But unfortunately, the sky was by no means empty. Hovering above the towering Prudential Building just a couple blocks to the north was a dark metal pyramid the size of several football fields. It cast an ominous shadow over most of the city.

And despite the fact it was beyond terrifying to see such a thing floating in the air with no indication of propulsion to explain how it was hovering there to begin with, it was also somewhat majestic. To use the word colossal wouldn't begin to describe the sheer size and grandeur of the mind-blowing structure. It was huge. So huge that it could conceivably contain an entire city the size of Boston inside its polished walls that glinted and gleamed in the sunlight like a giant disco ball.

Somewhat enamored with the displaced heavenly structure, Erin and I stood on the sidewalk, staring at it as passersby darted throughout the maze of abandoned cars that filled the streets in complete and utter panic. "It's mesmerizing," Doc said.

I nodded. "It is. You should have seen Tenth Heaven. Whole land-scape full of those things in different configurations. Some on the ground. Some stacked on top of each other forming sky scrapers. Some floating in the air like that one. It was insane."

"Heaven's full of pyramids?"

"Yup. Bobby said something about how tetrahedrons represent the perfect symmetry between nature and technology. It's apparently how they build everything. They call them lodestones."

"Lodestones," she muttered. "What are they made of?"

"Barzel. The metal of Heaven."

"It's exquisite."

"And virtually indestructible. How many angels do you think are in one of those things?"

"More than enough to kick your sorry ass, schmendrick," replied a gruff voice that I hadn't heard in a while. "But that's not saying much, now is it?"

Spinning around to find a familiar crotchety figure perched on a foldout chair and puffing on a pipe, I just shook my head. "Fred Binkowicz. You're back. Oh, good."

"Don't sound so excited."

"I'm not. It's called sarcasm."

He just glared at me. "I don't think you're funny, schmendrick."

"I'm so disappointed to hear that, Fred. I really am. Where've you been, anyway?"

"Where I've been is none of your business. But it looks like I got back just in time to watch you end the world. Congrats on that, by the way."

Holding out her hand, Doc said, "Hi, we haven't met. I'm Erin."

"Yeah, yeah," Binkowicz muttered, begrudgingly shaking hands. "I know who you are."

"Fred here is a prophet," I said to Doc. "So, in addition to being a cantankerous jackass, he *knows* things. Or maybe he doesn't. Maybe he's just a cantankerous jackass."

Shooting me an icy glare, he said nothing as he leaned back on the foldout chair and sucked on his pipe.

I smiled. "Okay, good talk. Always a pleasure. Yours, not mine. And welcome back from wherever the hell you were. We all missed you terribly."

Leaving Binkowicz to go on about his business of being a snarky bastard, Doc and I made our way across the street through a small but growing crowd of frantic people and ducked into an alley that cut between two sizable brownstones.

"So," she said as a cool summer breeze blew through the dank space, assaulting my nostrils with the overpowering stench pouring out of the dumpster ahead. "You doing OK?"

"Me? Yeah, I'm good."

"You sure?"

"Yup. Why?"

"Well, it just seems like you're a little wound up. I mean, more so than usual."

I chuckled. "Well, I can't imagine why, Doc. It's not like anything earth-shatteringly insane happened in the past few days. Except for the world about to end thing. And the whole Lucifer thing. Then there was the meeting God thing. Then he did the kicking all the angels out of Heaven thing. And then there was the—"

"You know what I mean."

I chuckled again. "I know what you mean."

"So, are you good?"

"I'm fine. Just trying to wrap my head around what's about to happen, I guess."

"I understand. It's a lot."

Kicking an empty beer can out of my path, I said, "And I feel like we should be doing something."

"Doing what?"

"I don't know. Something. Anything."

She sighed. "You have no patience at all, do you?"

"None whatsoever."

"Well, I don't think *God* works according to your schedule, so you better relax before you drive yourself nuts. What's he like, anyway?"

"Who?"

"God."

"Well, first off, he prefers to be called Ethan. Which I find incredibly odd. And he apparently has an affinity for flannel shirts and books. Make of that what you will."

"And?"

"And he's, ah, okay, I guess."

"Okay?"

"Yeah, sort of."

"God is *sort of* okay. Really?"

"No, not really. If I'm being honest, he's a dick. A real snarky jackass that seems to get a legitimate kick out of always being right and not giving a shit about what other people think of him. But there's something about the bastard that makes you want to like him, anyway. It's infuriating."

"So, he's a sarcastic egomaniac that likes to run his mouth but is also endearing to the point where you kind of love him."

"Yeah, that's about right."

She grinned ear to ear. "And does that not remind you of anybody?"

Thinking on that for a second, I said, "Holy shit, you're right. He's just like MacCawill!"

"Yeah," she snickered. "*MacCawill.* You really are a dope."

And as I made the mental note that Doc might have been talking about somebody else entirely, we strolled out of the alley and found ourselves in a small parking lot tucked between a bank and a neighborhood bar on the outskirts of the Northeastern University campus.

And it was right about then when an ear-splitting scream rang out from somewhere in the near vicinity and Doc instinctively pulled the pistol from her jeans and chambered a round as she scanned the area. Picking up a flash of movement toward the side of the bank, she nodded at me, and we crossed the parking lot at superhuman speed to find a group of college kids cowering against a wall in various stages of consciousness.

Their faces were bloodied. And they were naked.

And standing over them were three exceptionally tall assholes who were also naked but trying their damnedest to put the college kids' clothes on. Awkward?

Yeah, it was a bit awkward.

At any rate, as Doc and I rolled up on them, they didn't so much as give us a passing glance, which just added to the general obscurity of the whole scenario.

"Leave us," one of the three muttered, not bothering to turn in our direction. His torso rippled with muscles that seemed to have their own muscles.

Raising her pistol, Doc wasn't quite sure what to make of the situation. "Dean, who the hell are these guys? And what the fuck are they doing?"

"I don't think they're guys. I think they're angels."

"Hmm, you sure?"

"Pretty sure."

She grinned. "What do you say we kick their ass and find out?"

How do I love thee, Doc Kelly?

Let me count the ways.

2

"I SAID LEAVE US!" the head jackass barked as he spun toward us wearing a pair of cargo shorts that were six sizes too small for him and a 'Kiss me I'm Irish' tee-shirt that was on backwards. "I command you!"

Doc laughed. "He sounds mad."

Grinning, I said, "Yeah, he does. Are you mad, bro? Are your shorts too tight?"

And that really seemed to piss him off. "Do you *mock* me, human?"

"Yes, I *mock* you."

Doc raised her hand. "Me too."

"And your sphincter brothers," I added. "I *mock* them, too. Just in case you were wondering."

"Same," Doc said. "They're a mess. Very mock worthy."

In various stages of dress, the three angels apparently didn't appreciate those comments, as they stopped trying to clothe themselves and collectively glared at us. Massive armored wings sprouted from their backs and oversized swords appeared in their hands as they stood shoulder to shoulder and took a menacing step in our direction.

"Such insolence will not be tolerated," the jackass in the cargo shorts said. "You have made a terrible mistake."

"Hey!" I protested. "That's my line!"

While I don't think they were quite seven feet tall, the highly pissed off warrior seraphs were every bit of six-foot-ten, give or take an inch or two. And despite the fact they were beyond terrifying to gaze upon with their glowing eyes, unnatural armored wings, and super-sized swords waving about, it was kind of hard to take them seriously.

They looked like grown men who, for some reason, decided to dress in children's clothing despite the fact that it clearly didn't fit. It wasn't even close. Their shorts looked like speedos and their tee-shirts looked like demented bikini tops. And better yet was the fact they had no idea they looked like complete and utter morons.

Which, in retrospect, is probably why I found it so funny.

At any rate, I couldn't stop laughing as the triumvirate of semi-dressed weirdos fanned out like apex predators and surrounded me and Doc. "Everybody just take it easy," I said between chuckles. "Field trip's over. Why don't you boys be good little halos and go back to your flying pharaoh box before somebody gets hurt. And by somebody, I mean you. Just so we're clear."

"Do not presume to give us orders, human," the 'Kiss me I'm Irish,' jackass said. His voice dripped superiority. "We will do as we please in this realm."

I grinned. "Let's agree to disagree on that, Lucky Charms. And in case you haven't heard, there's a truce in effect. You shouldn't even be here."

"A *truce*." He scoffed. "We are not beholden to any such truce."

"Ah, but you should be. It was put in place by God himself."

He spit on the ground. "That means nothing."

Doc smiled. "Seems like diplomacy's failed, Dean."

I nodded. "Some people just can't be reasoned with."

And it was right about then when the three angels launched at us in a blur of motion.

Apparently ready for some ass whooping, Erin's seamless suit of ethereal golden armor manifested on her body like a glove that hugged every last contour of her physique before flowing up her neck and encasing her head in a featureless, full-faced helmet. Almost like a metal ski mask, the menacing headgear coated everything except her eyes, which balefully blazed like sentient white orbs set against the golden carapace. It was sexy and terrifying all at the same time.

With her otherworldly combat suit in full effect, she drifted to her left and ducked under the enormous sword swinging toward her face at blinding speed before driving her kneecap straight into the ball sac of its owner. And just as the poor bastard let out a heartfelt groan that actually made my ball sac hurt, Doc throat chopped his ass before sweeping his legs. The overzealous seraph plummeted to the sidewalk with a horrendous thud as Doc methodically squeezed off rounds from her H&K hand cannon at his winged cohorts that were now within inches of taking my head off.

Willing the cloak into being, my face curled into a dark grin as it manifested in a spectral flash and flared about my shoulders like a caged animal set free. A surge of adrenaline fired through my already amped up body as I called for the gauntlets and felt the argent metal fluidly coat my hands and forearms.

Drifting to my right as the hail of gold-plated bullets from Doc's pistol zipped past my face like pissed off hornets, I felt as much as heard the guttural scream that erupted from my immediate rear as they struck their intended target. Spinning around to find a jackass standing there with several holes in his chest and a confused look on his face, I simply said, "Hi," before slugging him in the gut so hard that he pissed himself before passing out.

Thinking that worked out rather nicely, I felt the cloak ripple anxiously on my shoulders and instinctively stepped to the left to avoid being decapitated by the third degenerate seraph. Pulling my hands into tight fists, I sunk all my weight into a crushing uppercut that slammed into his chin like a goddamn sledgehammer before tagging him with a left hook that sent the jackass straight to the ground in an unconscious heap.

"That looked like it hurt," Erin yelled as she bobbed and weaved her way through a volley of sword strikes from Lucky Charms, who was back on his feet and now officially pissed. Ripping the massive sword from his hand and flinging it clear across the parking lot like it was a twig, she holstered her pistol and unleashed a blinding barrage of punches, elbows, and kicks that sent him reeling backwards into the brick wall of the bank. It looked like she was about to knock him out when large serrated blades sprouted from each of her golden fists like dueling machetes. It was almost like she was willing the armor into a different shape. Something I'd not seen her do before.

The featureless helmet melted from her face to reveal a shit-eating grin as she held both blades to the smarmy seraph's neck. "You ready to honor the truce now, shithead?" And when he eagerly nodded in the affirmative, she said, "Good boy." Then she blasted him in the balls again with her armored knee and threw him to the ground like a rag doll.

"Not bad," I said, promising myself to never get in a fight with Erin Kelly.

"Not bad yourself. You good?"

"Yeah, I'm good. Just wondering what else you can do with that armor nowadays."

With a droll grin, she said, "You'd be surprised."

Making the mental note to figure out what the hell that meant at some point down the road, the uncanny armor melted from existence and she bent down to help the college kids to their feet. Looking like they were about to shit themselves, the twenty-something hipsters took off down Gainsborough Street wearing nothing but boxer shorts and flip flops.

Glancing at the pile of stunned, dazed, and confused seraphs, I just shook my head. "So, what do we do with these idiots now?"

It was right about then when the three amigos snapped back into consciousness and scrambled to their feet as their various wounds healed before our eyes.

Slapping a fresh magazine into her H&K as her armor returned, Doc said, "Well, we better figure out something fast because they're apparently ready for round two."

And as we contemplated that for a couple seconds, a vortex of swirling white light manifested in front of us, and out stepped a dark-haired figure of average build and height dressed like he just strolled off a golf course. And although he didn't look like much, he was apparently someone of extreme importance because the sphincter triplets turned white as a ghost as soon as they saw him. Grunting something at them under his breath in Enochian, he quickly turned to Doc and me with a charming smile.

"Greetings and apologies," he said. His voice was deep, yet cheerful. And his vivid green eyes were kindly yet hardened. "I am Uriel."

"Uriel," I said. "As in the archangel."

He nodded. "And I'm afraid these are my soldiers. It was quite fortunate that you were here to *deter* them from doing anything foolish. Or *more* foolish, I should say. And for that, I'm quite grateful to you both, Dean Robinson and Erin Kelly."

"You know who we are," Doc said as her armor once again vanished and she holstered her pistol.

Uriel nodded again. "It is common practice for the seraphic court to keep record of humans of great significance."

Pointing, at the floating monstrosity in the sky above the Prudential building, I said, "And that's yours, I take it?"

"It is one of many lodestones that I am responsible for, yes. And it seems that not all my legionnaires are properly embracing the terms of Father's armistice as we sort out the particulars of our new habitation arrangement. But please rest assured that I will personally deal with these *dissenters* swiftly and forcefully. The last thing any of us want is for matters to become uncivilized."

"So, you think there's more of your minions running around the city stealing clothes and trying to blend in with the locals?"

Grinning, he pointed at the portal and his underlings scampered through it like scolded toddlers. "For their sake, Dean Robinson, I should hope not. Thank you again for your assistance. I'm sure we'll be seeing each other again sooner than not."

Offering an appreciative nod to Erin, he stepped through the portal himself, and it snapped shut behind him with a distinctive popping sound.

"He was nice," Doc said as we turned down Gainsborough Street and started maneuvering through the labyrinth of abandoned cars.

"Little too nice."

"How so?"

"He's an archangel. Archangel's are dicks."

"Is there anybody you don't consider to be a dick?"

"Besides you?" And when she offered nothing in response besides an icy stare, I just grinned for an awkward second or two. "Look, all I'm saying is that archangels hate humans. It's in their nature."

"Maybe they just hate you."

"Nah."

"You sure?"

"Ok, name one archangel that hates me."

"Gabriel."

"He doesn't *hate* me. He just dislikes me. A lot."

"He put a bounty on your head, Dean."

"That doesn't count. It was all part of the plan to find the Ark of the Covenant, remember?"

"Ok, fine. Michael then. He hated you. Before Bobby cut his head off, that is."

"No, I don't think Michael *hated* me, hated me."

"Are you serious? He literally tried to kill you. Twice."

"True. But that was just business."

"Then what about Remiel? He also tried to kill you. At least twice. He hated you."

"Right, but he was being controlled by Lucifer, so…"

"So what?"

"So, it doesn't count."

"Why not?"

"Because the Devil made him do it. That shouldn't count, right?"

"Ok, fine. So how about Raguel and Saraqael?"

"What about them?"

"They both tried to kill you in the Arizona desert. They *clearly* hate you."

"No, they were working for Remiel at the time."

"How is that relevant?"

"It's relevant because Remiel was working for Lucifer."

"So, it doesn't count either?"

"Clearly not. See what I mean?"

"Ah, no?"

"This is undeniable proof."

She let out a series of exasperated sighs. "Proof of what?"

"That archangels are dicks that hate humans."

And then she groaned rather loudly. "Just because every archangel you've met has tried to kill you doesn't mean that they inherently hate all humans."

"I beg to differ, Doc."

"You really are impossible." She chuckled. "You know that, right?"

"I'm just saying there has to be a reason why Gabriel is the only one on the seraphic court that Stephen and Abernethy trust."

"Well, maybe that will change now that *Ethan's* about to make us all move in together."

Reaching the intersection of Gainsborough and Hemenway, we were about to cross the street and head toward the Fenway Victory Gardens when I stopped and grabbed her hand. "Speaking of moving in, does this mean you and Billy are sticking around the Quartermaster? I mean, until this whole mess gets sorted out a bit."

"Of course we're staying," she said emphatically.

My face curled into a wide smile. "That's great."

"Where else would we be, right? The Horseman of War could very likely be at these peace talks."

And the smile vanished from my face. "Oh, that's right. I almost forgot about the whole Witness and the Four Horsemen thing."

"But since we'll be here a while, I thought maybe you and I could share a room."

My face curled into a wide smile again. "Really?"

"Yep. So, imagine my disappointment when Charlie said you were bunking with him nowadays."

And the smile vanished from my face. "Ah, what?"

"So, I guess I'll just room with Billy."

"Wait, what just happened?"

"He really looks up to you, you know."

"Charlie?"

"It's almost like you're his big brother. Even though he's like nine feet tall. So cute!"

"Seriously though, I'm not rooming with Charlie—"

"It's so sweet the way you're taking him under your wing and all."

"I don't even like Charlie."

"Oh, stop it. You love him."

"Did Charlie say we're rooming together? Because if he did, that fat bastard is totally lying—"

And unfortunately, I never got to finish that sentence because a brief crackle of static chirped in the RoosterTech-infused communications device buried in my right ear.

After a second or two, I heard the voice of my enigmatic ginger colleague say, "Dean, you copy?"

"Yeah. But it's not a great time. I'll call you back—"

"You and Erin better get back here. We just got word from Ethan. The meeting's been set."

"When?"

"One hour."

"OK," I muttered, glancing at Erin. "We're on our way."

"Time to go to work," she said.

I nodded. "Yup."

"I guess we'll figure out our sleeping arrangements when the future of mankind isn't on the cusp of total disaster, huh?"

"Yeah." I chuckled. "Whenever the hell that is."

Typical.

3

MAKING the mental note to punch Charlie in the face the next time I saw him, Doc and I entered the Reliquary to find Big A and a few others huddled around the makeshift conference table on the far side of the expansive stone rotunda.

"This place creeps me out," she said as we strolled past one of countless towering bookshelves filled with ancient manuscripts and arcane artifacts that lined the hand-hewn walls of our otherworldly command center. "It's like Hogwarts Castle on crack. And it smells funny."

"I'm not sure what Hogwarts Castle is, but it does smell like ass here. I think Abernethy needs a shower. He was a little ripe earlier."

"Do you really not know what Hogwarts Castle is? From Harry Potter?"

"Harry who?"

And when it was pretty clear I had no idea what the hell she was talking about, she said, "Oh, sorry, that must've been during your blackout period."

"Blackout period."

"Yeah, you know the time that you missed after—"

"Are you talking about the fourteen-year involuntary hiatus I took between the time I was murdered by a demented fallen angel and then miraculously resurrected as a semi-divine super soldier only to learn that the Red Sox won two World Series and screen legends like Patrick Swayze kicked the bucket in my absence? Is *that* what you're referring to?"

She grinned. "Still a sore topic?"

I grimaced. "Yeah, little bit."

"Sorry."

"It's OK. You are right about the Reliquary, though. It is creepy. And a lot creepier since Rooster built his quasi-sentient mutant mainframe."

"You talking about the Contraption?"

Weaving our way through the sprawling labyrinth of flickering monitors, humming server racks, and other jury-rigged misfit parts of unknown origin or purpose, I said, "Yeah, I mean, look at all this shit. It's insane. I swear every time I come in here, it's bigger. And I think it watches me."

She laughed. "You think maybe you're being a little paranoid? It's just a computer."

"That's exactly what *she* wants you to think."

"She?"

"Trust me, Doc, the Contraption is no computer. It's a cybernetic miscreant of epic proportion. And somehow it makes really good coffee. That's not natural. I definitely miss the old days when Skyphos was around."

"Well," she said as we walked past a series of ginormous dot matrix printers, "I miss Skyphos too, but I'm quite sure the Contraption isn't *watching* you." And no sooner did she say those very words than one of the printers roared to life and spit out a piece of paper. Ripping it free and quickly scanning it, she chuckled. "Then again..."

"What does it say?"

"It says, 'I see you, Dean.'"

"That's exactly what I'm talking about!"

And right on cue, another sheet of paper flew from the printer.

Grabbing it and chuckling again, Erin read it aloud. "You look tired today, Dean."

I shook my head. "What were you just saying about me being paranoid?"

And then another piece of paper came flying out with the words 'I'm watching' printed in large, bold text next to a big smiley face. And at the bottom of the page, in very small font, it said, 'Always watching...'

Doc shrugged. "And I stand corrected. You might be on to something."

Making a mental note to have a discussion with Rooster some point down the road about his maniacal pet computer, we pulled up to the conference table to find him busy sifting through various stacks of documents while MacCawill perched near the industrial-sized coffee pot sucking on a cigar.

Pulling up next to Abernethy, I said, "Where's everybody else?"

"Preparing," he replied, handing me a stack of files. "How was yer wee stroll?"

"It was fine."

"Anything to report?"

"Aside from the rogue halos running amuck terrorizing the locals? No, not really."

"Rogue halos? Well, bloody hell!"

"Oh, and we met Uriel. He seemed nice."

"Uriel," the burly Scotsman grunted as his face curled into a deep scowl. "Silver-tongued charlatan. Just like the rest of his ilk on the seraphic court save for Gabriel. They're all daft."

I winked at Doc. "Told ya."

Abernethy stroked his beard a few times, and I could almost see the wheels turning in his head. "Tell me, Deanie, what was Uriel doing in Boston?"

"Some of his cronies jumped ship. He was policing them up."

"So that's his lodestone floating over the Prudential Building, is it?"

"One of many, apparently. He was very appreciative that Doc and I helped him out."

"And how did you *help* him exactly?"

I grinned. "By beating the living shit out of three of his minions."

He snickered. "Well, it seems Ethan's truce is a bit more fragile than I thought. It's a good thing the parley's soon."

Doc grabbed a couple files from my hand. "Is that what these are for? The parley?"

"Aye, Erin dearie, it's all the information we have on the key players."

"Key players," she said somewhat rhetorically as she flipped through the folders and scanned the contents.

Big A nodded. "From all the interested parties. Humans, angels, and nephilim alike."

"Ambassadors of sorts," Stephen said, joining the conversation as he picked up a steaming cup of coffee from the conference table that I swear wasn't there a second earlier. "They will represent their kind at the accords."

Wondering why the hell cups of coffee never randomly appeared for me, I said, "And what do these *ambassadors* have to do with us?"

Dressed in his signature black suit and crisp white shirt motif, the briefest hint of a grin formed on his stoic face. "Well, among other things, Ethan's asked us to maintain order during the negotiation process."

"Maintain order, huh?"

"Yes, Dean. Maintain order."

"So, we're supposed to keep the peace at the peace summit."

He took a sip of coffee. "Among other things."

"Which are?"

"To be revealed at the appropriate time, apparently."

And when it was pretty clear Stephen wasn't sure what Ethan

was up to either, I flipped open one of the files. "So, are these peculiar peace accords happening here at the Quartermaster?"

"Nae, lad," Big A said. "They're to occur on neutral ground agreed upon by all parties."

"Where's that? And please don't say Nod. I still have nightmares about those deranged leprechaun guys that tried to slow roast me."

"Nod is hardly neutral ground, Mr. Sunshine," replied a velvety voice in a peculiar accent that I truly hoped never to hear again in my unnatural lifetime, much less so soon. "A momentous occasion such as this can only be held at a venue where everyone feels *comfortable*. And where better to feel comfortable than the Medmenham Lounge."

Spinning around to find a familiar gaunt weirdo in a well-fitted suit with an oversized black touring cap cocked proudly on his head, I said, "Metatron. It's, ah, good to see you again. And so soon."

Puffing on a cigarette, he just glared at me for a long moment with his beady eyes. One of which was a radiant green and the other a chilling blue. "Is it?" he said between puffs.

"Is it what?"

"Good to see me."

"Yeah. Definitely. How've you been?"

"Do you mean how have I been since being ripped from my home against my will and interrogated at gunpoint by you and your belligerent crew of reprobates last week?"

"Still upset about that, eh?"

"It was *last week*."

I shrugged. "Desperate times and desperate measures?"

He grinned, making sure I got a good look at his mouth full of gold teeth. "Fortunately for you, I don't hold grudges. And more fortunately for you, *Ethan* has asked me to play nice in the sandbox."

I grinned back. "All water under the bridge then. So, I take it you're not at the QM because you miss me."

"Metatron is here at my request to provide counsel," Stephen said before clearing his throat, causing Rooster and MacCawill to stop what they were doing and gather around the table. "By virtue of his duties as the Heavenly scribe, and subsequent exploits as the Black Swan, he's in the unique position of knowing each of the key players that will be in attendance at the accords. So, before the negotiations begin, let's get grounded on what we're walking into. John, if you would be so kind as to get us started."

Taking a seat at the conference table, Rooster nodded as his fingers flew across an old clunky keyboard. Within seconds, all the monitors within eyeshot flared to life, displaying images of what appeared to be Gabriel and Uriel aside from another figure I didn't recognize.

"Let's start with the angels," he said. "From what we can tell, they're split into three factions. The first of which is aligned with Gabriel and still loyal to Ethan. The second faction seems to hate Ethan's guts and *were* loyal to Michael before his untimely demise. They have since gravitated to the archangel Uriel as their de facto leader."

"Daft scunner," Abernethy grumbled under his breath but still loud enough for everybody to hear, which made me chuckle despite the situation.

"And the last faction," Rooster continued, "are the Watchers who are seemingly loyal to no one and led by Semyaza now that Azazel's apparently out of the picture."

Doc raised her hand. "What do you mean Azazel's out of the picture? What happened to him?"

Metatron shrugged. "That, my dear, is the topic du jour. From what I've been able to discern from my sources, our dear friend Azazel has not been seen nor heard from since the unfortunate events at the Washington Monument last winter."

"Wait," I said. "Are you saying he didn't go with Lew to sack Heaven after they freed the Watchers?"

"That's precisely what I'm saying."

"Is he dead?"

"It's possible. I heard whispers about a falling out between him and Lucifer, but nothing definitive. But if you ask me, Azazel's far too clever to simply *die*. He'll turn up sooner or later. Mark my words." And as I made the mental note that it couldn't be good given my least favorite fallen angel's malevolent track record, Metatron continued, "That said, one could argue that Semyaza has always been the Watcher's alpha dog going all the way back to the early days. Azazel was more of a figurehead."

"He looks like a real peach," MacCawill muttered, studying the portrait on one of the countless computer screens of a crazy-eyed weirdo with nineties punk rocker hair and eyeshadow. "Or a real crack head."

"Apparently, the six millennia he spent locked away in the depths of Tartarus didn't do much for his temperament. Or his mental state."

"Look forward to meeting him," Rooster muttered as he pounded on the keyboard again and a portrait of a grizzled, muscle-clad giant appeared. "Moving on to the nephilim, there's two primary camps that'll be represented at the accords. The anakim and the '*Others*.'"

"The anakim?" I scoffed. "Are you shittin' me? How exactly do the man-eating giants get a seat at the table?"

"Since Ethan decreed it," Stephen said. "They, like us and everyone else, will be sharing the Earth, and it only behooves us to try to come to an arrangement with them."

"And what if they can't be reasoned with?"

"I think you'd be surprised to find that anakim are quite reasonable given the proper motivation."

I shook my head. "I doubt that."

"Would you say that of High Commander Hon based on your recent experience with him and the Carolingian Knights of Nod?"

"Hon's different."

Stephen slid his hands into his pockets. "He wasn't always."

"So, the *anakim*," Rooster said, moving the conversation along, "will be represented by Mortog, who apparently earned the right to speak for his giant brethren by beating the living shit out of anyone else who wanted the honors. Fortunately, High Commander Hon has agreed to assist Mortog at the peace talks in the event Mortog gets confused, as he's apparently not very bright. Any questions? Ok, great. And for the rest of the nephilim, they'll be represented by—

"Janser Berinhart," Metatron said as a picture of a brawny, broad-shouldered woman with a thick mane of raven hair and stunning yellow eyes appeared on the monitors. "Queen of the Others."

Somewhat taken aback by the grotesque series of deep scars that ran clear across her chiseled face in the shape of harrowing claw marks, I said, "Who the hell is she?"

He lit a cigarette and took a long draw. "No one to be trifled with, Mr. Sunshine. I promise you that. Half varangian and half draugr, Janser Berinhart is a living, breathing reminder of a time when the Earth was a bit more *primal*."

"So, you're saying she's a really old vampire berserker bear beastie that's also a queen. That sounds pretty terrible."

He smiled. "More or less."

"Queen of what exactly?" Doc asked, intently studying the picture of the menacing maiden who looked like she could drink Big A under the table, then beat him in an arm-wrestling contest with ease.

"Queen of the nephilim underworld," Metatron replied. "Although that's more of a nickname than an actual moniker. That said, she's generally considered to be the shadowy leader of the Others."

"And why have we never heard of her?"

"Because she didn't want you to. It's all part of her *charm*, shall we say."

"And just so everybody's straight," MacCawill said, chewing on a stogie, "the Others are inclusive of any and all nephers that aren't of the unnaturally large and stupid persuasion."

Metatron nodded. "Well said."

Checking his old-fashioned pocket watch, Rooster started tapping a finger on the table as the computer screens went blank.

"Ok. Last and probably least, because we're about out of time, are the humans who are represented by Mr. Blue Sky and the Academy."

I chuckled. "That sounds like the name of some shitty eighties band. Where's their picture?"

"There's no picture."

"Well, who are they?"

He held up an empty file. "That's the thing, we have no idea."

I shrugged. "But they're world leaders, right? How do we not know who they are?"

"The truth is, we've never known," Stephen said with a furrowed brow. "All that's certain is that at some point during the High Middle Ages, the Academy came into being, and over the course of a few centuries, they managed to methodically infiltrate every power structure across the civilized and uncivilized world. Clans, tribes, fiefdoms, kingdoms, monarchies, oligarchies, dictatorships, democracies. All of them. Everywhere."

"Sorry, I'm still not following."

"It's rather simple, Dean. The *Academy* are the people who rule the rulers. The proverbial hand that rocks the cradle."

I shook my head a couple of times. "Wait, are you saying that the conspiracy theories about a secret group of nameless, faceless people that 'run the world' are actually true? Come on, man." And when he offered no response besides a solemn nod, I muttered, "Are the Men in Black real? You can tell me."

"We may not know their identities," Metatron said, glazing right over my Men in Black comment, "but we do know that there's always seven members of the Academy. No more, no less. When one dies, a new one takes their place. And *Mr. Blue Sky* is not a name. It's a rank. A mantle of power that rotates between the seven."

Checking his watch again, Rooster said, "All right, it's about that time. You guys better head to the Medmenham. Good luck. We're all counting on you."

"Wait," I said, still trying to wrap my head around the mind-bending secret society scenario, "are you not coming?"

"I'm staying here to run some more scans on the Earth's core. Doesn't really matter if everyone figures out how to live in harmony if the planet's about to shit itself into a gazillion pieces, does it?"

Making the mental note that my enigmatic ginger colleague had a pretty valid point, I turned to Stephen. "So, what's the plan, boss? What you need me to do?"

He grinned a wolfish grin that instantly made me regret asking. "I have a very special job for you."

"Special job, huh?"

That didn't sound so bad.

4

"Special job my ass," I grumbled, trying like hell to ignore the incessant waves of cigarette smoke that rolled through Samson's Bar like a smoldering forest fire. "Can't believe we're back in this shithole. And on *welcoming duty* of all things."

A random Journey song crackled and hissed through the dilapidated speakers dangling from the ceiling as I took a good look around the ramshackle watering hole that served as the worldly entrance to Metatron's infamous Medmenham Lounge. Neatly tucked into the eclectic cityscape of New York City's Greenwich Village, the unnatural clientele drawn to Samson's Bar ironically blended right into the backdrop of everyday life, as did the establishment itself.

"What's a shithole, Dean?" Bobby asked as he tried to get comfortable on the creaking bar stool next to me that had seen better days. Wearing jeans and a faded tee-shirt that showed off his sinewy biceps and distinct rows of Enochian glyphs tattooed on both sides of his neck, my displaced angelic battle buddy nonchalantly ran a hand through his schwoopy, reverse mullet.

"A *shithole*, Bobby, is a place that sucks really badly."

"And what does it suck?"

I took a painful gulp from the piss warm mug of flat beer sitting on the bar in front of me. "No, it doesn't suck as in *suck*. It just plain *sucks*. You get it?"

He nodded somewhat unconvincingly. "Well, I, for one, am happy to be back at Samson's Bar. I don't mind in the least that it's a sucking hole of shit."

I chuckled. "And why's that exactly?"

"Because this time I am not pretending to be in handcuffs."

Holding up my mug, I said, "Well, cheers to that, my friend. And hopefully we won't be putting any shoes in anuses this time either. Now keep your eyes peeled for our esteemed VIPs. They should be here any minute."

Pulling up next to us and tossing his chewed-up stogie on the floor, MacCawill grumbled, "What's a guy gotta do to get a beer around here?"

"Where the hell did you go?" I said, flagging down the bartender.

"Had to see a man about a horse."

Looking perplexed, Bobby just kind of tilted his head and gazed at him for an awkward sec or two. "What do you need a horse for, Roy?"

"What? No. I meant I had to drain the lizard. Take a whiz."

And when it was abundantly clear Bobby had absolutely no idea what idea what he was talking about, MacCawill said, "You know, syphon the python? Squeeze the lemon? Splash the pirate. Wash the mongoose. Water the weasel? Unbutton the mutton. Point Percy at the porcelain. Shake hands with an old friend? Beat the piss out of the little guy—"

"He had to pee, for Christ's sake," I said as the heavily tattooed beefcake of a bartender sauntered over like he owned the joint and grunted something at me.

"What?" I grunted back.

"I *said*, do you want another *beer*?"

"Please. Make it nice and warm like the first one. And a round for my friends too."

He grinned. "Coming right up, dumbass."

"Wait, I thought I was smartass, and you were dumbass."

Promptly flipping me off, he grumbled something of a snide nature under his breath as he retreated to the dilapidated taps and tried his best to coax some life into them.

Lighting up a fresh cigar, MacCawill snickered. "Making friends everywhere you go, mancho. Nice."

"Are you seriously giving me shit about giving other people shit? That's rich. Hi, pot. Meet kettle."

"Whatever." He scoffed. "Remind me again why I'm stuck here babysitting you and the halo hair god instead of being out in the field with the rest of the crew?"

"Maybe it's got something to do with the fact we're supposed to greet Semyaza and Janser Berinhart and escort them downstairs to the Medmenham Lounge."

"And what's that got to do with me?"

Slapping him on the shoulder, I said, "Who better to greet a couple underworld degenerates than a bona fide underworld degenerate himself."

Rolling his eyes, he said nothing as the bartender dropped off three beers before placing an old ass rotary telephone on the bar.

"You got a call, dumbass."

"A call. Me?"

"Yeah, you. Somebody named O'Dargan. Sounds important."

Thinking it rather odd that Rooster would use a land line to call me, I put the phone to my ear. "John?"

"Yeah, it's me," Rooster said. "I've been trying to reach you guys on our comms devices, but they apparently can't penetrate the wards around Metatron's bar."

"What's up?"

"It's the scanner me and MacCawill just built. Something's wrong with it."

"How do mean?"

"Well, it's sending back some wonky readings that can't be right. It either needs to be calibrated, or the Earth's core is literally turning into Jell-O."

"What did you just say?"

"Forget it, it's fine. I just need MacCawill back here to check it out. Can you manage without him?"

"It'll be tough," I said with just a touch of sarcasm. "But me and Bobby can probably handle things. I'll let him know. Anything else?"

"Yeah, one more thing. Hurry the fuck up already." And then he hung up.

Making the mental note that Rooster was wound up pretty friggin tight at the moment, I put the archaic phone back on the cradle before grabbing MacCawill's beer just as he was reaching for it. Draining it in a single gulp, I handed him the empty mug with a satisfied smirk. "Rooster needs you back at the QM. Pronto."

Shaking his head, he said, "Please tell me that ginger jackass didn't break the seismic accelerograph we literally just finished building."

"He said it was acting wonky or something to that effect."

"Goddamnit," he muttered, getting up from his stool and waving his hands. "I bet he connected the fiber optic cable to the sonar array after I specifically told him *not* to do that because it would skew the linear refractive geomapping!" And then he stomped toward the door and faded from sight, grumbling under his breath the whole time.

"Is Roy alright?" Bobby asked, taking a reluctant sip of beer.

I grinned. "He's fine. Probably needs to water his weasel again."

Contemplating that for a second or two, he said, "He must have a very thirsty weasel."

"Or just a really small one," I chuckled before glancing at the clock haphazardly tacked on the wall above the bar. "The accords start in ten minutes and still no sign of the demented leader of the

Watchers or the shady queen of the nephers. I can't imagine showing up late to a meeting called by God is a good thing, right?"

"Semyaza will not be late," he said, quite matter-of-factly. "He was always known for his punctuality."

"I didn't realize you knew him."

He nodded. "We served together at the Acropolis long before he became a Watcher. He was a great warrior. And my friend. Prior to his fall from grace, that is."

And it was right about then when I noticed an unnaturally thin weirdo in a sullied trench coat and combat boots sliding through the crowd of rowdy patrons. With spiky hair that looked like he stuck his finger in an electric socket and bloodshot eyes that were accented with a ridiculous amount of eye shadow, he was making a beeline for us with a goofy smile plastered across his gaunt face.

Instantly recognizing him to be Semyaza from the less then flattering picture we saw at the QM, I was more than surprised when he crawled up on the bar like it was a couch and sprawled out in front of us like he owned the place.

"Hiya, hiya, Kerubiel!" he said in a smokey voice full of nasally inflection as he rested his face upon his palm. "Old buddy, old friend, old *pal o' mine*. Been a while! Long, *long* while. What do you think, six thousand years, give or take? Take!"

"Hello, brother," Bobby said. His words were emotionless. Cold, even. "It has been quite some time, yes. Time that has not been kind to you."

Blinking erratically, Semyaza yelled, "Time! Time! Time! No, no, it has not. But I again breathe the free air, little brother. And that's *magic* in and of itself."

"It's better than you deserve given your betrayal."

Hopping off the bar in a blur of motion, the neurotic angel pouted like a disappointed child. "Aw, don't tell me you're still mad, little brother. I thought we were past that."

Bobby shook his head as his eyes flashed bluish white. "No, brother. We are not."

Which prompted Semyaza to stick his tongue out in response. "Well *boohoo* to you! You self-righteous prick! You always were so *high and mighty*. And what the hell do you know, anyway? You spent your whole miserable existence in the *Acropolis* doing your *duty* and sucking from Gabriel's teat. *Teat*, teat!"

Apparently not appreciating that comment in the least, Bobby jumped to his feet and wrapped a hand around his estranged buddy's pencil neck. "Do not speak to me of duty," he snarled as the glyph tattoos lining his neck glowed a searing white. "Nor mention Gabriel's name in my presence ever again. Do — you — understand?"

Gasping for breath yet somehow still smiling, Semyaza muttered, "Well, somebody got cranky in their old age, huh? Huh!"

Releasing his death grip, Bobby crossed his arms and glared at him for a long moment. "You're a disgrace to our kind. You and all the Watchers."

"*Disgrace*." He scoffed. "For what? What! What did we do that was *so* bad, huh?"

"You corrupted mankind! You taught them the Forbidden Knowledge."

Waving his hands and starting to dance, Semyaza yelled, "Well whoop-dee-fucking-doo! We *taught* them. And for that unspeakably *heinous* crime against humanity, Father locked us away for all eternity and threw away the key. Whoop-dee-fuck!"

"And you fornicated with the women of Earth!"

"Yeah, we did. Did! So what? They had fun. We had fun. All good, right?"

"It resulted in the nephilim! And the Earth was infested with your half-bred giant offspring for generations to come!"

"Ok, now *that* part was unfortunate. But we could have fixed it if *Father* hadn't thrown the book at us. Book!"

Apparently done with the obscure walk down memory lane, Bobby just shook his head a few times before grabbing his beer and turning his back to Semyaza.

And then, unfortunately, the weirdo turned his attention to me. "So, are you the little *godling* I keep hearing about? Hello, little godling. You don't look like much. Godling!"

I chuckled. "Me? Well, I hate to break it you, asshole, but you look like the stick figure version of a crackhead that got kicked out of a Depeche Mode concert for being too goth."

Apparently appreciating that description of himself, Semyaza laughed for a solid ten seconds before saying, "Funny, funny little godling."

Figuring he was clearly a couple sammiches shy of a picnic, I just grinned. "OK, well, good talk. It's time for your old pal Kerubiel to escort you to the Medmenham Lounge, where the others are gathered. The accords are about to start. Wouldn't want you to be late. I mean, you're already on the big guy's shit list, right?"

"Not yet, godling," he said, plopping down on the stool next to Bobby and waving at the bartender.

I shook my head. "You sure a drink is a good idea? I mean, you're kind of a mess, pal."

And right on cue, the bartender slid a double shot of whisky across the bar. Semyaza reached into his trench coat and pulled out a small vial of glowing liquid. Grinning at me, he then emptied it into the shot glass before slamming it in a single gulp. Closing his eyes for a quick second, he took a couple of deliberate breaths before opening them.

"Ah, much better," he said sitting up straight and fixing his hair. His eyes were no longer bloodshot and his voice no longer sounded like a jonesing heroin addict. Despite his ridiculous outfit and eye makeup, he seemed kind of normal in a mildly deranged sort of way. "How do I look?"

"Are you kidding?"

He sighed. "Do I *look* like I'm kidding?

I shrugged. "I thought we already established that you looked like a stick figure crackhead."

"Tell you what, funny little godling." He chuckled. "Why don't *you* spend a few millennia locked away in the dark depths of Tartarus." Then he started tapping on his forehead with an index finger. "It's not so good for the *psyche,* if you know what I'm saying. That's where my go juice comes in handy."

"Go juice, eh? You mean the stuff in the vile?"

"Yeah, yeah, *now* you're getting it. It helps with the cobwebs. And the shadows. And the *screaming.*"

"And apparently the tic. That was really annoying, by the way. Like Tourette's Syndrome, but the crackhead version. So, what does this *go juice* consist of, anyway?"

Semyaza grinned. "Oh, it's just a little something to take the edge off."

"Made from what?"

"The usual stuff. Venom of an Egyptian Mau, blood of an honest man, tears of a pregnant virgin, yada yada."

"You serious?"

"No, dumdum! It's horse tranquilizers and heroin with a splash of concentrated fentanyl."

As I made the mental note that Semyaza actually was a crackhead, Bobby announced, "It's time to go. The accords start in two minutes."

With a cliched bow, the narcotic swilling fallen angel said, "Then by all means, *little brother,* lead the way to Father's hypocritical hostage negotiation."

Grabbing him by the scruff of the neck, Bobby grumbled, "It's a peace summit, you anushole," as he gave his prodigal brother a healthy push toward the very back of the bar in the direction of the portal to the Medmenham lounge.

"Be right behind you," I called after him, making the mental note that Bobby hadn't quite grasped the nuance between ass and anus. "If the nepher queen isn't here in the next sixty seconds, she's on her own."

Thinking sixty seconds was plenty of time for one more beer, I reached down and grabbed my mug as a deep, throaty voice from behind me said, "And what makes you think she's not here already?"

And then a powerful hand grabbed the back of my head and repeatedly slammed my face into the wooden bar.

I really hate this shithole.

Check, please!

5

About tired of having my forehead bounced off the bar like a goddamn basketball, I willed the cloak into being and clenched my fists as it manifested in a spectral flash and billowed about my shoulders. The blaring music came to a screeching halt, and the surrounding crowd of ruffians scattered as I rose to my feet.

Now officially pissed, a jolt of unnatural adrenaline surged through my body as I focused all my supernatural strength and threw my head back as hard as I could. And as I felt it smack into the face of the jackass standing behind me with a horrid clacking sound, I couldn't help but grin. Spinning around and ready to pummel the stupid bastard with the balls to blindside me, I was more than surprised to find that it was, in fact, someone without balls.

It was a woman.

A broad-shouldered, husky woman with flowing raven hair and haunting yellow eyes that were somehow jovial and terrifying at the same time. Wearing skin-tight pants made of tanned leather and an ornate animal skin vest that was barely holding her bulging breasts at bay, I suddenly felt a bit inadequate at the sight of her massive, toned biceps.

And despite the fact that her nose was broken in several places and blood was gushing down her scar-riddled face like water pouring from a faucet, she was laughing. Heartily laughing. Almost like she enjoyed getting head-butted so hard it exploded her nose. And it turned her on. "Oh, baby!" She howled between chuckles. "Don't *tease* a girl like that!"

Not quite sure what to make of the leather-clad buxom badass, I just stood there for an awkward moment or two before reluctantly dropping my fists and willing the cloak into retreat. As the music returned and the sketchy bar patrons went back to whatever the hell they were doing, I said, "You're Janser Berinhart."

She smiled widely to reveal a mouth full of blood-stained teeth. "I am."

"You're late."

"*Janser Berinhart* is never late, baby blue." Her voice was deep and rich and could easily be mistaken for that of a man if not for its playful singsong nature that was clearly feminine. Albeit alpha feminine. "Janser Berinhart just *is*."

Crossing my arms, I said, "And why did *Janser Berinhart* slam my head into the fucking bar?"

Casually wiping the blood from her mouth with her forearm, she smiled again before waltzing right past me, slapping my ass, and sitting on my stool. "Foreplay." Then she grabbed my beer and drained it in a single gulp before smashing the mug on the floor.

I shook my head. "That was my beer."

"*Was* being the optimal word," she said, grabbing her nose and snapping it back into place without so much as a wince as the bartender lined up two shot glasses before handing her a bottle of bourbon. "Come, sit. Drink with me, Dean Robinson."

"You know my name?"

Taking a healthy swig from the bottle, she then poured two shots before tapping on the empty stool next to her. "I know all about you, soldier boy. Now, sit."

"We don't have time for this," I grumbled, looking at the clock on the wall. "We're already late for—"

"Sit!"

Figuring it was no use arguing, I begrudgingly plopped down on the stool next to her. "One drink. Then we go."

"One drink," she agreed, handing me a shot. "Then we go."

"I can't imagine the big guy is going to appreciate this very much."

She smirked. "The *big guy* can suck my left tit. He shows his face for the first time in five hundred years, and we're all supposed to kiss his ass? No. I think not. And besides, I sent my delegates ahead of me. They can handle things at the *grand parley* until I'm done playing."

"Wait, who are your delegates? And what do you mean by *playing*?"

Ignoring both questions, she said, "Raise your glass!"

Getting the distinct feeling that she was used to doing whatever the hell she wanted and absolutely nothing else, I shrugged in defeat. "Ok, fine. And what are we drinking to?"

"To change. And freedom. And the hope of a world where my people are not hunted — by *your* people. Or anyone else!" Downing the shot, she then smashed the glass on the floor before grabbing the bottle and emptying it into her mouth. Smashing it on the floor as well, she jumped to her feet and let loose with a booming guttural growl like something you'd expect to hear from a pissed-off grizzly bear.

Smiling at me to make sure I got a good look at her rather impressive fangs that I hadn't noticed earlier, she said, "Ready when you are, baby blue," before she tossed a couple gold coins on the bar and made her way toward the back of the smoke-filled room.

Making the mental note that I really needed a damn vacation, I threw the shot back and tossed the empty glass on the bar as I jumped to my feet. Casually flipping the bartender off, I followed Janser through the crowd of drunken patrons until we reached a curiously out of place booth tucked up next to a series of vintage arcade games. Fully realizing that the booth was actually a gateway to the Medmenham Lounge from my last misadventure at Samson's Bar, I waited for her to take a seat when she said, "You first. Age before beauty and all."

Shaking my head, I reluctantly crawled into the narrow booth, only to be smothered by her couple hundred pounds of muscle-clad girth as she squeezed in right next to me and threw a meaty arm over my shoulder. Just as I was about to tell her to quit manhandling me, the booth started spinning at an alarming rate before rising several feet into the air as the floor below us morphed into a swirling vortex of muted, dark colors.

And despite the fact I already knew it was about to plummet downward at breakneck speed into a bottomless abyss and that I shouldn't start screaming, it was right about then when the goddamn booth started plummeting downward at breakneck speed into a bottomless abyss and I started screaming.

For the record, it was a manly scream.

Like a valiant knight charging into battle.

Or a frenzied gladiator locked in mortal combat.

Or a prepubescent boy that just got kicked in the balls so hard that his already high-pitched voice sounded that much more shrill.

Wait, what?

No, not like that.

But if it was, Janser was roaring or whatever hybrid bear beasties do at the top of her lungs the entire time, so I'm pretty sure she didn't notice.

At any rate, after a few seconds of pure terror, the interdimensional vortex slowed to a very gradual halt before spitting out the obscure booth into the Medmenham Lounge's very high-end sitting room. Lit only by the faint glow of gas lamps, the otherworldly cocktail lounge sprawled out in either direction for as far as the eye could see, with the fragrant aroma of incense lingering in the air.

Blissfully engaged in drinking, smoking, and all manner of more extreme vices, well-dressed patrons congregated in intimate pockets of swanky leather chairs and dark wooden furniture spread throughout the lavish space. Some appeared human. Others not so much.

Nimbly hopping from the booth with a feline grace that shouldn't have been possible for a person of Janser's size and physique, she snapped her fingers, and within a literal second, a waiter in a tuxedo was standing there with a bottle of bourbon and a Cuban cigar. "Welcome back to the Medmenham Lounge, my queen," he said, striking a match and holding it while Janser puffed on the stogie a few times. "May I bring you anything else to make your stay more amenable?"

She blew a large, ornate smoke ring and smiled. "Not unless you're on the menu, *tiger.*"

He smiled back. "Everything is on the menu at the Medmenham, my queen."

Pulling a few gold coins from her vest, she then placed them in the waiter's mouth one by one as she licked her lips. "Then why don't you go find a couple *friends* and meet me at my table."

Thinking that was beyond gross, I squirmed out of the booth. "No, no, no. You don't have time for that. We're late—"

"I'm never late," she said, biting the cork off the bottle of booze and spitting it at me before taking a big swig. "I just am, remember?" Then she started casually strolling through the posh establishment and chatting with people like she owned the joint.

Ignoring my repeated protests to go to the accords, she continued to do this for a solid ten minutes until we reached a secluded alcove with its own bar sitting next to a roaring hearth that was encircled by three very ornate oversized couches. And sprawled out on the very ornate oversized couches were the waiter and several of his friends of various nephilim species going to town on each other in a full-on fur-flying orgy. A furgy?

Really, really, really hoping that the mental image of hairy tits, fuzzy dicks, and a whole new disgusting spin on 'doggie style' wasn't permanently seared into my memory, I spun around and covered my mouth in an attempt to stop from puking. "Aw, for fuck's sake!" I barked. "You could've warned me about that!"

Saying nothing, she puffed on the cigar clenched in her teeth and stared at me with her intense yellow eyes as she methodically removed her clothes until her brawny yet voluptuous form was completely naked.

In the buff.

In the raw.

Topless.

Bottomless.

Full friggin monty.

Wearing nothing but a smile.

Nakie!

And as I did my very best not to gawk, she held up her right hand, and within a blur of motion, it morphed into a fur-covered claw. Almost like that of a grizzly bear, but still somewhat human-like. And jet black.

Then the same happened to her left hand. And then both her feet.

Then her already hefty legs and torso got even heftier as her near six-foot burly frame grew in height and girth and sprouted thick, raven fur. And lastly, although her deeply scarred face kept its human appearance for the most part, her mouth and jawline sprouted into a ghastly gaping maw accentuated with four-inch fangs that dripped and drooled like an apex predator about to feast on its prey.

Still smiling at me, which was beyond terrifying at this point, she pulled the cigar from her mouth and tossed it on the floor. "Your turn, baby blue," she said in a gravelly guttural voice that literally made the hair on the back of my neck stand up.

Backpedaling several steps, I did my very best to force a grin. "Me? Nah, I'm good. Thanks though?"

With a wink of her now glowing yellow eye, she belted out a sultry roar as she turned and sunk her razor-tipped claws into the waiter's chest before mounting him. About to lose my lunch, I covered my mouth again and continued to backpedal. "So, I'll just meet you at the accords whenever you're finished with, ah, whatever it is you're doing there. Good talk!"

Then I spun around and ran as fast as I could until I was out of earshot of the unnatural grunting and whatnot. And as I tried like hell to erase the last ninety seconds from my memory banks, I walked straight into Metatron.

"Excuse you, Mr. Sunshine!" he protested, as I practically tackled him without even noticing.

"Shit, sorry," I muttered, helping him back to his feet.

Grumbling under his breath, he adjusted his touring cap and glared at me for an awkward second or two. "Where have you been? And *where* is Janser Berinhart? Her entourage of *delegates* is causing quite the stir."

And no sooner did those words exit his mouth than an ear-splitting roar followed by a round of sensual howls echoed through the swanky lounge space, causing everyone to stop whatever they were doing and look for the source. "She's, ah, busy," I said.

He shook his head. "Good grief. Is she really doing *that — now?*"

I nodded. "Yup. She is. Whatever *that* is, I mean. It's not like I watched or anything. Just so you know."

He sighed. "Do you know how much it cost me to replace the upholstery after the last time she—"

"Please don't finish that sentence," I grumbled.

"Right, well, you'd better join the others. Fortunately for you, Ethan has not arrived yet. I'll deal with Janser Berinhart myself." And as the former scribe of God-turned-underworld nightclub owner stomped off to break up the aforementioned furgy, he tossed me an old ass coin as a large door manifested a few feet away.

Oddly, the door was not set in a wall. It was just kind of standing there in the middle of the goddamned room amidst various clusters of the Medmenham's peculiar clientele. Made of polished bronze and covered with layer upon layer of ornate markings, it was something you'd expect to find on an ancient church. And as I carefully slid the arcane coin into a slot carved into one of the mighty panels, the door swung open to reveal a breathtaking atrium like something straight out of Ancient Rome.

And standing within the breathtaking atrium was a raucous gaggle of angels, humans, and nephilim of assorted sizes screaming at each other at the very top of their lungs.

Perfect.

Nothing like kicking off a peace summit on the verge of fisticuffs.

6

Now granted, I've never been known for my diplomacy skills.

And if I'm being honest, my concept of peace-keeping was predicated on heavily armed troops and intimidation tactics.

So, although I had no idea what a peace summit was supposed to look like, I was pretty sure this wasn't it. I stepped foot into the grandiose marble atrium to find the so-called *ambassadors* perched around a gargantuan horseshoe-shaped table screaming at each other.

It was absolutely classic.

Angels yelling at humans.

Humans yelling at nephilim.

Nephilim yelling at everybody.

And giants yelling at no one in particular but doing it very loudly and menacingly.

Chuckling at the sight of Stephen and Abernethy, who were doing their damnedest to keep things civil by screaming back at the lot of them, I pulled up next to Doc Kelly, who was quietly observing from the periphery of the chaos.

"This looks like fun," I muttered.

She smiled. "Yeah, they've been at it since Bobby dropped off Semyaza twenty minutes ago. Speaking of, where the hell have you been?"

"With the *queen*."

"And?"

"And aside from being a royal pain in the ass, she's kind of on her own schedule."

Pointing at a hulking man and a woman with blue hair and clawed hands who were having a rather heated conversation with Gabriel and Uriel, she said, "Well, if her cronies are any indication of her temperament, she must be a real gem."

"Are those morons her esteemed delegates?"

"Yeah, and there's a couple more of them floating around here somewhere. They're little people like—"

"Wait, you mean korrigans? Like those demented leprechaun fuckers in Nod?"

And before she had a chance to answer, I felt a sharp pain in my right knee cap followed by a peculiar voice that said, "Oi! Blighter boy! Who you calling leprechaun, eh? Eh!"

Looking down to find a pair of oddly dressed three-foot-tall mini-men with shaggy blonde hair, scraggly beards, and huge noses, I felt a turbo shot of adrenaline pulse through my system. "No fucking way," I grumbled. "Hof and Yaw? I thought we killed you assholes."

And as they both studied me for an awkward moment, the first one turned to the second one and nonchalantly covered his mouth with his hand. "I think we know this blighter boy, Hof. His ugly mugly looks familiar to me."

The second one nodded. "Oi, we know him. That be the Dean blighter, Yaw."

"Yeah, yer right. The *Dean* blighter. We caught him in the bog. And we were gonna slow roast him on the smoker, you 'member, Hof?"

"Yeah, I 'member, Yaw. But he escaped."

"Oi, he escaped. Maybe you should get yer hammer."

"Oi, then I'll whack him on the head—"

"Boys!" One of the blue-haired jackasses called out from across the atrium, causing the miscreant korrigans to forget about me and scurry across the ornate room to join their colleagues.

I scoffed. "Unbelievable."

Doc grinned. "Friends of yours?"

"Of all the goddamn nephers to pick from, leave it to Janser Berinhart to bring those two assholes with her. She's got some nerve."

She chuckled. "And apparently a gigantic pair of balls to be late to a meeting called by *God*."

"Balls? No. But she does have a gigantic pair of something else."

And as Doc gave me a funny look, the enigmatic door appeared a few feet away and out stepped a really pissed-off looking Metatron with Janser right behind him carrying a half empty bottle of bourbon. And although she was back in her human form, she was still buck ass naked, which caused everyone to stop screaming at each other and collectively gawk at her for an awkward moment or several.

"Oh my," Doc muttered, as the burly queen of the Others sauntered by us with her buxom full-figured form on full display.

And as Janser took her place at the table amidst her entourage of weirdos, she guzzled what remained of her bourbon before smashing the bottle on the floor, causing everybody to start yelling again.

Taking note of Hon, the armored giant and high commander of the Carolingian Knights of Nod, who was doing his very best to keep Mortog, his somewhat brutish counterpart, in check, I said, "Honsel doesn't look very happy."

Doc smiled. "Yeah, I think he's regretting his decision to assist Mortog with the negotiation process."

"Why's that?"

"Well, Mortog apparently has the intellect of a ten-year-old who amuses himself by pulling his finger and farting. And then he promptly announces that he pulled his finger and farted."

Making the mental note that you can't beat the classics, I shifted my attention to the unimpressive group of seven humans of varying age, gender, and ethnic background clumped together in a tight gaggle. "Who are those jokers?"

"That would be the Academy."

"Seriously?" I scoffed, taking note of their nondescript outfits and bland appearance. "That mundane collection of exceptionally average people is the secret society of über powerful kingmakers?"

Erin nodded. "Yep. Although they look more like a parent-teacher organization than a global shadow regime."

"Yeah, you'd think one of them would have an eye patch. Or a hairless cat. Or at the very least be wearing fancy suits."

"You know better than that," said a gruff yet very familiar voice from behind me. "People with power, *real* power, don't wear suits."

Turning to find Tony Coates, my former brother in arms-turned-leader of the mechanized strike team known as the Biological Anomaly Retaliation Task Force, or B.A.R.T. for short, I couldn't help but grin. "Is that a fact?"

He grinned back. "That, my simple friend, is a fact."

"Ok, smart ass, then what do people with real power wear?"

Grinning again for good measure, he said, "Whatever the fuck they want." Built like a linebacker and looking unnaturally fit for a fifty-year-old former infantryman, he ran a hand through his bushy beard that was artfully speckled with a few noticeable streaks of gray as he nodded at Erin. "Hello again, Doc."

She chuckled. "Hello again, Tony."

"Again?" I said, somewhat confused.

"Tony and I were catching up earlier. You know, because we got here on time and you were *late*."

"No, we've already been over this. I wasn't late. I was detained— at the bar. With the nymphomaniacal nepher queen. And that sentence sounded so much better in my head."

Tony chuckled. "Just like the old days."

"What is?"

"You making excuses for some shit or another while me and Doc Kelly take care of business."

Offering him a spirited hand gesture, I said, "Speaking of business, *Big Sarge*, what the hell are you doing here, anyway?"

"I'm here at the behest of my employer to ensure their safety in the event things become uncivilized."

"Your employer," I muttered, connecting a few dots. "Wait, the Academy? You work for the Academy?"

"I can neither confirm nor deny the existence of such an organization, nor whether I'm in their loyal service."

"But you are."

"Yeah, totally. They bankroll my entire operation."

"You mean the B.A.R.T.? I thought that was a government outfit."

"Government sponsored. Privately funded."

"And the Academy is the private funding."

He nodded. "Money, resources, equipment, anything we need, they provide. And I don't ask any questions. Neither does the government. Easier that way."

"Interesting," I muttered. "So, the Academy built the fleet of Praetorian. What's their interest in hunting giants?"

"Like I said, I don't ask questions. Blue Sky calls the shots, and we deliver."

"What's his deal?" Doc asked. "This enigmatic Mr. Blue Sky person."

Inconspicuously nodding at a slightly overweight woman with curly dark hair who sat at the conference table quietly studying everyone, he said, "Well, for starters, he's not a *he*. He's a she."

"So, the leader of the Academy is a woman." Erin smiled, noting her loose-fitting denim dress and Birkenstocks. "That looks like a hippy soccer Mom from middle America."

Tony smiled. "Yup."

"So, it's *Mrs.* Blue Sky then."

"Nope. She still goes by Mr. And, no, I don't know why."

Doc chuckled. "Ok, so, what's she like?"

"She's nice."

"Nice. That's all you have to say about the lady that runs the organization that, besides not existing, kind of runs the world?"

"Well, aside from being the literal smartest person on the planet who has the uncanny ability to stay twenty moves ahead of anybody and everybody at any given moment, yeah, she's nice."

I smiled. "You almost sound like you're afraid of her."

He smiled back. "Blue Sky doesn't scare me. She fucking terrifies me. Just wait until you see her in action. It's something to behold."

"Well, I hope you're right because she's gonna need some big balls to negotiate with this crew."

"Please." He scoffed. "These negotiations will go exactly how she wants them to. And if I know her, she's already gamed out every possible scenario."

"And how's she done that?"

"I guarantee she's got detailed files on everyone here. Strengths. Weaknesses. Motivations. Fears. Skeletons in the closet. Pressure points to exploit. She's already in their heads. Believe it."

Scanning the arcane crowd of otherworldly beings, I shook my head. "Come on, man, you're saying that the Academy has detailed files on *everyone* here?"

"That's precisely what I'm saying."

"Including giants and nephers?"

"Definitely."

"Even the archangels?"

"*Especially* the archangels. Shit, I wouldn't be surprised if she had a file on God himself."

"But how? I mean, that's not remotely possible—"

"Like I told you before, I don't ask questions. Easier that way."

As I made the mental note that perhaps the human race had more of a chance in this new world order than I originally thought they did, I couldn't help but chuckle as Abernethy jumped on top of the ginormous horseshoe-shaped table in an attempt to get everyone to stop berating each other.

Waving his massive arms back and forth, he very Scottishly barked, "Everyone haud yer wheesht!"

And when the entire group flat out ignored him, he again barked, "Haud yer wheesht!"

And when everybody flat out ignored him for a second time, he jumped to the floor and drew his mighty claymore broadsword before holding it high above his head. "Bloody hell, people! I said be quiet!" Then he simply lopped the table in half with one herculean strike.

While I wasn't sure if it was the fact he literally cut the goddamn conference table in half with his friggin sword or it was more the fact that everyone finally understood what the hell he was saying, it seemed to work as all the *distinguished* ambassadors stopped their shouting and glared at him.

"Now that's better," he grumbled, as everyone took their respective posts around the jacked-up table. "Ethan will be here any moment, and he need not see this incessant bickering."

"The highlander is quite right," Uriel said, dripping of sarcasm. "Perhaps we should all take our respective seats at Father's negotiation table and await his distinguished arrival in revered silence." Then his face curled into an exaggerated frown. "If only *someone* hadn't destroyed the table in a fit of rage. What are we to do now, noble Abernethy?"

Thinking that was rather funny, Mortog the eighteen-foot behemoth and distinguished representative of the anakim starting laughing so hard that the floor shook. "Abernethy has bad bad temper," he said in a booming, guttural voice as his massive chest heaved up and down. "And he talk talk funny."

"The godling may talk funny," Semyaza said. "But he's got *style*. I mean look at the dress he's wearing. It's fantastic!"

Sheathing his claymore broadsword in a blur of motion, the burly Scotsman forced a grin as his hands curled into tight fists. "It's not a bloody dress. It's a kilt!"

Semyaza grinned back. "Call it what you want, godling. I think crossdressing's *sexy!*"

And just as Big A was about to punch a hole through Semyaza's heroine-addled head, Stephen stepped between them. "That's enough," he said in signature stoic fashion. "And that goes for every-one. You'd all be well served to show some respect—"

"*Respect.*" Janser scoffed, still standing there buck naked. "Respect for what, Stephen? For God? Or Ethan. *Please.* He deserves many things, but our respect is not among them."

Apparently not appreciating those comments in the least, Gabriel stepped forward with a deep scowl on his chiseled face. "Mind your tongue, Janser Berinhart."

Giving one of her extra-large breasts a healthy squeeze, the uncanny queen grinned a wolfish grin. "Suck it, Gabriel."

Which, of course, struck Mortog funny, causing him to erupt into obnoxious, booming laughter for the second time in as many minutes. "Queen J told Gabriel to suck her booby booby! Hey, wanna pull pull my finger?"

And as the situation devolved back into a frenetic free-for-all complete with pushing, shoving, shouting, farting, and the occa-sional flapping of unusually large breasts, the commanding tone of a familiar voice cut the air like a clap of thunder, causing everyone to instantly stop. "Quit acting like children," muttered Ethan Roy as everyone looked up to find him standing between Stephen and Big A like he'd been there the entire time.

Wearing his usual flannel shirt and carpenter jeans ensemble, a deep frown was clearly visible from under his stately beard as his intense, icy blue eyes scanned the room. With a simple wave of his hand, the mighty horseshoe-shaped table was restored to pristine condition as he continued to glare at the bizarre group. "Sit the hell down and shut up."

And there was just something about the way he said it that made everybody do exactly that.

7

Sitting in perfect silence, the entire crew, regardless of size, shape, species or bloodline, gawked at Ethan Roy, almost like they were trying to figure out if he was actually standing there. Or not.

It didn't matter one bit whether they loved him, hated him, loved to hate him, or hated to love him. They were all equally awestruck by his dominating yet humble presence as he stood before them like an ominous statue.

"Damn," Doc whispered, admiring the wiry, athletic frame of the great creator as he ran a hand through his impressive mane of white speckled hair. "God kind of looks like a sexy Santa Claus."

Making the mental note that Erin may have a thing for older guys and perhaps beards, I watched with great anticipation as Ethan rolled up the sleeves on his flannel shirt and nodded at Stephen and Abernethy before positioning himself in the center of the ginormous horseshoe-shaped table.

"So, here's the thing," he said, breaking the deafening silence. "I was wrong. Wrong about a lot of things, apparently. And it's time for some changes. In fact, it's past time." His words had a distinct, deliberate cadence that was both eloquent and curt at the same time. It was reminiscent of John Wayne, but with a detectable intellect that you could almost feel as he spoke.

Slowly pacing, he methodically made eye contact with everyone sitting around the table. "For longer than you know, I've walked among you. From the Heavens to the Earth and all places in between. Watching. Listening. I've seen your actions. Heard your words." And as everyone literally hung on each and every syllable coming out of his mouth, he said, "And it makes me sick. Every last bit of it. Your insatiable, unrelenting desire to consume everything in your grasp. It literally sickens me. And *somehow*, despite all your vast differences, you're all the same. You share the same greed. The same hate. I can't make any damn sense of it. And believe me, it's not from lack of trying."

He grinned in a way that was more menacing than friendly. "I used to think that separation was the key. Angels in Heaven. Humans on Earth." Pausing to glare at Semyaza, who sunk low in his chair, he said, "Then the nephilim entered the picture thanks to the Watchers. So, I created the Deacons. My own wrath incarnate. Servants of mankind to maintain the Balance. And they did. But to what end?" He chuckled. "I dare say to no goddamn end. So, here we are. All these years later. Same bullshit. Day in and day out. And despite it all, I find myself asking one simple question — what's next?"

Clearing his throat, Uriel stood up. "May I offer a suggestion, Father?" And when he received nothing but an icy stare in response, he promptly returned to his seat and placed his hands on his lap. "Perhaps later."

Rubbing his temples for a couple of long seconds, Ethan said, "The truth is, I don't know what comes next. That's for you all to decide. But unlike in the old days, you'll be figuring it out together. And you'll be doing it on Earth. No more separation. No more intervention. Flourish, prosper, or don't. This is the one and only time I'll convene this group. You have my word on that. I only ask for one thing in return — please try. *Try* to reach an accord amongst yourselves. The Earth was once an Eden for all who walked upon it. It can be that way again."

Letting out a deep sigh, he then scanned the room once more. "At my request, Stephen and Abernethy will serve as masters of ceremony for these—these Eden Accords. The rest is up to you. Good luck."

And before anyone could get a word in edgewise, he was gone.

Almost like the air was returned to the room, the group seemed to take a welcomed breath as Uriel again rose to his feet and grinned at everyone. "Well, that was pleasant. How very nice if not entirely hypocritical of father to drop in and set the tone for this truly historical gathering. Now that the pleasantries are over, I'd like to recommend that we begin the proceedings by—"

"Oh, *shut it*, Uriel," Semyaza said as he also rose to his feet. "No one wants to listen to your ingratiating bullshit. And besides, the way I figure it, there isn't anything to talk about."

"Incorrect," Stephen said, annoyed by the deranged seraph but remaining stoned-faced, nonetheless. "There is much to discuss if we are to successfully negotiate—"

"Negotiation!" Semyaza shouted. "An interactive process in which parties of *equal* standing or stature seek common ground on issues of *mutual interest* to reach an agreement that will be honored by all."

Stephen sighed. "What is your point, Semyaza?"

"My point, little godling, is simple," he replied, nodding at Uriel and Gabriel. "We are sons of Heaven. And sons of Heaven inherently have no common ground nor mutual interests with humans or half breeds. We will do as we please. And that is simply *that*."

Uriel grinned. "As much as it dismays me to agree with my prodigal brother, I do believe he is correct in this particular matter. As it turns out, we are the mighty and—"

"*We* will not abuse our power as such," Gabriel declared, as he also sprung to his feet and glared at his two brothers. "Did you hear nothing Father just said? The seraphim once lived in concert with

Earth's lesser species, and we must find a way to do it again —peacefully."

Not appreciating that comment in the least, Janser Berinhart stood up as her creepy yellow eyes flashed a creepier yellow, and thick, raven fur instantly covered her naked body. "Who are you calling *lesser*, daddy's boy?"

"Anakim are mighty!" Mortog grunted, grabbing his chair and smashing it on the floor. "We pluck pluck your halo head off shoulder and shit down your neck neck!"

And despite Stephen's and Abernethy's best attempts to get control of the situation, it was right about then when the newly coined Eden Accords turned into a deafening cacophony of shouts, insults, and otherwise calamity.

"Christ," Doc grumbled. "This is a disaster."

I shook my head. "You ain't kidding."

"Check it out," Tony said, pointing across the atrium at the frumpy soccer mom who apparently ran the secret society that apparently ran the world. Seated at the table with her hands on her lap, she had a telling smirk on her face that gave the impression she was thoroughly enjoying herself. "Blue Sky's about to let 'em know who's really in charge."

"Come on, man." I chuckled. "She may be all *scary* and whatnot in the regular world, but the world's not regular anymore. I mean, hell, there's two archangels standing there and a fucking giant and—"

And I never finished that sentence because it was at that exact moment when Mr. Blue Sky, who was actually a Mrs., reached into her purse and pulled out what looked like a metal baseball. Holding it close to her mouth, she gave it a delicate kiss before casually placing it on the floor and rolling it toward the gaggle of über beings who were too busy screaming at each other to notice. And as the peculiar object reached the center of the group, it slowly rose roughly six feet in the air before erupting in a blinding flash of ethereal green light that not only caused everybody to stop arguing, it froze them in place like statues. All of them.

Stephen and Big A.

Gabriel, Uriel, and Semyaza.

Mortog and Hon.

Queen Janser and her unnatural delegation of weirdos.

All frozen in place like surreal mannequins only able to move their eyeballs.

As I tried to wrap my head around just how in the hell Blue Sky managed to do that, Tony slapped me on the shoulder with a shit-eating grin on his face. "You were saying?"

I shrugged. "I was saying that she officially terrifies me now, too."

Rising to her feet as the rest of the Academy remained seated behind her, Blue Sky adjusted her dress and very carefully climbed on top of the horseshoe-shaped table. Strolling to where Semyaza sat frozen mid-rant, she looked down at him with a smug grin on her face.

"Negotiation," she said. Her voice was silvery, but her tone was brazen. "An interactive process in which parties of *equal* standing or stature seek common ground on issues of *mutual interest* to reach an agreement that will be honored by all."

Then she condescendingly patted him on the head like a child. "Now that we've established we're all of equal standing, I recommend we seek common ground on issues of mutual interest. Any objections?" And when nobody answered primarily because nobody could friggin talk, she smiled ear to ear. "Wonderful."

Climbing down from the table and returning to her chair, she snapped her fingers, and everyone was instantly released from the unseen force holding them at bay. Shocked that a mere human, nonetheless one that looked like she should be baking cookies for a Girl Scout troop, was able to assert total dominance over them, everyone just kind of glared at the peculiar leader of the Academy for an awkward second or two.

"Do not do that again," Stephen said, finally breaking the silence with his intense gaze focused on Blue Sky.

Using her index finger to draw an imaginary X over her chest, she grinned. "Cross my heart."

"Very well," he muttered, facing the group. "If everyone would please take your seats, we can begin the discussions. In my opinion, the first order of business should be—"

"Nexus points," Blue Sky said, rather matter-of-factly. "That's the first order of business."

Clearly annoyed that she cut him off mid-sentence, Stephen shrugged. "I don't understand."

"No, I imagine you don't. But fortunately, I do." Reaching into her pocketbook, she pulled out a series of satellite photos that were overlaid with mysterious grid patterns and tossed them on the table. "It's rather simple. All that fancy angel technology tucked away in the lodestones lurking about in our skies is powered by the primal energy grid that encircles the Earth in the form of ley lines. This same energy also provides the angels themselves, and apparently their offspring, with their enhanced strength, size, speed, and otherwise supernatural abilities. It's not some arcane *magic*, you see. It's science. Albeit high-dimensional quantum science, but science nonetheless."

"That's all very nice, lassie," Abernethy grumbled, clearly losing patience. "But what is yer point?"

"My *point* is that there's exactly two physical locations on the entire planet where the ley lines converge to form a literal vortex of limitless, elemental power. Two nexus points that, if controlled by any faction of our winged colleagues, would—"

"Would be exceptionally bad for the rest of us," Janser Berinhart said, connecting the dots.

Blue Sky nodded. "Precisely." Grabbing two of the photos from the table, she held them up side by side. "Zion Canyon in Utah. And the Great Pyramid of Giza in Egypt. These are the nexus points. And I propose the first official act of the *Eden Accords* is to immediately place both areas summarily off limits to all parties until proper protocols are agreed to and enacted."

Janser slammed her fist on the table. "I agree!"

Which was closely followed by, "Agree! Agree!" from Mortog.

"This is unwise," Gabriel said, shaking his head. "Places of such power cannot be left unguarded given the current instability. They could easily be exploited by—"

"By *whom*, brother?" Uriel cut in. "By me and my legions? Or Semyaza and his Watchers? It almost sounds like you doubt our otherwise good intentions."

Semyaza laughed. "No, it more so sounds like big brother wants to keep them for himself."

"Yes," Janser said, glaring at the archangel. "It does, doesn't it?"

"I want no such thing," Gabriel replied, devoid of emotion. "But given my brothers' history of treachery, deceit, and otherwise malfeasance, you would be better served to leave the protection of the nexus points to my legions."

Blue Sky's face curled into a wide smile. "*Protection* says the archangel. And who will protect us from you, should your legendary altruism falter, Gabriel?"

As the group continued the spirited debate with slightly more civility than the first few attempts, Doc nodded at Tony. "Your boss is one hell of a shrewd operator."

"That she is." He chuckled. "And she's just getting warmed up."

I groaned. "Why do I get the feeling we're going to be here for a long, long time?"

He chuckled again. "I see you still have the patience of a six-year-old kid."

With a big smile on my face, I was about to tell him to piss off when the atrium floor began to violently quake, causing the ornate marble columns circling the room to crack and moan in protest. Bracing ourselves against the wall, we were barely able to keep our feet as a second and third wave rolled through the sprawling room. Just as it felt like the entire atrium was going to come crumbling down on top of us, the shaking stopped. And sprinting through one of the archways, holding a crumpled stack of papers was Rooster with MacCawill on his heels.

"What in the bloody blue blazes is going on, Jackie?" Abernethy grunted as he wiped dust from his face.

Dumping the papers on what remained of the table, Rooster started frantically sifting through them until he found one in particular and held it up. "Look at these readings! They're off the charts. It's toast! Shit, we're toast! Look at these goddamn readings!"

"Take a breath, John," Stephen said, trying his best to study the chart Rooster was frantically pointing at. "What are you saying?"

"He's saying that the Earth's core is steadily turning into cream cheese," MacCawill said, snatching the chart and laying it on the table for all to see. "The damage done by the Acropolis is much worse than we originally thought. These seismic readings prove it."

"And unless we figure out a way to fix it," Rooster added, "the planet will literally rip itself apart."

"How long do we have?" I asked, joining the conversation with Doc and Tony on my flanks.

Rooster shrugged. "Maybe a week. Maybe more?"

"Maybe less," MacCawill muttered.

"Then we must take action," Stephen said. "How do we repair the damage?"

And after an excruciatingly long moment as everyone exchanged blank stares and shrugged their shoulders, Metatron stepped forward with a deep frown on his face. "A task of such magnitude can only be addressed by Ethan himself or those who were here at the very beginning with him—the Builders."

"The Builders?" Stephen asked, clearly not following the plot.

"The first angels, the Anunnaki. The prolific builders of the ancient world."

Semyaza grinned almost like he was oddly enjoying the doomsday scenario. "Well, I can't imagine that daddy dearest is going to intercede given his epic *tough love* speech and subsequent mic drop. Apparently, we *sicken* him."

Gabriel sighed. "It seems the Anunnaki are our best and only hope. Their skill is legend."

Almost afraid to ask judging by the looks on their faces, I said, "Then why does it feel like this isn't good news?"

"Because, Mr. Sunshine," Metatron replied, lighting a cigarette and taking a long drag. "The Anunnaki have not been seen nor heard from in three millennia. Maybe four."

Well, shit.

8

"An entire race of *super angels* cannot simply disappear," Blue Sky said, with a detectable edge, as she glared at Metatron. "Especially one as powerful as you insinuate. And I find it hard to believe that you don't know what became of them. You're the scribe of *God* after all."

"I *was* the scribe of God, good lady," he rebutted, clearly not appreciating her tone. "That was quite a long time ago. And I did not say the Anunnaki disappeared. I said they've not been seen nor heard from for—"

"Four thousand years, blah blah, yada yada," Semyaza grumbled as he rolled his eyes. "It's not like the *great and powerful* Anunnaki would help us even if they were standing in this very room. A greater collection of egomaniacal prima donnas has never existed! Peculiar shaped heads and all. They're probably the cause of these earthquakes to begin with!"

"Nae," Abernethy grunted. "Yer failed angel mutiny is the cause of these earthquakes."

"Mutiny? I know nothing of that, I assure you."

"Is yer mind so muddled to where you don't remember two days ago when Michael and your best mate Lucifer stole the bloody Acropolis from Tenth Heaven and tried to blow the Earth to wee bits?"

The deranged seraph grinned. "That was not a mutiny, godling. That was a long overdue liberation. And I'd say it was quite successful, actually."

Looking like he was about to blow a gasket, Gabriel barked, "Enough! There's no time for this. If we are to locate the Builders, we must band together."

And after an awkward second or two where everyone reluctantly nodded agreement, Stephen said, "Perhaps we should take a step back. Pardon my ignorance, but aside from the Watchers, I was unaware that another race of angels lived upon the Earth. Who exactly are these Anunnaki?"

Metatron sighed before lighting another cigarette from the one hanging out of the corner of his mouth. "I'm afraid that's a question not easily answered." After a long drag from the fresh smoke, he said, "The Anunnaki were Ethan's first creation. Generation zero. The original angels, so to speak. Some say they're the best of us. Others say quite the opposite. It's difficult to know either way."

Looking more confused by the second, Stephen simply shrugged. "And why is that, Metatron?"

"Well, they're somewhat of an enigma. Even to the seraphim. And as they spent most of their time on Earth, precious little information about them exists. Aside, of course, from what they left behind."

"And what was that?" said Blue Sky, interjecting herself back into the conversation. "What did they leave behind?"

Metatron chuckled. "Literally or metaphorically?" And after a long silence accompanied by icy stares from the entire group, he said, "From the beginning, then. The Anunnaki were prolific builders. That much we do know. As such, they helped Ethan literally shape the Earth. And upon its surface — they built. And they built. And they built."

"They built what?"

"Structures. Cultures. Civilizations. Myth and legend. Legend and lore. If you look hard enough throughout history, mainstream or otherwise, you'll find a definite link back to the Anunnaki in some form or fashion."

Blue Sky's eyes danced with thought as she apparently started to connect a series of dots. "Pyramids," she muttered, fixated on Metatron. "The ruins of the Acropolis sitting on the desert floor in Zion Canyon. And the lodestones hovering above our cities. They're trapezoidal shaped structures. Pyramids."

Metatron grinned. "An interesting and unique architectural style, wouldn't you say?"

Blue Sky grinned back. "Yes, I would. It's also the very same architecture inexplicably littered throughout ancient civilizations spanning all corners of the planet. Like the Sumerians. Persians. Egyptians. Romans. Greeks. Incans. Mayans. So on and so forth."

Apparently very impressed that Blue Sky put all that together so fast, Metatron said, "Well done, good lady. But don't forget the Akkadians, Assyrians, or the Babylonians. They actually worshipped the Anunnaki as gods, as did the Sumerians, of course."

"Wait," Rooster cut in, looking like his head was about to implode. "Are you saying that the Anunnaki are the Sumerian 'sky gods'? Like, literally?"

"That's precisely what I'm saying, Mr. O'Dargan."

"And they're literally responsible for the all the mind-blowing ancient structures that modern day science still can't explain?"

"Only the good ones."

"The good ones? You mean like the Egyptian pyramids scattered across the Valley of the Kings?

Metatron nodded. "And the great Ziggurat of Ur in Iraq. And the majestic cities of Chichen Itza, Pumapunku, and Macchu Picchu. And don't forget Easter Island. Oh, did I already mention Atlantis?"

"Wait, Atlantis? As in the mythical lost island colony?"

"It's only lost if you don't know how to find it."

And as the group thought about that for an awkward second or two, and Rooster now looked like he was about to piss himself, Uriel said, "Enough already, brother! Unless the Anunnaki have been slumming with those derelict Atlanteans for the last four thousand years, I fail to see how any of this titillating history lesson is helping with our current predicament."

"That's because you're not listening, *brother*. The Anunnaki helped Ethan *shape* the Earth."

"Yes, yes, we're all very impressed with their body of work. And?"

"And rumor has it that they didn't just build upon the Earth's surface. There are tales. Tales of great, thriving metropolises deep within the very ground we walk upon. Tell me, have you ever heard the of the Hollow Earth concept?"

"Big big caves," Mortog said, nodding emphatically. "Underground. Where anakim go. Nobody follow."

"Where anakim go," I muttered, thinking back over the past year, and our multiple failed attempts to figure out where the super-sized malevolent miscreants were concealing their ranks. "Wait, are you saying that you assholes have been hiding underground this whole time?"

"Like under the goddamn Grand Canyon, for example?" Rooster added.

Getting an apparent kick out of the fact that he and his band of giant marauders managed to outsmart us, Mortog broke into a hearty laughter. "Dumb dumb Deacons never found us. Anakim smarter!"

As Rooster and I stewed on that, Stephen turned to Metatron with an inquisitive gaze. "So, you're hypothesizing that the Anunnaki took up residence deep within the Earth itself in these massive cave structures?"

Metatron nodded. "Yes, but not in caves like our dear friend Mortog here and his oversized ilk. I believe the Anunnaki retreated to Hollow Earth — the world within the world. The subterranean paradise they ever so skillfully created when the Earth was formed."

Looking Metatron up and down with her creepy yellow eyes like she didn't believe a word coming out of his mouth, Janser Berinhart said, "And why would you think that?"

"Why, the stories of course. Have you not heard them over the years, my good queen?"

"Stories of what?"

"Nibiru. The netherworld nirvana. Otherwise known as Kur or Fennario. A place beyond time, space, and comprehension, they say. A place of wonderment and awe, they say. A place not unlike the Medmenham Lounge, but on a much, much grander scale. A hedonistic heaven on Earth — or, in it, I should say."

Janser dismissively waved her hands. "Of course I've heard the stories of *Nibiru*. But such a place does not exist. If it had, I would've been there. You know this."

"Ah, but they also say that it's a place you cannot travel to without proper invitation."

"Invitation." She chucked. "And after all these many years, am I to understand that you, the great Black Swan, never warranted an invitation? Nor have I, the Queen of the Others? *Please.* There is no such place."

Metatron grinned, making sure Janser got a good look at his gold teeth. "Let's agree to disagree, my dear. Dollars to donuts the Anunnaki can be found in Nibiru."

Semyaza began to clap. Obnoxiously. "Perfect! So, our collective salvation awaits us in a clandestine, or perhaps farcical, land of deceit and debauchery that no one knows how to reach. Well done, scribe. Well, well done!"

"Wait," Rooster said. "If the Anunnaki do live in this subterranean realm, then they must be severely impacted by the damage to the Earth's core just like we are. Probably more so, actually. Maybe they'll just fix everything, right?"

"That is highly doubtful, John O'Dargan," Gabriel replied. "If the Builders retreated to this netherworld as Metatron believes, then I'm quite certain they would have taken any and all precautions to maintain their independence from the rest of the planet."

"So, you're saying they would've built their home to withstand the destruction of the actual Earth?"

He nodded. "Indeed. Although I don't recall much about them, I do recall their extreme dissatisfaction with both mankind and the seraphim alike."

"Is there anything else, Gabriel?" asked Stephen. "Do you recall anything else about the Anunnaki that might help us?"

The archangel shrugged. "I'm afraid not. Their leader, Enki, went to great lengths to keep their exploits private. Perhaps they left clues to the whereabouts of Nibiru in one of the many structures they left behind. Perhaps we should start searching them—"

"Wait!" Metatron gasped, like he just had an enlightened epiphany. "Enki! That's right. He's the key."

"No, scribe," Semyaza grumbled. "Enki is an insufferable windbag. More so than even you!"

Ignoring his prodigal brother's snide commentary, Metatron said, "Enki might have been disillusioned with human beings, but there was one in particular that he was hopelessly enthralled by. And it was rather scandalous, as I recall." Then he swung his gaze toward Rooster. "Perhaps you've heard of her. Her name is—"

"Lilith," Rooster muttered, reading between the lines. "Ugh. Should've seen that coming."

"Lilith," Semyaza said after perking up a bit. "As in *the* Lilith? The delectable ginger minx that put the original '*wowza*' in *wo*man with her bodacious—"

"She's Rooster's mom," I grumbled, causing Semyaza to stop talking and offer my enigmatic ginger colleague an awkward shrug.

Metatron shook his head a few times. "Lilith and Enki were a bit of a power couple as memory serves. I mean, when she and Lucifer were on the rocks, that is."

"Your point?" Rooster grumbled, now beet red from head to toe.

"My *point* is that if anyone would know how to reach Enki or travel to Nibiru, it would be Lilith."

"And this *Lilith* person," Blue Sky said, looking like a child that wandered into the middle of a movie. "Who is she exactly?"

I groaned. "Let's just say that she's been around for a while. A long, long while."

"How long?"

"Garden of Eden kinda long."

"And what are her credentials?"

"Credentials? Well, she's kind of the first woman. Ever. Technically speaking, that is."

Blue Sky's brow furrowed. "Technically speaking?"

"Yeah. She kind of left Adam holding a fig leaf over his dick and stormed out of the Garden of Eden. Then shacked up with Lucifer for a few millennia. But then she ditched Lew's sorry ass, too. Rumor has it she cleaned him out in the divorce, by the way. And now she lives in a painting. With a snake. Did I mention she's kind of crazy pants?"

Not quite sure how to take that, Blue Sky said, "Can we trust her to assist us?"

"Trust?" I scoffed. "Hell no! Did you hear anything I just friggin said? Only way Lil's helping us is if her darling baby boy asks super nice."

Now it was Rooster's turn to groan. "Fine," he said. "I'll do it. But this is the last time. And if memory serves, you're still in debt to her from the last time she *helped* us."

"Yeah," I muttered, recalling the unnatural pact I made with Lilith when we were searching for the Ark of the Covenant back in the winter. "Maybe she's forgotten about that."

"Don't count it," Doc grumbled, shaking her head.

As another earthquake rumbled through the atrium, reminding all of us that time was of the essence, Stephen said, "If a consultation with Lilith is our agreed upon course of action, then I propose the Eden Accords continue while John O'Dargan goes to see her immediately. And as Dean Robinson and Erin Kelly have history with her as well, I suggest they accompany him."

Blue Sky grinned. "Not that I don't trust your good intentions, Stephen. But I don't trust your good intentions. So, I'll be sending Commander Coates along with your entourage. Just to keep everyone honest. You understand, of course."

And before Stephen could get a word in edgewise, Janser Berinhart said, "And I will also be sending representation, as I don't trust any of you!" Which was echoed by Mortog, Semyaza, Uriel, and Gabriel affirming that nobody trusts anybody to do anything without sending their respective cronies along.

"Very well," Stephen muttered after an exasperated sigh as he turned to Rooster. "How would you like to proceed, John?"

Pulling his signature antique pocket watch from his weathered bomber jacket and giving it a quick glance, Rooster said, "Anybody that's going with me be at the Quartermaster in twenty minutes. I need to figure out where my mom is on display nowadays. Then we'll pay her a visit."

And as everyone kind of gawked at him for a few awkward seconds, I made the mental note that the Eden Accords weren't exactly off to the greatest start. With that in mind, I also made the note that there was literally nowhere to go from here but up.

Unless, of course, we had to go to this Hollow Earth place. Which would be down.

Either way, I really just wanted Janser Berinhart to put some goddamn clothes on. Her furry tits were really starting to creep me out.

Just saying.

9

More than happy to leave the Medmenham Lounge in the rearview mirror for the time being, I nodded at Stephen before following Rooster and MacCawill through a portal that flared to life on the outskirts of the ginormous horseshoe-shaped table. With Doc and Tony on my heels, we stepped foot into the Quartermaster's main hall to find a few hundred clerics and acolytes seated throughout the sea of wooden tables scarfing down food while a few hundred more huddled around the mighty bar.

And for some reason, they were clapping.

And shouting.

And laughing their asses off.

As we got a little closer, I heard a couple shrill voices belting out a really, bad rendition of a Fleetwood Mac song I couldn't quite place.

"Christ," MacCawill grumbled, fighting his way through the labyrinth of people on his way to the bar. "What the hell's going on here?"

Covering her ears, Doc yelled, "Apparently the world's absolute worst karaoke!"

Tony chuckled. "Karaoke, my ass! That sounds more like coyotes having hate sex with Yoko Ono."

We finally burst through the crowd only to find Hof and Yaw standing atop the bar slamming beers and trading verses of "Gold Dust Women" as everyone cheered them on like they were demented leprechaun rock stars. I just about shit myself.

But instead, I decided to simply lose my shit.

Willing the shotgun into being, I felt the presence of the scabbard-like holster on my back as I reached back and pulled the semi-divine 1887 Winchester free in a blur of motion. The double barrels glowed and hissed with the white fire of Judgement as I focused my will and cocked the lever.

Swinging the muzzle toward the malevolent midgets with a big-ass smile on my face, I just stood there for a long moment as they stopped singing and gawked at me. Shaking my head, I muttered, "I don't know what you two jackasses are doing here, but if either one of you so much as utters another word of that song, I will shove this gun so far down your throat, you'll be shitting fire for a month. Are we clear?"

Saying nothing, they emphatically nodded as the surrounding crowd quickly dispersed and Coop popped his head up from behind the bar. "Don't shoot, hoss. I'm coming out."

With my unnatural shotgun still trained on my least favorite korrigans, I said, "Coop, please tell me why these assholes are river dancing on our bar. You know who they are, right?"

Looking like he was about to piss himself, Coop just shrugged. "Friends of yours?"

"Friends?" I barked. "Are you kidding me?"

"Ah, no?" He shrugged again. "They showed up right before y'all did. Janser Berinhart sent them. Said something about going with you and Rooster to see Lilith. Figured you knew."

Holstering the shotgun, I just glared at the wannabe leprechauns. "This true?"

Hof nodded. "Oi!" Which was quickly followed by, "Oi! Oi!" from Yaw.

Chuckling under his breath as he plopped on a barstool and poured himself a frothy beer, MacCawill said, "Lemme guess, mancho, these are the korrigans that kicked your ass in Nod, huh?"

Now it was my turn to shrug. "No idea what you're talking about, Roy. I've never seen these two assholes before in my life. That said, the shithead on the left is Hof and the other one's Yaw. Now, can somebody please get me a beer before I want to kill them again?"

"*Kill us?*" Hof snickered under his breath, yet still loud enough for everybody to hear. "The Dean blighter's dafty, Yaw."

"Oi!" Yaw snickered back. "He is a dafty, crafty blighter, Hof. But we could still whack him on the head with me hammer when he's not looking. Then we could slow roast him on the rotisserie—"

"And that's enough of that," I grumbled before grabbing both of them by the scruff of the neck and flinging them into the crowd. "Go and play for a while. And maybe wash up. You smell like cabbage. And old lady pants."

As the disgruntled korrigans flipped me off in unison before fading from sight for the moment, Rooster said, "Great. I wonder who else we can look forward to tagging along with us."

"Ah, y'all," Coop said as he stuffed a man-sized wad of chewing tobacco in his cheek. "What the hell's going on?"

After we took the next couple of minutes to explain the current state of affairs, he poured himself a tall beer and took a healthy gulp. "So, you're basically saying that these so-called peace talks are about as worthless as a sidesaddle on a sow. The Earth is falling apart faster than a sneeze through a screen door. And the only ones that can help us are these ancient angels that nobody's seen in four thousand years. Except, of course, for Rooster's momma, who's more slippery than a pocketful of pudding. No offense, pard."

"None taken," Rooster muttered. "And yes, that's about the state of things."

"Well, I hate to say it, but that sounds worse than having a dagum yellow jacket in your outhouse."

Thinking that Coop's redneckisms were really getting better, I turned to Rooster. "Speaking of pudding, we need to find Lilith."

"Shouldn't take the Contraption but a couple minutes to locate where her painting is on display. Why doesn't everybody grab some chow and meet me and Dean in the Reliquary when the rest of our tagalongs show up."

Already leaning over the bar to pour myself a tall, frothy beverage, I said, "Sounds like a plan, buddy. I'll be right here if you need me."

He groaned. "No, you'll be with me. In the Reliquary. Did you not hear what I just said?"

"Reliquary? For what? I got a beverage here."

It was right about then, Tony grabbed my prized pint and chugged it in a single gulp. "Thanks, Cap. That hit the spot." Then he hopped onto my stool with a shit-eating grin on his face as Doc, MacCawill, and Coop joined him.

Calling my old Ranger buddy an asshole a couple times for good measure, I followed a chuckling Rooster through the bustling crowd until we reached the massive door leading to the Reliquary. "So, what's this about?" I grumbled now that we were able to hold a conversation without shouting.

"We need a plan," he said, as the door swung open and we crossed the threshold into our otherworldly war room.

"A plan? To find your mom?"

Shaking his head, he just glared at me like I was a complete dumbass. "Ah, no. We need a plan to ditch our unwanted company."

Pulling to an abrupt halt, I glared right back at him. "Wait, are you seriously suggesting that we betray the trust of the Eden Accords by ditching their duly appointed cronies that we just agreed to take with us for the express purpose of keeping everyone from ripping each other to shreds? Is that what you're proposing here?"

He shrugged. "Bad idea?"

I grinned. "No, it's fucking brilliant. I'm in. They'll just be in the way."

He grinned back. "Exactly! And what happens if Lilith actually tells us how to find the Anunnaki? What then?"

Thinking on that for a second or two, I said, "Damn, you're right. The whereabouts of the only beings capable of repairing the Earth is the ultimate bargaining chip, isn't it?"

"Yes. Yes, it is. And in the wrong hands, it could be catastrophic. I mean, not more catastrophic than the planet literally shitting itself into a gazillion pieces, but you get the point. The Eden Accords would be toast for sure."

"All right, so what are you suggesting?"

"Well, assuming my mother knows how to reach Enki and the Anunnaki, I'm suggesting we trust no one with that information — except us."

"Us?"

"Me, you, and the team. That's it."

"So, we steal the information."

He shrugged. "Kinda sorta. But it's for the greater good, right?"

"And then what?"

"Then we go to Nibiru ourselves and convince these *Builders* to fix things."

"And what do we tell Stephen and Abernethy?"

"Nothing."

"We have to tell them something."

"Ok, so we make something up."

"Like what?"

"I don't know. Something that's not the truth but not exactly a lie either."

I chuckled. "This is classic."

"What?"

"*What?* Think about it. We're convinced that the group of über beings tasked with achieving world peace and prosperity will weaponize the location of the Anunnaki as leverage against each other."

"Exactly. Because they're liars. And cheats. And thieves. The whole lot of them."

"I don't disagree."

"Then what's so goddamn funny?"

"Well, since we think they'll steal the information, we're going to cheat and steal it first. Then we're going to lie about it so we don't get caught in the thievery or the cheatery."

He shrugged. "Yeah, and? Are you in or not?"

My face curled into a wide smile. "Oh, I'm totally in. I just want it on the record that, for once, a plan of epically bad design that reeks of tragic irony was not my idea. It was yours."

"Noted," he grumbled, taking a seat behind a computer terminal surrounded by a sprawling array of computer screens before pounding away on an old-ass keyboard for a few seconds. "All right. According to the Contraption, my mom's in San Francisco. Museum of Modern Art. Dialing up the coordinates now."

And right on cue, the Contraption's infamous portal generator roared to life in a barrage of hissing sparks and black smoke as my enigmatic ginger colleague continued typing at a feverish pace.

That's right, we had a portal generator.

It's kind of a long story, but somehow Rooster, MacCawill, and Ziggy built a quantum transportation device out of a dilapidated phone booth, a laptop computer, a couple beer kegs filled with plutonium, and a semi-functional temporal compass that Double OT won in a game of strip poker. And for the record, he won because he stripped *before* they started playing poker.

At any rate, we had a portal generator. And as a swirling blueish white light began to radiate from the arcane phone booth, I looked up to see MacCawill, Doc, and Tony strolling toward us with a collection of miscreants in tow to include my least favorite leprechauns.

"Better hurry," I muttered. "The crew's here."

"Did they bring the tagalongs?"

"Yup."

Rooster nodded, still typing away. "Perfect."

"Perfect? I thought our whole plan was predicated on ditching the goddamn tagalongs. Are they coming to San Fransisco with us?"

He grinned. "No. No, they are not."

Figuring I was better off not knowing what Rooster was up to, I just shrugged as everyone huddled around us.

"The gang's all here, mancho," MacCawill grumbled as the korrigans hid behind him, grinning at me. "Representing Janser Berinhart is Hof and Yaw, whom you've apparently met." Then he nodded at the three pissed-off angels, standing shoulder to shoulder and looking exceptionally disgruntled. "Tweedle Dickhead, Tweedle Doucheball, and Tweedle Fuck Face here represent Gabriel, Uriel, and Semyaza, respectively." And then he grinned at the fifteen-foot behemoth standing next to him wearing a ginormous pair of sweat pants and a hoodie. "And the big man here is Mortog's brother, Jim."

"Jim?" I chuckled as the anakim looked down at me and smiled to reveal his double rows of big teeth. "Your name's Jim? For real?"

To which he simply gave me a big thumbs up and said, "Jim Jim."

MacCawill shrugged. "From what we can tell, that's pretty much all he says."

Not quite sure what to say to all that, I just kind of waved at the big oaf as Rooster finished whatever the hell he was doing behind the computer terminal and faced the group. "All right, listen up," he said before pointing at the swirling vortex surrounding our interdimensional phone booth. "The goal of our little journey here is to locate Lilith and ascertain the current whereabouts of the Anunnaki. This portal will take us to her. But when we get there, I suggest we try to keep a low profile so as to not freak out any civilians out and about. Agreed?"

"And where are we going exactly?" one of the angels asked in a tone that was less than pleasant.

"Alaska," Rooster said, as he turned and winked at me. "Fortunately, my mother is in a somewhat remote location on the outskirts of Anchorage at the moment, so it should be an uneventful trip. Once we get there, everybody follow my lead. And most importantly, don't say anything. I'll do the talking. Any more questions?"

Looking somewhat concerned, Jim raised his hand. "Jim Jim?"

"No," Rooster replied. "We don't have time for snacks."

"Jim *Jim?*"

"Yes, I'm sure."

"Jim Jim!"

"No, goddamnit! The phone booth isn't a vending machine. It's a portal generator! Does anyone besides Jim have any questions?"

As we all just kinda shrugged, and I made the mental note to ask Rooster when he learned how to speak Jim Jim, my enigmatic ginger colleague said, "Good. Then let's go. Me and Dean will go first—"

"Oi!" Hof yelled. "You're not going first, ginger boy blighter! Hof and Yaw go first!" Which, of course, Yaw added, "Oi! Ginger boy blighter can't trick Yaw and Hof! You go last, ginger boy! Nice try."

"Agreed," said another one of the three angels. "Although korrigans inherently disgust me, they have a point. We will go first to ensure no foul play is afoot. Unless, of course, you disagree?"

"Fine," Rooster grumbled. "Have it your way."

And as our esteemed delegation of tagalongs started to file into the interdimensional phone booth and fade from sight, including Jim, who had to get on all fours to fit, Rooster grabbed Tony's shoulder just before he stepped through. "Trust me, Big Sarge. You don't want to go where they're going."

As the portal snapped shut, Tony said, "And where's that?"

"My summer place," MacCawill grinned. "On the moon."

"The moon, eh? As in, the one in space?"

"What are you guys up to?" asked Doc as she skeptically gazed at me and Rooster while Tony scratched his head. "Wait, I don't want to know. Where's Lilith actually hanging around these days?"

"San Francisco," Rooster said as the phone booth flared to life with a new portal. "At the Museum of Modern Art."

"Museum?" Tony said, clearly not following the plot. "Your mom's at a museum? What, does she work there or something?"

"It's more of a residency."

"So, she lives there?"

I grinned. "No. She *lives* in a painting. With a big ass snake. And she's always naked." And after he offered no response besides a glazed look, I said, "Yeah, never mind. Time to go?"

"Definitely," MacCawill replied. "No telling when your new pals will be back."

"How much time you think we got?"

"Well, seeing that my moon cottage is nothing short of a highly secured bunker, they should be stuck there a good while. But you never know. Halos are resourceful bastards. Either way, me and Ziggy will hang out here and keep an eye on shit."

"Speaking of my favorite kegbot," I said. "Where the hell is Ziggy? I haven't seen him all day."

"Yeah, me neither, come to think of it. And I could use some goddamn fig newtons. I haven't had a proper shit for days. Hey, Zig! Where you at? You better not be watching robot porn again! Fig newtons!"

"On that note," Rooster said. "We should get going." Then he offered Erin a clichéd bow. "Ladies first."

Shaking her head and grumbling something of a snide nature under her breath, she stepped into the portal's swirling vortex as Tony, Rooster, and I followed.

And just like that, we were off to California to try to save the world from certain apocalyptic demise. Again.

This was definitely the wrong week to quit drinking.

Good thing I never really considered it in the first place.

10

Given the current state of affairs, you'd think most folks would be cowering in the safety of their homes with their heads tucked between their legs as they kissed their asses goodbye and muttered Hail Mary's in rapid succession.

I mean, for starters, the entire planet was being relentlessly pummeled by earthquakes.

And then there was the off-the-charts volcanic activity popping up everywhere.

And don't forget the inexplicable flying pyramids the size of city blocks that ominously darkened the skies like nightmarish storm clouds.

But as the portal deposited us on the outskirts of a rather grandiose botanical garden of some sort, it was pretty clear that the good people of San Francisco didn't give a shit about any of that. Because if the scene laid out before us was any indication of what the rest of the city was doing, nobody was at home cowering. They were out and about.

Singing.

And dancing.

And barbecuing.

And drinking.

And partying their collective asses off.

"Now that's a proper fiesta." Tony chuckled as the portal snapped shut, leaving us in a modest grove of redwood trees overlooking an ornate and quite massive reflection pond that was teeming with people. Some in bathing suits. Others in birthday suits. And yet others still wearing all their clothes.

Not quite sure what to make of it, Doc said, "I guess this is how they panic in California?"

I groaned. "Friggin West Coast weirdos." And then some dude tossed me a can of beer as he ran past us in a speedo screaming, "End of the world party, bro! Drink up!" Nodding my appreciation, I cracked the beer and drained it in a single gulp. "Although, I kinda like their style."

Erin shook her head. "What is this place, anyway?"

Scanning the stunning park of manicured gardens and stepped terraces laid out before us for a good quarter mile or so, Rooster said, "Yerba Buena Gardens. The museum is north of the park a few blocks, if memory serves. We should get moving."

Making our way through the hopping crowd and past the reflection pond-turned-impromptu swimming pool, I began to sweat as the sticky mid-afternoon heat seemed to wrap around my damn body like a wet blanket. "You spend much time around here?" I asked Rooster.

He nodded. "Yeah, I used to try to visit a couple times a month."

"Couple times a month, eh?"

"Yep. And I lived here for a few years back in the day. Me and Caveman had a place on the bay."

"When was that, John?" asked Erin.

"1848. Or was it 1849? I forget. At any rate, we had a little mining operation. Made some good money until shit got crazy with all the forty-niners. Then we headed back east."

"Mining operation," Doc said somewhat pensively. "Wait, are

you saying that you were here during the California Gold Rush of 1848? Seriously?"

"And what about more recently?" I asked before my enigmatic ginger colleague had the opportunity to slip into bloviation mode and give us a history lesson that I wasn't in the mood for. "Who were you visiting a couple times a month? A lady friend perhaps?"

"Lady friend," he replied, like I was a complete dumbass. "You know I'm a foodie, right?"

I shrugged. "Yeah, so?"

"*So*? This is San Francisco."

"Yeah, and? Is the food good?"

"Not good." He scoffed. "It's exceptional. San Francisco is foodie Mecca." Realizing I just opened the door for a bloviation opportunity on a completely different topic, I just shook my head as he repeated, "Foodie—Mecca." And before I could get a word in edgewise, he said, "The cioppino or Swedish pancakes alone are worth a trip. The mouthfeel is purely orgasmic."

"Please don't say mouthfeel again. Or orgasmic. Like, ever again. Just don't."

Ignoring my snide commentary, he said, "But that's the very tip of the iceberg. I mean, the *sweet and savory* baked goods? Don't even get me started. The cheese cake melts in your mouth. And the apple fritter? Out of body experience. Every time. Oh, and they invented bread here."

"I'm pretty sure bread wasn't invented in friggin San Francisco," I grumbled.

"From sour dough to focaccia to pan dulce, the flavor profile is life-altering. Mind-melting, even."

"Please stop."

"And the Dutch crunch bread? Dude, forget about it. My mouth is watering just thinking about the layers upon layers of flaky bliss."

"I know what you mean," Tony muttered as we walked past a group of scantily clad women playing a rather spirited game of volleyball as a couple guys with acoustic guitars serenaded them with an Eagles song I couldn't quite place. "My mouth is watering too, buddy."

I'm pretty sure Rooster was about to give us another unrelenting dose of foodie logic when we reached the north end of the park, coasted through a modest alley, and found ourselves standing on the corner of a four-lane street filled with abandoned cars for as far as the eye could see in either direction. Directly across the street from us was a towering building with a reddish brown and white stone facade that just screamed, 'Look at me! I'm a pretentious museum filled with art and snooty hipsters. Art!'

Making our way across the street as people flitted about like they didn't have a care in the world, Rooster said, "Hey, guys, check out that coffee shop next to the museum."

"Hell no," I grumbled. "We are not stopping for foodie froufrou lattes and hifalutin strudel—"

"Wait," Doc said, peering in the window at an ivory-haired bombshell waving us. "Is that Billy?"

And sure as shit, as we closed the distance and stepped into the posh coffee shop that was bustling with people like everywhere else in the city, I was more than surprised to find our resident she-dragon all dolled up in her typical white leather pants, biker boots, and a white tee-shirt perched at a high-top table watching the news on a television mounted on the wall. "What took you so long?" she said in her goofy Nordic accent as we huddled around the table and she exchanged fist bumps with Erin.

I shrugged. "What are you doing here, Puff?"

"Watching your back," she replied, clearly not appreciating the magic dragon moniker.

"Thanks, but I don't need my back watched."

Grinning rather smugly, she rose to her feet and looked down at me with her electric blue eyes as the tattooed scales that elegantly covered her sculpted arms raised like hackles. "I wasn't talking to you, *little man*."

"What's going on, Billy?" asked Doc. "Did something happen?"

"Your scruffy cowboy sent me."

I chuckled. "You mean MacCawill?"

She nodded. "He said to tell you that your *new friends* broke out of his safehouse."

"Shit," we all grumbled in unison upon hearing that excellent bit of news.

"That didn't take long," Rooster said. "Where are they now?"

Billy shrugged. "MacCawill said they were still on 'the moon,' wherever that is. I mean, it's not like they're on the actual moon, right?"

Apparently feeling that was a question better left unanswered, Doc muttered, "New plan. Me and Billy will stay here and keep an eye out for the tagalongs while you guys deal with Lilith."

"I'll stay, too," Tony said before winking at the ladies. "I hate museums. And the company seems exponentially better here, if I'm being honest."

Figuring Tony had a valid point, I turned to Rooster. "All right, guess it's just us then. You ready?"

Fixated on the TV, he said, "Yeah, one sec. Check this shit out."

"Breaking news!" The newscaster blurted. With bloodshot eyes and wrinkled clothing, he looked like he hadn't slept for a week. "Buzz Shea here, folks. And the latest buzz? Don't panic! It's all good! Or at least that's what our *esteemed leaders* are saying. In a press conference held at the White House, which is ironically surrounded by countless legions of super-sized Praetorian mechanized warriors, our fearless President and his Secretary of Defense just told the American public that the flying pyramids are nothing to worry about."

I shook my head. "Nothing to worry about, huh?"

"Exactly!" The reporter shouted. "Nothing—to—worry—about! It's simply a test of an elaborate 'global defense network' intended to shield the Earth from future meteor strikes. So, everybody can just go back to normal. We're definitely not being invaded by space aliens. Oh, and with regard to the earthquakes, volcanoes, giant sightings, and all the other weird shit happening — just ignore it. It's all good, folks! All good! Christ, can somebody get me a goddamn drink?"

"That's Blue Sky's work," Tony said. "I guarantee it."

"Blue Sky," Rooster muttered. "Wait, are you saying that the Academy controls the messaging coming from the American president?"

Tony chuckled. "Not just the American president. Every president. And prime ministers, leaders of state, royal families, random dictators, and so forth. They have their hands on everything. The messaging, the media, and everything up and down the chain. It's all part of the process."

"Ugh," I grumbled. "And how did you find these guys again?"

He grinned. "Like I told you before, I didn't. They found me."

Pulling his antique pocket watch from his bomber jacket he insisted on wearing despite the sweltering heat, Rooster said, "We should get going, Dean. Time's wasting."

I spun toward Erin. "You good?"

She nodded. "We'll call at the first sign of trouble. You guys watch your back."

"It's not my back I'm worried about," I muttered as Rooster and I turned to go.

And after a short walk from the coffee shop as he regaled me with tales of his favorite cheesecake, apple fritters, and something called a French Huguenot Torte, we found ourselves standing in the lobby of the San Francisco Museum of Modern Art. And much like the Guggenheim in New York City we visited the last time we dropped in on his mom, it was a thing of absolute wonder. Despite the fact it was beyond pretentious and pretty much represented everything I hated in life.

That said, as we stood in the grandiose lobby that boasted a polished gray stone floor complimented by stunning white columns that jutted far into the towering parquet-style ceiling before melding into an arched dome style skylight, I couldn't help but be impressed. Ginormous abstract canvasses of swirling muted colors hung on either side of an elegant staircase like proud sentries as countless people scampered about the expansive space, talking and laughing. As much as I hated to admit it, the place was breathtaking. Not that I was a damn hipster or anything.

At any rate, following Rooster toward a large oblong desk near the center of the lobby, we pulled to a halt as he picked up a directory and scanned it for a second or two. "Her exhibit is on the second floor," he said. "So far, so good. Let's go."

Making our way up the aforementioned staircase and through a few peculiar exhibits, including one that resembled a giant room of mirrors like something you'd see at a low budget carnival and another one that looked like somebody covered themselves in paint and rolled around on the floor, we pulled into a sterile, white alcove adorned with several paintings. And in the dead center of a series of other portraits by the prominent British painter John Collier, which also seemed to be of naked women throughout history and literature such as Lady Godiva, Clytemnestra, and Circe, was Rooster's mommy dearest, Lilith.

Pulling to a halt amidst a crowd of folks gawking at the collection of naked beauties, Rooster slid his hands into the pockets of his bomber jacket and began to fish around for something. After a few seconds, he produced one of those analog cooking timers and began to carefully wind it.

"What does your magic egg timer do again?" I asked.

"It's a warding device," he said. "Makes everyone in the near vicinity instantly want to go somewhere else. And it's not a *magic egg timer*. It's a highly sophisticated piece of Roostertech that sends out a mild, yet highly suggestive, feeling of dread compliments of some nifty magus mojo."

Grinning at me, he then wound it a few more times before carefully placing it on the floor. And within a second or two, all the surrounding patrons abruptly stopped whatever they were doing and un-assed the immediate area with great haste.

Now finding ourselves alone, I grinned back. "It's a real nifty magic egg timer, buddy."

Ignoring my commentary, he let out a deep breath and focused all of his attention on the incredibly lifelike portrait of the nubile enchantress hanging on the wall before us. And despite the fact that I'd already seen the painting, I was instantly mesmerized by the haunting depiction of a pale, yet voluptuous femme fatale standing seductively deep within a dark woodland.

With a face of dominating beauty, her head was erotically tilted to the side, allowing her ravishing red hair to flow down her back and clear past her thighs. Showing absolutely no attempt at modesty, her arms alluringly cradled her torso in a rather brazen display of her impressive bare breasts. In fact, the only thing preventing her from being buck ass naked was the ginormous snake inappropriately positioned around her waist and curled about her legs. With her eyes closed and the ever-so-faint glimmer of a sultry smile on her pursed lips, she nestled the sizable head of the serpent under her chin.

The longer I stared at the portrait, the deeper I seemed to fall under its unnatural power until something happened to snap me out of it — the young seductress opened her eyes and looked straight at me. And despite the fact that I knew it was going to happen, it still scared the living shit out of me.

Instinctively backpedaling, I think I might have actually peed a little when Lilith straightened her head and carefully released the big ass snake to happily slither along the forest floor of the painting. Before I knew what the hell was happening, the now stark-naked Old Testament exhibitionist casually stepped out of the portrait and into real life, leaving behind a noticeable void on the canvas in the shape of her silhouette.

With a cunning smile on her face, she stood there before us, large as life.

Rooster's mom.

Nakie!

II

LETTING out an eccentric yet highly spirited, "My darling, Eóin! My dearest baby boy! Come here and give mama some sugar!" Lilith, who looked five years younger than Rooster, then proceeded to wrap herself around him in a creepy, full-body hug much like she did the last time we saw her.

Trying his best to wrestle free of the maternal mixed martial arts leg lock, my enigmatic ginger colleague muttered, "Hello, mother. It's, ah, nice to see you too. How've you been?"

"Wonderful," she replied in an alluring, nasally accent that was something in between Michelle Pfeiffer's Catwoman, Marilyn Monroe, and any one of the Spice Girls as she unfurled herself from Rooster and fixated on me. "Simply wonderful."

Doing my damnedest to maintain strict eye contact while trying to ignore the fact that she was buck ass naked, I just kind of stood there and awkwardly waved. "Ah, hi, Lil. Good to see ya again. Looking very limber. You maybe want to put some clothes on? Or not. That's cool too."

Circling me like a praying mantis while running her hands through her lavish ginger mane, her smile morphed into a flirtatious grin as her pristine blue eyes danced with an intoxicating fiery madness. "Dean Robinson," she purred. "You silly, silly boy. What an absolute delight it is to lay my eyes upon you and your strapping physique." And then she playfully tapped my nose with her finger a few times as she held me hostage with her vexing gaze. "You do remember our arrangement, yes?"

Backpedaling several steps, I just grinned. "I remember."

"You owe me a favor."

"Like I said, I remember."

"Is that why you've come to see me? To settle your debt?"

"So, about that," Rooster said, fortunately stepping between me and his vampish mom. "We kind of need your help."

Lilith pouted. "Oh, drat! I should've known. Why else would you come to see your dearest mother?"

"Well, I could've come just to say hi."

"Did you?"

"Well, no. But—"

"Have you ever?"

"Of course, I have."

"Have you?"

"Maybe?"

"*Have* you?"

"No?"

"No, Eóin. You have not."

"Right. Sorry."

"Oh, it's fine," she said somewhat insincerely, as she stroked Rooster's cheek. "I suppose I understand. Despite all your tendencies to be mommy's little boy, you've always been more prodigal than not. Tell me, dearest, do you remember when I used to dress you up as a princess and we'd play—"

"New topic!" Rooster blurted out. "I assume you've been keeping track of current events, right?"

She shrugged. "Current events?"

"Yeah, you know how Michael, as in the archangel, kind of

started an angel mutiny with the help of my dad and his pals, the Watchers, who he sprung from Tartarus? Then they kind of stole the Acropolis from Paradise City and attacked Earth. And then God kicked all the angels out of Heaven and—"

"Boring, boring, boring!" Lilith scoffed as a silken, shoulder-cut dress of pure white gracefully appeared over her pale body. "Although I do find it exceptionally gratifying that Lucifer was defeated in such grand fashion, I'm beyond annoyed with the fact that Ethan Roy had the audacity to send his multitudes of mundane seraphs to Earth. Gag me! And I've heard whispers of some peculiar peace summit he's convened at the Medmenham Lounge of all places. What—a—dump!"

"You mean the Eden Accords."

"I'm sorry, the *what*?"

"The, ah, peace summit. Ethan's dubbed them the Eden Accords."

"Good grief." She groaned before feigning to puke. "As if Eden turned out so great the first time around! Just whom does Ethan Roy think he is, anyway?"

Rooster shrugged. "Well, he's kind of God so..."

Lil giggled. "Yes, I suppose he is. For now, at least."

Making the mental note to figure out what the hell that meant at some point in the future, I said, "Sorry to break up the reunion here, but in case you haven't noticed, Lil, the planet is kind of shitting itself into a gazillion pieces and—"

"And what, pray tell, does that have to do with little ole moi, lovie?"

"Well, that's why we're here. Consensus has it you're in the unique position to help fix it."

She giggled again. This time more obnoxious than the last. "Fix it? I haven't *fixed* anything since getting the Clintons elected to the White House — twice. And that was exhausting! Talk about hanging chads..."

Rooster groaned. "Mother! Please! This is serious."

"Fine," she muttered. "Tell me, then. What is it you need from me that's so important?"

"We need to find the Anunnaki," I said. "And quickly."

"Very quickly," Rooster emphasized. "They're the only ones that can repair the Earth's core before it goes thermonuclear and snuffs out life as we know it in a world-shattering cataclysmic event."

After a super awkward second or two as Lil studied us almost like she was looking straight into our souls, she muttered, "Interesting."

"Interesting?" I grumbled. "What the hell does that mean? Can you help or not?"

"Tell me," she said, like a skilled lawyer leading a witness, "what do you know of the Anunnaki?"

Rooster shrugged. "Not much. Metatron said they were the first angels and prolific builders. As such, they helped Ethan build the planet. And they built pyramids and other shit. Yada yada, so on and so forth."

"They did much more than that, dearest. And I'm not sure you could quantify them as angels, per se. Nor are they like men. The Anunnaki are definitely something else. And the males have these oddly shaped, incredibly huge—"

"Don't!" Rooster shouted. "Please don't say it."

"Get your head out of the gutter, Eóin. I was talking about their heads."

"And you said it anyway. Awesome. Thanks for that."

"Not *those* heads, silly. Although, now that I think about it, those heads were massive, too. And they were bright blue, which I never really understood. But I digress. My point is that the males all had these very peculiar elongated skulls."

"Wait, you mean like Egyptian pharaohs?"

"Well, yeah. Especially since most of the pharaohs *were* Anunnaki. Or their direct descendants."

"Wait, what? You serious?"

"Come now, dear. I thought you were supposed to be the smart one."

"Oh, he's super smart," I said, trying to get the conversation back on track. "Everybody says so. Even the dumbasses. But back to the reason for our visit. Rumor has it that you might know where the Anunnaki live. A place called—"

"Nibiru," she said.

"So, you do know."

"Of course, I do. Nibiru is a hedonist's paradise of unmatched proportion. A true Eden. It's my kind of place, lovie. Although I haven't been there in ages. Ever since I broke things off with my paramour, Enki. A more delicious being has never existed. Yum, yum, yummy! Now he had a head worth—"

"Mother!" Rooster scoffed as Lil little began to lick her lips.

"So, this Enki character," I said, recalling Metatron's explanation back at the Medmenham Lounge. "He's their leader, right?"

"He certainly is," she said. "So charismatic. And brilliant. And manly. A true renaissance man. Albeit one with a terrifying temper."

"You think you could get us an audience with him?"

"An audience with Enki? Are you mad, Dean Robinson? He'd more likely gut you alive and feed your entrails to his dogs at first sight. He *loathes* humans. Almost as much as he loathes angels."

"But he liked you, right?"

"Come now, lovie," she said before rubbing her breasts and grinning. "What's not to like?"

"So, can you get us an audience with him or not?"

"Even if I wanted to help, which I don't, it's been eons since I've spoken with him."

"Wait," Rooster grumbled. "What do you mean that you don't want to help?"

"Why would I?"

"Oh, I don't know. Maybe because the goddamn Earth is literally falling apart?"

"And?"

"Are you serious right now?"

"Yes, and?"

"And we're all going to freaking die! Even you, mother."

Lilith shrugged and grinned. "And?"

Looking like he was about to blow a gasket, Rooster shook his head and paced back and forth at a feverish pace. After several belabored seconds of muttering expletives under his breath in rapid succession and flailing his arms around like a madman, he pulled to an abrupt halt and glared at his mom, who seemed to be enjoying his extreme frustration. And then he lost his shit.

And I mean, he *completely* lost his shit.

It was like all the frustration of dealing with a batshit crazy mother for his entire unnatural lifetime just erupted in his brain and spewed from his mouth like a raging volcano.

I'm not sure how long he ranted for, but it was at least a solid couple minutes. And the string of profanity that flowed from his mouth in prolific prose was unlike anything I'd ever heard before in all my days as a soldier. It was almost Shakespearean. That is, if Shakespeare only used four letter words followed by a lot of exclamation points.

His eyes glowed like fiery red Christmas lights until they actually started spitting fire. His skin turned bright red and formed scales like he was making the transformation to his liderc form. But instead of turning into the fifteen-foot infernal behemoth, he remained his normal size with one small but noticeable difference — he burst into flames.

And I'm not talking like normal flames. I'm talking like unnatural orange flames that reeked of sulfur and slithered around his body like a thousand pissed-off snakes. It was quite the spectacle. As I backpedaled several steps, wondering just what in the hell to do next, Rooster yelled something to the effect of 'Goddamn you, Mother!' before slamming his fiery fist straight into her prized painting.

Completely shocked and somewhat terrified, I took several steps backward as Lilith rolled her head back on her shoulders, almost like she was creepily soaking in the infernal power emanating from Rooster's hellish form.

"My, my, Eóin," she said as her eyes glowed a harrowing red and she gazed at the charred remnants of her painting that smoldered on the floor in a pile of ash. "Such anger. I simply love it!"

"You're *going* to help us!" Rooster snarled, orange flame spewing from his mouth as he pointed at Lilith with a bright red, scaly finger. "Right now!"

And after a couple excruciatingly long seconds in which I wasn't quite sure whether or not Rooster and his mom were going to start trading blows, Lilith simply said, "Fine. I'll help you."

And just like that, the unnatural flames vanished from Rooster's physique and he returned to his normal jovial ginger self. "Wait, you will? Really?"

She nodded. "I will." And as her eyes flashed back to their regular intoxicating blue tint, she added, "On one condition."

"Which is?"

"Dean Robinson now owes me *two* favors. Two teeny, tiny favors whose nature will be disclosed at the time of their necessity, which is for me to decide when I decide it. And, of course, in accordance with the terms of our previous pact, Dean will willingly forfeit his soul in recompense upon refusal to comply."

I'm pretty sure Rooster was about to completely lose his shit again when I said, "Deal." And shook Lil's outstretched hand. Which, for the record, was unexpectedly cold and clammy.

"Deal," she confirmed before starting to clap and twirl around like a child on Christmas morning as Rooster grumbled something unpleasant under his breath. When she was done with her impromptu, obnoxious celebration, she said, "Ok, boys, so what is it you'd like to know?"

"The Anunnaki," I grumbled. "We need to find the goddamn Anunnaki, remember?"

"And quickly," Rooster halfheartedly muttered, apparently now at his wits' end.

Still smiling like she won the friggin lottery, Lilith reached into her dress for an awkward moment or two before pulling out what looked like a medallion roughly the size of a hockey puck covered with an intricate series of ornate sigils and glyphs. Tossing it to Rooster, she said, "Nibiru is a place you can only travel to with a proper *invitation.*"

Intently studying the arcane artifact, he asked, "Is that what this thing is? An invitation?"

Lilith grinned. "That, my dear boy, is the VIP back stage pass of invitations. Issued by Enki himself, mind you, it bears his seal and is encrypted with his blood. And with it in your possession, you can travel anywhere, and I do mean anywhere, within the boundless realms of Nibiru without challenge."

"Wow," Rooster said, perking up a bit. "That's actually incredibly helpful. Thank you, Mother."

"Why, you're quite welcome, dearest."

"So, how do we get there?"

"Where?"

"Nibiru."

She shrugged. "How would I know?"

"Wait, what do you mean?"

"About what, dearest?"

"About getting to Nibiru! How did you get there before?"

"Well, *naturally*, Enki used to send his personal envoys to escort me. And by envoys, I mean delectable man servants that were far too eager to pleasure me as we travelled, so—"

"I quit," Rooster grumbled with his head hung low. "Good bye, Mother." And then he flipped me the peculiar medallion and walked out of the alcove, leaving me alone with Lilith, who sort of looked like somebody just stole her lunch money.

"Oh dear," she frowned. "What's gotten into Eóin?"

I chuckled a bit despite the situation. "Are you serious?"

"Quite serious. Why is he so upset with me, Dean Robinson? Have I done something wrong?"

I took a deep breath. "Well, just spit-balling here, but maybe he's upset because you're always trying to scam us. Or trick us. Or take advantage of a situation to fuel your deviant exploits, whatever the hell they are. Or maybe it's the relentless sexual innuendo constantly spewing from your mouth. It's gross. And honestly, kinda cliché at this point. I mean, you're his mom for Christ's sake. Quit being such an asshole. And quit hugging him when you're naked. That ain't right."

And after a long moment or two of her glaring at me with her icy blue eyes, in which I was fully expecting her to rip my throat out at any second, her face curled into a contrite grin. "The gates of Nibiru are scattered across time. While there are many, I only remember one. August 18th, 1969. Bethel, New York. The gate was in some sort of peculiar school bus. At a farm. Or maybe near a farm. And there was something about pigs or hogs. And a voodoo child. Perhaps both. Or neither. I can't recall. At any rate, the medallion you're holding contains a blood cipher that will open the gate. Good luck, lovie."

Without so much as another word, she then turned and gazed at the smoldering remnants of her famed portrait. And as it was pretty clear she needed a new home, she swung her attention to the rather sizable portrait of Lady Godiva hanging on the wall, which, of course, displayed the thirteenth century exhibitionist who rode nude atop a white horse through the streets of Coventry, England in protest of oppressive taxation.

Turning to blow me a kiss as her dress vanished in a spectral flash, she said, "And Dean, you'd be wise to tread lightly. The Anunnaki may provide the salvation you seek. But it will come at a cost."

Then she simply snapped her fingers, and within a subtle flash of light, there were now two naked beauties perched atop the white horse in the portrait. Make that two, naked beauties, and a rather large snake that somehow survived the destruction of Lil's former portrait and was happily draped across their shoulders. And it kind of looked like it was smiling.

"Friggin Lil," I muttered under my breath as I made my way out of the alcove to find Rooster. "You can't make this shit up."

No. You really can't.

12

Shaking my head at the latest mind-bending encounter with Rooster's mom, I took a hard look at the arcane medallion she gave us. Covered with a stunning of array of interlocking crimson glyphs, the obscure object almost looked alien, and as I held it in my hand, I swore it was pulsing like it had a heartbeat.

Thinking that was rather odd, I carefully tucked it in the pocket of my sullied jeans for safe keeping because despite being a rather snazzy trinket, it was also the key to getting us into Nibiru and finding the Anunnaki. So, we had that going for us. Which was nice. Thanks, Lil.

But before we could use the key, we had to find the lock.

And to the best of Lilith's recollection, the lock was in 1969. In some podunk town, no less.

And it was hidden inside a school bus. That was on a farm.

Or perhaps near a farm.

And this farm might have pigs. Or maybe hogs.

Or maybe neither.

And there might be voodoo involved.

Or not.

Or Lilith may have just made all that up for shits and giggles. So, we had all that going for us, too. Which was not so nice. So, yeah. Thanks, Lil.

With my thoughts racing on overdrive as the past few minutes played in my head on a recurring loop, I made my way out of the alcove and backtracked through the eclectic conglomeration of junk otherwise known as modern art until I was again standing in the main lobby of the museum. But unlike the last time I was here, just mere minutes earlier, it was no longer filled with people. It was completely vacant.

And it was quiet.

Unnaturally quiet.

Wondering what the hell happened to my enigmatic ginger colleague, I tapped on the Roostertech-infused communications device buried in my ear. "John, you copy? Where you at?" And after a few seconds of nothing but static, I tried calling Doc and Tony with no success either. Figuring that couldn't be a good sign, I flew down the stairs and started to cross the vast lobby when a familiar voice stopped me dead in my tracks.

"Jim Jim!" yelled a booming, guttural voice as I spun around to find a certain fifteen-foot behemoth standing there glaring at me. His eyes were black, like pools of oil, and his massive chest bulged from under his oversized hoodie.

I grinned. Albeit somewhat nervously. "Oh, hey there, Jim. Where you been, buddy?"

"*Jim* Jim!" He grunted, taking a menacing few steps in my direction. Apparently, he didn't appreciate being sent to the moon.

"Whoa, easy there," I said, backpedaling to maintain a safe distance from the big oaf. "Just relax. We're all friends here, right?"

Without so much as another word, the menacing miscreant then waded into a sprawling exhibit on the lobby floor and plucked the statue at its center. A statue that kind of looked like a gigantic bronze penis with a pineapple growing out of the top of it.

And before I could lodge a spirited protest, he raised the giant phallic symbol high above his head and charged at me, screaming something to the effect of *"Jim Jim!"* over and over and over.

Awesome.

So now I was in a real pickle.

Although I hardly knew Jim, I kind of liked him. No, I don't know why. He wasn't exactly a jolly giant. He was just strangely endearing for some inexplicable reason. And there was also the small factor of the Eden Accords to consider. I mean, he was Mortog's brother, and it probably wouldn't bode so well for negotiations if I fried him with a blast of Judgement fire. That would most likely be frowned upon.

On the other hand, I wasn't about to let the crazy fucker whack me with a giant bronze penis, either. Especially one with a pineapple growing out of it. And in a goddamn museum of all places. That's just wrong.

As the unnatural beastie charged at me with reckless abandon, I stood my ground and willed the cloak into being. Its otherworldly power coursed through my body as it appeared in a spectral flash of white luminescence and billowed about my shoulders. Feeling the mental switch flip to the on position, I slowly pulled in a long, deliberate breath.

Cleared my mind.

Focused my thoughts.

Found the Balance — the perfect balance between wrath and clarity.

As the unfathomable power welled up in the deep recess of my soul and the expected sensation of calmative awareness washed over me, I stepped out of the path of Jim's brutish assault and tripped the big bastard as he careened by me in a blur of motion. He kept shouting his single-syllable battle cry right up until he executed a perfect nose dive into the pristine, polished floor and the big metal dick flew out of his massive hands only to land on the back of his head, knocking him unconscious.

Thinking that worked out pretty well, I was doing my damnedest to come up with a suitable one-liner like, 'Hey Jimbo, you got cold cocked!' as the cloak anxiously flared out, causing me to instinctively spin around and duck just before a battle hammer slammed me in the face.

A miniature battle hammer.

Like something that would be wielded by...

"Demented leprechaun, carnie bastards," I grumbled, as I looked up to find Hof and Yaw standing there grinning at me.

"Oi! Who you calling a carnie, blighter boy?" shouted Hof, which was immediately followed by, "Oi! Who you calling a — wait, what's a carnie?" from Yaw, who looked confused.

"Carnies," I grunted as the argent metal gauntlets manifested on my forearms and fluidly encased my fisted hands in seamless, indestructible barzel. "Small hands. Smell like cabbage."

Apparently taking great offense to that description, the wannabe hobbits then morphed from pale, frail munchkin men into something that resembled demented garden gnomes with grayish, leathery skin and an oddly impressive physique.

Their grotesque faces stretched into devious grins, bearing two rows of unevenly-spaced jagged teeth, as Hof sauntered straight toward me and Yaw casually drifted to my right flank. "We went easy on you last time, Dean blighter," said Hof as he held up his clawed hands. "This time, we finish the job! Right, Yaw?"

"Oi!" Yaw replied, producing two daggers from his goofy overcoat. "We're gonna finish the job, blighter boy! You smell like cabbage! Oi!"

Pulling my metal hands into tight fists, I smiled back at the macabre midgets. "Bring it, Mr. Frodo."

Grinning again for good measure, the derelict duo sprang into action and closed the ten-foot gap between us in a matter of a split second. Opting for an airborne assault, Hof leapt through the air with catlike dexterity and was just about to sink his disgusting, venom-tipped claws into my forehead when I spun to my left and swatted the fucker with my metal fist. As the wee bastard plummeted to the stone floor with a groaning thud, I felt Yaw charging in from my right flank and side-stepped him like a bull fighter just in time to avoid being shish kabobbed by his dueling daggers.

Focusing all my supernatural strength, I took a couple of powerful steps and kicked that sorry bastard in the ass as hard as I could. Sailing through the lobby like a freakish football, he screamed bloody murder until he smacked into a wall and slunk to the floor. Throwing my hands up like a referee, I couldn't help but shout, "And the kick is good!"

Back on his feet and now officially pissed, Hof was about to take another run at me when a scratchy, throaty voice called out, "That's enough fun for now, boys. You can finish him off later."

Spinning around, I found an unusually tall, crack skinny angel standing there with a shit-eating grin on his face, holding a sword to Rooster's neck. A pulse of anger fired through my already amped up body and judging by the look on Rooster's face, he wasn't too pleased about the situation either.

Recognizing the angel as one of the tagalongs we sent to MacCawill's place on the moon, I said, "That's a bad idea, pal."

"Gadreel."

"Sorry?"

He grinned and gave me a good look at his mouth full of super yellow, jacked-up teeth. "My name," he said, "is *Gadreel*." And he said it like I should know who he is.

I grinned back. "Gadreel. So, you're a Watcher, huh?"

"You've heard of me then, I take it."

"No. It's just that you got that whole crackhead thing going on like your boss. And you stink. Might I recommend a long shower? And perhaps some toothpaste. Actually, you should just go see a dentist. Looks like you're a few thousand years overdue."

He grinned a second time. "Semyaza said you were a funny little godling, Dean Robinson."

I chuckled. "Did he now? That's really sweet of him. What else did he say about me? Actually, I don't give a fuck. Tell you what, jack-ass, how about you lower your sword, and I'll make sure Rooster doesn't rip your goddamn lungs out of your chest until *after* he kills you."

Shaking his head, he pressed the blade into my enigmatic ginger colleague's neck until a fine layer of blood formed. "This sword was forged by the dark magi of the ancient realms. It's hexed with the blood of a thousand fallen gods. And, trust me, it will slice through your liderc's neck long before he takes his true form."

Rooster's face flickered with pain as his eyes flashed a harrowing deep red. Figuring it was time to quit screwing around, I called for the shotgun and immediately felt the leather scabbard manifest on my back. Pulling the 1887 semi-divine Winchester free in a blur of motion, the double barrels glowed and hissed with the white fires of Judgement as I focused my will and cocked the lever.

Clearly unfazed, he said, "Is that really necessary?"

"Well, you're trying to kill us, so, yeah."

"We could just negotiate."

"OK. What do you want?"

"We simply want the location of the Anunnaki."

"*We*? Wait, don't tell me you're working with Jim Jim and the carnies. Aren't angels a little too high and mighty for that kind of shit?"

"The Watchers are outcasts," he said, somewhat sincerely. "And so are the nephilim. Let's just say we're kindred spirits."

"And what about Gabriel's and Uriel's cronies? Where are they?"

He shrugged. "Still on the moon, I imagine. You know, where you sent us so you could keep the location of Nibiru to yourselves. Humans, you're just so predictable."

I shrugged. "Yeah, you got me. Too bad Lilith didn't know anything. So, we're back to square one. All of us."

"You're lying."

"That's the truth. Go ask her yourself if you don't believe me. Up the stairs and hang a left. She's in the third painting from the right. The one with the snake. And the horse. And the tits."

"You're lying," he repeated.

"We were just about to head back to the Medmenham Lounge to give everybody the bad news. We can go together. You, me, Rooster and the carnies. It'll be fun."

"Do you take me for a fool, godling?"

"No, jackass. I take you for a crackhead, remember?"

And as the peculiar angel stood there smiling at me while continuing to press the arcane blade deeper and deeper into Rooster's neck, it occurred to me I was out of options. He knew I was lying and apparently had no qualms about slowly slicing Rooster's head off until I gave him what he wanted. Digging into my pocket, I was about to toss him the blood cipher medallion when a strange sound permeated through the lobby.

It was faint at first, but seemed to grow louder and louder with each fleeting second. Almost like it was getting closer. And the louder it got, the more I thought it sounded like the clattering of hooves. Galloping hooves. Like from a horse.

It was right about then something rather unexpected happened. As I stood there contemplating what to do, a massive white stallion flashed by me in a blur of motion and pulled to an abrupt halt directly in front of Gadreel. Before the poor bastard even had a chance to blink, the uncanny horse reared back on its mighty hind legs and snorted a few times before it pummeled the smarmy seraph's face with its front hooves like Mike Tyson working a speed bag.

Resembling a life-sized bobblehead doll, Gadreel dropped his sword and Rooster ducked to safety amongst the general calamity. Rushing to his side, I helped him to his feet, and we both just kind of stood there for an awkward second or two, gawking at the mysterious horse when something else rather unexpected happened. Lilith and Lady Godiva, in all their nubile nakedness, appeared atop the great white beast.

"What the fuck?" Rooster blurted out. "Mother? Wait, *Mother*?"

"Of course it's me, Eóin!" she replied, thoroughly enjoying herself. "Are you quite all right, dearest?"

"I'm fine," he said, wiping blood from his throat. "Thanks?"

"You're quite welcome. Now run along. I'll keep this Watcher and his pets occupied for the moment. You and Dean have work to do!" Then her eyes glowed a terrifying shade of red, and her body was silhouetted by hissing infernal flame as she focused on Gadreel. "No one hurts my baby boy!"

Turning to me in complete bewilderment, I think Rooster was about to ask me what in the hell was happening when I holstered the shotgun and shrugged. "Yeah, I got nothing. Time to go?"

And then we hauled ass through the lobby with unnatural speed and burst through the exit onto the perceived safety of the streets of San Francisco. Turning for one last look before slamming the door shut behind us, I couldn't help but chuckle.

I mean, hell, it isn't every day you see two naked ladies riding a horse that's happily kicking the shit of out an angel, a giant, and a pair of carnie leprechauns.

Now if that ain't modern art, I don't know what is.

If only somebody brought a gigantic bronze penis.

Now *that* would be something.

Art!

13

"So," Rooster said as the museum doors slammed shut behind us and we stood on the sidewalk catching our breath. "My mom has a horse."

I shrugged. "And apparently, a new friend. One that shares her affinity for public nudity."

"Was that really Lady Godiva?"

"Do you really wanna know?"

"Point taken," he muttered as the sizable gash on his neck healed and all but vanished. "I guess I should just be happy she showed up when she did, huh?"

"You kidding me? We didn't need her help. I had that situation completely under control."

Nonchalantly wiping away any remaining blood from his throat, he grinned at me rather snidely. "Yeah, you sure did."

I matched his snide grin with one of my own. "How'd that Watcher get the drop on you, anyway?"

"The damn korrigans distracted me," he grumbled. "Carny bastards."

"You know, they do smell like cabbage. It ain't right."

"It's really not. Anyway, before I knew it, Gadreel had that hexed sword to my neck. How the hell did they get off the moon, anyway?"

I tossed him the blood cipher medallion. "Forget the tagalongs. We have bigger fish to fry. Like finding Nibiru."

"Nibiru. Wait, did my mom actually tell you how to get there?"

I shrugged. "Sort of. In her not so great, super vague, and signature ambiguous kind of way."

"Ugh," he muttered, "so we have another puzzle to solve. Awesome. Let's cut our losses and get out of here before anything else happens."

And no sooner had those words exited Rooster's mouth than the museum doors blew off their hinges. Smashing his way through the surrounding wall was a pissed off giant with several distinctive hoof marks scattered across his sweatsuit. And perched on his shoulders, cackling like a pair of deranged howler monkeys were Hof and friggin Yaw.

"Jim Jim!" snarled the fuming anakim as he fixated on me and Rooster.

It was right about then when every person on the street for a solid quarter mile in either direction started to completely lose their shit at the sight of the enraged mammoth beastie. The casual West Coast 'end of the world party' vibe was replaced by a distinct 'zombie apocalypse' panic as people scattered in any and all directions while screaming, shouting, breaking windows, starting fires, and acting like complete lunatics.

Ripping my shotgun free of its holster, I cocked the lever and trained both searing barrels on Jim's massive chest. "Not another step, big fella! Just take it easy, and nobody gets hurt. Except maybe Hof and Yaw. I'd really like to shoot them in the face. Several times."

"Jim *Jim*!" He grunted as the korrigans pulled their pants down and mooned me. Carny bastards.

"Look, we're sorry," Rooster said, trying to reason with Jim. "That was a total mistake."

"*Jim* Jim?"

"Of course not. Why would we send you to the moon on purpose? I was just a big, ah, misunderstanding."

"Jim *Jim!*"

"What do you mean you don't believe me?"

"Jim — Jim!"

"Because I'm a ginger? *Really*? That's just rude, Jim. And border-line racist."

As I made the mental note that Jim was apparently a good judge of character, Doc Kelly pulled up alongside me with Tony and Billy in tow as Rooster kept trying to talk the big dope down from his 'roid rage.

"Shit," Doc grumbled, with her H&K hand cannon at the ready. "They found us after all."

I nodded. "Yup. And we need to get out of here. Now."

"Please tell me you got the location of the Anunnaki."

"I got it. Kinda sorta. Generally speaking. I think, anyway."

"Is that good?"

I shrugged. "It could be worse."

"Then let's get out of here. Why aren't you shooting him?"

"Who, Jim?"

"Ah, yeah. He's a giant. You kill giants. It's kind of your thing."

"I can't shoot Jim. He's Jim. And he's Mortog's brother."

"Yeah, yeah," Tony said, reaching into the assault pack propped on his back and pulling out a snazzy looking grenade. "I got this."

"That a flashbang?"

"Yup. B.A.R.T. standard issue. Nonlethal — *ish*." Pulling the pin, he then counted to three and gave it a casual toss toward the giant's face. "Catch!"

And right on cue, Jim started howling in primal pain as the flash-bang exploded in a searing array of blinding light mere inches from his eyes. Disoriented, the big oaf started flailing his arms around like a super-sized drunkard, causing Hof and Yaw to jump from his mammoth shoulders and land on the sidewalk, only to be trampled by a stampede of terrified people. Haha.

Thinking that worked out rather nicely, I nodded at the crew, and the five of us hauled ass across the street toward Yerba Buena Gardens amidst the general calamity. Busting through the alley and into the sprawling park, it seemed the news that a giant was in the general vicinity traveled fast because folks had transitioned from party mode to 'run for your fucking life' mode.

Flying past the reflection point at unnatural speed, I tapped the Roostertech-infused communications device buried in my ear. "Roy, you copy?"

And after a brief hiss of static, MacCawill replied, "Yeah, I'm here, mancho."

"Get us the fuck out of here, please."

"Roger that. You at the extraction point?"

"Almost there."

"Firing up the portal. Coming your way in three, two, one."

As we sprinted toward the modest grove of redwood trees where we started this grand misadventure an hour or so earlier, I was more than happy to see the swirling vortex of white light manifest before us. Making the mental note that even if the planet didn't shit itself to death over the next few days, I wouldn't be in any rush to visit San Francisco again, I followed the crew through the portal to the waiting safety of the Quartermaster.

But as we popped out the other side of the interdimensional gateway, there seemed to be a slight problem. We weren't at the Quartermaster.

We were somewhere else.

And it was dark.

"Ah, guys," Rooster muttered as the portal snapped shut. "Where the hell are we?"

Unable to see anything beyond a few feet in front of me because the only light in the mysterious location was being provided by a peculiar lamp shaped like a voluptuous woman's leg in the corner, I had a sneaking suspicion where we were.

A sneaking suspicion that was soon confirmed as my nostrils

were assaulted by the telltale stench of stale beer, cigars, and bacon that lingered in the dank, heavy air like the world's worse potpourri.

"We're in MacCawill's man cave," I said, fumbling around the dark in search of a light switch. "He brought me here last year when I had a bounty on my head. It's one of his safehouses."

"Man cave," Doc muttered. "Smells like an animal's cave."

"Smells like an animal's ass," Rooster grumbled.

"A dead animal," added Billy, holding her nose.

"That smoked a lot of cigars." Tony chuckled. "And really liked bacon."

"Oh dear," came a familiar voice with a detectable British accent from somewhere in the sprawling darkness. "I do apologize for the terrible odor! I've asked the Great Creator to stop *smoking* in here, but he simply refuses."

"Ziggy?" I called out. "That you?"

"It's me, Deacon Robinson. Give me one moment to turn on the lights." And within a second or two, an antique brass lantern fastened to the wall on our immediate left flickered to life, and a warm, orange glow began to overtake the darkness. As my eyes adjusted, another lantern farther down the wall followed suit. Then another. And another.

"Wow," Doc muttered, as we stepped out of the obscure alcove and into the main cavern of MacCawill's poshly furnished underground bolt hole hewn out of solid rock in a perfect rectangular shape. And as there were no visible entrances or exits, it was apparently carved from the inside out. Exactly how such a feat was possible still remained a mystery.

Roughly the size of a three-car garage with an arched ceiling looming a few feet above our head, the chiseled walls were inlaid with intricate carvings of sigils, glyphs, and Enochian script that ran from floor to ceiling throughout the entire cavity. The floor was a stunning pattern of alternating rich wooden panels that contrasted perfectly with the dark wooden bar that occupied the far wall.

To the right of the bar, which boasted five or so taps of delectable craft beer, was a collection of buzzing computers and gaming consoles complemented by a flickering arrangement of huge flat panel screens forming a cockpit around an oversized leather bean bag. And, of course, rounding out the obscure dwelling was a gun rack displaying enough firepower to conduct a frontal assault on the gates of Hell itself.

Tony's face curled into a big ass grin as he admired MacCawill's uncanny arsenal. "Nice. Very, very nice."

And before I could crack a joke about MacCawill overcompensating for something with his array of super-sized guns, I was distracted by a peculiar whirring and clicking sound coming from behind the bar. Turning to find a familiar kegbot speeding toward me on miniature tank treads, I couldn't help but grin as Ziggy pulled to a rather squeaky halt before running my foot over as he handed me a chilled mug of beer.

"Here you are, Deacon Robinson," he said, as a pair of digital eyes and a mouth appeared on the vintage seventies TV set that served as his head. "Welcome back to the Man Cave, sir! Cheers!"

I chuckled. "Thanks, Zig."

"You're quite welcome, sir! May your taste buds be tantalized by the first batch of Petulant Pig hazelnut chocolate stout."

"Petulant Pig?"

"Correct, sir. The Great Creator has partnered with our very own Duncan to create a uniquely innovative and extravagantly tasty line of specialty brews inspired by their combined epicurean exploits over the ages."

"Wait," Rooster butted in. "Are you saying that MacCawill's been secretly making beer with Duncan? As in Duncan, the pig? *That* Duncan?"

"Correct, sir. But not just beer. *Petulant Pig* beer. A uniquely innovative and extravagantly tasty line of specialty brews inspired by—"

"Yeah, yeah," Rooster grumbled, a bit miffed that Roosterbragh now had some legitimate competition in the category of arcane microbreweries. "I heard you the first time."

Thinking that was pretty goddamn funny, I took a healthy pull of the Petulant Pig stout and almost had an out-of-body experience as the frothy, chocolaty goodness slid down my throat like liquid happiness. "Holy shit!" I blurted out before taking another sip. And then another. And then draining the mug. "This stuff is friggin amazing!"

Ziggy's digital mouth curled into a wide smile. "Of course, it is, sir. Little D's Vanilla Nut Taps is a perfectly balanced chocolate stout yielding the delightfully sweet flavor of freshly procured cacao nibs while dazzling your palate with the intense aroma of Madagascar vanilla beans."

"Aw hell, I want some," Tony said, heading toward the bar.

"Yeah, same," Rooster added, apparently over his beer snobbery from a few minutes ago.

Not remotely impressed, Doc cleared her throat a few times rather loudly and obnoxiously. "Ah, guys, can we talk about the goddamn beer later?" Then she turned her attention to the kegbot. "How did we end up here, Ziggy?"

"I sent you," MacCawill answered as the conglomeration of screens and monitors in his gaming nook flickered to life and his image appeared. "Sorry, didn't have time to explain, but the Quartermaster isn't exactly a safe haven at the moment."

Doc nodded. "Because of the tagalongs."

"Yup. No telling when they'll show back up here. And there's some new faces hanging around the bar. I think your pals at the Eden Accords sent more cronies to keep tabs on their first set of cronies."

"Damn," I muttered. "So, the jig's up then. The Eden Accords know we tried to pull a fast one on them."

"Not necessarily," MacCawill said. "It's not like the tagalongs are going to report back to their bosses about being duped. So as long as we stay a step or two ahead of them, I think we'll be fine."

Rooster nodded. "He's right. We would have heard from Stephen or Abernethy if they thought anything was awry. We need to keep pushing forward with the plan."

"Agreed," Tony said, which was echoed by Doc and Billy. "So, how do we get to this Nibiru place?"

And so I took the next several minutes to replay my rather obscure conversation with Lilith and how we had to travel back to Bethel, New York in 1969 to find a portal in a peculiar school bus that should be located on a random farm that may or may not include pigs, hogs, and a voodoo baby. They all just kind of glared at me for an awkward second or two.

"No seriously, mancho," MacCawill grumbled. "How the fuck do we get to Nibiru?"

"That's it?" Rooster scoffed. "That's what my mother told you? I mean, there must be more, right? Is there more?"

I shrugged. "Not so much. That's all she remembered."

"Christ," Doc grumbled. "We're screwed."

Strangely unfazed by the concept of time travel, Tony looked like he was having a minor epiphany. "Did Lilith say voodoo *baby* or voodoo *child*?"

"Are you serious?" I chuckled. "What the hell does that matter?"

"Humor me."

"I think it was voodoo *child*."

"And what specific day in 1969 did she say the portal was located?"

"August, 18th. Is this meaning something to you?"

He grinned a wolfish grin, like he just connected a series of dots. "You're kidding me, right? August 18th, 1969. A farm in the ass crack of New York. Three days of peace, love, and music? Is this not ringing any bells?"

"Son of bitch," MacCawill muttered. "The Woodstock festival."

"Woodstock, baby!" Tony shouted, making me remember he was perhaps the biggest Jimi Hendrix fan to ever walk the face of the earth. "And better yet, the fourth and final day of Woodstock, where Jimi Hendrix and Gypsy Sun closed out the festival. And they played perhaps the greatest rendition of 'Voodoo Child' ever. Like ever. I'm talking *ever*!"

"This is good news," Doc said, matching Tony's grin with one of her own. "All we have to do now is find the school bus."

"Yeah," Rooster muttered like a total buzzkill. "One school bus amongst five hundred thousand people spread out over three or four hundred acres. And I think traffic was spread out over a twenty-mile radius around the farm. Piece of cake."

"That's the spirit, buddy," I said, slapping him on the back as I turned my attention to MacCawill. "First things first. If we're making a time jump, we need Owen. Is he at the Quartermaster?"

"Negative. He headed down to Tallahassee with the rest of the crew a few hours ago. Coop figured the MidKnight Jayde was a safer place to be until this whole Eden Accords shit show blows over."

"Tallahassee, eh?"

"Yup."

"Ugh," I muttered. "I bet it's hot as hell there."

He nodded. "It's definitely that. I'll meet you guys there in ten. Actually, make it twenty. I haven't taken a proper shit in a week. And, mancho, don't drink all my fucking beer, huh? That stuff ain't easy to make, you know. Me and Duncan got plans for it—"

"Sorry, Roy, you're breaking up," I muttered, turning off all the TV screens as Tony filled several pints and lined them up on the bar for everybody.

There's only one thing worse than not drinking good beer when the opportunity presented itself. Who am I kidding? There's nothing worse than that.

There is just beer.

And beer is good.

Amen.

14

THE LATEST PORTAL snapped shut behind us, and I started to sweat from the oppressive, humid heat that poured from the pavement in unrelenting waves, despite the fact the sun was about to go down. "God, I friggin hate Florida. Feels like a goddamn sauna out here."

Wondering why people chose to live in this kind of shit climate, I got a solid whiff of my armpits and decided I needed a fresh tee-shirt at some point in the near future. Because in addition to being spattered with blood, my white RoosterBragh tee bearing the iconic red rooster logo and catch phrase '*Have a Bragh, brah*' was now soaked in sweat. And it was ripe. Real ripe.

"Shit," Tony chuckled, wiping his forehead. "This is nothing. Remember summers at Fort Benning? Now *that* shit was hot. Georgia hot!"

"Yeah, I remember. I didn't much care for that, and I especially don't care for this."

He shook his head. "It's official. You've gone soft, my friend. The great and mighty Captain Dean Robinson is a complete and utter puss."

"Well, I kinda died, so..."

"So what?"

"So, I'm entitled."

"To be a puss?"

Apparently thinking that was rather hilarious, Billy gave Tony a fist bump as they both gazed at the artfully quaint, downtown block lined with upscale brew pubs, trendy bars, and eclectic eateries laid out before us in the early evening twilight. Seemingly done giving me shit for the moment, Tony said, "So this is Tallahassee, eh?"

Rooster nodded, taking note of the modest and dwindling crowd of locals meandering about the street and pointing at the gargantuan pyramid looming in the sky above. "Yeppers. We're in the college town district. Which is usually a bit more hopping. You know, when the planet isn't encumbered by space pyramids, earthquakes, and other unnatural disasters."

Tony nodded. "So, where's this MidKnight Jayde joint?"

"About a block or so north. I hope anyway. It kind of moves around."

"It moves? What the hell kind of place is it?"

Rooster grinned. "It's a karma cafe."

"Like a coffee shop?"

"Sorta?" And when it was pretty clear Tony wasn't following the plot, Rooster said, "It'll make sense when we get there. Or not. Aw, hell, let's just go."

So, after a quick jaunt up Gaines Street, in which I was forced to endure Tony's recanting of various and assorted Army stories about me being a whiney bitch while Doc, Billy, and Rooster laughed their asses off, we hooked a hard right onto Macomb into what appeared to be a vacant lot. Scanning the darkness for a quick sec, Rooster said, "This should be the place."

"What place?" asked Tony as he gawked at the disheveled dirt parking lot overrun by a small jungle of weeds with nothing but a sizable concrete slab in the corner. "There's nothing here."

"Give it a sec," Doc said as Rooster uttered a few words in

Enochian and the night air over the concrete slab shimmered like somebody dropped a pebble into a pool of still water.

Then, almost as if a pair of invisible curtains were slowly opening, a blurry vision came into focus and we found ourselves staring at a breathtakingly adorable teenage girl seated on a fold-out chair with her head buried in a Charles Dickens novel. A warm light, emanating from nowhere discernible, illuminated the general area surrounding her as she just sat there flipping pages without acknowledging our presence in the least.

Sporting some designer cut-off jean shorts and a black tank top, the teenage beauty queen of bronze skin and deep brown eyes continued reading at a feverish pace while running a hand through her blondish auburn hair highlighted with streaks of dazzling colors. As we all stood there waiting for her to do something, the intricate tattoos of the nine planets on her arms glided back and forth across her shoulders like they were alive on her skin.

Remembering the last time we were here when we watched the petite bouncer put an absolute beat down on a six-foot-four drunk jackass, Doc had a big smile on her face. "Hi, Mack. Remember us?"

"Of course. I never forgot a customer." Then she looked up from her book and glared at Rooster. "And I especially never forget a *ginger.*"

Grumbling something snide under his breath, Rooster just smiled and waved as Mack carefully closed her novel and placed it on her lap. "You guys are late," she said. "Coop and the rest of them got here hours ago."

"Yeah," I muttered. "We've been kind of busy, kid."

She grinned. "Yeah, I heard, *old man.*"

"I'm not old."

"I'm not a kid."

"Fine. What do you mean by you *heard*? Heard what?"

"I *heard* that you and ginger boy made a real mess of a museum in San Francisco."

"Wait, how the hell do you know that already?"

"I know stuff." Then she picked up her book and flipped through pages again. "I read. And I know stuff. It's kinda what I do."

"You know stuff?"

"Yup."

"Ok. So, what else do you know?"

"Well, I know you need a shower. You stink. So bad. And I know that the soldier boy with you is former First Sergeant Tony Coates, who's now commander of the Praetorian fleet. Big robots are badass, by the way. And I also know that Erin's new BFF is not only the second Witness, but she's also a draikina. Never met one of those. So cool. And I also know that—"

"OK, OK," I grumbled. "We get it. You read and you know shit. Great. You gonna let us in or what?"

Grinning again for good measure, she snapped her fingers, and a sizable wooden door began to subtly appear on the empty concrete slab. Within a quick second, the rest of the obscure dome-shaped building followed suit. "You guys be careful in there. And I hope you brought some earplugs."

I shrugged. "Why would we need earplugs?"

"Cuz."

"Cuz what?"

"Cuz Owen's been drinking whiskey. And you know what happens when he drinks whiskey."

"Christ," I grumbled. "Is he playing with himself?"

Mack nodded. "Beatles songs."

"Beatles, really?"

"He's doing the *Magical Mystery Tour* album on a loop. Song by song. Over and over and over. And the more he drinks, the worse it sounds."

"Good grief," Doc muttered.

"He's been at it for hours. Up on the stage, no less."

"On the stage?"

"The stage."

"Ugh. We'd better get in there. Thanks for the help, Mack. Be safe." Then Doc gave the badass teeny bopper bouncer a maternal pat on the shoulder before making a beeline for the MidKnight Jayde.

"Yeah, thanks, kid," I said, holding out my fist. "Take care of yourself."

Totally leaving me hanging, she just shook her head. "Nobody fist bumps anymore, old dude. But I will take care of myself. And you should, too. Starting with a shower and some fresh clothes. You smell like blue cheese. And cat farts. I think I just threw up a little thinking about it."

Saying nothing, I tried my very best to force a grin as I caught up with Erin while ignoring the incessant chuckling from my enigmatic ginger colleague.

"Ah, quick question," Tony said as we approached the mammoth door to the obscure supernatural roadhouse. "Did I hear you say that Owen was, ah, playing with himself?"

Doc nodded. "Yup."

"While on stage? Like in front of other people?"

"Nobody plays with themself like Double OT," Rooster said. "It's kind of legendary."

"*Legendary*?" Tony scoffed as he and Billy exchanged confused looks. "Am I missing something here?"

Chuckling to myself, I said nothing as we approached the massive dome-shaped corrugated metal structure covered in intricate, slithering patterns of neon otherworldly graffiti and riddled with bullet holes, claw marks, and blood spatter.

As we reached the ginormous wooden door that looked like it was ripped from a medieval castle, I couldn't help but smirk at the hand carved sign tacked haphazardly to one of the mighty panels. Amidst a very interesting array of sigils and glyphs that blazed bright with hissing white flame was etched 'The MidKnight Jayde. Karma, Whiskey, and Everything Ever After. All Are Welcome and Welcomed Are None. Shoes and Shirts Optional. Enter at Your Own Peril.'

The best part of it was that the word *Peril'* was crossed out and the word *Perdition'* was scratched above it.

Not quite sure what to think, Tony looked a tad on edge as he reached into his assault pack and pulled out a slick sidearm that he slipped into the waist of his jeans after chambering a round.

"Let's go," Doc said, as she wrapped her hand around the rusted handle and threw open the mammoth door. We all cringed at the cacophonous rendition of "I Am the Walrus" that blared from within at an ear-splitting volume. "Sounds like Owen's still going at it."

"You mean he's still playing with himself?" asked Tony.

"Yeah, we better hurry."

"Or we could just wait here. You know, until he's finished or what not. That kinda sounds like the right thing to do, yeah?"

Thoroughly enjoying the moment, I slapped him on the back. "And miss all the excitement? Not a chance." Then I lowered my shoulder and pushed him inside.

Crossing the threshold of the uncanny roadhouse kicking and screaming the whole way, I think he was about to punch me in the face when he got a good look at the surreal scene laid out before him.

And then he just about shit himself.

Because it was insane.

Beyond insane.

Starting with the fact that the interior of the MidKnight Jayde was a gazillion times bigger than what it appeared to be from the outside. And it was crammed full of people. Some that looked human. Others, not so much.

Then there was the fact that the place was lit by an armada of floating orbs composed of a subtle neon flame that systematically circled the ridiculous warehouse-like structure in a meandering orbit, giving everything a ghostly glow.

And *then*, there was the fact that since all the available floor space was maxed out, droves of sloshed patrons were standing on the surrounding walls and ceiling like the friggin law of gravity was on hiatus.

"What in the actual fuck?" Tony muttered, clearly perplexed by the mind-boggling venue.

I chuckled. "You'll get used to it, buddy. Or not. Probably not."

It was right about then our attention swung toward the stage where some asshole was screaming mangled Beatles lyrics into a microphone. And oddly, standing on either side of aforementioned asshole were two identical assholes. The first of which was playing an electric guitar and the second, a bass. And behind them, beating on a drum set with a bottle of whisky clenched in his teeth, was yet a fourth asshole.

Shaking his head in disbelief at the sight of the peculiar quadruplet of doppelgängers who seemed to flicker in and out of existence faster than our eyes could perceive what the hell was happening, Tony muttered, "What in the actual fuck," for a second time in as many minutes. "Why are there four Owens on the stage?"

"There's not. There's one."

"But there's — four Owens."

"Yeah, but the four are actually just one."

"So, there's only one Owen?"

"Yup."

"One Owen who's *playing* — with himself?"

"Now you're getting it."

"What the hell?"

"Legendary, right?" Rooster said. "I mean, minus the singing. That kind of blows. The whole thing's pretty terrible. He must be really drunk."

With his face completely blank, Tony just continued to gawk at the stage in utter disbelief. After an awkward second or two, the only thing he could seem to muster was, "What the hell?" for a second time.

Rooster grinned. "So, you know Owen's a time phantom, right?"

"Uh huh."

"So, time phantoms, or temporal jumpers, as they're also known, can move at will through the space-time continuum. Double OT is time phasing between the past and the future in such infinitesimal increments that it *appears* there's four of him in the present. Cool, right?"

After a long silence, as Tony tried like hell to make sense out of what Rooster just said, he just shook his head a few times. "The dude's literally playing with himself," he muttered under his breath. "Yeah, I got nothing." Then he waded into the dancing crowd of unnatural weirdos on a determined beeline for the bar.

Apparently, watching Owen play with himself made Tony thirsty.

That's awkward.

15

With Rooster on my heels, I pushed through the sea of sloshed patrons until reaching the MidKnight Jayde's pentagram-shaped bar that looked like it was made from the monoliths of Stone Henge. Pulling up next to Tony, who somehow already had three shots of whiskey and a beer chaser lined up in front of him, I couldn't help but smile as he scanned the unnatural crowd with a befuddled glaze over his eyes.

"Coffee shop, my ass," he grumbled before slamming a shot and following it with a healthy gulp of dark beer.

I chuckled. "What was that?"

Downing the second and third shots in a blur of motion, he carefully placed the empty glasses upside-down on the arcane bar top and grinned at me. "Just saying how you still take me to the nicest places after all these years."

I grinned back. "And don't you forget it, Big Sarge."

"Wait," Rooster said, joining the conversation and gawking at the elaborate row of taps lined up behind the bar amidst the towering racks of liquor bottles. "The MidKnight Jayde's a whisky joint. Since when do they serve beer?"

"Since now," said a deep voice as we all looked up to see a familiar, unusually young bartender wearing a vintage Pink Floyd concert
tee-shirt that looked authentic. With a pair of old school Colt
revolvers slung low around his waist like something out of a John
Wayne movie, he ran a hand through his floppy mane of dirty blonde
surfer hair before nodding at us. "Was wondering when you guys
were gonna show up. Things are getting crazy."

Rooster smiled at him like they were old pals. "Jesse Jameson.
Good to see you."

"Likewise," the suavely handsome teenager replied.

"We saw your sister outside."

"Yeah, she told me. You know Coop and the rest of them got here
an hour ago. We were getting worried."

"Don't worry about us, kid," I muttered. "We can take care of
ourselves."

He snickered. "Right."

"What the hell's that supposed to mean?"

"Nothing."

"Nothing?"

"Yeah. Nothing."

Studying his snarky smirk for an awkward few seconds, I said,
"What's so damn funny?"

"Well, it's just that you didn't particularly '*take care of yourself*'
last week when you got trapped in that korrigan death bog in Nod,
did you? I mean, you pissed yourself like twenty times. Then the
korrigans caught you and put you in carny jail. And you had to be
rescued by—"

"All right, all right," I grumbled, as Tony and Rooster enjoyed a
heartfelt chuckle. "How the hell do you know about that, anyway? I
mean, assuming it actually happened. Which, of course, it didn't,
so..."

"So, why don't I get you guys a round on the house before you
meet up with the rest of your crew. Sound good?"

I grinned. "Now you're talking. I take back all the bad shit I've been saying about you, kid."

He chuckled. "Thanks, old timer." And before I could rebut his snide remark, he said, "We got this new, super high-end craft beer on tap that's all the rage. Folks are coming out of the woodwork for it."

My ears perked up. "You had me at craft beer."

"What's it called?" asked Rooster, looking more than a bit skeptical.

Picking up a marketing brochure, Jesse began to read. "It's a uniquely innovative and extravagantly tasty line of specialty brews called—"

"No freaking way," Rooster scoffed. "Petulant Pig?"

The wise-cracking barkeep nodded as he dropped the brochure and grabbed some fresh pint glasses. "So, you've heard of it?"

My enigmatic ginger colleague nodded his head. "Yes. Yes, we have."

"People are drinking it like water. Lucky for you fellas, we got some fresh kegs a few hours ago."

Rooster groaned. "Yay."

"Starting from left to right," Jess said, pointing at the taps, "we got Little D's Vanilla Nut Taps, a designer chocolate stout with a killer mouthfeel."

"I wouldn't say *killer* mouthfeel. I mean, it was decent."

"And this next one is called Sweet Gourd Almighty."

"Sweet *Gourd* Almighty? Come on. Really?"

"Yeah, it's a spiced pumpkin ale. Total palate dazzler. Clever name, right?"

Rooster groaned a second time. "Yeah, clever."

"Then there's an Imperial IPA called Sloppy Hoppy Hog Grog. Big, huge hoppy punch followed by a malty, sweet finish. So good."

"You guys know RoosterBragh has an Imperial IPA too, right? Remember the Double Talon? It's—"

"Yeah, never heard of it," Jesse said. "Back to Petulant Pig. Our last brew on tap is a summer seasonal dry hopped wheat called Sublime Beachtime Swine. It's like sunshine in a glass. Highly recommend."

With my mouth watering at the description of the delectable brews, I was about to ask for six pints of all of them when another familiar voice broke me from my hoppy, malty trance. "There you guys are!" said a distinct, old school Massachusetts accent.

Turning to find all six feet of Willa Knightly, the MidKnight Jayde's resident vexen and arcane proprietor standing there in all her witchy glory, I stood up and smiled. All decked out in her signature black sundress complimented by several layers of primal necklaces, her vibrant skin and glimmering blonde hair gave her a distinct celebrity vibe.

Giving her a quick hug, I said, "Hey, Willa. How you been?"

"Oh, sorry, Dean! I don't have a fountain pen."

"What do you mean?"

"A canteen? Are you thirsty?"

"Well, sort of, but—"

"Marmot? Shit! Are they back? I thought I got rid of them all last year! Did my spell wear off?"

"What the hell are you talking about?"

"Rooster has gout? That's terrible! I've got a spell for that, too. No worries!"

"OK. I give up. I don't know what else to say."

"Erin, Coop, and everyone else are this way! Come on, you guys! Follow me!"

Turning toward a chuckling Jesse Jameson, who slid a couple pints of aforementioned Petulant Pig my way, I slammed them in two seconds flat. Smiling at me, he held up a black tee-shirt with the catchphrase '*Quit dicking with the chicken. Swig some Pig!*' accompanied by the image of a super buff cartoon pig grinning ear to ear. The really funny part was that the pig was holding a gargantuan mug of beer in one hand and strangling a rooster with the other. "Here," he said, holding his nose as he handed it to me. "You should really change."

Nodding my appreciation, I ripped off my sullied RoosterBragh tee and slid on the Petulant Pig swag before following Willa through the eclectic crowd.

"So," Tony said, as he and Rooster pulled up alongside me. "Who's Willa again?"

"Willa Knightly," I replied. "She's Jesse and Mack's aunt. She also runs the MidKnight Jayde. And her hearing hasn't been the same since the witch trials. Long story."

"Witch trials? You talking about the Salem witch trials?"

"Apparently."

"But that was like three hundred years ago."

"Yeah."

"But she looks like a twenty-five-year-old swimsuit model."

"And?"

"She's a three-hundred-year-old witch?"

"Not a witch," Rooster said. "A vexen. And a scary powerful one."

Tony shrugged. "And what the hell's a vexen?"

"They're a type of elemental magi. Capable of manipulating the four elements — fire, water, earth, and air. And they can do other stuff."

"Like magic?"

"Well, yeah, kinda. But—"

"So, they turn people into newts, fly around on brooms, makes potions. Stuff like that?"

Rooster smiled. "A couple days ago when we were at Zion Canyon getting our asses kicked by Lucifer and his butt buddies, remember all that blue lighting?"

"Yeah, I remember. It rolled through the desert like an artillery barrage and French-fried giants by the hundreds. Why?"

"That was Willa."

"Vexen," Tony muttered, as the color drained from his face. "Not a witch. Got it."

We pulled up to a smaller, more private setting laid out like a cozy diner decorated with an impressive array of eighties cult movie posters. We found Coop sitting in silence and sharpening his quiver of uncanny arrows as Doc Kelly and Billy intently stared at a newscast on a modest black and white television. Conversely, Caveman and Charlie were huddled around a vintage Donkey Kong arcade game and cheering on our resident miniature feral hog, who was somehow working the joysticks with his front hooves. The physics of that particular act are still unexplained to this very day.

"Hey, everyone," Willa said, smiling a bright smile. "Look who I found at the bar."

Doc glared at me. "You guys take the scenic route? Me and Billy have been sitting here for ten minutes."

I shrugged. "Sorry, Tony got lost. And there was beer."

"Good to see, y'all," Coop said, stowing his arrows and standing up to greet us. "Doc said you had a close call in San Francisco."

"That we did, Cooper. But we got what we needed. Sort of."

"Is that good?"

"Hold that thought until you hear the plan. Where's the rest of the crew?"

"Stoner sent word that he'd catch up with us in a few days. Magic Bus still getting put back together after last week's excitement. MacCawill's on his way. And I thought Bobby was with y'all."

"He was. But I haven't seen him since Samson's Bar before he escorted Semyaza to the Eden Accords."

"He didn't stay at the accords for very long," Doc said. "He had a chat with Gabriel, then he left with Mariel."

"Well, if he left with M, I'm sure they'll turn up at some point. Or not. Friggin angels."

And as I contemplated on that for a second or two, all six-foot-three of Roy MacCawill's apocalyptic cowboy frame pulled up alongside me with a pint of frothy beer in each hand and Ziggy on his flank. "Nice tee-shirt, mancho. Sorry we're late. Had to drop the kids off at the pool."

The kegbot sighed. "Must you *always* tell people about your bowel movements? It's uncouth."

"Uncouth my ass," MacCawill grumbled. "Nothing better than taking a massive dump. It's natural. And beautiful. And better out than in, I always say."

"Yes, of course, sir." And then he waved at us with his robotic claw. "Hello, everyone. Apologies for our tardiness. The Great Creator had to take a massive dump."

Chuckling under my breath as Charlie, Caveman and Duncan joined the group, I said, "All we need now is Owen. Any thoughts on how we get him to stop playing with himself? And that's the last time I actually say that out loud. Just so everybody knows."

Without so much as a word, Willa snapped her fingers, and within the blink of an eye, Owen Octavius Trask was standing before us happily wailing away on a vintage, white Fender Stratocaster and screaming the iconic chorus to "I Am the Walrus" at the top of his lungs. He wore nothing but Captain America boxer shorts, a pair of bedazzled cowboy boots, and a tee shirt depicting Yoda's head on a sasquatch. The time travelling rock star's majestic mane of dark brown, shoulder-length hair epically flopped and tossed about his shoulders like that Fabio guy from the nineties commercials. Realizing he was no longer on stage, nor still accompanying himself with his other time straddling personas, he looked up to find us all awkwardly waving at him.

Putting an unceremonious end to his Beatles tribute, he stopped singing and placed his prized guitar in a case that I swear wasn't there a second earlier. Tugging on the thick, gangly beard that protruded from his chin like hairy tentacles, he gazed at us for a long moment with a furrowed brow. "All right, you rascals. I know that look. Y'all jokers want something, don't ya? So, spit it out already. What is it? What can NecroMaster, Lord and Commander of the Lost Dungeon Realms of Antioch do for you today, huh?"

"NecroMaster?" Billy scoffed in her goofy Nordic accent, followed by, "Lord of *what*, exactly?" from Doc.

Owen flipped his hair back and puffed out his chest. "I believe you meant lord and *commander*, little miss sassy pants."

"Owen," I grumbled.

"Yes, monkey man?"

"Nobody's going to call you that."

"But it's kind of my name now, dig?"

"That's not your name."

"I beg to differ, Dean bean. I kinda changed it."

"No, you didn't."

"Ha! You caught me! But, seriously, monkey man, you gotta call me that. The fans demand it."

"The fans?"

"The book fans, whistlebritches! Gilmore's groupies. They seriously *love* my character, bro. But they want more! I think that a spin-off series is more than warranted." And when it was abundantly clear that I had no idea what the hell he was talking about, he said, "Ok, so no spinoff. But I'm totally evolving my character again with a snazzy new stage name and a tragic yet heartfelt backstory that I intend to sprinkle into various scenes throughout the next couple chapters. Dig?"

Tony leaned in close to me. "How drunk is he?"

I groaned. "He sounds annoyingly sober."

"Sober? He thinks he's a character in a fucking book."

"Yup."

"And we're trusting him to transport us through time?"

"You have a better idea?"

"Well, no, but—"

Owen cleared his throat. "Ahem, although I totally can't *hear* you guys because you're whispering and all, I kinda already read this chapter, so I know what you're saying. And it's awkward. So, why don't we just skip to the part where Dean tells everybody *the plan,* and we get on with it, huh?"

Now it my turn to clear my throat. "Right, the plan. Everybody, listen up." And just as I was about to explain that we needed to time jump back to Woodstock and find a random school bus that contained the portal to the mythical land of Nibiru, Billy said, "Oh, my god! Look at this." Then she turned up the volume on the small TV set before repositioning it so we could all see the screen.

"What are we looking at?" I grumbled, unable to make any sense out of the blurry video and frenetic voice of the newscaster.

"Mount St. Helens just erupted," Doc said. "And most of the Pacific Northwest is now an island off the coast of Idaho."

Oh.

Is that all?

16

MacCawill did a spit-take. "What the hell did you just say?"

"You heard me," Doc grumbled as she stared at the television footage of a volcano spewing apocalyptic lava bursts several miles into the sky. A volcano, mind you, that should have been surrounded by hundreds of miles of rocky forest in every direction, but was inexplicably sitting on the very edge of the Pacific Ocean.

As we all tried to wrap our heads around what was happening, the camera panned to my least favorite newscaster. "Buzz Shea here, folks! And holy *bleep*! Just look at this *bleep*ing *bleep*! Not only did Mount St. Helens erupt for the first time since nineteen-*bleeping*-eighty, it somehow caused most of Washington state to break apart from the rest of the *bleeping* country and drift into the *bleeping* ocean! I mean, *bleep*! This is nuts, right? Somebody get me a *bleeping* drink. And stop with the goddamn bleeps already! They know what I'm saying! *Bleep*!"

"Christ," Rooster muttered, as Billy turned the television off. "It's happening much faster than I thought."

"What is, cuz?" asked Coop as he tucked a healthy wad of chewing tobacco in his cheek.

"The deterioration of the Earth's core. This is how it starts. Mega volcanos. Shifting of the tectonic plates. Oceans boiling. Land masses splitting apart at the fault lines."

"And don't forget about the Jell-O rain," Owen said rather matter-of-factly.

Caveman raised a bushy eyebrow. "Jell-O rain?" Which was accompanied by an inquisitive snort from Duncan.

"Yessiree, the stuff of nightmares. When the skies open up with Jell-O rain, it is game *over*. Done and done. And then, *really* done."

"Come on, Odie," Charlie, our resident mini-giant, said as he shook his massive head back and forth.

Double OT shrugged. "What?"

"There's no such thing as Jell-O rain."

"I beg to differ, Cosmic Carlos. I've seen it. It's real!"

The giant chuckled, and his gargantuan gut jiggled like a demented Santa Claus. "OK, so maybe it is. But what's so bad about it raining Jell-O?"

Owen chuckled, too. "That's what I thought, too." And then his face flashed with terror. "Until the damn Jell-O rain took out my entire family!"

"Wait, what?"

"And my cats, too!"

Charlie gasped. "Not the cats!"

"And then, I was alone."

"Alone?"

"Just a poor, orphan child. All alone."

"Orphan? You weren't an orphan, Odie."

"Of course, I was a damn orphan! An adorable yet super sexy orphan with nothing but his wits and his fabulous hair trying to make his way in this cruel, cruel world."

"Owen!" I grunted.

"Yes, monkey man?"

"Not now."

"Cool origin story though, right?" And when I offered nothing in response besides an icy stare, he sagely nodded a couple of times. "That whole orphan thing was too much, wasn't it? Yeah. Got it."

"All those people in Washington," Billy said, moving the conversation away from Owen's tragic yet heartfelt backstory. Her electric blue eyes hardened with intensity. "We need to help them."

Coop nodded. "Durn skippy. Gotta be something we can do."

"Trust me," Tony said. "If there's anything to be done, Blue Sky and the Academy already have a plan in motion."

"Tony's right," I muttered. "We need to push forward with our mission."

Erin nodded. "If the Anunnaki are the only beings who can fix the Earth before things get worse, then we need to find them. Right fucking now."

MacCawill fired up a stogie and grinned. "Then what are we waiting for? What's the plan?"

And before I could respond, Owen said, "Listen up, bitchachos, here's the plan—"

"Hold on," I cut in. "How the hell do you know the plan?"

"Der! I read this chapter, too! More like skimmed it. Kinda sorta. Anywho, the gist of the plan is that we're going to Woodstock to find a bus. Or something like that. Any questions? No? Perfect. Cue the music!"

And, much to our chagrin, "Stayin' Alive" from the Bee Gees filled the air at an ear-splitting volume as Owen reached into his boxer shorts and pulled out a peculiar gadget that I knew from past experience was his infamous temporal compass. After making a few quick adjustments, a marble-sized ball of swirling white light popped out of the arcane device and started spinning at a mind-blowing pace while exponentially growing in size.

"What's happening?" Billy yelled as her dragon scale tattoos morphed into actual dragon scales and she jumped between Doc and the unnatural spectacle.

"Temporal vortex, baby!" Owen yelled back as he tossed out packs of bubblegum that I hoped weren't also pulled from the nether regions of his undergarments. "Chew it like you stole it! It'll help with the spatial acclimation."

"Spatial what the fuck?" Tony grunted with his eyes about to pop out of his head.

As the ball of ethereal light fluidly morphed into a man-sized, gyrating cyclone and began to suck us in like a surreal vacuum cleaner, Owen said, "Everybody hold on! Here — we — go!"

And before anyone could lodge another spirited protest, an ungodly screeching sound filled the room and the vortex voraciously swallowed us like a spectral whale.

Feeling like I'd been tossed into a goddamn washing machine in the middle of a turbo spin cycle, I was blinded by the waves of pulsing light as sensory overload kicked in with extreme prejudice. The brilliant light then transitioned to harrowing darkness, and despite my best efforts to focus, I drifted into the ether.

Right before everything faded to black, I'm pretty sure I heard Coop say something to the effect of, "Dagum, y'all. Is it just me or did it get darker than the inside of a bull's ass in here?"

THE UNMISTAKABLE SMELL of campfires accompanied by the sound of people laughing coaxed me back to consciousness as the low drone of music softly hummed from somewhere in the general vicinity. Feeling like I'd lost a bare-knuckled boxing match with Rocky Balboa, I rubbed my eyes a few times to restore my muddled vision as aching pain shot through every square inch of my body. Making the *very detailed* mental note to punch Owen really hard the next time I saw him, it took all my strength to roll over and sit up.

"Easy does it," a mellow voice called out from behind me as I felt two hands grab my shoulders and guide me to my feet. "Looking pretty gnarly there, my man. You OK?"

"I'm good," I muttered as my vision snapped into focus and I found myself looking at a shirtless, shoeless skinny dude complete with frayed bell bottom jeans, scraggly beard, and shoulder length hair held up with a dirty bandana. "Thanks for the help."

He smiled to reveal a mouth full of yellow teeth. "No problemo, my brother. Anytime."

Quickly scanning my new surroundings, I couldn't help but chuckle at the sea of genuine American hippies spread across the sprawling vista of muddy fields and rolling hills for as far as the eye could see. "It worked. This is Woodstock."

Awkwardly grinning at me for a second or two, my new buddy said, "Come again?"

"We're at Woodstock, right?"

"Ah, yeah."

"And it's 1969."

"It is."

"And today, it's August 18th?"

He scratched his chin for a second or two. "Yeah, man. I think so, anyway. I kinda just woke up."

With my head still pounding, I muttered, "At least that jackass brought us back to the right day."

"You sure you're OK?"

"I'm fine. Just need to find my friends."

"Your friends, huh? Maybe I can help. I might've seen them around."

"Trust me, you'd remember if you had."

"Yeah, why's that?"

"For starters, one of them's a giant. Albeit a short, fat one."

"A giant? That's righteous."

"And another one's a dragon. But she kind of looks like an albino version of Xena the Warrior Princess. Then there's Ziggy, who's a robotic beer keg. And—"

"Whoa, that's heavy, my brother. Like totally far out."

"Yeah. That. So, you seen them or not?"

"Nah, man. Maybe I will if you gimme some of that stuff you're on, though."

"What do you mean?"

"That stuff you're tripping on. You got any left?"

"Tripping?"

"Is it acid? Shrooms?" He started routing through the pockets of his sullied jeans. "I got some weed I can trade ya."

"Look I'm not on friggin drugs."

"Come on, man. I wanna see dragons and giants, too."

It was right about then, a familiar voice called out, "Dean, over here!" and I spun around to find Doc Kelly standing on the edge of some thick woods that bordered the field to my rear. "Hurry!"

"Whoa," my beatnik buddy muttered. "Who's that foxy lady?"

I chuckled. "You're not her type, pal. But take care of yourself, huh? Hang loose. Ah, give peace a chance. And stuff." And then I left my beatnik buddy to go on about his business of being a hygienically challenged counter culturist and maneuvered through the surrounding mine field of sleeping hippies until I reached the wood line.

"You look like shit," Erin said, pulling some clumps of grass off my tee-shirt and wiping some mud from my face. "You OK?"

I shrugged. "Think so. You?"

She rubbed the back of her neck. "Little sore, but good. Everybody else is this way. Come on."

Following her into the woods, I muttered, "If we survive the next couple days, I may kill Owen."

As we reached the rest of the crew to find pretty much everybody shouting various and assorted obscenities at our resident time traveling rock star, I thought that somebody may actually beat me to it. "All right, all right already," I grumbled in an attempt to calm everyone down a bit. "Just take it easy."

The entire group summarily ignored me, so I repeated myself.

Then I repeated myself again.

And then one more time for good measure.

And then I got really pissed and shouted, "Shut the hell up, goddamnit!" which caused everyone to stop yelling and glare at me.

Taking post next to Owen, I forced a grin. "OK, so that wasn't exactly the best start to the mission."

MacCawill grunted. "You talking about the part where Double O'Douchewagon jumped us through time without any warning or the part where I woke up with eight hundred pounds of mutton clad mini-giant flopped on top of me like Shamu?"

"I already said sorry, dude," Charlie protested.

Trying to erase the mental image of a MacCawill and Charlie manwich, I said, "Like I said, it wasn't the best start to the mission but we're all here. And we're in the right place. At least I think so."

Giving his temporal compass a quick tap, Owen studied it for a second or two. "It's Monday morning. August, 18th, 1968. We're time on target, monkey man. Boomsauce! Necromaster does it again, folks! You're welcome, by the way. Tip your waiter. I'll be here all week."

"1969."

"That's what I said."

"You said 1968."

"Did not."

"OK," I said, trying like hell to remain somewhat calm. "We need to get moving."

"Yes. Yes, we do," Rooster said. "Check this out." Grabbing a twig from the forest floor, he then used it to point to a section of a map he was holding up.

"What are we looking at, pard?" asked Coop as we all huddled around Rooster and squinted at the crumpled document that was missing a large section.

"This is a map of the festival grounds and the surrounding area in Bethel, New York. The Contraption created it based on historical documents, first-hand accounts, and pretty much any other information floating around the ether. It's without a doubt the most accurate mapping of Woodstock ever rendered."

Coop tucked a wad of tobacco in his cheek. "And that big chunk missing from the top?"

Rooster shrugged. "I was holding the map when Owen decided to randomly jump everybody back in time without so much as a 'Hey, guys, we're going to jump back in time now. Maybe put all your important stuff safely in your pockets and try not to fucking puke.'"

Owen grinned. "My bad?"

"Half a map is better than no map," I muttered. "Where do you think we are?"

"Right here," Rooster said, pointing to the outskirts of a sprawling field separated from the main stage by a few acres of woods and a small pond.

"That makes sense. There's like a thousand hippies camped out in that field. They were sprawled out everywhere in various stages of consciousness."

"That makes sense, too," Tony said. "The festival was supposed to end Sunday night, but the weather was so bad that everything got pushed back several hours. That's why Jimi Hendrix and Gypsy Sun didn't play until Monday morning. Folks are probably catching some shut eye before the grand finale."

"The grand finale," Doc said. "And when is that, exactly?"

"Hendrix took the stage around nine and finished up around noon."

Doc turned to Owen. "And what time is it now?"

After a quick glance at his temporal compass, he said, "About six thirty. Give or take?"

"Then we need to move. The clock's ticking, guys."

"Let's split up," I grumbled. "Four teams. Each team takes a quadrant of the map. We need to find the portal to Nibiru. According to Lilith, it's in a bus somewhere on the festival grounds."

Coop hawked some tobacco juice on the ground. "Any distinguishing features to this bus, hoss?"

"All we know is that it may or may not have something to do with pigs. Or hogs." To which Duncan snorted a few times, then shook his little pigly head.

"No joy," Caveman said. "Lil' D says there's not a pig or hog within fifty square miles of here. He'd smell 'em. The snout don't lie, bro."

"Awesome. Then apparently there's no distinguishing features about the goddamn bus."

Willa cleared her throat. "I don't know about your friend Gus, Deano, but if this bus is harboring a portal, then it must be pumping out elemental energy of some form or another. Even if the portal's inactive."

"Willa's right," Rooster said, before routing around the innards of his bomber jacket and producing several packs of cigarettes that he began to hand out. "And these will help us lock in on the energy signature."

"A pack of smokes," MacCawill muttered. "Really?"

Rooster grinned. "That's not a mere pack of smokes. It's Rooster-Tech. A rather ingenious device that I invented several centuries ago when the wannabe wizard Merlin was causing trouble by—"

"What does it do?" I asked, just about at my wits' end.

Clearly not appreciating being robbed of a rather juicy bloviation opportunity, my enigmatic ginger colleague muttered, "It detects the inverse molecular field produced by concentrated ions of elemental energy." And when it was pretty clear that nobody had any idea what he was talking about, he let out a loud sigh. "It *beeps* when you get close to a portal. Active or inactive."

"How close?"

"Within ten feet or so."

Nodding approval, I stuffed the hifalutin pack of smokes in the back pocket of my jeans. "Tony and Rooster are with me. We'll take the northeast quadrant that's missing from the map."

Doc nodded. "Then Willa, Billy, and I will take the southwest quadrant where the stage is."

I turned my attention to Coop, Caveman, and Duncan. "Why don't you guys get the campsite and the bordering roads in the southwest corner." To which they all flashed a thumbs up, including Duncan, who didn't have any thumbs.

As I contemplated that for an awkward second, MacCawill said, "Me and Ziggy will take the southeast quadrant."

Rooster tore the map into sections and handed them out to their respective owners as Charlie cleared his throat. "And what about me, Deano? Where do I go?"

I shrugged. "Maybe you should just stay here? I mean, history would probably notice if a giant showed up at Woodstock, right?"

It was right about then, Owen reached into his boxer shorts and pulled out an aerosol can that I knew from prior experience was his mysterious time traveler urban camouflage known as Garb Gas. And before anyone could ask him just what in the hell he was doing, he shook the can a couple of times and covered the group with the obscure mist. As the fog cleared, I found myself looking like something straight out of a Cheech and Chong movie. I couldn't help but chuckle at the rest of the crew, who looked like a really pissed off version of the Brady Bunch. Even more impressive were Charlie and Ziggy, who morphed into a couple of bushy haired beatnik dudes in tie-dyed shirts and ratty jean shorts.

Figuring it was past time to get a move on, I said, "Let's roll. Everybody stay on comms. Holler if you get a hit on the bus. And hurry. We only have a few hours to find it. Charlie, you're with me."

"And me?" asked Owen.

I grinned a shit-eating grin. "Go with MacCawill." To which Owen grinned a shit-eating grin himself and slapped MacCawill on the shoulder. "Oh, hells yeah. Let's roll Royster, you big sexy bastard! Roy and Owen sitting in a tree..."

And as we all split up in search of the interdimensional portal that was hidden somewhere in the bowels of the Woodstock festival, I'm pretty sure I heard MacCawill mutter something very snide under his breath as he shot me the middle finger.

Classic.

17

"Any luck, guys?" The voice of Doc Kelly chirped from the RoosterTech-infused communications device buried in my right ear.

"Negative," MacCawill replied after a brief hiss of static, which was followed by, "Same here," from Coop.

"Nothing to report here either," I muttered as I followed Rooster and Charlie out of yet another wooded area to find a conglomeration of weary festivalgoers huddled around a camp fire in a small clearing.

"We've got about an hour until Hendrix comes on stage," Erin grumbled. You could practically feel the frustration in her voice. "Pick up the pace."

"Roger that," we responded in unison as the line fell silent.

Pulling up alongside me and gazing at the collection of sullied people in various stages of consciousness and dress, Tony just shook his head. "I can't get over all the people here. The history books really don't do it any justice at all."

"It is impressive," I said.

"Impressive? It's insane. I mean, there's people everywhere. In the woods. In the fields. Crawling around in the mud. Bathing in the goddamn ponds. Perched on top of cars on the side of the roads. I'm not even sure you could take a piss without hitting somebody, for Christ's sake."

"Speaking of taking a piss, is it me or does this whole place reek?"

"It ain't you. Stinks worse than a third world country in the heat of summer. That's what happens when five hundred thousand people spend three days together without toilets. Or trash cans." He chuckled. "Friggin hipsters. Filthy bastards."

"Hippies," Charlie corrected.

"That's what I said."

"No, you said hipsters. There's a difference."

Tony grinned. "Do enlighten."

Charlie grinned back. "Ok, so *hippies* are bell bottom-wearing nonconformists that smoke a lot of pot and are generally amicable folks. While *hipsters* are skinny jean wearing douchebags that don't eat meat and drive electric cars. And unlike hippies, hipsters are über hygiene conscious as a matter of principle, ergo these folks are *hippies* and not *hipsters*."

Not quite grasping the nuance, Tony just kind of grunted as Rooster pulled to a halt on the outskirts of a small crowd listening to a couple guys doing a piss poor acoustic cover of Janice Joplin's "Me and Bobby McGee." Scanning the area, he pointed to a clump of woods to our front. "I think there's one more clearing on the other side of these trees that makes up the eastern border of the farm, if memory serves. I suggest we split up and cover the remaining ground as quickly as possible. If the bus isn't here, we can redirect our search to another quadrant."

I turned to Tony and Charlie. "Me and Rooster will push through those woods and start searching the eastern edge. Meet us there after you guys sweep this area."

Nodding acknowledgment, they each produced their Rooster-Tech powered packs of cigarettes and pushed their way through the foul-smelling crowd to check the countless vehicles strewn about the periphery of the field. With time of the essence, me and Rooster made our way around the partying counter culturists until we reached the wood line. Darting into the thick evergreen forest, we navigated another series of ramshackle campsites without disturbing their semi-coherent occupants until we reached a sizable clearing on the far side.

And unlike the rest of the festival grounds, this part looked organized. It was almost carnival-like in appearance, with rows upon rows of ginormous circus tents sporadically placed throughout the sprawling field. String lights were haphazardly strung through a series of poles zigzagging the grounds, and the smell of food cooking on charcoal grills lingered heavy in the air. Countless clusters of people wandered from tent to tent talking and laughing while others patiently stood in lines waiting for something to eat as music hummed from large speakers on a stage in the far corner.

"Check this out," I muttered, taking it all in. "It's almost like a festival within the festival."

"Yes. Yes, it is."

"Was all this on the map?"

Rooster shrugged. "I think so. But all I really remember about it is that stage in the corner. I think they called it the 'Free Stage.'"

"Free Stage? Who played on it?"

"I think I read something about a house band. Nobody famous though. I also read that some folks never even made it to the main stage and just stayed here the whole time."

"That's crazy."

"I'm guessing various and assorted mind-altering drugs were involved."

"I imagine that's a safe bet," I muttered as a couple of strung-out hippies, completely oblivious to their surroundings, strolled past us wearing nothing but their underwear and humming the theme song to *Gilligan's Island* in perfect harmony.

"On that note," my enigmatic colleague muttered as he scanned the perimeter of the hippie circus, "let's get moving. There's at least twenty buses here. We might get lucky."

I nodded. "I'll get the southern half." Then I pulled out my faux pack of smokes and flicked the On switch, only to hear the infamous RoosterTech portal tracker make a horrid whistling sound before bursting into flames. Tossing it on the ground, I looked up to find Rooster shaking his head. "You broke it," he grumbled. "Nice."

"Sorry."

Grumbling under his breath, he reached into the pocket of his bell bottom jeans and pulled out the blood cipher medallion given to us by Lilith and tossed it to me. "Here. The medallion is mated with the portal, so it should react to it when in close proximity."

Snatching the arcane object from the air, I clutched it tightly in my hand. "React how?"

"It might glow. Or vibrate. No telling. Just don't break it. Or lose it. Actually, maybe you should give it back to me."

Flipping him off, I tucked the medallion in my pocket. "Don't forget who got us the blood cipher in the first place. I'll check the southern half. Meet back here in fifteen." Then I beelined for the conglomeration of vehicles about a hundred yards to my left. Passing by a gigantic green and white striped tent that reeked of marijuana, I was about to glance inside when the sound of a couple of assholes humming the *Gilligan's Island* theme song caught my attention. It was right about then the scantily clad weirdos I'd seen a few minutes earlier barreled straight into me, causing all three of us to tumble to the ground in a hippy heap.

Letting loose with a barrage of obscenities, I scampered to my feet while my tripped-out assailants snapped back into a semi-lucid state and followed suit.

"Oh, man," the guy hippie said as he brushed his flowing hair away from his face. "Didn't see you there." Which was followed by the lady hippie incessantly giggling as she adjusted the flower head-band that sat on her head like a peculiar crown.

"It's fine," I grumbled. "No problem."

He gawked at me with glazed eyes, and his girlfriend continued to giggle like she was a few sammiches shy of a picnic. "You sure, man?"

"Yeah, all good. Just watch where you're going."

"I'll try. My mind's melting. Everything's wavy gravy."

"Sorry to hear that."

"It's groovy, man."

"Great. Then good luck with all that. I gotta go."

"It's from the fairy dust, ya know."

"Fairy dust, eh?"

"Yeah, you want a hit?"

"Thanks, but no. I'm allergic to fairies. And dust. And hippies in their underwear that smell like ass."

Ignoring my snide commentary, my strung-out beatnik buddies stood there smiling at me for what felt like an eternity before the dude slapped me on the shoulder like we were old friends. "Hey, man, we're on our way to see the Hog Farm folks and get some food. You wanna come with?"

And as his words registered with my brain, I just about shit myself. "Hog farm? There's a hog farm here?"

"I mean, there's not like actual hogs or anything. That's just what they call themselves."

"Who?"

"The Hog Farm. They're the festival security. But they're super groovy. They got fairy dust. And food. And fairy dust."

"Do they have a bus?"

He grinned. "Of course, they have a bus, man. You can't have a party without a party bus. You wanna go or what? They're right through the *enchanted forest* over there."

More than a bit skeptical, but figuring I didn't have much to lose at this point, I nodded. "Lead the way."

Following my new pals to the rear of the Free Stage on the eastern border of the festival grounds, we ducked into the woods to find a well-worn trail marked by strands of Christmas lights. After a short walk and a lot of humming later, we popped out into yet another clearing. And although it had a similar carnival feel to its larger counterpart, it definitely had all the aspects of a well-formed commune, complete with several tents, impromptu food kiosks, wash stations, and other back woods amenities to include porta potties.

Without so much as a wave goodbye, the humming hippies skipped off toward a makeshift stage where an acoustic band was setting up their instruments as my eyes eagerly scanned the apparent Hog Farm. And wouldn't you know, parked adjacent to one of the oversized tents was a school bus. A school bus that had undergone a full-on flower power makeover with every color in the rainbow eclectically blended together in an obnoxiously awesome paint job. And there were peace signs everywhere. And by everywhere, I meant *everywhere*.

The walls.

The wheels.

The windows.

And most likely the goddamn windshield wipers, too.

Pulling the blood cipher medallion from my pocket, I felt it throb with a warm, almost electric pulse as a distinct ethereal glow formed around its roughhewn edges. "I found it," I muttered under my breath as a feeling of complete elation washed over me.

Sliding it back in my pocket, I was about to tap the RoosterTech communications device buried in my ear and tell the crew that I'd found the portal when a friendly voice called out, "Hidey hodey, friend. Cup of joe on this fine morning?"

Looking to my right to find a rather goofy looking gent in a pair of overalls and a floppy hat handing out drinks, I just politely waved at him. "Thanks, but I'm good."

"Nonsense!" he shouted with a big smile that revealed a mouth lacking all but a couple of teeth. "How about some coffee? Fresh brewed by the good people of the Hog Farm. Come on, don't be shy, fella. It's on the house."

Getting the sense that he wasn't going to take no for an answer, I made the short walk to his improvised serving station. "Coffee, huh? Got anything stronger?"

He chuckled. "Like what, my friend?"

"Beer?"

He checked his watch. "You know it's eight thirty in the morning, right?"

I shrugged. "Light beer?" The puzzled look on his face made me realize that light beer apparently wasn't a thing in 1969. "Forget it. Coffee's good."

"Coffee it is," he said, grabbing a Styrofoam cup from a tray on the end of the table and handing it to me. "Here you go."

Nodding my appreciation, I took a healthy gulp of the dark liquid and was more than surprised to find that it was not coffee at all. "What is this?"

"Come again?"

"This isn't coffee. It tastes like punch or something."

"Oh shit," he said, grabbing the cup from my hand and inspecting its contents.

"Oh shit, what?"

"Oh shit, I may have accidentally given you some electric punch instead of coffee."

"Is that bad?"

"That depends."

"On?"

He grinned. Sheepishly. "Whether or not you were planning on having your mind melted this morning."

"Oh shit," I muttered. "Did I just get fairy dusted?"

And there was just something about the look on his face that told me everything I needed to know.

Friggin hipsters.

Hippies.

Whatever.

18

Now granted, I'd been on my fair share of high stakes missions over the years.

And I'd like to think I was pretty adept at dealing with unforeseen circumstances. It was just a matter of time before the best laid plans went to complete shit, and the more you embraced that tried-and-true tenet, the better off you were.

So, I was fully expecting our epic quest to seek out the Anunnaki and save the planet to go off the proverbial rails in any number of ways. But, if I'm being honest, I kind of thought our problems would come in the form of conniving angels.

Or disgruntled giants.

Or overzealous half-bred beasties.

Or meddling human shadow regimes.

Not being inadvertently dosed with a mind-altering substance by some floppy hat wearing trippy hippy at friggin Woodstock.

That one wasn't on the radar.

Until right now, of course.

Because as I stood there glaring at the aforementioned floppy hat wearing weirdo, it occurred to me I couldn't remember what the hell I was doing there in the first place.

Awkwardly waving at me from across the table, he said, "You doing all right there, friend?"

As his words somewhat registered with my muddled brain, I felt my mouth curl into a wide smile. Or at least I think I did. I couldn't quite feel my face. But it felt like I was smiling. If I had a face, that is.

"Oh, boy," he muttered, "You must've got a strong dose. Can you hear me?" Holding his hand up, he snapped his fingers a couple of times. "You in there, man?"

It was right about then my right ear hissed with static, causing me to jump backward. And then there was a voice in my head. "Dean, you copy?"

It was Rooster's voice. And it was loud as hell. "John? That you?"

"Yeah," he said. "You having any luck?"

"With what?"

"What do you mean *with what*? Finding the freaking bus!"

"What bus?"

After a long pause, he muttered, "What's wrong with you?"

"Nothing. I mean, I can't feel my face. And you're in my ear. That's kinda weird. How'd you get in there by the way? And why are you yelling at me?"

"Where the hell are you?"

"Stop yelling."

"I'm not yelling!"

"Totally yelling." Then I rubbed my ear a few times and everything went silent as floppy hat man came around the table and put a hand on my shoulder, "You OK, fella?"

"Yeah, I'm great. Why?"

"It's just that you were kind of talking to yourself."

I shook my head. "That was just Rooster."

"You were talking to a chicken?"

"No, I was talking to *Rooster*."

"Uh-huh."

"He's in my ear."

"So, you're hearing voices in your head?"

"Yup. Rooster's voice. He was yelling at me."

"The chicken was yelling at you, huh?"

"Yeah, what a dick, right?"

"Oh, boy," he muttered for a second time in as many minutes. "Why don't you come with me."

"Where we going?"

"We're going to find a nice, quiet place for you to sit down for a while. That sound good?"

"Yeah, that sounds *great*. Hey, do I still have a face?"

Ignoring the question, floppy hat man then ushered me through a crowd of people who all looked like the original cast of *Gilligan's Island*. It was uncanny. First there was Gilligan. Then the Skipper. Then the Professor, Mary Ann, and Ginger. And then friggin Thurston Howell III and his deranged wife, Lovey.

They were everywhere. And everyone. And they were all smiling at me like they knew something I didn't. Sons of bitches!

"Here we are," he said as we skirted around the back of the acoustic band made up of life-sized teddy bears of varying shades of psychedelic colors. Meticulously tuning their instruments, they all stopped and looked at me as we strolled past. And wouldn't you know they smiled at me like they knew something I didn't. Snarky sons of bitches! Fucking life-sized teddy bear assholes!

Pushing open a sizable door that creaked and moaned in protest, floppy hat man climbed a couple steps and motioned for me to follow. "Come on, fella. Almost there."

"What is this place?" I asked, not quite convinced I should follow him.

"Just a place to relax for a while. Come on up. It's OK."

Figuring I didn't have any other choice, given the zombie-like infestation of *Gilligan's Island* cast members and the creepy teddy bear band, I reluctantly climbed the steps to find a dimly lit, cozy space. There were several bench seats laid out on either side of a long aisle that seemed to disappear behind a huge wall of beads hanging from the ceiling. And the only light provided was pulsing from a series of pink and blue lava lamps complemented by a strand or two of Christmas lights draped from the blackout windows.

Guiding me to one of the seats, floppy hat guy then patted me on the shoulder and smiled. "You stay here, friend. I'll be back to check on you in a bit." Then he turned and left me alone in the peculiar room, as the overpowering aroma of incense gave me an instant headache.

As my foggy mind struggled to maintain a functional thought pattern, the sound of an old blues song filled the air. And although I couldn't see them from the confines of my tripped-out hippy hide-away, I assumed it was the teddy bear band doing a warm up set as the twang of acoustic guitars accompanied by a mandolin and a stand-up bass rang out in perfect harmony. And almost immediately, I started humming.

It was right about then a mellow, velvety voice from somewhere behind me said, "You like that song, huh?"

Spinning around, I was more than surprised to find yet another man-sized teddy bear pushing his way through the wall of beads. Shorter and chubbier than the ones I'd seen outside, this one had thick tufts of dark, curly hair that somewhat resembled a majestic lion's mane sprouting from its head. Parted in the middle, the unruly mop almost reached his shoulders before melding into a bushy beard that exploded from his face in all directions.

Not sure whether to be terrified or not, I just kind of gawked at him as he adjusted his circular, wire-framed glasses and took a long drag from a joint he was holding in one of his teddy bear paws. "Hey there," he said, as his furry face curled into a wide smile to reveal a mouthful of human teeth.

Not really sure what to say, I continued to gawk as the obscure figure chuckled a few times before taking a seat on the bench next to me. After an awkward moment or two, I worked up the courage to utter, "Hey there yourself?"

"You a friend of Gravy?" he asked.

"I mean, I like gravy. Friends might be a stretch, though. Being that it's a condiment and all."

He chuckled. "Not *that* gravy. Gravy. The guy with the overalls and the—"

"Floppy hat?"

"Yup, that's him."

"Huh, he never actually told me his name. But, yeah, I guess we're friends. I mean, he gave me coffee."

Looking down over the rim of his glasses that had slid down his nose, he held out one of his paws. "Any friend of Gravy is a friend of mine. I'm Jerry."

I gave his paw an obligatory shake. "Nice to meet you, Dean. I'm Jerry. Wait, that's not right. Is it? Shit, do I have a face?"

He grinned and stroked his beard a few times. "Relax, my friend. If I had to guess, you've been fairy dusted. It'll wear off in a little while. In the meantime, try to enjoy the trip. It's best that way. Trust me." His voice was warm and welcoming. And his words had a distinct melody to them as they flowed from his mouth with a level of intelligence that was almost palpable.

I shrugged. "Enjoy the trip?"

He nodded. "Best that way."

"It's just that I was in the middle of something really important."

"Everybody is, my friend. Maybe this is the universe telling you that whatever it is you were doing just isn't that important after all. Let it go."

"You think?"

"Absolutely."

"Hmm, maybe you're right. You certainly are wise for a five-foot-tall talking teddy bear. Hey, can I call you Jer-bear?"

Tapping one of his fluffy feet to the music coming from outside, he smiled at me again. "Man, I love this song. It's an old twelve-bar blues tune called—"

"'Good Morning, Little School Girl,'" I blurted out as the song's name popped into my head at that exact moment. "The Grateful Dead covered it on their first album. Might've been the second."

Smiling again, my fluffy friend nodded his approval. "Impressive. You like the Dead, huh?"

I scoffed. "Hell yeah, I like the Dead. Although, if I'm being honest, I prefer their earlier stuff."

"Earlier stuff?"

"Yeah, anything after 1975 was kind of crap."

"Crap?"

"Total crap."

He chuckled. Heartily. "You do realize it's 1969, right?"

"Is it?"

"Ah, yeah."

"That's weird. Maybe I'm from the future?"

"Ok, so what's your favorite album in the future?"

"Live or studio."

"Studio."

"That's easy. *American Beauty*. Hands down."

"*American Beauty?* Wow, cool title."

"Yup, got all the classics. *Friend of the Devil. Box of Rain. Sugar Magnolia. Ripple.*"

"And when was that released?"

"1970. Maybe 1971?"

Chuckling again, he hopped to his feet and patted me on the head. "Well, it was a genuine pleasure to meet you, Dean from the future. You've given me much to think on for sure."

"Wait, you're leaving?"

Pulling an acoustic guitar out of a case by his feet, he strapped it over his shoulder and grinned. "Duty calls." Then he disappeared down the steps to join the rest of his fluffy band buddies.

Making the mental note that there was something strangely familiar about that talking stuffed animal of unusual size, I drifted in and out of conscious thought as song after song after song floated through my head like a parade of magic carpets. And then, almost like he appeared out of thin air, Rooster was standing in front of me. And he did not look happy.

Letting out an exasperated sigh, he tapped his right ear a couple of times. "I'm with Dean," he said. "There's a path in the woods behind the Free Stage. Everybody get here, now. He found the portal. And I think he's high — or stoned. Or something else."

I smiled. "Hey, man, how'd you get out of my ear?"

Rolling his eyes, he fished around the pockets of his bell bottoms until he produced a small vial of glowing green liquid. Tossing it to me, he said, "Drink this."

"What is it?"

"It's beer."

Pulling out the cork and taking a whiff, I was repulsed by the horrible odor. "No. Not beer."

Apparently not in the mood, Rooster grunted something under his breath before grabbing the vial and pouring it down my throat. Feeling like I just inhaled a liquified skunk, my entire body began to convulse as whatever arcane tonic my enigmatic ginger colleague just forced down my gullet started to work. A few seconds and one hell of a splitting headache later, I was back to normal.

"Fuck me," I grumbled, spitting out the remnants of the horrid liquid still lingering in my mouth. "What the hell was that shit?"

"That, my friend, was a concentrated dose of Rooster Psychia-Tea guaranteed to negate the psychedelic effects of any and all hallucinogens."

"Hallucinogens?"

"It appears you were roofied. What the hell happened?"

"Not sure. It's all kind of a blur after I got some coffee from Gravy."

"Gravy?"

"Yeah, he gave me coffee."

"So, gravy gave you coffee."

"Yeah, but it was actually punch."

"So, gravy gave you punch?"

"Yup. Pretty sure."

"And then?"

"The cast from *Gilligan's Island* was everywhere. And there were these creepy teddy bears. Then I ended up here."

"Yeah, you were definitely roofied."

"Ugh."

Grinning, he held up his RoosterTech-infused pack of cigarettes. It was beeping off the hook. "On the bright side, at least you found the bus."

"Right," I muttered under my breath. "The bus." It was right about then my muddled brain connected a series of dots, and I realized I'd been sitting on the bus this entire friggin time. "We're on the bus! I mean, of course, we're on the damn bus. I found it, then you found me. How did you find me, by the way?"

He shrugged. "Luck. When your comms went dead, the whole team started searching the area. Then I overheard a guy talking to his buddies about a dude who was rambling about his favorite *Grateful Dead* albums 'from the future.' Figured that had to be you."

"Wait, you mean the talking teddy bear with the glasses and the goofy beard? That guy was real?"

"Not sure about a talking teddy bear, but he was real, all right. And a spitting image of Jerry Garcia. It was uncanny. Crazy, right?"

"Yeah," I muttered. "Crazy." Then I played back the strange conversation I had with the obscure teddy bear with the crazy hair, goofy beard, and round rimmed glasses. "Wait, you don't think that guy was actually Jerry Garcia, right?"

We never finished that particular conversation because it was right about then Doc came flying up the steps with her face curled into a deep scowl. "We have a problem. The tagalongs found us again."

"They're here?" Rooster scoffed. "In 1969? Are you sure?" And when Doc offered nothing in response besides an icy stare, he muttered, "Of course, you're sure. Sorry?"

"We can't fight them here," she said. "And we're just about out of time. We need a plan."

I grinned. "We have a plan."

"Which is?"

Pulling the arcane blood cipher medallion from my pocket, I held it up. "We get the crew on the bus and we fire up the portal. The tagalongs can't follow us to Nibiru."

And before anyone could say anything else on the matter, the peculiar medallion began to violently pulse like an unnatural strobe light, and we were bathed in a creepy crimson glow. Then there was an obnoxiously loud popping sound.

And just like that, we were somewhere else.

Awesome.

19

"Run that plan by me again, Dean," Doc grumbled as we found ourselves standing in a hotel lobby amidst a bustling crowd of people. Some of them looked human. Others not so much.

Fighting back the urge to mutter something snide under my breath, I simply grinned at her and slid the blood cipher medallion into the pocket of my jeans. And in doing so, it occurred to me I was no longer wearing bell bottoms nor clad in faux hippy gear. Neither was Rooster nor Erin.

"The garb gas wore off," Rooster said like he was reading my mind. "I think that means we're back in the present. But where? Is this Nibiru?"

Looking around the peculiar lobby, I couldn't help but chuckle at the cheesy wood paneled walls, horrific orange and green carpeting, and reception desk painted bright yellow. And there was this awful music playing. It was like elevator music, but somehow exponentially worse. "Unless the famed Anunnaki live in a hotel that looks like something straight out of a '70s sitcom, I think the portal misfired."

Stepping out of the way of a nine-foot shaggy behemoth in a

plaid housecoat that strolled past us with a cigar hanging out of its fang-filled mouth and its face buried in a ginormous newspaper, Erin said, "Misfired or not, I get the feeling we're not on Earth."

Rooster shrugged. "Then where the hell are we?"

"Number *twenty*-three!" shouted the clerk perched behind the reception desk as she meticulously scanned the crowd with a determined squint magnified through thick bifocal glasses. She looked old. Actually, she looked ancient. And her shrill voice reverberated through the lobby with a piercing echo as veins popped from her gaunt neck. "Now serving number twenty-three!" And when nobody stepped forward, she barked, "Will everyone kindly check your tickets for number — twenty-three!"

It was right about then when I felt the medallion vibrate in my pocket, and when I pulled it out to investigate, it was no longer a hockey puck-sized hunk of metal. It was a small, white slip of paper with the number twenty-three stenciled on it. Clearly as surprised as I was by the unusual turn of events, but not in the mood to dick around, Erin grabbed the ticket and held it up. "Twenty-three," she said, pushing her way through the crowd. "I'm number twenty-three."

Figuring it best to follow, I scampered after her with Rooster on my heels. No sooner had we reached the desk than the clerk's face turned white as a ghost. It was almost like she recognized us. Then, unfortunately, she picked up the handset of a rotary telephone and screamed, "Security to the lobby! Security! Lobby, now! It's *them*. They're back!"

And before we knew what the hell was happening, the crowd instantly dispersed, and we were surrounded by a couple dozen goons on high protein diets toting razor-tipped spears and covered from head to foot in unnatural armor. Although jet-black instead of golden, it resembled Doc's armor in the way it fit its occupants, revealing nothing but two eyes that glowed a harrowing white from behind a faceless helmet. To say it was creepy didn't do it any justice. It was downright unnerving.

"Whoa," I protested, taking a step forward and holding up my hands. "I think there's been some kind of mistake."

The old woman grinned and waved her finger at me. "The only mistake, young man, is yours. I explicitly warned you what would happen if you ever returned to the Hotel Shasta, did I not?" Then she nodded at her security detail. "And now, you may kill them. *Kill them!* Now!"

"Wait!" yelled Doc. "Please! We've never been here before. I swear it." To which, one of the faceless security guards bent down and whispered something into the receptionist's ear.

"Hmm," she said, studying each of us for an awkward second or two. "I believe you're right, Percival. Carry on then." And right on cue, the security force vanished as the eerie music resumed and the crowd instantly returned.

Glaring at the old bat, I grumbled, "What the hell was that about?"

She groaned. "Alternate timelines are so terribly confusing."

"I'm sorry, what?"

She groaned again. This time louder. "A future version of you has already been here. In the past."

I shrugged. "I'm sorry, what?"

As I stood there trying to make some sense of what she just said, Rooster cleared his throat. "Ah, ma'am, how is it you can tell that we're from an alternate timeline?"

"That is quite simple." Then she looked at me. "*He* doesn't have a scar running across his face." Then she looked at Doc. "*She* still has kind eyes." And then she looked back at Rooster. "And *you* still have both of your arms."

"I'm sorry, what? Both of my arms? Did you say arms?"

"I've said quite enough on that particular topic," the receptionist said, looking around the lobby. "In the event you haven't noticed, you three are not the only guests requiring assistance." Then she forced a smile. "Allow me to properly welcome you to the Hotel Shasta. I am your hostess, Vee."

"The Hotel Shasta," Rooster muttered as his eyes danced with rapid thought. "I've heard of this place. Supposed to be some kind of interdimensional waystation. I always thought it was a myth."

"*Waystation*." Vee scoffed. "Would you describe a quintessential realm away from home providing unlimited complimentary services to its honored guests as a mere *waystation*?"

Rooster shrugged. "I feel like that's a trick question."

Groaning for a third time, our enigmatic hostess muttered, "Are you in need of lodging, passage, or provisions?"

"Passage," Doc said.

"Passage to where?"

"Nibiru."

Vee raised an eyebrow. "And I assume you have a proper invitation?" To which Doc placed the ticket with the number twenty-three on the desk as it morphed into the blood cipher medallion. Apparently satisfied with our credentials, Vee nodded. "Tell me, are you *gods* of some sort or another?"

"Gods?" asked Doc as she grabbed the medallion and tucked it into the pocket of her jeans.

"Yes, yes, you know, gods. Old gods. New gods. Greater gods. Lesser gods. Sky gods. Underworld gods. Elemental gods. Celestial gods. Death gods. Life gods. Primordial gods. Nature gods. Vengeful gods. Guardian gods. So on and so forth."

Doc shook her head. "Ah, no. We're not *gods*. Why?"

"Because, young lady, if you're not a *god*, you're typically food or fodder in the good lands of *Nibiru*."

"We can take care of ourselves," I said, which caused Vee's wrinkled face to curl into a shit-eating grin. "Yes, well, I supposed we'll see. We *always* see." Then she punched a few keys on something that looked like an old-fashioned cash register, and it printed three tickets. Handing them to us, she said, "The elevator bay is down the hall and to the left. Hand these to the operator."

"And then what?"

Groaning yet again, Vee muttered, "And *then*, the operator will escort you to an *elevator* that will transport you to the great game halls of Agartha in the highlands of Nibiru."

"Is that where we can find Enki?"

She laughed. "Enki? Are you quite mad? What business could you three possibly have with the ruler of the Anunnaki?" And before I could respond, she said, "Actually, don't tell me. I simply don't care. If it is Enki you seek, then you must venture to Aventine City, where you will find him, and his *esteemed* court, at the Ziggurat of Anshar. I suggest you find a guide, as the journey will be treacherous and unforgiving, to say the very least. Good luck and *good day*." Then she scanned the crowd. "Now serving number twenty-four. Twenty-four!"

"Wait," Doc said. "A guide. Where do we find a guide?"

Shooing us away as the next guests made their way to the reception desk, she said, "Try the bar. Down the hall to the right. Good day!"

Leaving Vee to go about her business of being a crotchety old crow, we bid her farewell and followed the orange and green carpet down a grand hallway lined with pedestal chairs and ashtrays on either side.

"I don't like this," Rooster said, shaking his head. "We should go back and get the rest of the team."

"We're on our own," I muttered. "And so are they, unfortunately."

"Maybe not. I mean, we're in the *Hotel Shasta*. This place is legend. Literally. There's gotta be some kind of being here that can send us back to 1969."

"There's no time for that, John," Erin said. Her voice was resolute. "We have to push forward. I don't like it either, but we have no choice."

I nodded. "Speaking of time, what the hell was the old lady rambling on about future versions of us showing up and shit?"

Rooster grinned. "Do you want me to explain it?"

Nonchalantly flipping him the middle finger, I muttered, "No, I really fucking don't. Let's just agree to never come back here. Problem solved."

I'm pretty sure my enigmatic ginger colleague was about to school me on the many nuances of the space-time continuum to include temporal incursions and predestination paradoxes when Doc said, "And what's the deal with those security guards? Did you see their armor?"

"I did. Looked just like yours."

"And there was something about the way they moved. It was almost like they were—"

"Ghosts," Rooster said, rather emphatically, which caused both Doc and me to stop dead in our tracks.

"Ghosts," she repeated. "That's a metaphor, right? You don't mean like actual *ghosts*."

"Maybe?"

"Wait, are you saying ghosts are real? Seriously?"

Rooster shrugged. "It's entirely possible. I mean, we're at the Hotel Shasta, which up until five minutes ago I didn't think was real either."

"And the old lady," I said. "She's a ghost too?"

"No, she's something else. Definitely among the living, but not human. Her aura was off the charts."

Doc shook her head. "But if the guards are freaking ghosts, then how are they in physical form? Aren't ghosts supposed to be incorporeal? That's kind of their defining factor."

"Now that's the interesting part," my enigmatic ginger colleague replied as we continued strolling down the corridor. "I suspect it's got something to do with that armor. Maybe it's god-powered. Kind of like yours, but instead of being powered by Ethan Roy, it's powered by somebody else. Somebody with the juice to create a small army of undead knights." Then his eyes shot wide open like he'd had an empowered epiphany. "Holy shit! The Dead Knights of Londinium! It's gotta be them. They're real? They're here! Holy shit!"

I chuckled. "The Dead Knights of Londinium? Sounds like a Monty Python movie. Or British zombie porn."

"Well, it's not." He scoffed. "I mean, it could be, I guess, but that's not the point. We need to tread very, very carefully, guys."

I chuckled again. "Because of the friggin ghost knights?"

"The Dead Knights! And they're seriously bad news."

"And who are these Dead Knights, John?" asked Erin, clearly a bit skeptical.

"Well, according to legend, they were followers of Sir Percival."

"Percival. As in the knight from Arthur's round table? That guy?"

"Exactly. And, supposedly, after several fruitless years into his quest for the Holy Grail, he ended up making a deal with a witch of some sort who claimed she could give him an enchanted map that would lead him straight to it."

"And I'm guessing that backfired?"

"In spectacular fashion. Unable to decipher the map, Percival was driven mad. In a fit of rage, he then murdered all his knights in one bloody swoop before falling upon his own sword. But, given the deal with the witch, their spirits were unable to move on. Instead, they were compelled to do her bidding for eternity — as ghosts."

I rolled my eyes. "And then some random *god* came along and stuffed them into magical armored suits and they ended up being rent-a-cops for some whacked-out hotel in the middle of nowhere? Bullshit. Those guys aren't dead. And they're certainly not knights. They're just dicks."

Rooster sighed. "Did you hear what the old lady called the one that spoke to her back at the reception desk?"

"She called him Percival," Doc said.

"Exactly! That can't be a coincidence. You know how many bloodbaths are attributed to the Dead Knights over the past millennia? A shit load. You can't kill them. They're already dead!"

"Undead knights or not," Doc said as we reached the end of the hallway, "I think we can all agree that we need to keep a low profile and get the hell out of here as quickly as possible. We good?"

"We're good," Rooster and I muttered in unison as we hooked a right and were greeted with a rolling barrage of cigarette smoke that poured from the hotel bar like a smoldering forest fire.

Doc nodded. "Then let's find a guide and get gone."

Literally parting the smoke with our hands, we carefully wove our way through the crowd of unnatural beings as an instrumental, pseudo-jazz version of "Kickstart My Heart" from Mötley Crüe rang out from an electric guitar somewhere in the near vicinity. Reaching the somewhat lavish bar and scoring some real estate next to a couple dudes with big ass horns sprouting out of their heads, and furry, hooved feet, I said, "Hey, fellas, how's Narnia?" before plopping down on a stool.

Sitting down next to me, Erin jabbed me in the ribs with her elbow. "Really?"

I shrugged. "What?"

"Didn't I just say to keep a low profile?"

"Lighten up, Doc. Everybody loves a good C. S. Lewis joke. Even goat people." To which she jabbed me in the ribs again. This time, harder. Much harder.

"Welcome, welcome, noble travelers," came a familiar voice from behind the bar. "May I interest you in one of our house martinis? They're simply fabulous. Shaken not stirred, of course."

And as I looked up to find the Hotel Shasta's resident bartender grinning at us with a mouth full of unnaturally white teeth, I did a triple take. And then I about shit myself.

Like a male model, his near seven-foot frame was statuesque to say the very least, and his perfectly cut, black suit hugged his body like a glove. His celebrity-grade, raven hair was meticulously styled and, unlike the last time I'd seen him, it was tied in a pony tail that draped over his shoulder.

But it was his eyes that really got me. For not only were they crimson, snakelike, and utterly soulless — they were the eyes of my executioner.

Jumping to my feet in a blur of motion, the cloak manifested in a spectral flash as a turbo shot of adrenaline fired through my body like an electric current. "You son of a bitch!"

It was right about then the grin vanished from Azazel's flawless face. "Dean Robinson," he muttered in his signature sycophantic British dialect. "Well, this is more than a bit awkward."

You fucking think?

20

With the cloak billowing about my shoulders like a caged animal doing everything in its power to break free, I felt the metal gauntlets form over my hands as the scabbard-like holster manifested on my back. My face curled into a dark grin as I ripped the semi-divine 1887 Winchester shotgun free and cocked the lever. Both barrels glowed and hissed with the white fires of Judgement as I jabbed them into Azazel's sculpted torso. "It's nice to see you, asshole. Any last words?"

The music came to a screeching halt and everyone in the near vicinity backpedaled several steps as my least favorite fallen angel looked like he was about to piss himself. "Ah, Dean," he said, in an atypically sincere tone. "I appreciate that you're upset, but might I suggest you lower your weapon. This isn't the kind of place that tolerates such behavior."

"Put your gun away, Dean," growled Doc, decked out in golden armor and apparently ready for some payback with extreme interest. "This piece of shit is mine."

Vaulting over the bar in a blur of motion, she wrapped one hand around Azazel's throat and curled the other one into a tight fist that sprouted a razor sharp, machete-sized blade from its golden knuckles. I'm pretty sure she was about to filet the poor bastard from his testicles to his spectacles when we were somehow completely surrounded by the armored, super creepy hotel security force. And they didn't look happy.

Not that we could really tell because, like Erin, they were wearing super creepy, featureless helmets, but you get the point. And speaking of points, they had at least a couple dozen glinting spears tactically positioned about an inch from all our vital organs. Nice touch.

"Trouble, Nigel?" asked the head security dude in a guttural, almost grating voice with his glowing white eyes fixated on me and Doc.

Azazel forced a grin. "*Trouble?* No, no, nothing of the sort, Percival."

"That's good. You know how the Hotel feels about trouble."

"Of course, no trouble here. Just catching up with some old friends."

He grunted. "Friends, eh?"

"Yes, yes. Most certainly *friends*. The very best of. Always kidding around with each other, we are. Isn't that *right*, dear Erin. Erin?"

And after a long silence where Doc realized that Azazel was more afraid of the hotel security weirdos than he was of us, she released her death grip on his neck as her golden armor melted from existence.

Then she vaulted back over the bar.

And then she started laughing.

But it wasn't a funny, light-hearted kind of laugh.

It was much more of a super fake, '*I wish I was anywhere but here*' kind of laugh.

"Yeah, sorry, guys," she said. "Totally kidding around. We go way back with Myles here."

"*Nigel*," Azazel muttered under his breath.

"Yup, Nigel. We go way back with Nigel. Always joking about 'killing each other.' It's a little game we play. Super fun. Kind of like tag but with guns. And knives. Hilarious, right? Am I right, John?"

Rooster nodded. "Oh, yeah. Totally hilarious."

Doc smiled. "Hilarious! Right, Dean?" And when I just shrugged in response, she nonchalantly whacked me in the ribs hard.

"Hilarious!" I blurted out, figuring it best to play along as I tried my damnedest to downplay the throbbing pain. "Old Nigel here's a real pal, you know. I mean, we just love the crazy fucker to death. And what a nice surprise to find him here. Our old buddy, Nigel." Then I holstered the shotgun and willed the cloak and gauntlets into retreat. "So, we good here, fellas? I could really go for one of those house martinis. Or six."

Poking me in the chest with his armored finger, Percival muttered, "No *trouble*. No problem." And within the literal blink of an eye, he and his inexplicable cohorts were gone. It was goddamn unnerving.

With the unpleasantries concluded, the crowd returned to their perches at the bar as the guitarist sitting in the far corner resumed his jazz tribute to eighties power ballads with "Love Bites" from Def Leppard. Figuring that was a nice touch, I glared at Azazel, who was standing behind the bar, awkwardly grinning at us. "Start talking," I grumbled. "What the fuck are you doing here, *Nigel*?"

"Isn't it obvious?" he replied rather sheepishly. "I'm *hiding*. Or trying to, at the very least. No thanks to you three." Then he very carefully scanned the area before whispering, "You do realize those were the Dead Knights of Londinium, right? They absolutely terrify me."

To which Rooster jumped to his feet and pumped his fist. "I knew it! Told you so. I was totally right, for the record. And nobody cares..."

"Who are you *hiding* from?" asked Doc as she glared at Azazel. Her words were cold and her glare was colder.

"Why Lucifer, of course," he said with his voice just above a whisper. "Do you believe he *betrayed* me? *Me!* After all I did for him. He turned the Watchers against me and left me for dead. Dead!"

I shook my head. "How long have been here?"

He shrugged. "I'm not quite sure. Time doesn't quite work at the Hotel Shasta. That's precisely why I came. Have I missed much back in the world, as they say? Never mind. Don't tell me. I don't want to know. I'm quite content with my new life. I very much enjoy tending bar. I'm quite good at it. And the clientele that pass through here are stimulating."

"Your new life," I muttered. "So, you're a friggin good guy now? Just like that?"

"Good. Bad. Or otherwise. I simply am. And, for what's it worth, please accept my sincerest apologies for our past *conflict*."

I started laughing hard. "Past conflict? You mean like in Bosnia. When you fucking killed me. Shot me in the chest five times with my own shotgun. That kind of past conflict?"

He grimaced. "Sorry?"

"And you *kidnapped* me," Doc growled. "And made me deliver those freak show baby giants as you tortured Father Watson to death. Remember that, you asshole? Are you sorry for that, too?"

"Quite sorry, actually, Doctor Kelly."

Rooster cleared his throat. "And then there's the three thousand years of horrible shit you did to mankind in general. Don't even get me started on that. I was there for most of it."

"Yes, yes, I am well aware," Azazel muttered as his crimson gaze fell toward the floor. "I can only apologize for what I've done, not what I am. But one day soon—"

"One day soon," I said, grinning a wolfish grin. "When you're not *hiding* anymore, you and me are going to finish this conversation. But right now, you're going to fucking help us."

Azazel perked up. "How may I be of service?"

"We're going to Nibiru, and we need—"

"Nibiru," he gasped. "Whatever for? The Anunnaki are not to be trifled with."

"We need a guide," Erin said. "The receptionist said there would be one here."

Getting the sense Doc wasn't in the mood, Azazel nodded. "But of course." Then he pointed at the dude playing guitar in the corner. "That gentleman's name is George. The folks around here call him *Five Finger*. I believe he's a minor deity of some sort or another."

"He's a god?"

"He is indeed. And one who's been known to traverse the realms of Nibiru on occasion."

"Is he for hire?"

He smiled. "My dear Doctor, this is the Hotel Shasta. Everyone is for hire. It's just a matter of determining their particular price." Then he reached under the bar and produced a round leather purse, presumably full of coin. Tossing it to her, he said, "That should cover his fee, plus a very generous tip."

Doc nodded somewhat appreciatively. "Be seeing ya, *Nigel*."

"May I offer any of you a drink before you go? House martini? Oh, and we have this fabulous new craft beer on tap that's all the rage. It's called Petulant—"

"We're good," she said, turning and making her way through the crowd with Rooster in tow.

I grinned at Azazel. "I'll take a pint for the road."

"No, he won't!" Doc yelled back. "Let's go, Dean."

"Just one."

"Dean!"

Figuring the beer would have to wait, I gave my least favorite fallen angel- turned pseudo-benevolent barkeep a parting glare before catching up with Rooster and Erin. "So, Azazel's gone straight," my enigmatic ginger colleague grumbled. "Didn't see that coming."

I scoffed. "Gone straight, my ass. That son of a bitch is up to something."

"We'll deal with him later," Doc said. "Count on it."

And after a short jaunt through the labyrinth of unnatural bar patrons, we reached the aforementioned Five Finger George, who was perched on a stool and now playing a funky jazz version of "We're Not Gonna Take It" by Twisted Sister. He was fit with a wiry frame and looked to be twenty-five years old. Thirty tops. With vibrant, almost glowing green eyes and dark brown hair formed into an audacious fauxhawk, he had an undeniable rockstar vibe about him. But the best part was his outfit. It was epic.

And by epic, I meant that if Jon Bon Jovi and David Lee Roth somehow conceived a love child circa 1986, this is what he would have been wearing when he popped out of the womb. I'm talking black leather pants, snakeskin boots, and a leopard print tee-shirt crudely cut into a tank top with a pair of scissors. And if that wasn't enough, he was rocking an acid-washed jean jacket vest, a purple pinstriped scarf, and a pair of aviator sunglasses with mirrored lenses. It was almost too much for reality to accept.

"Ugh," Doc grumbled. "He looks like a total douche." Followed by, "That jackass is a god?" from Rooster. "Really?"

I shrugged. "I'm kind of digging the look. Just saying."

Swaying to the rhythm, George's hand effortlessly flew up and down the neck of his vintage Paul Reed Smith electric guitar adorned with a stunning sunburst finish, giving it a distinct flame-like appearance. But the longer I stared at it, the more I was convinced it wasn't a *flame-like* appearance after all. It was actual flame.

Which would kind of insinuate that his otherworldly guitar was made of fire.

Either that or I was completely losing my mind.

Or better yet, I was still under the influence of the hippy, trippy fairy dust.

At any rate, as George expertly picked the final few notes of the song, he leaned into the microphone and chuckled. "We're not gonna take, take, take it!" His voice was smooth and matched his retro eighties vibe to a tee. "Nothing like a little jazz-fusionated Twisted Sister, right? Am I right, folks?"

Absolutely nobody clapped or acknowledged him in the least. He chuckled again. "OK, gonna take a quick break now. Be back in ten. Until then, this is *Five Finger*, the righteous six stringer and your favorite rock 'n' roll *bringer*, signing off!"

And when absolutely nobody clapped or acknowledged him in the least for a second time, he muttered, "Seriously though, be back in ten."

Hopping off the stool, he muttered something unpleasant under his breath as his uncanny guitar hovered in the air for a second or two before shrinking to the size of a comb and sliding into the breast pocket of his jean vest. Lighting a cigarette that sort of just appeared in his mouth, he took a couple of puffs before noticing us standing there gawking at him. Then he took off his sunglasses and grinned. "Hey there, rock stars, you digging the righteous tuneage?"

Doc grinned back. "You George?"

He took another drag from his smoke and blew an ornate smoke ring that looked rather like an erect penis. "Depends on who's asking?"

To which, Doc replied by grinning a second time as she casually tossed the bag of coin up and down a few times. "That's who's asking."

"Well then, sex kitten," he said before flipping his cigarette to the floor and snuffing it out with his boot. "Five Finger George I am. And I am, *most triumphantly*, at your service. So, what's the gig?"

"We need a guide to take us to—"

"Say no more. I'm your man."

"Don't you want to know where we're going?"

"Nope. I'm in."

"So, we have a deal?"

"We totally have a deal, sex kitten. Now, how about you hand over that mo-mo-mo-*ney* and we grab ourselves a drinky drink to celebrate. Hey, I didn't get your name."

And it was right about then when Doc wound up like a softball pitcher and slung the hefty purse into Five Finger's leather clad crotch at breakneck speed. "My name's Erin," she muttered. "But you can call me Doc, *sex kitten*."

Collapsing to the floor with his hands cradling his nethers, the poor bastard started to hyperventilate as Rooster and I winced on his behalf.

Talk about a first impression making a lasting impression.

21

Pushing himself off the ground and easing back onto his stool, George groaned a few more times as he popped the cap off a bottle of Coors Light that somehow appeared in his hand. After a gulp or two, he muttered, "I'm gonna need a minute here."

"Take your time," I said. "We've all been there. Except for Doc, of course. Not to say she doesn't have any balls, per se. She totally does. They're just more of the metaphorical nature. You know, because she's a woman."

He took another sip of beer and glared at me for an awkward second or two. "I didn't get your name."

"Right, sorry. I'm Dean. That's Rooster. And you've already met Doc, also known as—"

"Yup," he said, cradling his crotch. "I remember."

I grinned. "And you're, ah, George, right? Five Finger?"

He drained his beer only to have a fresh one appear in his hand. "The righteous six stringer. Your favorite rock 'n' roll bringer." Then he burped.

"Catchy slogan."

"You like?"

"Oh, yeah. It's clever — ish. And sort of original."

"Yeah, well, Five Finger George is nothing if not *original*."

Not sure if he was being serious, I just nodded a couple of times. "Speaking of, I've never heard anybody do a jazz rendition of a Mötley Crüe song before. It was really—"

"Righteous?"

"I was going to say interesting, but sure. Righteous works."

He perked up. "Finally! Somebody with some actual taste around here!" Then he drained his second beer, only to be replaced by a third. "Righteous!"

I chuckled. "Gotta say, love the outfit, too."

"Hell yeah, my man! I mean, I am a guitar god, after all. Gotta look the part, right?"

"Wait," Rooster said, "You're the guitar god?

"No, no, no, I'm *a* guitar god. There's quite a few of us, actually."

"So, are you like the 1980s version or something?"

"Hell yeah! Well, sort of. I mean, there's quite a few of *us* nowadays, too. But I've been building my brand, you know. I got the primo look. I got the catchphrase. I do the whole 'hair band jazz fusion' thing, which chicks totally dig, by the way. So, I pretty much have the '80s glam rock market cornered."

Doc cleared her throat. "I'm sorry, but is a guitar god like a god whose *power* is being really good at playing guitar?"

"Ah, no." George scoffed, clearly offended. "OK, somewhat. But we do other stuff too."

"Like?"

Draining his beer to have yet another full one appear in its place, he said, "Like *that*."

"So, you have the power to summon bottles of beer? Wow. That's amazing."

"Not just *any* beer — Coors Light! Righteous, right?" And when Doc offered nothing besides an icy stare in response, he said, "OK. Well, I also perform miracles. And answer prayers. That's a *huge* part of the job."

"Prayers," I muttered. "Are you saying that people actually pray to you?"

"Ah, yeah. I'm a *god*. It's kinda my thing."

"What do they pray for?"

"Are you serious right now? How do you think people get crazy good at playing guitar?"

"They practice?"

"They don't *practice*. They *pray* to a guitar god. Like me!"

"And that actually works?"

"Sure it works. If they pray hard enough. For several years. And make the appropriate monetary donations. Then maybe, just maybe, I'll bestow them with some righteous rock star skills. Restrictions apply. Terms and conditions may vary. You know the drill, Dan."

"It's Dean."

"Exactly."

Rooster shook his head. "You have a lot of followers, George?"

"Me? Oh, yeah. Tons of followers, Schuster."

"It's Rooster."

"But seriously, my followers are the best. They love me. All of my many, many beloved followers."

"How many are there?"

"Way too many to count. Or put a number on. So much math involved."

"Name one."

"Of what?"

"Your beloved followers."

"Ok, well, there's, ah, Jeff. Or is it Jack? Maybe Jeremy? No, definitely Jeff. I think."

"Jeff, huh?"

"Yeah, he's a real sweetheart. Lives in Florida. Good ole Jeff. He's aces all around. Aces!"

"And is Jeff a rockstar?"

"Well, I wouldn't exactly call him a rockstar. I mean, he works in sales. But he has a band!"

"A band? Like a famous band?"

"Sure, they're famous. Don't tell me you've never heard of Nature Makes a Correction. NMaC for short? Ringing any bells?"

"Sorry, no. Do they have a lot of fans?"

George sighed. "Not especially. I mean, there's Nancy, of course. But she thinks they kinda suck. And they aren't really a band, per se. It's just Jeremy."

"You mean Jeff."

"Yeah, him."

"You don't have many followers, do you, George?"

"*What*? Of course, I do." And when we all just glared at him, he muttered, "All right, all right, all right. So maybe I don't. So what? You think it's easy to get followers nowadays with every jackass and their mom posting 'free guitar lessons' on YouTube? You can learn every goddamned *Green Day* song ever written in like fifteen minutes! How am I supposed to compete with that shit? It's not fair! Why do you think I'm stuck at the Hotel *fucking* Shasta playing jazz fusion for a bunch of off-world malcontents and taking odd jobs from strangers, huh?"

"Speaking of odd jobs," I said. "We need to get moving. Are your balls in working order or what?"

"Yeah, yeah," he muttered. "I'm good. Erica said that you said needed a guide, right?"

"It's Erin," Doc grumbled. "And yes, we need a guide."

Draining his current beer, Five Finger then took a healthy gulp of the one that replaced it. "So, where we going? Somewhere nice, I hope."

"Nibiru."

And then he did a spit take. "I'm sorry, but it almost sounded like you just said, *Nibiru*."

"That's exactly what I said."

"No, that can't be what you said, because *that* would be absolutely insane."

"Sane or otherwise, we need to see Enki. It's beyond important."

And George apparently found that hilarious because he started to laugh. Hysterically. "OK, wow. That's good! You totally had me there. So good!"

Doc shrugged. "What?"

"*What?* Did Nigel put you guys up to this? Oh man, that crazy bastard. This isn't even real money, is it? Is it?" Then he opened the purse and realized the money was very much real. Then he stopped laughing. And then he tossed the bag back to Doc. "Nope. No, thank you. No way. No can do. Hard pass. Gotta go." Putting his sunglasses back on, he then hopped to his feet and headed toward the bar.

I stepped in front of him. "Not so fast, Jon Bon Jerkoff. You made a deal."

"I did. And now I'm unmaking it. Besides, you have to be invited to Nibiru. The Anunnaki don't just let anybody stroll into the place. So, you crazy kids take care. Or, as we say in the business, piss off!"

I'm pretty sure he was about to snap his fingers and pull a godly vanishing act when Doc pulled the blood cipher medallion out of her pocket and held it up. And that stopped Five Finger George dead in his tracks.

"Whoa," he muttered, unable to avert his eyes from the arcane trinket. "Righteous."

"You know what this is, right?"

"A royal token bearing the seal of Enki? Yeah, I know what it is. Question is, where did you get it?"

"It's not stolen, if that's what you mean."

Rooster cleared his throat. "It's *probably* not stolen." After we all glared at him, he said, "What? Remember who gave us the medallion in the first place. No telling how she got it. Just saying."

"Who are you guys talking about?" asked a very curious George.

"Rooster's mom," I muttered.

"Oh, cool. Who's your mom, Brewster?"

"She's nobody. Nobody you'd know, anyway."

After intently studying my enigmatic ginger colleague's face for a second or two, George grinned a wolfish grin. "I don't freaking believe it! You're Lilith's kid, aren't you? You're a spitting image of her. It's uncanny!"

"Wait, what? You know my mother?"

"Hell yeah, I do. Say, how's she doing, by the way? She ever mention me?"

"Ah, why would she?"

"Let's just say we used to unskinny bop a bit back in the day—"

"Nibiru," Doc barked, thankfully moving the conversation away from the fact that our pal George apparently used to bang Rooster's mom. "We need to go there. Now."

Backpedaling a step or two, George covered his crotch. "Not a great idea, Karen."

"Erin!"

"But, seriously, even with a royal token, we have one small problem to overcome."

"Which is?"

"Well, from the Hotel we can get to the game halls of Agartha easy-peasy. But Enki hangs out in Aventine City."

"At the Ziggurat of Anshar. The receptionist already told us that. Which is why I gave you all that fucking money to take us there!"

"Right, but to get to Aventine, we have to cross the barrens."

"Yeah, and?"

"And that's pretty much impossible nowadays given the civil war that's broken out between Enki and his super deranged brother, Enlil."

"There's an Anunnaki civil war going on? For real?"

"Yeah, and the barrens are controlled by Enlil for the most part. So, flashing that royal token around may just as likely get your head lopped off as get you free passage." As we all stood their stewing on what George just dropped on us, the peculiar guitar god added, "Unless..."

"Unless what?" I asked.

"Unless we take a less traditional route."

"Meaning?"

"Meaning that we might be able to barter passage with a smuggler. But it won't come cheap."

"How much?"

George tossed the bag of coin up and down a few times. "It'll probably take most of this, if not all of it."

"That's all the money we have."

He grinned. "But it's not the only thing of value you have now, is it?"

"You want Enki's medallion," Doc said, connecting the dots.

"Bingo."

"Why?"

"That's my business, Sharon."

"Erin!"

"Exactly, so do we have a deal?"

I nodded. "If, and only if, you get us to Aventine City in one piece. Then we have a deal. No exceptions."

"Agreed." Then Five Finger George leaned into his microphone and tapped it a couple of times. "Hey there, folks, it seems that I've got some *rock'n* business to attend to, so tonight's show is over. But don't worry, I'll be back tomorrow."

When absolutely nobody clapped or acknowledged him in the least, he said, "Until then, this is *Five Finger*, the righteous six *stringer* and your favorite rock 'n' roll *bringer,* signing off!" And after a few seconds of silence, someone shouted, "Stick your five fingers up your ass!" from somewhere within the sprawling, smoke-filled room. "You suck, George!"

Hopping off his stool and scanning the crowd, George's face curled into a dark grin as he locked on to the heckler, who appeared to be one of the goat guys I was sitting next to earlier. Saying nothing, the peculiar god of glam rock then clapped three times, and right on cue, his miniaturized flaming guitar flew out of his pocket, only to zip around his head several times like a demented hummingbird. And without so much as a warning, it darted across the bar in a blur of motion only to lop the goat guy's head clean off his shoulders.

Tapping the microphone a couple of times, George said, "Anyone else have something to say?" And after the place erupted into a barrage of deafening applause, he snapped his fingers and his magical musical instrument returned to the pocket of his jean jacket like a macabre pet.

Making the mental note that there might be a bit more to Five Finger George than meets the eye, I nodded at Erin and Rooster, who were apparently thinking the same thing.

And as for the headless goat guy?

I'm not sure I felt bad for him.

He was kind of a dick.

And that whole hooves for feet thing ain't right.

22

As the terrified crowd continued to applaud like George was the next coming of Eddie Van Halen, the peculiar guitar god winked at us and grinned. "I don't know, guys. Feels like an encore is in order. We got time for *one more* song?"

Expecting the creepy Hotel security cronies to show up at any second, I said, "Are you serious? We need to leave."

"*Leave*? Come on, Dennis. Listen to this crowd! They love me."

"You just decapitated one of the fucking goat guys."

"Dude! They're called *satyrs*. What are you, racist or something?"

"What? No, I'm not racist."

"Kinda sounds like it, Danny. Just saying. Words hurt, man."

I groaned. "My point is, won't those ghost knights be kind of pissed about the fact you cut somebody's head off as they were sipping a house martini?"

"Fair point," he grumbled. "We should probably bounce." Then he put on his mirrored sunglasses and made a beeline for the exit.

Figuring it best to follow, we fought our way through the thick haze of cigarette smoke until we were once again standing in the Hotel Shasta's main corridor amidst the retro seventies décor. After a quick jaunt across the orange and green carpet, we pulled up to a secluded alcove that was completely empty except for an elevator. A vintage elevator with stunning wooden doors encased within an ornate cage of polished metal of some sort.

Standing in front of it was a gaunt elderly man with a bushy mustache, wearing an orange and green valet outfit easily three sizes too big for him. Squinting at us through a pair of thick glasses, he said, "That you, Georgie boy?"

"Hey, Winston. It's me."

"Man, oh man! Molly's gonna be so happy."

"You sure? She was kind of pissed at me the last time I stopped by."

Winston chuckled. "You know she can't stay mad at you. Hey, who are your friends?"

"Just some folks I'm taking on a little sightseeing venture."

"Oh, yeah? Where to?"

"Nibiru," Doc said, handing him the tickets we received from the receptionist earlier.

The old man smiled. "The great game halls of Agartha. Oh, boy! You folks are in for a genuine adventure. Or a truly horrible death. Or an eternity of indentured servitude to a pissed-off god. Either way, I'm sure it'll be memorable!" Stepping aside, he pulled on a lever protruding from the floor, and the metal cage surrounding the elevator retracted as the mighty wooden doors opened. "Remember to keep your hands and feet inside during transit. Oh, and never use the 'e' word. She will not appreciate that one bit."

Wondering what the hell all that was supposed to mean, I reluctantly followed George onto the elevator, as did Erin and Rooster. And just as the doors closed, an alluring and somewhat nasally female voice said, "Well, well, well, what do we have here?"

George grinned. "Hiya, Molly."

"Hi yourself, Georgie," replied the disembodied voice. "Been a while."

"Yeah, you know how it is. Rock, rock, never stop. I'm a slave to the music."

She giggled. "I know you are, baby! So, where ya headed, you sexy, *sexy* man?"

"Nibiru."

Right on cue, several lights on the panel flickered to life, and the peculiar elevator began to move upward at a steady pace. "Then, Nibiru, here we come. Aren't you going to introduce me to your traveling companions?"

"Absolutely. The big guy here is Don."

"Dean," I grumbled.

"Right. And this is his girlfriend, Emma."

"Erin," Doc muttered.

"Exactly. And the carrot-topped dude is Scooter. Or Shooter. Maybe Hooter?"

Rooster groaned. "Just call me John."

"Perfect." Then George gently patted the wall of the elevator. "And *this* is my Molly."

I shrugged. "Sorry, who's Molly?"

"Why, I am, darling," the mysterious voice responded as the buttons on the panel lit up in the shape of a smiley face.

"Wait," Rooster said, "Is *Molly* the name of the elevator?"

It was right about then when Five Finger's face completely drained of all color and his eyes shot wide open. "Shit," he muttered as we all exchanged confused looks. "You guys should hold on to something. Now!"

We'd later learn that Molly was *indeed* the name of the elevator.

We'd also learn that Molly was not an elevator at all. She was an interdimensional sentient being. An interdimensional sentient being that apparently considered the term 'elevator' beyond offensive and bordering on hate speech. Which, in retrospect, explained why things got super interesting from that point forward.

And by super interesting, I mean Molly screeched to an abrupt halt, and before we knew what the hell was happening, she started to spin like one of those shitty Tilt-A-Whirl rides you'd find at a carnival. It was slow at first, but within a few seconds, it accelerated to the point where we were thrown against the walls by the crushing g-force that pinned us there like sardines in a can. It was unbearable to say the very least. And every time I thought it was going to stop, it just kept going.

And going.

And going.

I'm pretty sure we all started screaming.

Some more than others.

OK, so maybe it was just me that was screaming. I might've had a really traumatic Tilt-A-Whirl experience when I was a kid. You have a fucking problem with that? Those things are friggin death traps.

At any rate, just as it felt like my head was going to implode under the extreme gravitational force, we slammed to an unceremonious halt.

Then the doors flew open.

Then we were ejected from the elevator like bags of trash.

Then Molly shouted a string of obscenities at us and called Rooster a racist.

Then she blew a series of kisses to George.

And then the doors closed again as the enigmatic, sentient elevator vanished in a poof of smoke and a flash of light.

Pushing myself off the ground, I turned to Doc and Rooster. "You guys good?"

"Yeah," Rooster grumbled. "I guess? What the hell just happened?"

George shook his head. "You used the 'e' word. That's what just happened!"

"The 'e' word? You mean *elevator*?"

"Dude! Don't say it again! What the hell's wrong with you, Brewster?" And after George went on to explain Molly's backstory to include some rather seedy details about their relationship that I still haven't come to terms with, we all just kind of glared at him for an awkward second or two.

"Wait," Rooster said. "Are you saying that you had sex with the—"

"Don't you dare say elevator! Goddammit! Now you made me say it!"

"Ah guys," Doc said as she scanned our new set of surroundings. "Are you seeing this?"

As I did my very best to erase the mental image of Five Finger George getting jiggy with a horny elevator, I looked up to find a surreal dreamscape of neon lit buildings jutting into a night sky for as far as the eye could see.

The architecture was like nothing I'd ever seen before in the Heavens or on Earth. Pyramidal in nature, it was futuristic yet somehow maintained an old-world charm like you'd expect to find in Ancient Rome. Or Ancient Egypt.

Perfectly placed within a stunning backdrop of floating water-falls and thick pockets of lush greenery, the mind-blowing array of structures seemed to form a meandering circle around a glowing reflection pond teeming with fountains of all sizes and neon colors. Some of them were positioned on the ground, while others floated in the air at varying altitudes.

It was insane.

Perhaps beyond insane.

Almost too much to wrap my brain around.

"Fuck me," Rooster muttered. "Is this Nibiru?"

George nodded. "Welcome to Agartha. Home of Nibiru's great game halls. It's kind of like Vegas meets Disney World meets... Hell?"

Rooster gazed at the night sky. "Why don't I recognize any of those stars? Wait, there's *two* moons. Ah, why are there two moons?"

"How are we seeing the sky at all?" asked Doc. "I thought Nibiru was an underground city?" Which gave George a good chuckle. "Come on, Sharon," he said, "Don't tell me you guys fell for the old

Hollow Earth bit. Nibiru, the netherworld nirvana. The Anunnaki's subterranean paradise. Blah, blah, blah…"

"Are you saying that we're not in Hollow Earth?"

"Ah, yeah! Because there's no such thing. I mean, hell, if you guys are impressed with the dueling moons, just wait until the suns come up."

"Wait, suns?" Rooster muttered. "Did you say suns? As in plural. Are we on a different planet right now? Or is this some kind of bizzaro shadow realm?"

George shrugged. "Realms. Planets. What's the difference, really?"

We never got the opportunity to finish that conversation because it was right about then an elaborate firework display erupted from the center of the fountain-filled reflection pond and people starting pouring out of the buildings in droves. Some of them appeared to be human. Others not so much.

"We need to get moving," George said. "Unless you're a being of stature, traipsing about the streets of Agartha is bad for your health."

"Who the hell are all these people?" I asked as we followed him across a narrow street paved with metallic bricks and into a dark alleyway between two high-rises that looked straight out of a futuristic yet slightly dystopian Las Vegas.

"Well, that's the thing, Dave, there's no telling who could show up in Agartha. It's kind of like a perpetual party town for gods, monsters, and legendary figures from across the known universe. When they get bored, or they lose their mojo, they come here and party their collective asses off. They catch a couple shows. And gamble. And terrorize the occasional human. You know, fun stuff."

"What do you mean by they lose their mojo?"

He grinned. "You guys really don't know shit, do you?" And when Doc, Rooster, and I just kind of shrugged in response, he said, "There's power, true *power*, in belief. And when that belief is gone, so is the power. Get it?"

"Wait," Rooster muttered. "Are you saying that *gods* come here when they lose their followers?"

Five Finger grinned again. "Just trust me, we need to keep a low profile."

Making the mental note to figure that out at some point down the road, I exchanged an uneasy glance with Doc as we reached the end of the alley and George pointed at a mammoth statue in the near distance. Illuminated by a series of levitating spotlights, it was surrounded by an ornate garden of sculpted trees and flowing fountains. It appeared to be the statue of an angel. Or so I thought.

With razor tipped wings that spread far into the sky in either direction, the figure was dressed in some form of sleek armor that accentuated its absurdly muscular physique to a tee. Its face was long and thin and boasted a thick, braided beard that rested proudly on its heaving chest. But perhaps the most impressive thing about it was its head.

Although covered in an ornate helmet, it wasn't shaped like a normal head. Instead, it was elongated. Sort of like an Egyptian pharaoh. Or a football. And if that wasn't enough, the armored figure was holding the severed head of some horrific beastie in one hand and a battle axe in the other.

"If we're going to find a smuggler," George said, "That's where we start."

I nodded. "Cute statue. Now I know what would happen if Arnold Schwarzenegger fucked the Sphinx."

"That would be Enki," he said, ignoring my snide commentary. "He's got a thing for very large statues of himself. And severed heads."

"Who doesn't," Doc muttered.

"Is that what all the Anunnaki look like?" asked Rooster.

George nodded. "If you mean terrifyingly buff über beings with funky-shaped skulls and homicidal tendencies, then yes, that's pretty much what they look like."

"They sound like a real barrel of laughs."

"They are that indeed," he said as we made the short walk to the gardens on the periphery of the statue and began to make our way down a cobblestoned pathway bordered by towering hedgerows of thick shrubs on either side.

"So," I muttered, swatting at some large and strange looking flies that seemed to be following us, "What's the plan?"

"The plan, Dirk—"

"Dean!"

"Right, but the plan is to connect with my old pal, Walter."

"Walter, eh?"

"Yeah, me and Walter go way back. Thick as thieves."

"He a smuggler?"

"A smuggler? No, he's more of a broker—of sorts."

"And what does he broker exactly?"

George grinned. "I think the better question is what *doesn't* he broker."

And there was just something about the way he said it that made me think Walter and I weren't going to get along. Typical.

23

"So," George said as we hooked a left at a towering shrubbery and closed in on the statue's stone feet, which were roughly the size of small cars. "Best to let me do the talking when we find Walter. You guys just play it cool, *cool?*"

"Yeah, whatever," I grumbled, swatting at the glowing, dragon-fly-sized insects buzzing around my head like low flying aircraft. "What the hell's up with these bugs? They're relentless."

"And fast," Rooster added. "What are they?"

George chuckled. "Well, for starters, they're not bugs. They're pixies. Akkadian pixies, to be precise."

"Wait, pixies? As in — fairies?"

"Yeah, and you should definitely stop swatting at them if you value your fingers."

"Pixies are real? Like for *real?*"

Doc rolled her eyes. "Come on, you mean like *Tinkerbell* or something? Bullshit." Which caused one of the minuscule marauders to break from the pack and hover in front of us at eye level for a few seconds.

Squinting until its tiny frame came into focus, I couldn't quite believe what I was seeing.

It looked like a man.

A miniature, winged man who was no taller than a few inches and dressed in miniature clothes. Surrounded by an orb of soft white light, he floated in the air before us like a hummingbird with a big ass smile on his face.

And as I stood there wondering what the hell he was so happy about, the rotten bastard whipped out his little pixie penis and shouted something to the effect of, "Tinkerbell *this*, bitches!" before rejoining his pals, who were collectively laughing their asses off at our expense.

Apparently not finding that as funny as the rest of us did, Doc pulled out both of her H&K pistols. With a dark grin on her face, she then swung them at the swarm of airborne miscreants, causing the wee bastards to scatter to the wind in a flurry of high-pitched obscenities and extended middle fingers. Classic Doc Kelly.

George grinned. "Akkadian pixies are legendary assholes. Let's just hope they've already eaten today."

"They haven't," said a deep, breathy voice from somewhere in the darkness before us. "Not yet anyway."

"Walter? That you?"

"Of course, it's me. What do you want?"

Pulling to an abrupt halt while motioning for us to do the same, George chuckled. Nervously. "Here to do some business, buddy. You maybe want to come out and talk for a minute or two?"

"What do you *want*?" The voice came from the shadows with a detectable edge as I could almost feel the hum of the pixie's wings circling above us in an unnerving orbit.

"Come on, man. Is that any way to talk to old your pal? It's me! Five Finger. Your favorite *six stringer* and—"

"What do you fucking want, George?"

"Aw, dude, don't tell me you're still pissed about that poker game?"

"Should I not be?"

"I just got lucky that night. Already told you I was sorry, man."

"*Lucky*, my balls. You pulled that royal flush out of nowhere. Damned if I know how you did it, but you cheated your *six-stringing* ass off."

George scoffed. "Did not!"

"Did so!"

"Did not and you know it, buddy!"

"Then swear it."

"I'm sorry, what?"

"You heard me. Swear on the name of your sweet Molly."

"I'm happy to."

"Then do it."

"Sorry, do what now?"

Apparently done listening to George's bullshit, Walter huffed and puffed a few times before stepping out of the shadows.

And damned if all four of us didn't instinctively backpedal several steps in response.

For it seemed that Walter wasn't so much a man as he was a—"

"*Horse*," Rooster blurted out, pointing at the hybrid being with the lower body of a hulking Clydesdale and the upper body of a grizzled, middle-aged dude sporting a beer gut and a five o'clock shadow. "Horse?"

"Schuster!" George shouted. "We *do not* use that word around these parts. My dear friend, *Walter* here, is a *centaur*, you racist son of a bitch!"

"Don't change the subject, George," Walter grumbled.

And as our resident guitar god fumbled around for something to say, one of the pixies swooped down from above and perched himself on Walter's shoulder. Crossing his arms, he then sniffed the air like he was a friggin blood hound. "You smell that, boss?"

"What's it smell like, Bodie?"

"Smells like diamonds, boss." And then he leapt into the air and circled George a few times before diving into one of the back pockets of his prized leather pants. Crawling out a second or two later, he appeared to be holding several playing cards that he then delivered to Walter, much to George's chagrin.

"And what do we have here?" The seedy centaur muttered as he flipped through the cards with a scowl on his face. "An ace of diamonds."

"Now hold on," Five Finger protested. "I can explain that."

"And how about this ten of diamonds? You explain that too?"

"Definitely. OK, probably."

Walter groaned as he tossed the final three cards on the ground. "What about the king, the queen, and the jack? Quite an uncanny, fucking coincidence, you just walking around with a royal flush in your back pocket, eh?"

George backpedaled several more steps as the pixie squadron formed a menacing attack formation on Walter's flanks. "Ok, so let's not overreact here. Everybody just chill. There's a perfectly good explanation for that."

"Which is?"

It was right about then George's faced curled into a shit-eating grin. "I fucking cheated!" And then he, Walter, and all the pixies broke into a roaring barrage of laughter.

Wondering just what in the hell was happening, I exchanged confused looks with Erin and Rooster as George exchanged high fives with Walter and his flying army of mini malcontents. And when they were done celebrating, George reached into his jean jacket and pulled out a small leather satchel that he tossed to his buddy. "One hundred talents, as promised. Those dumb ass elves had no idea they were being hustled."

"Nope, they did not."

"As always, it's been a pleasure doing business with you."

Catching the bag and handing it to his pixie henchman, Walter grinned. "The pleasure is all mine, my friend. But I thought the deal was for *two* hundred talents, no?"

I think they were about to start faux arguing again when I

stepped forward and cleared my throat. "Excuse me, I don't mean to interrupt whatever it is that's happening here, but my friends and I need to hire a smuggler. And we're in a rush, so…"

Glaring at me like I just kicked him in the balls, Walter said, "Not sure I appreciate your tone, boy."

I grinned. "You'll appreciate it a lot less with my fist up your horse ass." Which earned me a jab in the ribs from Doc and an inadvertent chuckle from Rooster.

"I didn't catch your name," the centaur muttered as he forced a grin back.

George stepped in front of me. "He's nobody. Just a tourist. I'm taking him and his pals here on a little sightseeing venture to the Aventine."

Finding that rather hilarious, Walter and his flying minions broke into another round of hearty laughter. "The *Aventine*? Good one! Even if you could get across the barrens, Aventine City is no place for tourists." Then he glared at us and spit. "Especially Earth-dwellers."

Shoving George out of the way, I was about to will the cloak into being and punch his gift horse right in the fucking mouth when Doc held up the blood cipher medallion. "You *will* help us," she said. "Now!"

Fixating on the arcane object bearing the royal seal of Enki, Walter's eyes shot wide open as the pixies collectively gasped. And then, much to my surprise, he said, "My apologies. I was unaware of your stature with Enki's court. I meant no disrespect."

Doc slid the medallion back into the pocket of her jeans. "Apologies aren't necessary. But we do need the services of a smuggler. And time is of the essence."

"Of course," he said before turning to the mini minion still perched on his shoulder like a demented parrot. "Find Rita. Have her meet George and our new friends at the usual spot. Tell her it's urgent." Nodding acknowledgment, the pixie muttered something into Walter's ear before flying off in a blur of motion.

George squirmed. "Sorry, Walt, but I could have sworn that you just said *Rita?*"

"You know I did."

"As in *the* Rita?"

"She's the best. You can't argue with that."

"Oh, she's the best all right. It's just that I'm not so sure she'll be super happy to see me. You know, after—"

"Don't worry about it. Just get to the usual spot in back of the depot."

"You sure about this?"

Walter smiled to reveal a mouth full of shiny teeth. "Trust me. You have enough to pay her fee, right?"

"I do, but—"

"Then quit acting like such a puss. You're a *god,* for fuck's sake."

"Yeah, it's just that—"

"It'll be fine. Rita's a professional. Just remember to wear your seatbelt. All good."

Having had more than enough of the bromantic bickering, I cleared my throat for the second time in as many minutes. This time louder and much more obnoxious than the last. "All right, so we good here or what? We're burning daylight."

Five Finger nodded somewhat unconvincingly. "Yeah, we're good."

"Where's this depot place at?"

"It's on the other side of game halls," Walter replied. "Near the fighting pits. Not far from here."

"Then let's get moving," Doc said as she turned to George.

"Follow me," he muttered, exchanging glances with Walter before turning and backtracking down the cobblestone pathway with Erin and Rooster on his heels.

Giving the shady centaur a somewhat appreciative nod, I said, "Thanks, Pony Boy," before joining the crew.

"Stick to the shadows," he called after us as a wave of giggles rippled through the flying pixie formation. "No telling who you might run into on the streets of Agartha this time of night."

Making the mental note to figure out what that meant if we survived the next few hours, I slapped Rooster on the shoulder. "You OK?"

Still trying to come to terms with the fact that pixies were real, and we just had a close encounter with a centaur, he simply muttered, "Horse?" Figuring it was best to leave my enigmatic ginger colleague alone with his thoughts for a moment or two, I caught up with Erin. "Hey."

She smiled. "Hey yourself."

"You good?"

"Be better when we get to Aventine City."

"Word of advice," George said as we hooked a hard right at a spewing fountain and ducked under some hanging vines that lashed out at us as we passed. "If you keep flashing that medallion around, we'll never make it to the Aventine. Mainly because we'll be gutted. Or flayed. Or dead. Or something inconceivably worse! Remember what I told you before about the civil war?"

"I remember," Doc said. "Enki's brother, Enlil."

"Exactly, and the crazy bastard has spies everywhere. Even here in Agartha."

"It was worth the gamble. It didn't seem like your pal, *Walter*, was exceptionally interested in helping us."

"Nah, Walt was just playing hard to get. He would've come around sooner or later. Probably. Maybe not. Anywho..."

"So, what's the plan?" I grumbled.

"The plan is that we use the gardens as cover and get to the train depot unseen. Then we hook up with Rita, the best smuggler this side of the pirate port of Urukanu."

"She a friend of yours?"

"Yeah, you could say that."

"Girlfriend?"

He grimaced. "Let's just say that it's complicated."

I chuckled. "I know exactly what you mean." Which earned me an elbow to the ribs from you know who.

Snaking our way through the meandering gardens lit only by the waning light provided by the dueling moons above, we traversed path after path as George regaled us with sordid tales of his guitar god exploits in the 1980s. Interestingly, most of them consisted of him trading miracles for bathroom sex at Mötley Crüe concerts.

And Bon Jovi concerts.

And Poison concerts.

And Skid Row concerts.

And one time at a Cyndi Lauper concert.

Just when I thought my ears were going to start bleeding, we stepped out of the lush greenery and found ourselves standing on the outskirts of a chanting crowd. Some of which appeared human. Others very much the opposite. Screaming at the top of their lungs and placing bets, they were formed around a ginormous boxing ring adjacent to a train station. And inside the ginormous boxing ring were a couple ginormous combatants beating the absolute piss out of each other with ginormous, bloodied baseball bats.

"Whoa," Rooster muttered, "What's the hell's going on here?"

George grinned. "Agartha's fighting pits."

"Are those anakim?"

"Ogres. Actually, one of them might be a cyclops. They're like anakim, but dumber. And bigger. And dumber."

"You said dumber twice."

"Yeah, they're really dumb."

Doc shook her head. "They're going to kill each other."

"Probably. More gore, more money. But this is bush league bullshit. The *real* carnage is saved for the fighting pits of Aventine City. They say Enki himself presides over them. Absolute brutality from what I hear."

I pointed at the train station to the rear of the crowd. "Is that the depot?"

George nodded. "Yeah, party trains used to run between here and

Aventine City on a nonstop loop. Not so much anymore, though, compliments of the barrens being turned into a war zone and all."

"Where do we meet Rita?"

He scanned the area, looking uneasy. "This is the usual spot. Hopefully, she's around here somewhere."

And no sooner did those words exit his mouth than a shrill female voice called out, "Five Finger George? Oh, fuck no! I'm not taking your two-timing ass anywhere, you dirty son of a bitch!"

Oh good.

Looks like we found Rita.

She seems nice.

24

SPINNING AROUND, I was more than a bit surprised to find an iconic 1968 Ford Mustang fastback sitting in the shadows by the train tracks. Pearl white with a candy apple red racing stripe boldly emblazoned on the hood, the V8 engine roared to life and rumbled like only a vintage American muscle car could. And despite the near deafening noise emanating from the twin tail pipes, we could clearly hear Rita berating Five Finger George from somewhere behind the tinted windows.

"You've got some goddamned nerve showing up here, George!" she screamed. Her voice was shrill, yet somehow smokey at the same time. "You think I'm just gonna open my doors and let your sorry, leather pants-wearing ass back in after that *bullshit* you pulled? You must be out of your damn mind, *Five Finger*!"

George grinned and held his arms out in a hugging motion. "Hi, Rita. I've missed you too, baby. How've you been?"

Saying nothing, she pumped the gas pedal a few times, and the engine roared in response, almost like the car itself was telling George to piss off.

Turning toward us, George chuckled. Nervously. "Rita and I go way back, guys. I'll just go have a few words with her. We'll be ready to go in a minute. Two, tops. No worries." Then he approached the vehicle, only to have the hood pop open and squirt motor oil at him.

"Good grief," Doc muttered.

I chuckled. "Five Finger definitely has a way with women, eh?"

"We don't have time for this."

"Ah, guys," Rooster said, looking exceptionally disturbed. "I don't think Rita's a *woman*, per se."

Doc shrugged. "Then who do you think's in the car?"

"That's the thing," he said, pointing at George, who was now rubbing his hands up and down the Mustang's hood in a sultry caress. "I think she *is* the car."

"Good grief," Doc muttered for a second time in as many minutes. "You don't actually think that—"

"Elevators aren't the only piece of machinery that George's done the unskinny bop with?"

"Christ," I grumbled under my breath. "That guy ain't right. Although, the Mustang is a big step up from the elevator. Just saying." Which earned me a swat to the back of the head.

"Come on over, guys," George shouted as he waved at us. "It's all good."

Figuring we didn't have much choice in the matter, given the circumstances, we carefully approached the peculiar muscle car whose engine was now purring as opposed to rumbling. "Hey, everybody," Rita said. "Sorry you had to witness that. Me and Georgie had to work a few things out, if you know what I mean."

I smiled. Awkwardly. "No problem. We're actually kind of used to it by now after meeting a couple of George's other colleagues."

Nonchalantly flipping me off, Five Finger said, "Guys, meet Rita. And Rita, this is—"

"I'm Erin," Doc chimed in. "And this is Dean and Rooster."

"Rooster, huh?" she said, as her mighty engine revved a few times. "Mama just *loves* her some *ginger*. How about we take a quick ride, baby man?" To which Rooster kind of grinned and backpedaled several steps.

"Easy now," George said. "Let's try to keep it professional, Rita, dear. These are my clients, after all."

"Fine," she pouted as the engine reduced to a low hum. "And where am I smuggling your clients to?"

"Didn't Bodie give you the details?"

"*Bodie*," she scoffed. "That pencil dick pixie didn't tell me shit except to get here as fast as I could. So, what's the destination?"

With a sheepish grin, George pulled out the bag of coin we'd paid him and held it up. "I've got your fee here. Paid up front. No questions asked."

"George, where are we going?"

"Did I mention there's a nice tip, too?"

"Where are we fucking going, George?"

"So, we kind of need to get to Aventine—"

And before he could utter another word, Rita's engine roared to life, and she backed up several feet. "Oh, hell no! Mama ain't rolling to Aventine City, George. Not while this damn civil's going on. Not for all the damn coin in Nibiru. No way!"

"But, baby, you don't understand—"

"Don't you *baby* me, Five Finger! I barely made it across the barrens without having my chassis blown to bits by a damn landmine last week. And even if we did make it through, there ain't no way into the city. The Aventine's warded up tighter than a pixie's ass. So, unless you plan on strolling through the main gate like you own the joint—"

"That's exactly what we're going to do."

"Say what now?"

"Once we get there, we're gonna stroll right through the gate."

Apparently thinking that was rather hilarious, Rita laughed so hard that smoke billowed from her tailpipes for a solid five seconds. "And how exactly do you plan on doing that?"

George turned to Doc. "Show her the medallion."

Doc shook her head. "But you said—"

"It's OK, we can trust Rita." Then he leaned in close. "And we're kind of out of options."

Not sold but figuring there wasn't much choice in the matter, Doc reluctantly reached into the pocket of her jeans and pulled out the infamous blood cipher medallion bearing the seal of Enki.

Rita gasped. "Well, I'll be a Volkswagen Bug. Is that what I think it is?"

Doc nodded. "With you take us now?"

And after a long moment or two of deliberation, the passenger side door flew open. "All right, everybody in." Climbing into the back, Rooster was about to strap himself in when the driver's side door flew open. "Not so fast there, Red. You plop your ginger ass right behind my *steering* wheel."

Rooster blushed. "Thanks, but I'll just sit back here—"

The engine revved. "I'm not asking, baby man." To which, he very reluctantly crawled into the driver's seat only to have the seat belt snugly fasten itself around him.

"All right, folks," the enigmatic smuggler announced as the rest of us piled in just as she spun around to face the darkness of the surrounding desert. "Next stop — Aventine City. Buckle up and grab on to something. It's gonna be a bumpy ride." Then she floored the gas pedal and aggressively shifted through a series of gears as we raced through the night with reckless abandon.

Peering through the windshield, I took notice of distinct flashes peppering the night sky in the far distance, which I assumed were from the exchange of gunfire or something inexplicably worse. "Looks nasty out there," I said.

"It is that, indeed," Rita replied. "Only thing worse than a civil war is an *Anunnaki* civil war. Gives a whole new meaning to the concept of collateral damage. But don't worry. I'll get you Earth-dwellers to the Aventine safe and sound." Then she laughed. "I won't, however, vouch for what comes after that."

And there was just something about the way she said it that

made me think we'd made a horrible mistake. Unfortunately, it was right about then George let out a pronounced yawn before his head fell to his chest and he started snoring.

Then the same thing happened to Rooster.

And then Doc.

And the last thing I remember before passing out was thinking that for such a small person, Doc Kelly snored incredibly loudly. It almost sounded like a wild animal or something. Who knew?

WITH A SPLITTING HEADACHE and a foggy brain, I was coaxed back to consciousness by the sound of a deafening crowd as I sat up to find George, Erin, and Rooster in a similar state. Pushing off the sandy ground and getting to my feet, it took me a second or two to get my balance as my muddled mind struggled to understand what was happening.

It appeared we were no longer in the perceived safety of Rita, the sentient muscle car and our esteemed smuggler. Instead, we seemed to be sitting in the center of an arena of some sort. An arena that looked suspiciously like the Dreghorn, our otherworldly training facility, which was modeled after the Roman Colosseum. But as I slowly spun around and scanned our new set of surroundings, it was pretty clear this wasn't either location.

This was something else.

Something else entirely.

Akin to the Colosseum, it was a majestic marvel constructed with stunning white ornamental stone that surrounded an oblong sandy pit of massive proportion. But unlike its Ancient Roman counterpart, the stands in this arena jutted several *miles* into the surrounding skyline. And floating amongst them were semi-translucent jumbotron type screens that were apparently receiving live video feeds from the countless flying orbs that buzzed around the stadium like rabid birds.

But perhaps the most curious thing was the ginormous pyramidal structure that hovered high above the fray in a perpetual orbit. It somewhat resembled the seraphic lodestones hovering above our cities on Earth, but it had more of a temple-like feel to it.

"No, no, no," George muttered as he rose to his feet and looked around. "This is *not* good. Fuck, fuck, fuck! This is not good!"

Pushing herself off the ground, Doc grumbled, "What happened?"

"Rita happened!" he shouted. "She must've sold us out. Shit! Never trust a goddamned Ford!"

"Well, where are we?"

"OK, you want the good news or the bad news?" And when all three offered him no response besides an icy stare, he said, "Yeah, gotcha. So, the good news is that we made it to Aventine City. Yay? And, ah, the bad news is that we're apparently today's opening act in the fighting pits."

I groaned. "Opening act?"

"Yeah, they usually bring out some pathetic humans at the beginning of the fights and let the headliners rip them to shreds. Or eat them. Or both. You know, to get the crowd going and stuff."

"I really hate Nibiru," Rooster muttered. "Like seriously hate it. It's the worst."

"What about the medallion?" I said. "If this is Enki's city, all we have to do is show them the medallion and we're good, right?"

A lightbulb went off in George's head. "You're right! Good call, Derek. We're saved!" Then he pointed into the sky at the flying pyramid. "That's the Ziggurat of Anshar, which means Enki is probably watching us as we speak. All we have to do is—"

"The medallion's gone," Doc muttered, glaring at our resident guitar god. "*Rita* must've taken it when she sold us out."

"Goddamn it! We're fucked again!"

"Relax already," I grumbled. "We'll think of something. This isn't the worst situation we faced this week. Trust me."

"Yeah, *right*." George scoffed. "What the hell do three *dumbass* humans, no offense, know about anything anyway? And besides, even if I do make it out of this, Rita stole my only chance to get back to Earth!"

Rooster furrowed his ginger eyebrows. "What the hell's that supposed to mean?"

"The medallion, Brewster! Don't you get it? That was my ticket out."

"Out of what?"

"Out of perpetual purgatory at the *Hotel Shasta* and back to civilization! Back to my peeps. My followers. Back to being an actual god again and not some half-rate lounge act."

And as we all stood there for a second trying to understand what the hell George was talking about, a series of drums starting beating. It was slow at first, and as it increased in both tempo and volume, the crowd lost its collective mind to the point where you could almost feel the energy pouring out of the stands.

"That doesn't sound good," Rooster muttered. "In fact, it sounds really fucking bad."

George took a deep breath. "OK, I got this, guys." Then he took off his prized purple pinstriped scarf and tossed it on the ground. Facing the main gate at the far end of the arena, he rolled his neck back and forth on his shoulders a couple times before cracking his knuckles. Then he snapped his fingers, and right on cue, his enigmatic flaming guitar flew out of his pocket and grew to normal size as it hovered on his flank. "I'm the god here. So, whatever comes through that gate is all mine. Ole Five Finger's got this, rock stars. No worries."

And it was right about then the drums stopped beating. Smashing his way through the massive stone gate was a gargantuan, one-eyed giant. Larger than any anakim I'd ever encountered, it was easily thirty feet tall and its skin was an unnerving blue. Kind of like that of a Smurf.

A thirty-foot-tall Smurf.

With one big ass eyeball and a hulking, unnatural physique.

Who wanted to eat us for lunch.

As the crowd went completely apeshit and all four of us just stood there gawking at the mind-blowing beastie, it reared back its head and let loose with a bloodcurdling howl that made the hair on the back of my neck stand up.

George winked at us. "Watch and learn, young rock stars. This is how a god takes care of business." Then he grabbed his guitar by the neck and spun a couple times like he was throwing a shot put before flinging it at the cyclops. Hurtling through the air like a peculiar boomerang, the uncanny instrument tripled in size as it closed the hundred-yard distance in a blur of motion.

And just when it looked like it was going to decapitate the great blue beast with ease, the cyclops snatched it from the air and began to eat it like a sandwich. The crowd cheered him on as he took savage bite after bite until there was nothing left but a couple of guitar strings that he pulled from his teeth and discarded before burping.

Well, I think we can all agree that was a bit disappointing.

I wonder if George has another guitar?

Maybe it's time to go acoustic.

Five Finger Unplugged?

Kinda catchy.

25

Looking like somebody just kicked him squarely in the balls after taking his lunch money, George's jaw hit the ground as the crowd hit a fever pitch and the velvety voice of an announcer rang out through the stadium. "Well, *that* didn't go as planned, now did it, folks? Whatever will our *brave warriors* do now, I wonder? Whatever it is, they better do it fast because *Bluto* is almost done with his appetizer!"

Then the crowd started chanting something to the effect of, "Bluto! Bluto! Bluto!" which apparently was the name of the blue cyclops. How cute is that?

Then they started chanting, "Eat them! Eat them!" which made me question the moral compass of the inhabitants of Aventine City. This place just ain't right.

"He ate my guitar," George muttered with a blank stare.

I slapped him on the shoulder. "Bummer."

"I mean, who does that?"

"Evidently big blue monsters with one eye?"

And it was right about then our pal Bluto let out another blood-curdling howl and charged at us with reckless abandon. Awesome.

With his killer guitar out of commission, George apparently embraced the age-old adage that gingers make good human shields and nonchalantly backpedaled a few steps before ducking behind Rooster. Figuring it was high time to teach the oversized mutated Smurf some manners, I was just about to will the cloak into being when Doc sprang into action.

Saying nothing, she drew one of her H&K pistols and charged straight at the monocular monstrosity running towards us. Her seamless, golden armor snapped into place mid-stride and a harrowing sword-like machete sprouted from one of her fisted hands. Now within ten feet or so of the towering beast, she side-stepped a strike from his gigantic blue fist before running between the legs and pulling to an abrupt halt. Then, in a single, mighty swing of her golden blade, she severed his right foot from the rest of his leg.

Managing to take another clumsy step or two, Bluto then plummeted to the sandy floor of the stadium like a felled tree as he wailed in pain. The machete retracted into Doc's armor like it was never there, and she jumped on the beast's back as it writhed and floundered in protest. Walking along its spine until she reached its massive head, she held her pistol to the back of its skull and unloaded the entire magazine.

Jumping off the now deceased blue dope, Doc offered the crowd a spirited hand gesture before slapping a fresh mag into her pistol. In complete and utter shock, the stadium fell silent as the cyclops' carcass was carried off by a hundred or so short, stout, hooded figures that seemed to appear out of thin air.

Rejoining us, Doc holstered her pistol and grinned.

I grinned back. "Nicely done."

"Thanks. I guess these assholes aren't used to *lunch* fighting back." Then she turned her attention to George, who was still crouching behind Rooster. "How you doing there, *rockstar?*"

He jumped to his feet and dusted himself off. "Me? Oh yeah. I'm good! Just tying my shoe. You know, as I was getting ready for my next move."

I'm pretty sure Doc was about to give Five Finger a piece of her mind when the drums starting beating again and the booming voice of the announcer said, "Now, don't you worry about Bluto, folks. He's fine. Totally fine! Just needs a Band-Aid or two. And while we get him all patched up, how about a big round of applause for the *Grand Champion* of Aventine City! You know him. You *love* him! And *he* loves you! Let's hear it for the undefeated and undisputed *master* of the fighting pits — Gogmagog the Magnificent!"

And as the crowd went wild, a dark figure strolled out of the gate like he owned the joint. Unlike his brutish counterpart, he wasn't a howling, growling beast. And although he was every bit of seven feet tall, I wouldn't exactly call him a giant, either. He looked like a man. A handsome man with shoulder-length golden hair and a strapping physique, clad in a gladiator outfit accentuated by a dark armored breast plate. In fact, with the exception of his extreme height and build, the only other thing that suggested he wasn't quite human was his arms.

Granted, he had biceps the size of bowling balls, but that wasn't the odd part. It was more that he had four arms instead of two. And he was flexing and waving to his multitudes of adoring fans with all of them. It was unnerving.

Reaching the center of the arena, he drew all four of his swords and thrust them into the sand before him as the crowd screamed, "Gogmagog! Gogmagog! Gogmagog!"

Offering us a cliched bow, he said, "Come on then, mates. Let's get this over with, eh? One at a time. All of you at once. Whatever works. I'll make it quick, promise I will. Easy-peasy."

Doc chuckled. "What the hell's this guy supposed to be?"

Rooster shrugged. "I don't know. What do you call a seven-foot asshole with four arms and a cheesy British accent?"

"An asshole," I muttered. "You most definitely call him an asshole."

Ignoring my snide commentary, George said, "Ah, guys, what's the plan here? You do realize that Gogmagog's killed more people than the green plague, right?"

"I think you mean the *black* plague," Rooster corrected.

"Damn it, Schuster. You seriously need to work on this whole racist thing. Words hurt, man!"

"You guys stay here," I muttered. "Let me see if I can reason with this jackass."

"Are you crazy, Danny?" George protested. "You can't reason with Gogmagog! Look at him! He's walking death with celebrity hair and a killer smile. Pun intended!"

Exchanging nods with Doc and Rooster, I made the short walk to the center of the arena where the infamous Grand Champion of Aventine City was still blowing kisses to his fanbase. Pulling to a halt a few away from the statuesque figure, I smiled and waved. "Hey there, big fella. How are ya?"

"I'm quite good," he replied with a genuine smile. "How are you, mate? Circumstances withstanding, of course."

"I'm good — ish. Look, there's been some kind of misunderstanding. My friends and I aren't supposed to be here. It's a long story, but we came to see Enki about—"

"Let me stop you there, Earth-dweller," he said, smiling again. "There's nothing you can say to me that's going to change the events of the next few minutes. I'm afraid you've hit the end of the proverbial line. Lucky for you, it'll be painless. For I, Gogmagog, am a merciful champion, unlike that carnivorous brute, *Bluto*."

I chuckled. "Ah, you saw them carry his dead body out of here, right? You think you'll fare any better against us? He was like thirty feet tall."

He scoffed. "*Please.* You people did not damage Bluto. He simply tripped over his own feet and rendered himself unconscious."

"Foot."

"Sorry?"

"He only has one foot. The other one's still in the sand over there. See it? Pretty gross, eh?"

Gogmagog laughed. "You may be an inferior being, but you're an inferior being of great humor. I've quite enjoyed our little chat." Then he grabbed the hilts of his four broadswords and pulled them from the sand. "But now it is time to die. For the crowd demands blood. And blood they shall receive." When I offered no response besides a shrug and a snarky grin, he said, "Ah, just to be clear, you do realize I was talking about *your* blood, right?"

"Yeah, I got that."

"OK, good. Just checking." Then he assumed an overly dramatic fighting stance and twirled his swords around, causing the crowd to go nuts again. "On guard, sir!"

Figuring diplomacy had failed, and I really had no choice but to throw down with Sir Armsalot, I muttered, "Don't say I didn't warn you, pal," and willed the cloak into being. Manifesting in a spectral flash, it flared out from my shoulders as pulses of divine Wrath fired through my body like bolts of electricity. Feeling the calmative awareness wash over me, I called for the gauntlets, and my face curled into a dark grin as the otherworldly metal flowed over my hands and up my forearms.

Seemingly impressed, Gogmagog lowered his broadswords and gawked at me for a second or two. "Wonderful trick, Earth-dweller," he said as several orbs flew around us and our live images appeared on the countless jumbotrons floating about the arena. "What else can you do?"

I grinned. "This?" Then I curled my right hand into a tight fist and punched him in the gut so hard he dropped all four swords and doubled over in pain. And I think he might've pissed himself.

With his head now conveniently at eye level, I sunk my weight into a devastating uppercut that smashed into his square jaw with the force of a wrecking ball and shattered all his teeth. Then, just for fun, I treated his torso like that slab of meat in the training montage from the Rocky movies and unleashed a blinding torrent of punches until he collapsed.

The flying cameras swooped in like vultures as Gogmagog the Magnificent's unconscious body was sprawled out on the arena sand in a bloody heap. As the crowd fell dead silent again, I fought the urge to shout, "Are you not entertained?" at the top of my lungs. Figuring the classic Russell Crow reference would be lost on the derelicts of Aventine City, I just rejoined the crew as the hooded figures appeared and carried away the slumbering *Grand Champion*.

Exchanging fist bumps with Doc and Rooster, I was about to will the cloak into retreat when the goddamn drums started beating again. But unlike the other few times we'd heard them, this time was different. It was faster and somehow more violent. We weren't the only ones to notice because the crowd instantly transitioned from deafening silence to ear-splitting applause.

"Ah, guys," Rooster said, "What's happening now?"

George groaned. "Aw, shit. The dogs."

"Sorry, what? Did you say dogs?"

Before George could explain further, the arena floor shook like a stampede was heading straight for us. Then, busting out of the gate in a swirling dust storm, came a snarling pack of super-sized dog-like beasties. And by super-sized dog-like beasties, I meant rabid Rottweilers the size of elephants with gaping maws full of razor-tipped, jagged teeth and claws like you'd expect on a velociraptor. Oh, and they each had three heads. I probably should've led with that, in retrospect.

"We're super fucked now!" George shouted as the unnatural creatures raced toward us and the crowd roared in response.

"No," Rooster muttered. "No, we're not. Not yet."

I grinned. "Are you about to do what I think you're about to do."

Saying nothing, he took off his brown leather bomber jacket and carefully handed it to George. Then he ripped off his blue Rooster-Bragh tee-shirt bearing the iconic red rooster logo and catchphrase

'Bragh Is as Bragh Does, Brah' and kicked off his boots before sliding out of his jeans.

With his lanky, six-foot frame covered by nothing but a pair of boxer shorts, he winked at me and Doc. "What do you say we show these assholes what a proper monster looks like?"

And then his eyes flashed red as he dropped to his knees and buried his face in his hands. Letting out a primal scream that made all three of us backpedal a step or two, my enigmatic ginger colleague was overcome with uncontrollable convulsions as his entire body turned a deep, ghastly red.

Clearly freaked out by the turn of events, George barked, "Is Brewster OK? 'Cause he does *not* look OK! Guys? Guys!"

"He's fine," I said, backpedaling another couple of steps as Rooster grotesquely morphed from man to hulking beast before our eyes. "Just needs a minute. Two, tops."

"I don't think we have that much time," Doc muttered as the pack of mutant mutts was within fifty feet of pouncing on us and closing fast. Drawing both her pistols, the golden armor snapped into place around her as she faced down the coming onslaught. "Get ready!"

And it was right then the fully neph'd out Rooster slowly rose to his feet and turned to face us with a surreal, animal-like madness in his eyes. George's face went blank, and he turned pale white at the mind-blowing sight. Which was more than fair, given that Rooster's jovial ginger persona had been replaced by a fifteen-foot infernal creature with scaly, blotched red skin, chiseled muscle, and veiny tissue.

Its bony, deeply recessed shoulders were three times too wide for its frame, making its already taut torso look that much more sinister. And peering at us through eyes like orbs of blazing fire, its beaming face was a hellish compilation of spiny ears, barbed yellow teeth, and a hooked, beak-like nose. Totally traumatizing on all fronts.

"Get behind me," he said in a nightmarish, gravelly voice that sent a bone-chilling pulse through my spine. Then he looked down at George. "And don't let anything happen to my bomber jacket!" To which, George emphatically nodded several times.

Then, the Red Rooster let loose with a terrifying guttural growl and waded into the ravenous pack of mega dogs with his talon-tipped claws in the strike position. It was kind of hard to see what happened next given the swirling sandstorm that ensued from the titanic skirmish, but the outcome was fairly apparent given the outcry of puppy-like yelps. When the dust finally settled, I couldn't help but grin at the sight of Rooster standing amidst a heap of unconscious beasties in various states of disarray and disfigurement.

Joining us with a creepy smile on his really creepy face, we exchanged high fives before he fluidly morphed back into his stringy human form and slid his clothes back on. You could literally hear a pin drop in the entire stadium as we stood there wondering just what in the hell to expect next. But instead of being met by another barrage of unnatural creatures, something rather unexpected happened.

The gargantuan pyramidal structure, the Ziggurat of Anshar, circling high above the arena, broke out of its orbit and hovered near the top of the stands. From the structure emerged a winged figure who gracefully glided through the sky before descending into the pit and landing right in front of us with cat-like dexterity.

"Oh shit," George muttered. "That's *Enki*, guys. Oh shit. Oh shit. Oh shit. This is bad. This is *really* bad."

And as we all stood gawking at him, the statuesque leader of the famed Anunnaki took a long look at the pile of wounded dog beasties and shook his head in disappointment. Then, in a really high-pitched voice with a slight lisp that didn't match his near eight-foot, muscle-bound frame, he said, "OK, *seriously*, just who the hell are you people?"

Yeah.

Didn't see that coming.

26

Apparently upset that nobody answered him, Enki's razor-tipped, black wings melted from existence as he glared at us with his unnaturally blue eyes. Clapping several times as if to get our attention, he shouted, "*Hello*, people! Is anybody in there? I asked you guys a question. Answer! Answer now!"

Somewhat dumbstruck by his dominating presence, the longer I gazed at his strapping figure, the more I couldn't get over the fact that he looked just like the friggin statue we'd seen back in Agartha. It was downright uncanny. Minus, of course, the fact he was wearing a white tank top, khaki board shorts, and a pair of flipflops instead of sleek, futuristic armor. That was a bit unexpected, if I was being honest.

At any rate, standing easily eight feet tall, his face was long and thin and ageless. His majestic jet-black beard extended well below his barrel chest and was intricately braided with interwoven beads and colored trinkets. And the deep bronze hue of his skin seemed to glow in the afternoon sunlight. But it was his elongated head that I couldn't stop staring at. Just like the depictions of the Egyptian pharaohs, it was peculiar and bald and like nothing I'd ever seen in person.

Getting more agitated by the second because we were all just gawking at him, the Anunnaki overlord cleared his throat a couple of times. Each time louder and more intentional. Then, using his uncharacteristically high-pitched, nasal voice, he said, "OK, seriously, people. Somebody say something. You're making this awkward."

Then he noticed George, who was crouching behind Doc Kelly, and a big ass smile curled across his face. "No freaking way! Five Finger George? My favorite six stringer and righteous rock 'n' roll bringer. Is that *you*?"

With his eyes literally popping out of his head, George rose to his feet and waved. "You know who I am?"

"Of course, of course! I've caught your act a couple times at the Shasta." Then the revered leader of the Anunnaki started playing air guitar. "That hair band *jazz fusion* thing you do is fabulous! I absolutely love it! Too, too good."

George perked up a bit. "Oh, wow. That's, ah, great! Super great! Thank you. I really appreciate that."

"Sure, sure. So, tell me, what brings you and your friends to my fighting pits, huh?" Then he glanced at the pile of groaning three-headed mega mutts. "Oh, and I'm specifically interested in how you've single handedly incapacitated my champions and mutilated my beloved house pets! Speak! Now!"

As George crouched behind Doc again, I stepped forward and forced a grin. "Apologies for that. We didn't come here to fight, I assure you. It's been kind of a weird day."

Intently gazing at me, he said, "Then tell me all about it, Earth-dweller. And know that if you lie to me, I will know it. And then I will bathe in your entrails after ripping them from your feeble husk with a fork. And not a sharp fork. A very dull one. Now, proceed!"

Figuring Enki was either a few sammiches shy of a picnic or some kind of evil genius, I said, "OK, well, my name's Dean. Dean Robinson. And this is Erin Kelly and John O'Dargan."

"And the nature of your *business* in the Aventine?"

"It's kind of a long story."

"Then start at the beginning."

"OK, well, I'm the Seventh Deacon of the Seventh Line. Or at least I was before—"

"Wait, I knew it! I knew I smelled *his* stench upon you." Then he sniffed the air and pointed at Erin. "And her, too. You both wield the power of Ethan Roy. I can feel it pouring off you like that horrid Axe body spray you Earth-dwellers douse yourself with. Don't deny it!"

"It's true."

Anger flashed in his eyes. "Did *he* send you here? Tell me!"

"No," answered Doc. "He didn't. We came on our own. Well, sort of."

"For what purpose?"

"To seek your help."

"My help? How so? Tell me! Tell me now!"

Doc and I took turns explaining how Lucifer freed the Watchers and instigated an angel mutiny that led to an all-out assault on the Earth, which ultimately resulted in Ethan deporting the angels and forming the Eden Accords. Enki hung on every word. When we got to the part about how the planet was falling apart at the seams, compliments of the aforementioned angel mutiny, he started laughing.

And when we got to the part about how every governing member of the Eden Accords, to include his seraphic brothers, all agreed that the Anunnaki were their only hope for salvation, he *really* started laughing. Like slapping his knee and gasping for breath, kind of laughing. It was pretty obnoxious.

"Oh my," he said. "What an amazing tale of deceit and decline. How the *mighty* have fallen. I just love it! Too, too good. Thank you both. I really needed that. OK, so will you be leaving now?"

I shrugged. "I don't understand."

"Understand *what*, Earth-dweller?"

"Won't you help us?" To which he responded by laughing again, which I assumed was a resounding 'No.'

Not accepting that in the least, Doc said, "How could you sit idle and watch something like that happen when you have the power to prevent it? Billions of people will perish!"

Enki feigned a smile. "Your *people*, not mine. You see, *my* people were cast from both the Earth and the Heavens a long, long time ago by your precious *Ethan* and his second generation seraphs. So, we forged our own path. Here on Nibiru. And I should offer you the same advice, young lady. Now, leave here with my protection before I decide to bathe in your entrails after all. Toodles!"

Then Enki's majestic black wings appeared in a spectral flash, and just before he took to the skies, I said, "Name your price." Which got his attention.

"My price? My *price*? How *dare* you think that I, Enki, leader of the Anunnaki can be bought like some tawdry laborer! But, out of curiosity, whatcha offering, huh? *Huh*?"

And when I offered nothing in response but a shrug accompanied by an awkward grin, he said, "You know what? Let's talk about this over lunch. You guys hungry? I've got the most fabulous buffet going on right now in the Ziggurat. Although, before we do that, there is one thing that's been bothering me."

I shrugged again. "Which is?"

"How in the blue blazes did you *get* to Nibiru in the first place?"

Stepping forward, Rooster reluctantly cleared his throat. "My, ah, my mom used to come here in her younger days, and she told us where to find a portal. And, ah, she kind of loaned us one of your medallions that we might've lost in transit. Really long, pretty traumatic story."

After studying him for a long moment or two, Enki said, "And who's your mother exactly?"

"Well, her name's—"

"Wait, don't tell me. I can see it in your eyes! No freaking way!

You're *Lilith's* son, aren't you. I can hardly believe it! You're a spitting image of her! I mean, like, wow, right?"

"I said the same thing!" George said. "Crazy!"

"Wait, you know Lilith, too?"

George grinned. "Oh yeah. She's got it going on. I mean, like, *rawr*, right?"

Enki grinned back. "*Rawr* is right!

"Rawr!"

"*Rawr*!"

Rooster groaned. "OK, can you guys please stop doing that?"

Regaining a bit of composure, Enki said, "So, ah, how's dear Lilly been? She ever talk about me?"

"No. OK, maybe once."

"Interesting. Oh, and so sad to hear about your dad. Old *Lew Lew* and I were rather friendly back in the day. Kinda, sorta. Sounds like he's had a rough go as of late with the whole mutiny and all. Just terrible what happened to him."

Rooster shrugged. "Is it, though?"

"Yeah, no. Probably for the best. He's such a dick. Anywho, lunch?"

Before anyone had the chance to respond, he clapped his hands, and we were encircled by a beam of pure white light that radiated down from the Ziggurat hovering above.

And just like that, we were no longer standing on the arena floor.

We were seated next to each other at a table.

A gigantic, stone table in the dead center of a ginormous circular stone rotunda that had no visible entrances or exits. There were only windows which provided a stunning view of the afternoon sky and the landscape below.

And upon the table that appeared to be expertly hewn from solid rock was a literal feast that looked like it could feed fifty people. There were meats and cheeses and fruits of various size and color stacked several feet high. Some of it looked good. Some of it not so much.

"Welcome, welcome," Enki announced, holding up a stone goblet as he stood at the head of the table several feet from us. "Eat. Drink. Yada yada. So on and so forth. Do it! *Now!*" Then he drained his drink in a single gulp and slammed the empty cup on the table. "Oh my, that barley wine is simply fabulous. More!"

And within the blink of an eye, a short, stout, hooded figure similar to the ones we saw in the fighting pit appeared, holding a giant ceramic pitcher. He, or she, refilled Enki's goblet and vanished without so much as a word.

Making the mental note to figure out who the mysterious hooded munchkins were at some point down the road, I grabbed the goblet in front of me and took a healthy gulp. And then I promptly spit it out all over the table. "What did you say this stuff was?" I asked, trying to nonchalantly mop up the mess as Doc glared at me.

"It's Anunnaki barley wine, Dean Robinson. This particular batch was aged for two centuries. Isn't it fantastic?"

"Oh yeah. Smooth. Bit of an aftertaste, though."

"That would be the fermented goat urine."

"Sorry," George said, "But did you say goat urine?"

"Yes, yes, Five Finger. It's added for texture and provides a little extra *zing* for the palette."

George took a faux sip and forced a grin. "Oh, wow. That's good stuff."

Enki smiled. "And what of you, Erin Kelly and John O'Dargan? Do you like?" To which both Doc and Rooster replied with an energetic thumbs up as they slid their respective goblets to the other side of the table.

Holding up something that looked straight off of Fred Flintstone's table, he said, "Now everyone eat! I'd recommend the roasted centaur leg. It practically melts in the mouth. Oh, and do try the sautéed centaur tips. And, of course, there's the centaur chops cooked to a perfect medium rare. Dig in!" And then he proceeded to stuff his face with anything within arm's reach.

Exchanging awkward glances with Rooster, who muttered,

"Horse," under his breath before pushing away from the table, I cleared my throat. "Can we maybe talk a little business while we eat?"

"You Earth-dwellers are all alike," Enki jested, gnawing on a hunk of meat that looked suspiciously like a human thigh. "So terribly impatient. But, yes, *fine* — we can talk about your little *global catastrophe,* if you so insist."

"Have you considered your price for potentially helping us?" asked Doc.

"Well," Enki muttered, grabbing a handful of glowing purple berries of some sort and stuffing them in his mouth, "Under normal circumstances, I simply couldn't be bothered. I might even pop by and watch some of the devolution process for funsies." Then he spit out a bunch of seeds and wiped his mouth with his forearm. "But these are hardly normal times with my little brother, Enlil, trying to steal my throne and such. Civil wars are expensive! And no fun. And expensive!"

"So, you'll help?"

Finished eating for the moment, he took another slug of his piss-infused cocktail and grinned at us. "OK, let's say that I send my Builders to do what can be done for the Earth. Nothing more. And nothing less. If what you say is accurate, I'm not sure it can be *fixed,* but it can certainly be stabilized."

"And in return?"

"In return, Erin Kelly, you and your Eden Accords will return to me that which was taken all those many years ago when *Father* expelled us."

"Which is?"

"Zion Canyon. It was mine, and I want it back! *So,* that's my offer, and there will be no counter. Take it. Or *leave.*"

Doc nodded. "Understood. Would you mind if we took a moment to discuss amongst ourselves?"

"Please, please. Go right ahead. But not for too long! I'm terribly impatient."

As the four of us excused ourselves from the table and huddled up, Rooster said, "There's no way we can just promise him *Zion Canyon*, right? I mean, it's a nexus point of unlimited primal power, for Christ's sake."

Doc rubbed her temple. "Regardless, I'm pretty sure we don't have that kind of authority."

"And even if we did? Would we just hand it over to the *Anunnaki*? I mean, there must have been a pretty good goddamn reason why Ethan Roy kicked them out in the first place, right?"

"Yeah, but what's the alternative?"

"There is no alternative," I muttered. "We agree to the terms and deliver them to the Eden Accords. Then we deal with the blowback. That's the only play here."

Rooster shook his head. "And what if they say no? What then? We have another faction of pissed-off über angels to deal with? That sounds pretty horrible."

"And so does a world-ending fucking cataclysm. Pick your poison."

"Sounds like a total shit sandwich, guys," George chimed in. "And everybody knows that the only thing to do with a shit sandwich is to suck it up and take a big ole bite. You know what I mean?" And when we all just kind of glared at him for a couple seconds, he muttered, "And that feels like my cue to head back to the table."

As Five Finger scampered off, Doc said, "Dean's right. I don't think we have a choice but to accept Enki's terms on behalf of the Eden Accords."

"I guess," Rooster muttered. "There's just something about this whole situation that feels off."

I chuckled. "Which part? The whole thing's an unmitigated disaster."

"Yeah, but it just feels like we're handing the wolf the keys to the hen house."

Doc placed a hand on Rooster's shoulder. "I don't like it either, John, but unless you have a better idea, we're out of options."

Saying nothing, Rooster reluctantly nodded, and we rejoined Enki and George, who were discussing their favorite Mötley Crüe album while trying to decide whether or not the infamous Tommy Lee and Pamela Anderson sex tape from 1995 was authentic.

"And the verdict is?" asked Enki with bated breath.

I nodded. "You stabilize the planet, and Zion Canyon is yours. We have a deal."

With a big ass smile on his face, he rose to his feet and held up his goblet. "First, we drink to seal our arrangement. *Then*, Dean Robinson, we have a deal. Now, everyone raise your cups!"

Oh good.

More goat piss.

God, I hate Nibiru.

27

Forcing down another horrid sip of the *vintage* Anunnaki barley wine, I placed the stone goblet on the table and channeled all my inner strength to suppress the projectile vomit that was rumbling around in my esophagus. And judging by the dry heaving and green hue of everyone's else skin, it seemed they were doing the same thing.

Taking another healthy sip for good measure, Enki shouted, "Yum!" before grabbing George's goblet and draining the rest of its contents in a single gulp. Then he took a seat and cleared the table in front of him by casually tossing his plate on the floor. "Parchment. Quill! Now!"

And before we knew what the hell was happening, another one of the mysterious hooded figures appeared by his side and handed him just that. Dabbing the quill on the tip of his tongue, he then proceeded to scratch a few words on the parchment before handing it back to the servant. "Deliver this to Sargon. It is of the utmost importance. If you can't find him at the Temple of the Grand Architects, he's most likely at that brothel in Chinatown."

To which the servant replied by mumbling something in a

strange language that sounded like a series of hiccups strung together into syllables.

"No, no, no," Enki muttered, shaking his head. "Not *that* brothel. The one with the large breasted dragon wearing the leopard print G-string on the sign."

And when the servant mumbled something else, Enki shouted, "No, I don't know what it's called. And, *no*, I don't know why the dragon's wearing a G-string! Just go! Now!"

As the hooded minion bowed and vanished, Enki turned his attention to us. "Sargon is Nibiru's Chief Builder. I have requested that he devote his full attention to the small matter of mending your broken planet, which I'm sure he will attend to once his daily *activities* are complete."

Looking exceptionally perplexed, Rooster raised his hand.

"Do you have a question, John O'Dargan?"

"This may be off topic, but is there really a Chinatown in Aventine City?"

"Of course! There's a Chinatown in every city. It's a universal constant. Like Kevin Bacon movies. And reruns of Seinfeld. And Twinkies. Anywho, I believe now it is time to return you to Earth, yes?"

Remembering to revisit that Kevin Bacon comment at some point down the road, I said, "It's probably past time. Aside from wondering what the hell happened to us, the Eden Accords will be pleased to hear of our progress."

"Or they'll kill us on the spot," Rooster muttered under his breath, which earned him a jab to the ribs from Doc.

Enki smiled. "Excellent! And where are these famed *Accords* taking place?"

"A place called the Medmenham Lounge," I replied. "It's a pocket realm of sorts that's run by—"

"Metatron. Yes, yes, I know of it. And might I say, what a total dump! Ugh. Be that as it may, I'm ready when you are."

"You're coming with us?" asked Doc.

"Of course, of course. I now have a vested stake in this grand venture, and I will see it ratified. And besides, I can't wait to see the look on my brother's faces when they see me. It's gonna be *fabulous*! Ready to go?"

George cleared his throat. "So, I guess this is where we part ways. Good luck, guys, and, ah, drop by the Hotel Shasta sometime, huh? We can grab a drink or something." Then he halfheartedly waved at us and turned to leave. But as there were no doors in the stone rotunda, he didn't make it very far. "Can somebody let me out of here? And maybe gimme a lift to the Shasta?"

Enki smiled for a second time. "Absolutely not! The legend of *Five Finger George* should not be withering away at that mulitiversal roach motel! You should be out there in the wide world. Spreading joy and doing whatever it is an inconsequential deity such as yourself does."

George cocked his head to the side. "I don't understand."

Then Enki clapped his hands, and a hooded minion appeared holding an electric guitar. Similar to George's other guitar, this one was also a vintage model Paul Reed Smith, but instead of the sunburst flaming finish on the body, it was black. Jet black like a stunning onyx stone that seemed to hum with a tangible power as it gleamed in the sunlight. George's jaw hit the floor as the hooded munchkin handed it to him and disappeared.

"That is recompense for your six string that was unfortunately eaten by Bluto," Enki said. "I totally didn't see that coming, by the way. What a twist!"

Then he reached into the pocket of his board shorts and pulled out a blood cipher medallion bearing his royal seal. It was similar to the medallion we'd received from Lilith, but slightly different in size and color. Admiring it for a second, he handed it to George. "And *this* will give you the freedom to travel the realms and do your *godly* bidding once again. Simply focus on your destination, regardless of where it is in time or space, and you will find yourself there. Be careful, though, as the device is very sensitive."

Accepting the arcane trinket, George looked like he just won the lottery. "I, I don't know what to say," he muttered with his eyes welling up. "This is the absolute best thing that's ever happened to me. Look, I just gotta tell you guys how much I..."

And just like that, he was gone.

Enki sighed. "Did I not just finish telling him that the device was *very* sensitive? You guys heard me say that, right?"

"Wait," Rooster said as we all looked around the room. "Where'd he go?"

"Wherever it was that he was thinking about! Was *anybody* listening to me?"

"Will he be OK?"

"Oh sure. He'll be fine. Unless he was thinking about the bottom of a volcano. Or deep space. Then he's probably not fine. On that note, shall we?"

Then he clapped his hands again.

And just like that, we were no longer in the Ziggurat of Anshar on Nibiru.

We were in the grandiose marble atrium of the Medmenham Lounge where the esteemed members of the Eden Accords perched around a gargantuan horseshoe-shaped table.

And much like when we'd left them a very long day or so earlier, it was a total shitshow, complete with pushing, shoving, shouting, and the occasional farting compliments of Mortog pulling his own finger. At least Janser Berinhart had put some clothes on and her furry tits weren't flopping around with reckless abandon anymore. That was a small victory in and of itself.

At any rate, standing on the periphery of the general calamity, Doc and I tried our damnedest to get Stephen's or Abernethy's attention to no avail as Enki stood there observing the chaos with a satisfied smirk. "Would you look at this," he jested. "Ethan's mighty champions."

Apparently done trying to make a subtle entrance, Doc pulled out one of her pistols and pointed it toward the ceiling. And before I had the opportunity to lodge a spirited protest, she squeezed off several rounds which caused everyone to stop bickering.

Then, *unfortunately*, they spun around and collectively glared at us.

And then, almost on cue, all of their gazes drifted to the eight-foot tall weirdo with the football-shaped head who was standing there like he owned the joint.

While I wasn't sure whether it was a look of utter disbelief, outright shock, pure terror, or a combination thereof, I was sure about one thing. Every single being in that room had the exact same look plastered across their face.

Stephen and Abernethy.

Gabriel, Uriel, and Semyaza.

Mortog and Hon.

Queen Janser and her unnatural delegation of weirdos.

Mr. Blue Sky and her shadow rulers who constituted the infamous Academy.

And last but certainly not least, even good ole Metatron looked like he was about to shit himself at the mere sight of Enki.

It was almost like they were looking at the boogeyman, which made absolutely no sense given the context that they were a literal collection of interdimensional über beings themselves. The deafening silence continued for several seconds, and the tension in the room was beyond palpable. It was almost painful.

Fortunately, it was right about then when Enki waved at everyone and smiled. Then, in his falsetto voice, he said, "Hey, everybody. *Thanks* for having me. Seriously delighted to be here!" And when everyone just continued to gawk at him in silence, he added, "OK, seriously, people. Somebody say something. You're making this awkward. Speak! Now!"

Gabriel cleared his throat. "Welcome, brother. It's, ah, good to see you."

"Indeed," Uriel added. "And your timing is impeccable. Assuming you're here to *help*. Are you, brother? Here to help?"

Still smiling, Enki nodded. "Of course, of course. I've been fully informed of your predicament by Dean Robinson and Erin Kelly, whom I just *adore,* by the way, although they did make a real a mess out of my fighting pits. Anywho, I've dispatched my master Builders to assess the damage to the planet's core."

No sooner did he complete the sentence than the floor rumbled and shook as a quake rolled through. "And what of the repairs?" Semyaza asked, looking exceptionally haggard. "Your Builders will make them, yes?"

"Of course, of course. We'll mend what we can."

"Will that be enough?"

"It'll be enough to keep things from plummeting into a fiery abyss, if *that's* what you mean, Semyaza. You're looking pretty terrible, by the way. Are there no showers on Earth anymore? And are you wearing eye makeup? I strangely don't hate it."

"These repairs," Janser Berinhart said, stepping forward with detectable coldness in her deep voice. "What are you expecting in return for your efforts?"

"Oh, hello," Enki said, studying her broad-shouldered, husky physique, flowing raven hair, and haunting yellow eyes for a long moment. "And you are?"

"I am Janser. Queen of the Others."

"Oh my, that sounds simply exhausting."

"Answer the question, brother," Gabriel said. "What is the price of the Anunnaki's services?"

"Zion Canyon," I muttered.

And after another string of silence where I could just about feel everyone's icy glare piercing my skin, Stephen said, "What was that, Dean?"

I cleared my throat. "We made a deal with Enki. He fixes the Earth. And in return, the Eden Accords grant Zion Canyon to him and the Anunnaki." Which prompted a muffled yet definitive, "Bloody hell, laddie. You've surely stepped in it now," from Abernethy, followed by a series of more pointed comments from the rest of the group.

"You had no right!" Blue Sky shouted, jumping to her feet and adjusting her loose-fitting denim dress while kicking off her Birkenstocks in anger. "Your charge, *Mr. Robinson*, was to consult with Lilith and ascertain the location of Nibiru. *Not* to travel there and negotiate with the Anunnaki on behalf of the Eden Accords! And certainly not to barter away one of the two most strategic assets on the entire fucking globe!"

Getting in the frumpy soccer mom's face, Doc said, "We did what had to be done. So back off, bitch!"

"Or *what*? What'll you do, *Doctor* Kelly?"

Saying nothing, Doc just grinned. Then she grabbed a handful of Blue Sky's curly hair and slammed her head into the giant horseshoe table face first. And if that wasn't dead sexy, I don't know what it is. Just saying.

At any rate, with her nose profusely bleeding, the infamous Mr. Blue Sky muttered something of a very snide nature under her breath and joined her shadow regime pals as Mortog heartily chuckled. "Fancy lady got her ass kicked by Doc Doc!" Then he pulled his finger and farted as Hon, High Commander of the Carolingian Knights of Nod, swatted him on the back of the head.

Thoroughly enjoying the show, Enki said, "And I thought politics on Nibiru were entertaining! This is next level! But on a serious note, people, am I to understand that we *do not* have an agreement with regard to Zion Canyon? Because it that's the case, my Builders and I will leave you folks in peace. You know, to enjoy the impending doom of your broke ass planet. Toodles!"

"Wait," Gabriel grumbled, with his statuesque face curled into an atypical scowl. "Please wait, brother. I believe I speak for all parties when I say we will honor the agreement ment made on behalf of the Eden Accords." Then he scanned the room. "Am I correct in that assumption?"

And although nobody looked particularly happy about it, they all halfheartedly nodded in agreement. "Well then," Enki said, "It seems we have a deal after all."

"Not yet," Gabriel continued. "If you are to assume control of Zion Canyon, we need some assurances."

"Assurances? What kind of assurances, baby bro?"

"Assurances that your intentions are peaceful and, dare I say, unlike the *early days*."

Enki feigned a grin, and for the first time, I noticed a distinct coldness to his gaze. "Are you referring to the time when the Anunnaki prospered upon this very planet? This very planet that the *Anunnaki* designed and built with our very own hands alongside Father? Is that what you're referring to, *brother*?"

Gabriel matched Enki's glare. "No, brother. I'm referring to the time when the Anunnaki enslaved the human race before nearly wiping them out in a genocidal—"

"Let me stop you right there. Conquest for the sake of conquest is no longer the way of my people. We leave that *sort of thing* to you and the humans."

"And what is the way of your people nowadays?"

"Our *way* is prosperity. And you have my word that we will not seek war — nor will we cower should it seek *us*." Then his demeanor returned to the eccentrically strange overlord that I'd come to know over the past few hours. "So, we good here or what, guys? All set?"

"I believe we are," Janser Berinhart replied as Gabriel nodded. "And we thank you for your assistance."

Enki smiled. "It's my pleasure, queenie. We should definitely do lunch some time. I don't know why, but I feel like we'd be fast friends!" And it was right about then one of his peculiar hooded minions appeared at his side and mumbled something of an indecipherable nature before vanishing. "Well, gotta go, but you folks have fun with the rest of your dystopian peace conference, or whatever this is, exactly. And rest assured, my Builders are hard at work. The damage looks pretty severe, so it may be a little bumpy for a day or two, but things should level out. If you need anything in the mean-time, call me!"

Then he was gone in a powerful swoosh of air.

Semyaza scratched his head. "Sorry, but what the hell just happened here?"

"It appears we've solved one problem," Stephen said. "Thanks to the efforts of Dean. And Erin Kelly. And John O'Dargan." Then he glanced at me, and it was pretty clear that we'd be discussing the details of those aforementioned *efforts* later. Awesome.

"The Earth may be saved," Blue Sky muttered, "but at what cost? You've no idea what we've traded."

"The Anunnaki will honor their word," Gabriel said. "Or they will face my blade."

Semyaza scoffed. "Come on, bro. Enki may act like a fruitcake, but we all know what he's capable of. Let's just hope it doesn't come to that."

"Regardless," Blue Sky said, still holding a bloody tissue around her nose. "With control of Zion Canyon now in the hands of the Anunnaki, the scales are tipped in the wrong direction. I highly suggest we focus our efforts on preventing a similar debacle from happening to the second and final nexus point — the Great Pyramid of Giza."

As everyone agreed through a series of nods and grunts, Janser said, "Wait, we're missing somebody."

"It's Uriel," Gabriel muttered as he scanned the room. "He's gone."

And there was just something about the way he said it that made me think things were about to get a bit more interesting.

And by interesting I meant terrible.

28

"URIEL CAN'T BE GONE," Janser Berinhart grumbled. "I can still smell his putrid cologne! It's been giving me a headache all goddamn day."

"He was standing right there just a second ago," Metatron added. "I'm sure of it."

Semyaza shrugged. "Maybe he had to take a piss. What's the big deal?"

"He's a smooth-talking charlatan who I don't trust," Janser said as she glared at him with her creepy yellow eyes. "That's the *big deal*! And why would he just up and leave without saying anything?"

"Because he's betrayed us," Bobby announced as he walked in with Mariel and stood by his master. And despite the fact both he and M looked beyond exhausted, Bobby's schwoopy hair was perfect. It was uncanny.

Gabriel's stoic face flashed with concern as he placed a hand on his shoulder. "Betrayal is a strong word, Kerubiel. Are you certain?"

"I'm certain," Blue Sky muttered, with her face buried in her mobile phone. "It's all over the goddamn news." Then Metatron waved his hand, and a virtual screen appeared over the conference table. And within a second or so, the face of my least favorite newscaster appeared.

"Not good, folks!" Buzz Shea screamed into the camera. With bloodshot eyes and a scratchy voice, he looked like he'd been popping Adderall like candy. "Not good at all! The freaking *space pyramids* are on the move! And they seem to be congregating in Egypt at the *Great Pyramid*! Seriously? Is it time to panic yet? I don't know, but I seriously need a drink. And some meth. Can somebody get me meth? I mean, why not, right? Anyway, stay tuned, folks..."

Then the video shifted to an aerial view, and hundreds if not thousands of seraphic lodestones could be seen descending from the sky and forming a harrowing perimeter around the Great Pyramid. Systematically landing on the ground, the otherworldly structures melded together like a massive Lego set that formed a towering wall at least a mile high. And as the final lodestone touched down, completing the traumatizing barricade, a blinding flash of pure white light erupted from the center, and a dome-like force field of primal energy snapped into place around the whole thing.

"Well, shit," Semyaza muttered, as the translucent screen vanished with a wave of Metatron's hand. "That seems problematic. I guess Uriel wasn't taking a piss after all."

Shaking his head in anger as his gaze fell to the floor, Gabriel paced back and forth, muttering something to himself over and over. And the faster he paced, the madder he got. Unsure what to say to the fuming archangel, everyone just kind of stood there watching him in tentative silence until he'd apparently worked himself into a proper frenzy. Then, without so much as a word of warning, he tilted his head back and screamed at the very top of his lungs.

And I don't mind telling you it was fucking terrifying.

The sound the poured from his mouth was not only deafening, it was primal.

And guttural.

And it ripped the air apart like a clap of thunder as every single hair on my body stood up, and I found myself shaking. Backpedaling several steps as did everyone else in the atrium, I felt like my eardrums were going to burst when finally, he stopped.

"Before this day ends," he barked with eyes that glowed a searing white, "I *will* have his head on a pike. Do you hear me? I will have his head!"

Stepping forward with his hands held out, Semyaza said, "Easy, brother. We *hear* you. And I'm sure that no one here would be disappointed to see dear Uriel's head separated from his body. But you did see his defensive perimeter, yes? And his wards? They looked pretty impenetrable to me."

Metatron nodded. "He's clearly harnessing the power of the nexus to fuel them."

"Can they be breached?"

"Perhaps. Perhaps not."

"What are you saying, Metatron?" Stephen asked.

"I'm saying that Uriel has won the day."

"No," Gabriel snarled. "He has not!"

Semyaza grinned. "You never did know when to give up, big brother." Then he turned and faced the rest of the group and waved. "Nice meeting you all. I'd say this has been *fun*, but it really hasn't, has it? That said, I bid you farewell, and I sincerely hope to never see any of you again. Ever."

"You're not leaving, seraph," Janser muttered. "The Eden Accords are not concluded."

Semyaza responded with a round of hearty laughter. "Good one, lady. But I'm totally leaving, and you should, too. These *accords* are a joke. They were over before they started."

Taking a menacing step toward him, Janser's hands morphed into talon-tipped claws. "I disagree."

Semyaza grinned a second time. "You see, that's the problem right there. You can't have a goddamn peace conference when all anybody wants to do is fight each other! That's not how it works."

Thinking that he actually had a good point, I took a few steps forward and cleared my throat. "Where will you go?"

"Don't you worry, little godling. The Watchers and I will stay out of trouble. Promise. There's something about being imprisoned for six millennia that gives you a new perspective on things." Then he winked at me. "See ya around."

And then he was gone as a powerful swoosh of air swept through the room.

Blue Sky stood up and waved a finger at Gabriel. "You get him back here. Get him back here right now! The absolute *last thing* we need is another faction of rogue angels running amuck in the—"

"Mind your tongue, mortal," the archangel muttered as his eyes flashed white for a second time in as many minutes. "Or you may find yourself without it."

"Excuse me? Was that a *threat*? Did you *seriously* just threaten me?"

Stepping forward with an impressive scowl on his bearded face, Big A held his hands up. "Steady now! Everybody just take a wee minute to simmer down."

"Kilt man is right," Mortog added. "Everybody simmer down. We need a plan." Which earned him an encouraging nod from Hon. Then he farted and Hon slapped him on the back of the head.

"If Uriel is to be stopped, we need to band together."

"Your assistance is not required," Gabriel said with a cold edge. "My legionnaires will breach Uriel's wards. And I will have my vengeance."

"Oh, that's *brilliant*," Blue Sky muttered. "And the part about his wards being near impenetrable? Have you accounted for that small detail in your calculations?"

"Our lodestones are nigh indestructible," Bobby suggested. "Perhaps we could use one as battering ram of sorts. Or a projectile even?"

Metatron nodded. "That could work. Given the proper velocity and placement, it should punch right through the wards. Or create a sizable tear at the very least."

Gabriel's face curled into a wolfish grin. "And that is all we require." Then he turned to Bobby. "Ready our legions, Kerubiel. We leave at once."

"There is one more matter to discuss, master," he said. "Uriel's legionnaires outnumber ours three to one. I'm afraid we are greatly outmatched."

"No, you're not," said Janser Berinhart. "Not with my army at your back."

"And my anakim!" Mortog grunted.

Stephen stepped forward. "The remaining might of the Guild is at your disposal as well."

With all eyes falling to Blue Sky, she reluctantly nodded. "And you will have our Praetorian fleet. It is more than formidable."

Doc cleared her throat. "What about collateral damage? There's got to be a few million people in Giza and the other towns surrounding the pyramids."

"The total is closer to nine million," Blue Sky corrected. "And my people are already working on it. That said, we'll need time to conduct the evacuation properly."

"How much time?" I asked.

She glanced at her phone. "Four hours, thirty-two minutes, and ten seconds. Give or take."

"Then it's settled," Gabriel announced as he waved his hand and a map of Giza manifested on the conference table. "I will stage my legions in the desert south of the pyramids and well outside of Uriel's defenses. Meet me there in four hours. We attack when the humans have been cleared from the area. I lead. You follow."

"And what of the Eden Accords?" asked Janser. "Are they over?"

"Not over," replied Stephen, as he intently scanned the group. "Merely suspended until Uriel's treachery has been properly dealt with. Agreed?"

After a unanimous set of nods and a few muttered words, everyone started to filter out of the atrium.

Some used the door.

Others just kind of vanished mid-stride.

Anxiously waiting to catch up with Stephen and Abernethy, I was somewhat taken aback when they both followed Gabriel out of the room after what looked like a rather heated sidebar discussion.

"What do you think that was about?" asked Rooster.

I shrugged. "Not sure. Didn't look friendly, though."

"No. No, it didn't. You think we should follow?"

"Best to let to let them handle it. Whatever *it* is."

"So, what now?"

"I don't know about you guys," Doc said. "But I've about had it with the Eden Accords."

Rooster nodded. "Agreed. I'd rather be back in the Aventine City fighting pits than spend one more second listening to these *peace* talks. The only freaking thing they could actually agree on was to go to war. Kinda sorta."

"That certainly does feel like abject failure for a peace summit."

"At least the earthquakes stopped," I said. "And we're no longer worried about the planet breaking into tiny pieces in a maelstrom of fire and ash. That's a win, right?"

"Yeah, that's a win."

"And you smashed Blue Sky's smarmy face into the table. That was a definite win."

She grinned. "I really hate that bitch."

"Same."

"And I can't help but think she's up to something."

Rooster nodded. "You can almost see the conniving gears turning in her head."

"Yeah, she's a real peach," I muttered as my stomach growled and it occurred to me I couldn't remember the last time I ate something. "Since we have a few hours to kill, let's head back to the QM. I need some chow. And we should probably check in with the crew. Assuming they're not still roaming Woodstock, that is."

"That may be the smartest thing you've said all day," Rooster said.

"More like all week," Doc added.

"All month?"

"Maybe even all year."

Offering them both a spirited middle finger, I shook my head a few times as we headed back to the Medmenham's main bar in search of a portal. And although our long day was now about to get exponentially longer, I couldn't help but think things were starting to look up.

Either that, or we were totally hosed.

Typical.

"So lemme get this straight, mancho," MacCawill managed to force out amidst a barrage of roaring laughter. "A *pixie* pulled his dick out and told you guys to fuck off? That's priceless!" And then he started laughing again to the point where he had to lean against the Quartermaster's mighty wooden bar to avoid falling over. "Absolutely — friggin — priceless!"

Glaring at him in bewilderment after I'd just finished recapping the entire series of sordid events since we inadvertently parted ways with everyone at Woodstock, I shook my head and groaned. "Is that all you got from everything I just said?"

He shrugged. "What? It was the best part."

"I've always heard that Akkadian Pixies were legendary assholes," Ziggy added, rolling up on his mini tank treads and pulling to a squeaky halt before running over my foot. "You're lucky to have survived the encounter with all your fingers still attached. And I believe they're also known to throw their own feces."

"Those are Bohemian Pixies, Zig. Totally different species."

"Are you quite sure, sir?"

"Yeah, my third wife had one. Little bastard used to throw shit at me all the time. Took me years to get him to stop."

"Oh my. That's sounds terrible, sir. How did you break him of the habit?"

"I covered him with beer batter."

"And that worked?"

"Sure, after I deep fried his ass and dipped him in tartar sauce. Tasted like a fish stick."

Sliding me a pint of frothy beer, Coop intently scratched his scraggly goatee a few times as he stood behind the bar looking exceptionally curious. "Hey, hoss. So, this Five Finger George character y'all met. You said he was a god of some sort or another?"

Still trying to erase the mental image of MacCawill chomping on a flash-fried fairy, I said, "Yeah. Emphasis on the *some sort* or *another* part."

"Uh, huh. And you said he had sex with a car on an elevator?"

"No, I said that he had sex with a car *and* an elevator."

"Does he have a metal dick or something?"

Draining my beer in a single gulp, I looked around at everyone else. "Are there any *other* questions about Nibiru?"

Caveman raised a shaggy hand. "I got one, bromando."

"Does it involve unnatural fetishes with sentient machinery?"

"Nope."

"What about pixie penises?"

Then he promptly lowered his hand. "Maybe."

Finding that rather funny, Duncan let out a giggle-like snort from his perch on top of the bar where he was working the taps and handing out pints.

No, I don't know how he was doing it. He just was.

Clearly disgruntled that RoosterBragh had somehow been displaced by Petulant Pig as the Quartermaster's craft beer of choice, Rooster grumbled something snide under his breath as he slid his apron on. Waving his hand over the massive, cast-iron griddle lining the wall behind the bar, it sizzled and hissed with searing heat as he meticulously loaded it with juicy burgers. Liberally seasoning them with a variety of hifalutin foodie spices, he then produced his Herculean spatula and went to work flipping meat as a cloud of mouthwatering smoke filled the room.

"Although I'm kind of scared to ask," said Doc as my stomach growled like a wild animal, "what went down at Woodstock after we left?"

Billy crossed her arms. "You mean after you left *me* in 1969 with these idiots?"

"Yeah, sorry?"

Then our resident she-dragon, who doubled as an Icelandic warrior princess, chuckled as she traded fist bumps with everyone. "Just kidding. I kind of like these idiots."

MacCawill grinned. "And we like you, Puff."

Billy grinned back. "Call me that again, cowboy man, and I'll punch you in the dick."

And there was just something about her goofy Nordic accent that made it sound *that* much funnier.

With a contemptuous sneer and a spirited hand gesture, MacCawill hopped over the bar and helped Duncan sling beer as Coop and Caveman took turns explaining, in graphic detail, what happened in 1969 after we left and the infamous *tagalongs* showed up.

And I'll be damned if it wasn't one hell of an epic tale.

An epic tale that started with the serendipitous fact that Charlie and Jim Jim apparently knew each other from back in the day. More so than that, they were really good pals. So, when everything came to a head, and the slugfest was about to start, they wouldn't fight each other.

Instead, they started drinking.

And smoking.

And all manner of other things.

And while *that* was happening, Owen managed to negotiate a temporary truce with Gadreel, Hof, and Yaw that they sealed by drinking some electric punch that my ole buddy Gravy gave them. Then they all kind of forgot what they were doing in the first place.

So naturally, they started partying.

Partying, that is, in an unrelenting psychedelic haze that culminated in a series of absurd events starting with Hof and Yaw stage diving in front of Jimi Hendrix while he was playing the solo to Foxy Lady. Then there was Jim Jim, who got married to a beatnik lady named Hairy Hannah in a beautiful ceremony presided over by a life-sized teddy bear that was a spitting image of Jerry Garcia. And finally, Gadreel, the once psychotic fallen Watcher, changed his name to Gnat and joined a hippie commune en route to Salt Lake City.

After a long moment of stunned silence, Doc muttered, "OK, wow?" Then she started chuckling. "And where's everybody now?"

"Well," Coop said, hawking some tobacco juice into his trusted plastic cup spittoon, "Willa had to head back to the MidKnight Jayde. Apparently, they ran out of Petulant Pig and a minor riot broke out." Prompting another giggle-like snort from Duncan.

"And Charlie?"

"He and Owen kinda stayed."

"They stayed? In 1969?"

"Yup."

"But they're coming back, right?"

Billy shrugged. "We're not sure. But we started an over under. You want in?"

About to have a mild panic attack, I said, "What about Tony? Please don't tell me he's still chasing hippie chicks around Woodstock."

Caveman grinned. "Big Sarge came back with us all right. Headed back to his base, though." Then he reached into his pocket and handed me a small, thin device that looked like a futuristic walkie talkie. "He said to give you this, and he'd be in touch soon."

Sliding it into the back pocket of my jeans, I nodded at Caveman as Billy pointed to one of the countless tV screens lining the wall above the bar. "Have you guys seen this? The earthquakes have stopped. It's all over the news. You did it!"

Doc held up her beer. "We did it."

Intently flipping meat with the spatulas of destiny, Rooster muttered, "Yeah, and now all *we* have to do is evict an archangel and his countless legions of warrior minions from their mutinous mega fortress encompassing the Great Pyramid's limitless nexus of primal energy. No sweat."

"Speaking of," Billy said, grabbing a remote control and turning up the volume on the tV. "Check this shit out."

"Buzz Shea here, folks!" the newscaster screamed into the camera. Having taken off his suit and tie, he was wearing nothing but a white V-neck tee-shirt and looked like a haggard homeless person. "Guess who's got two thumbs and *loves* meth? This guy! And in more good news, reports are pouring in from across the globe, and it appears that *all* the unexplained seismic and volcanic activity has mysteriously stopped!"

"I hate this guy," I muttered. "You think he's actually on meth?"

"Meth!" Shea screamed with his eyes literally popping out of his head as a video feed of Uriel's barricade around the Great Pyramid came into focus. "And in the *bad news* category, it seems that all the space pyramids are flocking to Egypt like the Salmon of *fucking* Capistrano! Are you kidding me? Don't know about you, folks, but I'm so sick of these *fucking* pyramids—" And it was right about then he started frothing at the mouth and clutching his chest as the show cut to commercial.

MacCawill chuckled. "Yeah, definitely on meth."

"Dagummit," Coop muttered, still fixated on the tV. "Was that Thunderdome looking thing Uriel's handiwork?"

I nodded. "Yup."

"Looks like he and his boys are dug in deeper than an Alabama tick on a mule deer's nut sack."

"And not in a good way," Caveman muttered. "So, what's the plan?"

Shaking off both the latest Cooperism and Caveman's reaction to it, I said, "Gabriel and his legions are going to punch through the wards with a lodestone. Then we all storm the castle."

"That's kind of a shit plan."

"Feel free to tell that to good ole Gabe when we meet up with him and everybody else in Giza."

"Everybody else," MacCawill muttered. "Meaning?"

"Meaning we won't just be fighting alongside the halos."

"Who else is joining the party?"

"Janser Berinhart's army," Doc said. "And Mortog's anakim."

Still cooking, Rooster added, "And don't forget about the Praetorian fleet."

Thinking on that for a second or two, MacCawill said, "Maybe those Eden Accords weren't for total shit after all."

I shrugged. "What do you mean, Roy?"

"Think about it, mancho. This has gotta be the first time in history that angels, nephilim, and humans are fighting on the same side. That's gotta count for something."

As we all stood there in silence trying to come to terms with the fact that Roy MacCawill, apocalyptic bounty hunter and all-purpose asshole, just made one hell of a profound point, Rooster said, "Burgers are ready." And thankfully we all forgot about it as my enigmatic ginger colleague handed out plate after plate of hifalutin hamburgers and curly fries.

After stuffing my face for a solid ten minutes straight, I gulped another sip of Petulant Pig and took note of the time on the antique grandfather clock in the far corner. "Everybody listen up. We link up with Gabriel in three hours. Until then, prep your gear and get some rest. Meet in the Reliquary when it's time to go." Then I slugged back the rest of my beer and placed the glass on the bar.

"You OK?" asked Erin.

"Yeah, I'm good."

"You sure?"

"Yeah, why?"

"It's just that you look really pensive."

"Oh, sorry. Might've had one too many pints."

"Wait, so that's your '*I have to pee*' face?"

"You look disappointed."

She smiled. "Nope, all good. It's just that the next time I think that you're about to say something incredibly thoughtful, I'll know that you just have to take a piss."

Making the mental note that I really could have handled that better, I smiled back and excused myself before making the short walk to the little boy's room at the end of the bar. Pushing open the ginormous wooden door, I stepped inside and flipped on the lights as the door slammed behind me with a curious popping sound.

Thinking that was a bit odd, I made my way toward the row of urinals, only to find that they weren't there. They weren't there because I wasn't standing in the bathroom.

I was standing in a study.

A cozy study boasting rustic hard wood floors, wall-mounted oil lamps, and countless rows of stacked books that filled the entire floor space from floor to ceiling. And sitting in a rocking chair by a modest hearth against the far wall with his face buried in a newspaper was Ethan Roy.

Thinking you never hear about anybody getting summoned by God while they're trying to take a piss throughout the entire friggin Bible, I grumbled a snide word or two under my breath in protest.

After several seconds of me standing there and him ignoring me, he muttered, "You guys really cocked it up this time. What a disaster." Not quite sure how to respond to that or if a response was even warranted, I just kind of gawked at him until he looked up. "Well, sit down already."

Reluctantly taking a seat on a humble wooden chair opposite our snarky creator, I took note of the sizable pile of crinkled newspapers by his feet. All of which seemed to have horrific pictures of natural disasters, flying pyramids, and other such calamity plastered all over the front page.

Peering at me with his intense, icy blue eyes, he casually folded his paper and tossed it on the pile with the others before running his fingers through his stately, white beard a few times. "So, what do you have to say for yourself?"

I shrugged. "Mind if I use your pisser?"

"You can piss later," he grumbled. "First, we talk."

"About?"

"You can start by telling me why you morons thought calling on the *Anunnaki* was a good idea."

"You mean besides the fact that the planet was within days of shitting itself into a gazillion pieces?"

He grinned. "Don't get smart with me, Dean. I'm still not sure I like you very much."

Although slightly terrified, I grinned back. "That's really good to know. Thanks?"

After a prolonged sigh, he said, "Do you have any idea how diffi-cult it was to get rid of them in first place?"

"Ah, no, but—"

"But you do know they enslaved every human on the entire planet, though, right?"

"That was mentioned once or twice, but—"

"Then there was the slaughterhouses. Did you know about those?"

"Sorry, the what now?"

"The goddamn slaughterhouses! That's what I'm trying to tell you — the *Anunnaki* are a race of infinitely intelligent, warmon-gering savages who I banished to the far side of reality for good reason. Now they're back. And by invitation, no less."

"Well, we had to do something. I mean, you saw what happened to Washington State, didn't you? It's a fucking island."

He rolled his eyes. "Yeah, so?"

Making the mental note that even God hates the West Coast, I said, "Look, everyone agreed that Enki and *the Builders* were the only ones who could fix the damage."

"Did they now?"

"Yeah, they did. The entire Eden Accords. It was pretty much the only *goddamn* thing, no offense, they agreed on."

"Well, I guess that's something," he muttered. "Tell me about Enki."

"He seems nice. Totally batshit and slightly psychotic, but nice."

"Maybe he's mellowed out a bit since the early days. And his brother, Enlil?"

"Didn't have the pleasure of meeting him, but apparently they're fighting some kind of civil war."

Ethan groaned. "Speaking of civil war, what the hell's got into Uriel?"

"Well, spit balling here, but it seems that since we traded Zion Canyon to Enki as payment for his Builders to stabilize the Earth's core, Uriel figured the second and final nexus point was up for grabs. So, being an opportunist, he sort of moved into the Great Pyramid. And now Gabriel and pretty much everybody else are hell-bent on evicting his ass."

Ethan groaned a second time. "There's only one thing more dangerous than *having* absolute power. Do you know what that is?" And when I offered no response besides a blank stare, he said, "The fear of losing it."

"What are you saying?"

"I'm saying that by bringing the Anunnaki into the equation, you and the others changed the game."

"I don't disagree, but we had no choice."

"There's always a choice, Dean. Always. And you'd be well served to remember that."

"Fine, but why tell me this, huh? What the hell am I supposed to do?"

He shrugged. "Hell if I know. This is a top shelf shitshow. Good luck sorting it out."

I threw my hands up in frustration. "That's really fucking helpful! Did you bring me here just to be a dick?"

"No," he muttered as we locked gazes. "I brought you here to remind you that people tend to do incredibly *irrational* things when they think they're out of options." Then he waved at me. "Now get out."

And before I had the opportunity to get another word in edgewise, I found myself standing in the bathroom at the Quartermaster wondering what in the hell just happened.

"You OK, broseph?" asked Caveman as he walked in and admired himself in one of the mirrors before meticulously combing his thick mane of mansquatched hair. "Look like you saw a ghost."

"Not a ghost. A dickhead."

Albeit an almighty one.

30

With the words of Ethan Roy ringing in my head like a haunting echo, I made my way back to the bar and was just about to sit down next to Doc and catch the latest newscast when a powerful swoosh of air pelted me in the face. And standing before me was Mariel.

But in lieu of her signature naughty librarian outfit, beehive styled hair, and engaging smile, she was clad in seraphic combat armor with a deep frown on her face. "Hi, Bubullah," she said, placing her hand on my shoulder. "You must come with me. Now."

"M?" Doc said, hopping off her stool before I could get a word in edgewise. "Are you OK? What's wrong?"

Mariel forced a smile. "I'm fine. Thank you, Erin, dear. Nothing to worry about. Not yet, anyway."

"Do you need help?"

"At Stephen's request, I've come for Dean. His assistance is required."

"Assistance with what?" I asked. "What's going on, M?"

"I'll explain on the way. And we really must be going. Now, Bubullah."

Figuring that couldn't be good, I turned to Doc. "Stick to the plan. Get everybody to Egypt when it's time. Not before."

"I should go with you two," she said, to which, Mariel replied, "Best to stay here for now, Erin. I'll send word should we need more assistance."

Doc nodded. "But where are you going?"

"To talk some sense into a certain archangel who's gone meshugana." Then she placed a hand on my other shoulder, and just like that, we were somewhere else.

And, of course, by somewhere else, I meant we were on the other side of the globe, standing in the Egyptian desert on the outskirts of Giza. The dry air filled my lungs as we were greeted by a brisk morning breeze, and I found myself completely mesmerized by the unnatural mega-structure sprawled out before me. Despite the fact we were easily five miles away, the shiny metallic walls of Uriel's horrific Thunderdome jutted far into the cloudless sky, almost like a majestic mountain range that stretched on for as far as the eye could see. The sheer scale and grandeur of it was mindboggling, and a thousand times more terrifying in person than its depiction on television.

But perhaps the most impressive thing about it was the arcane force field that surrounded the entire structure in a giant bubble of humming, hissing primal energy. The translucent dome shimmered and flickered in the morning sun as it sporadically fired bolts of purple lighting into the desert sky like a pissed-off Tesla coil.

Wave after wave of arcane power pulsed through the desert with the uncanny rhythm of a beating heart, and I could literally feel them pass through me before dissipating in the ether. Feeling dizzy, I backpedaled a step or two as the cloak manifested in a spectral flash and flared out like it was trying to protect me.

"It might take a minute or two," Mariel said. "But you'll get used to it."

Struggling to keep my balance despite the cloak's protection, I placed a hand on her shoulder in an attempt to steady myself. "It's overpowering, almost intoxicating."

"It certainly is that."

"Is all that power coming from the nexus point under the Great Pyramid?"

She nodded. "It's fueled by the convergence of the ley lines. And harnessed by those who understand its properties, it's virtually limitless. Hence Gabriel's obsession with removing Uriel from the Pyramid."

"Speaking of, where are Gabe and the boys?"

Slowly turning around, she motioned for me to do the same.

So, I did.

And then I just about shit myself at the stunningly horrifying vision laid out before me.

Sort of like the Roman legions on steroids, Gabriel's forces were spread out for miles and miles across the desert in a seemingly endless formation. Muttering something to the effect of, "Holy fucking shit," under my breath, it took me a second or two to process what I was looking at.

Legion upon legion of heavily armored warrior seraphs toting ornate shields and all manner of sharp and pointy weapons of death were gathered in tight phalanxes that seemed to stretch beyond the horizon line. And interspersed within their ranks were futuristic catapult-like machines loaded with hissing spheres of swirling fire. If all that wasn't enough to make you shit yourself or go blind, the impromptu battle encampment was rounded out by hundreds upon hundreds of tactically positioned lodestones. Some of which were situated on the ground, while others circled the uncanny angel army in a tight orbit.

Mariel sighed. "That is a sight I hoped never to see again."

"It's, ah, slightly terrifying," I muttered, still trying to process the scene. "There's got to be ten thousand angels there. Maybe more."

She sighed for a second time. "When the archangels stood

against Lucifer during the great war, there was one thousand-fold that amount — on either side."

"Is that when Lew was cast out of the Heavens?"

"Yes. And the death toll that followed was catastrophic. The seraphic race has never quite recovered, even after all these many millennia. Yet here we are again, at the precipice of war. And for *what*, exactly? Power?" She scoffed. "It's unconscionable."

"So, how do we stop it?"

"With words, not actions." Then she grabbed my hand, and in a powerful swoosh of air, we'd traversed the countless legions of combat troops and were standing outside an elaborate tent at the rear of the formation. "This way," she said, casually dismissing the armed guards and pulling to a halt just before entering.

Taking a quick glance at my disheveled appearance highlighted by sullied jeans, jungle boots, and black Petulant Pig tee-shirt, which was pretty disgusting at this point, she shook her head. Muttering a few words in Enochian, she then snapped her fingers, and my ratty clothes were replaced with sleek black armor complete with a barzel breast plate and black fatigues. She smiled. "Much better, Bubullah. Are you ready?"

I shrugged. "Ready for what, exactly? Why am I here?"

Saying nothing, she turned and entered the tent. Figuring I should probably follow, I did just that and was more than a bit surprised to find Gabriel, the esteemed archangel and left hand of God, handcuffed and tied to a chair with a leather strap covering his mouth. And standing on his flanks with bloodied faces and blackened eyes were Bobby, Stephen, and Abernethy. None of whom looked exceptionally happy.

Fixating on me, Gabriel's eyes flashed jet black like pools of oil, and I could almost feel the anger and hatred pouring from his aura. He was clearly not in his right mind. If such a thing existed for a celestial über being, that is.

"Dean," Stephen said, stepping toward me. "Thank you for coming. We need your help."

"My help, eh?"

Big A nodded. "Aye, yer help, lad."

"Is anybody going to explain why Gabriel's in timeout? It's a bit awkward."

"My *master*," Bobby muttered, "is not thinking clearly at the current moment. As such, we have restrained him."

"Gabriel was about to launch his assault on the Great Pyramid," Mariel added. "Despite the fact Giza and the other cities have not been evacuated yet. The collateral damage would have been disastrous, to say the very least."

I nodded. "OK, so what do you need me for?"

"I'd like you to stay with Kerubiel in the event Gabriel *misbehaves* again," Stephen said.

"Where are you going?"

"To negotiate with Uriel."

"Negotiate. With the guy that stabbed everyone in the back and holds all the cards?"

"If there's a chance to avoid all-out war, then we must try. I thought you, of all people, would appreciate that."

"I do. It's just that we have no leverage."

"I can't imagine that Uriel wants a war on his hands. Perhaps he can be reasoned with and favorable terms can be agreed to."

Getting angrier by the second, Gabriel managed to bite through the strap covering his mouth and spit the remnants at Stephen in contempt. "There are no *favorable* terms," he snarled. "You insubordinate *simpletons!* I'll have your heads for this mutiny!" With his eyes fully transitioned to soulless black and his face curled into a hellish scowl, he glared at Bobby. "Kerubiel, release me now! I command you—"

"You *command* no one!" Bobby shouted with his eyes lit up like high beams on a car as every Enochian glyph tattooed on his neck glowed an ethereal bluish-white. "Not until you return to your senses. Please, master. Please be reasonable. I implore you."

And it was right about then things took an interesting turn. For as Gabriel's anger apparently reached Incredible Hulk level, a searing silhouette of white flame outlined the fuming archangel's powerful frame, and his eyes transitioned from black to blinding white. Then, unfortunately, he snapped the hex cuffs from his hands and rose to his feet as all the remaining bindings holding him at bay simply melted from existence.

Standing before us with his chest heaving, a super-sized sword manifested in Gabriel's hand as his armored wings flared out in a brazen show of force. "Listen to me," he said in a semi-rational tone. "Treachery such as Uriel's cannot be reasoned with. Like Lucifer and Michael, he is a cancer. A festering pestilence that preys on the goodness of others. He cannot be trusted by you or anyone else. Especially given the power he now wields. There is but one solution for the greater good. We must end him. Do you understand me?"

Stephen nodded as his cloak billowed about his shoulders and he carefully stepped forward. "We do, old friend. Believe me. But—"

"Then stand aside," he grumbled. "All of you. Stand aside now, and I will forget these misguided acts of mutiny."

Bobby's double-edged battle axe manifested in his hand. "What is it you mean to do, master?"

Gabriel's flawless face curled into a dark grin as he took a menacing step toward him. "I mean to finish what I started, Kerubiel."

"You cannot!" Mariel shouted, taking post on Bobby's flank. "It is a fool's errand, Gabriel! You cannot defeat Uriel alone. If you will not negotiate, then we must wait for reinforcements, at the very least."

"And allow the evacuation to complete," Bobby added. "If not, the loss of human life will be—"

"Acceptable," the archangel snarled.

And as I stood there waiting for the other proverbial shoe to drop, Gabriel apparently decided the conversation was over, and it was now time for deeds. He grabbed Bobby by the neck and lifted him off his feet before body slamming the poor bastard on the ground with a horrid thud. In a blur of motion, a golden staff manifested in Mariel's hands, and just as she was about to strike Gabriel in the throat, he slammed the hilt of his mighty sword into her forehead, sending her plummeting backward in an unconscious heap.

With their swords drawn and cloaks flaring, both Stephen and Big A descended on the pissed-off über seraph in unison. Sparks sprayed throughout the tent as the otherworldly swords collided in a blinding barrage of strikes barely perceptible to the human eye until it was pretty clear Gabriel wasn't going to be overpowered for a second time today. Holstering his sword, the archangel then backhanded Stephen with one of his armored wings, rendering him unconscious. And without missing a step, he grabbed Abernethy by the collar and headbutted him so hard, the massive Scotsman fell limp and slunk to the ground.

A turbo shot of adrenaline fired through my already amped up system as I placed myself between Gabriel and the exit. Figuring I wouldn't fare very well in a sword fight nor a boxing match given everyone else's misfortune, I willed the shotgun into being and instantly felt the presence of the scabbard-like holster on my back. Ripping the semi-divine 1887 Winchester free, I focused my will and cocked the lever as both barrels hissed and glowed with the white fire of Judgement.

Swinging the muzzle at Gabriel, I muttered, "Don't. Please."

He sneered at me. "Or *what?* Do you honestly think that *you*, a pitiable husk of a man, are worthy to cast Judgement upon me — an archangel of the Lord?" And when I offered no response besides an icy stare, he shouted. "I'm the left of hand of God! Not you, *Dean Robinson!* Not these *Deacons*. Me! It has always been me. And I will have my vengeance if it stains my hands red with the blood of every human and half-breed in this wretched realm!"

Raising the shotgun to my shoulder as my heart raced in overdrive, I trained both barrels on his chest. "Stand down, Gabe. I don't want to end you, but I will."

With my finger on the trigger, I locked gazes with the enraged archangel and waited with bated breath for him to make his next move. As we stood there, face to face, glaring at each other for what felt like an eternity, the unmistakable sound of explosions could be heard from outside the tent. It was faint at first, but the longer we stood there, the louder it grew. Almost like it was getting closer. And there was just something about the look of complete befuddlement on Gabriel's face that made me think his folks weren't responsible for it.

"Is that your handwork?" I asked.

He shook his head. "I assure you, it is not."

Figuring that couldn't be a good thing, I lowered the shotgun, and before I could get another word out of my mouth, Gabriel had already blown past me. Following him in a state of panic, I burst out of the tent, only to find his sprawling legions in a state of complete disarray as the desert floor erupted in blinding explosions of white fire, almost like we were standing on top of a giant minefield. And somebody just detonated it.

"Uriel," he snarled, surveying the carnage. "What have you done?"

"It's not him," I said, pointing at the massive dome structure in the near distance that was also riddled with explosions both inside and outside the translucent energy field. "Someone else is doing this."

"Someone else," he muttered, as his eyes flashed black and he scanned the chaos. Then his face went absolutely blank. "Someone who knew that every angel on the planet would be right here. Right now."

And as I stood there trying to figure out what the hell he was talking about, the back pocket of my fatigues began to vibrate, and I pulled out the sleek walkie talkie device that Tony had left for me at the Quartermaster. Turning it on, I immediately heard him scream, "Dean, get out! Get out now! She's gonna blow the pyramid! Get the fuck out…"

Then, almost like he knew exactly what was going to happen next, Gabriel turned to face the dome, just as an explosion ripped through the air like the loudest, most violent clap of thunder I'd ever heard.

Then there was a blinding flash of pure white light, followed by a searing blast of heat.

And then there was nothing.

Well, shit.

I think I might've just died again.

Goddammit.

31

IN THE REALM of possible outcomes resulting from my impromptu jaunt to the Egyptian desert with Mariel, being vaporized by an angel-killing nuclear blast was definitely not at the top of the list.

In fact, up until five short seconds ago, I was blissfully unaware that angel-killing nuclear blasts were even a thing. But as I stood there watching the whole tragic event replay in super slow motion like I was having a trippy out-of-body experience, it was really hard to deny.

Why exactly I was standing there watching the whole tragic event replay in super slow motion like I was having a trippy out-of-body experience was another mystery in and of itself.

At any rate, there I stood, watching myself. Or at least the version of myself from a few seconds ago that was standing next to Gabriel, trying to figure out what in the hell was happening. Then came the blinding flash. And although neither one of us realized it at the time, I could now see that the flash originated from somewhere in the center of Uriel's monumental barricade.

It was quickly followed by a raging pillar of white fire and black smoke that blasted through the very top of the impenetrable dome of arcane energy and morphed into a nightmarish mushroom cloud that literally filled the sky.

And last, but not least, came the wall of pissed-off, unnatural flame that raced through the desert like a rogue tidal wave vaporizing everything and everyone in its path.

Thinking that the slow-motion series of events was so much more terrifying than its real time counterpart, I shook my head in protest as the fiery apocalypse crept to within a few feet of turning me and Gabe into crispy critters.

So, imagine my surprise when someone tapped me on the shoulder, and a familiar voice said, "This is my favorite part, Danny. Check it out!"

Turning to find a leather pant-clad jackass standing there with a bottle of Coors Light and a shit-eating grin, I did a double take.

Then I did a triple take.

Then I slapped myself in the face a few times.

Then I muttered, "George?"

Pointing at the version of me that was about to get microwaved, he said, "Dude, look!"

Completely bewildered as to what the fuck was actually happening, I looked up just in time to see another version of him manifest behind the other version of me and place his hand on my shoulder. And right before the flame overtook us, we both vanished.

"Righteous!" he shouted, draining his beer as a full bottle appeared in his hand. "No need to thank me, Dan. Just doing my job. So..."

Still trying to process what the hell was happening, all I could muster was, "George?"

"You're totally welcome, by the way. Even though you don't need to thank me. But you can if you want. Or not. That's fine, too. Anyway, we should probably leave. Like now. Before we're both barbecued like all those poor angels." Then he held up the medallion that Enki gave him back in Aventine City. "This little baby can't slow down time forever, you know?"

And that's when it hit me like a ton of bricks. "Slow down time," I muttered. "Wait, so I'm not dead. And this is actually happening?"

"Hell yeah, it's happening! I just time jumped in and saved your ass, bro. Righteous, right?"

I grinned. "Yeah, that's really great, George." Then I ran toward Gabriel, who now was within literal inches of being consumed by the hissing flame. Grabbing his arm, I pulled him backwards when he turned his head and locked gazes with me. "Perhaps I misjudged you, Dean Robinson," he said, as the faintest hint of a smile formed on his chiseled face. "Do take better care of your people than I have of mine." Then he broke free of my grip, only to step into the wall of unnatural fire and turn to ash.

"Dude!" George shouted, as the heat pouring off the towering inferno was unbearable. "We seriously need to go, Danny! Now!"

Still trying to come to terms with what just happened, I turned and glared at the peculiar deity. "It's Dean!"

He shrugged. "What?"

"My name is Dean! Not Danny. Or Donny. Or Dennis. Or fucking Dirk. It's Dean, for fuck's sake!"

"OK, sure. Can we go now? Please? Dean?"

"Follow me," I grumbled, walking back into the tent to find the Stephen, Big A, Bobby, and Mariel still passed out on the ground. Pulling them all to within arm's reach of me, I joined their hands and nodded at George. "Now we can go."

"Destination?"

"The Quartermaster."

"Sweet. I've always wanted to play there." Then he placed his hand on my shoulder and rubbed the medallion a few times as the wall of flame inched its way into the tent.

And just like that, we were back in the QM.

More so than that, we were back in the QM to find everyone staring at the wall of tVs in stunned silence as they watched the apocalyptic explosion decimate everything within twenty square miles of the Great Pyramid. Erin, Billy, Rooster, Coop, MacCawill, Caveman, and Duncan all stood there like sullen statues.

"No, no, no," Rooster repeated over and over like he was trying to convince himself that it didn't happen. "Just no. No!"

"And Dean," Doc muttered, still blankly staring at the newscast. "You guys don't think he was—"

"Whisked from death's door by some time-hopping jackass in leather pants?" I said as the crew spun around to find me standing there with Five Finger George on my flank and our unconscious pals piled by my feet.

And to this day, I'm still not quite sure whether Erin punched me in the face before hugging me or vice versa, but it was a total Hallmark moment. Mostly, anyway.

"Wait," Rooster said, gawking at the enigmatic god of glam rock. "How did you know that—"

"Deano was in trouble?" George grinned. "Somebody prayed to me. Asked me to save him. You know, because I'm a god and stuff."

I chuckled despite the situation. "Are you serious?"

"Hell yeah, I'm serious, Don. Dean!"

"Who?" asked Doc. "Who prayed to you, George?"

He shrugged. "Dunno. Didn't get a name. But, even if I did, it's kinda protected by client-god confidentiality laws. You know the deal, Sharon." And when Doc offered nothing in response besides an icy glare, he said, "Erin. I meant Erin!"

Making the mental note to figure that out later, I looked up to find a portal spinning to life behind the bar, and out stepped a pissed-off Janser Berinhart with the lumbering frame of Mortog on her heels. "What's happening?" she barked, pointing at the newscasts flittering on the countless tV screens. "Is Gabriel responsible for this?"

"No," I muttered. "Gabriel's gone. As is Uriel, I presume."

"Gone, as in…"

"Dead."

"And their legions?"

"Same."

She grunted. "Then who? Who did this?"

"I did," replied a silvery voice with a brazen tone as all the tV's flashed with static before displaying the image of the enigmatic Mr. Blue Sky. Still wearing her denim skirt, she appeared to be sitting in what looked like a posh coffee shop enjoying a scone and a double shot of espresso.

"*You*," both Janser and Doc snarled in unison.

Running a hand through her dark, curly hair, the shadowy leader of the Academy triumphantly chomped on her pastry and grinned. "Me."

"That was a fucking massacre!" I shouted.

"Says the man who hunts and kills others in the name of a higher power who can't be bothered to mind his flock anymore. Get off your high horse, Mr. Robinson! You're not a soldier. You're an assassin. A murderer."

"You had no goddamn right to do what you did!"

She scoffed. "I had every right! Do you not think that *Gabriel* would have done the same to us, if given the opportunity? And besides, I didn't end those angels. They were ended by their lust for power. I simply had the foresight to plan appropriately."

"By rigging the Great Pyramid with a nuke?"

"Nuke," she jested. "You know a nuke wouldn't do the trick. Angels are terribly hard to kill. We had to be a bit more *creative*."

"Bitch!" Janser screamed. "You listen to me—"

"Hmm, no. You listen to me. All of you. As far as I'm concerned, the *Eden Accords* are now concluded. And it has been decided that the Earth is not your home. It's *my* home. And now you understand the consequence of assuming otherwise. So, in conclusion, I suggest you crawl back whence you came or face systematic extinction. Your call. Bye now."

As the tV screens faded to black, we all just kind of stood there in silence for a long moment and exchanged pissed-off glares.

"So, what now?" asked Doc after what felt like an eternity.

Janser turned to Mortog. "That sounds like our cue, big boy."

The giant nodded. "Time to go, queenie."

"What'll you do?" I asked.

She winked at me. "What we always do." And right before she stepped through the portal and disappeared, she said, "Survive."

And there was just something about the way she said it that made me think I'd not seen the last of Janser Berinhart.

Erin sighed. "We can't let Blue Sky get away with this."

"We won't, Doc," I muttered. "She'll answer for what she's done."

"Until then," Rooster said, "I suggest we all lie low." Then he glanced at the unconscious heap that was Stephen, Abernethy, Bobby, and Mariel before looking me square in the eye. "Today was truly horrible, but it could've been worse."

"A lot worse," Doc added, grabbing my hand.

I glanced at George. "I never thanked you."

He grinned. "That's OK, Deano. Just doing my job. You know, as a god and stuff. Righteous!"

"Hold on a sec," Coop said, hopping over the bar and slapping him on the shoulder. "Are you that Five Finger guitar god fella with the elevator girlfriend?"

And before George could chastise him for using the 'e' word, Coop, Caveman, MacCawill, and Ziggy started peppering him with questions about his seedy exploits with sentient machinery amidst other arcane absurdities. Chuckling at the repeated mention of pixie penises, Rooster and Billy quietly listened while shaking their heads.

Doc chuckled. "You think he'll stay?"

"George? I guess we can only hope."

"I still can't believe he saved you."

"Yeah, that," I muttered, plopping down on a stool as Duncan slid me a pint. "Good thing Enki gave him that medallion. And I'd still like to figure out who exactly *prayed* to him about me at some point. You sure it wasn't you?"

She pulled up a seat next to me. "Did I pray to the god of leather pants and bathroom sex? Oddly enough, that *really* didn't seem like a viable option."

Now it was my turn to chuckle. "You can't make this shit up, huh?"

"Nope, you can't. Hell of a couple of days, though."

"You ain't kidding."

"I might sleep for a week straight."

Draining the pint in a single, mighty gulp, I placed the empty glass on the bar. "Same."

"But first, I'm going to take a very, very, *very* long shower."

"That sounds pretty amazing."

Saying nothing, she then hopped off the stool and kissed me on the forehead before heading toward the back of the QM's massive hall where our rooms were located. And as I sat there watching her walk, she stopped mid-stride and looked back. "So?"

I shrugged. "So?"

"Are you coming?"

"Coming? Wait, do you mean—"

She grinned a wolfish grin. "Very, very, *very* long shower."

And it was right about then I realized that my semi-cursed pseudo afterlife was about to get exponentially better.

So, I had that going for me.

Which was nice.

Really, really, *really* nice.

32

A few weeks later...

The bar was an absolute shithole.

But it was my favorite shithole.

Or it least it used to be.

A lifetime ago, of sorts.

"How you doing over there, young man?" Asked the aging bartender as he meticulously arranged the various and assorted bottles of booze stacked on the wall behind the cash register.

His name was Milt. He was an old soldier from a bygone era. And this was his bar.

Whether or not it had an actual name, I was never really sure. Everybody just called it Milt's Place and left it at that.

Situated between a pawn shop and a tattoo parlor on the outskirts of Fort Campbell, Kentucky, home of the U.S. Army's mighty 101st Airborne Division, it wasn't much to look at. The floor was bare concrete, and the walls hadn't been painted since the Reagan administration. Instead, they were aptly covered from top to bottom with American flags, military paraphernalia, and pictures of deployed soldiers ranging from World War I to the present day. And aside from the dilapidated pool table in the back, there wasn't much else to the place besides the bar itself and a few tables. Oh, and it reeked of cigarettes and stale beer.

So, like I said, it was a shithole.

But it was a soldier's bar.

And that was always good enough for me.

Clearing my throat, I held up my empty shot glass. "I think somebody must've knocked this over when I wasn't looking."

Shaking his head, Milt shuffled toward me with a bottle of bourbon in hand and a lit cigarette hanging out of his mouth. With a crooked smile, he peered at me over the rim of his reading glasses. "I'd really like to know who that son of a bitch is that keeps knocking your drinks over."

"Me too. It's really starting to piss me off."

He grinned. "You do realize you're the only one here, right?"

"Hmm, good point. Maybe the glass has a hole in it then."

"Maybe so. Maybe I'll just leave the bottle here and save myself a couple trips. You know, in case of anymore *leaks.*"

I grinned back. "That sounds like a plan, Milt. Thank you kindly."

Just about to walk away, he stopped and peered at me again. "This might sound crazy, but you're the goddamn spitting image of a fella that used to come in all the time."

"Yeah, good looking bastard?"

He chuckled. "Not sure about all that, but he was a tough son of a bitch. Went by the name of Dean. Dean Robinson. He was a Ranger. He and his boys were part of some unit that nobody ever talked about."

"Never heard of him."

"Well, it was a long time ago. He'd probably be pushing fifty nowadays." Then he shuffled to the cash register and plucked a picture off the wall. "Yup, that's him right there." Sliding the picture across the bar, he added, "This was taken after a boxing match on base. They say he was quite the fighter."

Looking at the picture of myself from sixteen years ago, I couldn't help but chuckle. "I don't see the resemblance."

"You kidding me?"

"Maybe a little bit."

"Trust me, kid, you look just like him. It's uncanny. Anyway, I need to step out back. You all set for the moment?"

I nodded. "Thanks, Milt. I'm perfect."

Handing me a remote control, he pointed at an old ass TV haphazardly tacked to the wall. "Feel free to turn it on." Then he took a drag from his smoke and disappeared through a door behind the bar.

Pouring myself another shot of bourbon, I fumbled around with the remote for a second or two until the TV came to life. Flipping the channels until I landed on a newscast, I drained the shot and poured myself another.

"More *questions* than *answers*," the female reporter said in an overly dramatic tone. Wearing a red power suit and a black shirt that was unbuttoned enough to show substantial cleavage, she had an unusually deep voice for a woman. "Good afternoon and welcome to the *Buzz Source*. I'm Kitty Collingsworth in for Buzz Shea. We send our thoughts and prayers as he recovers from his unfortunate *methamphetamine*-induced stroke. Poor, poor Buzz."

I chuckled. "Yeah, *poor* Buzz... asshole."

"Well," the newscaster continued, "it's now been several weeks since the infamous *space pyramid* incident, and we're still searching for answers. While the White House has confirmed that an unclassified nuclear weapon was indeed discharged in Egypt's Giza Plateau, destroying all of the known enigmatic pyramidal structures, scientists are still baffled as to how the blast resulted in zero nuclear fallout. That small inconsistency coupled with the fact that no civilians were injured or killed during the horrific incident are leading many to believe it was a legitimate *miracle*. Or better yet, a sign from God himself."

"Good grief," I muttered, slamming the shot and pouring myself another. "Miracle my ass."

"In other news, although the unexplained wave of seismic and volcanic activity of late has ceased, the massive clean-up efforts continue around the globe. And closer to home, significant efforts are underway to somehow '*re-annex*' Washington State as it's still floating off the Idaho coast." She chuckled. "Sorry, I really can't get used to saying '*Idaho coast.*' Oh well, I guess that's a sign of these unusual and *unprecedented* times we live in. Giants, space pyramids, and unnatural disasters! What's next? I'm not sure I want to know. Do you?"

Chuckling under my breath, I turned the TV off and shook my head when the front door swung open and in stepped Tony Coates. Wearing black fatigue pants and a black polo shirt that showed off his bulging biceps, he sat down next to me and was about to grab my shot glass when I slapped his hand. "Don't you fucking think about it, Big Sarge."

He grinned as he ran his fingers through his bushy, grey beard. "Just checking your reflexes, old man."

"Old man," I scoffed, reaching over the bar and grabbing another shot glass. Promptly filling it with bourbon, I slid it in front of him. "You're the one in need of a prostate exam."

"Maybe so, but at least I'm not a friggin zombie."

"Being *undead* doesn't make me a friggin zombie."

"Then what does it make you?"

I shrugged. "Special."

"You've always been *special.*"

"I'm about to put a *special* boot in your ass."

Chuckling, he grabbed his shot and held it high. "Here's to your zombie ass trying."

Following suit, I said, "And your old ass crying."

A drink or two later, as we continued to trade barbs and share a few laughs at each other's expense, I muttered, "So, I got your message. What's going on with your *employer*?"

He groaned. "Nothing good."

"Meaning?"

"Meaning that the Academy is about to declare open season on anything of the non-human persuasion. That stunt at the Great Pyramid was apparently the tip of the iceberg."

"Awesome."

"Yeah."

"How in the hell did Blue Sky manage that, anyway?"

"You mean vaporizing tens of thousands of angels and their indestructible lodestones alike without turning northern Africa and the Middle East into a post-apocalyptic fallout zone in the process?"

"Yeah, that."

"Well, that's the thing. She had help."

"Help, from who?"

Reaching into his pocket, he pulled out a picture and laid it on the bar. "Does the name Enlil mean anything to you?"

Studying the image for a second or two, I felt a pit form in the bottom of my stomach at the sight of the eight-foot, hulking über warrior with an elongated head. Holding an oversized spear, he was perched atop a pale horse roughly the size of an elephant.

"Enlil is Enki's brother," I muttered. "They're fighting some kind of civil war on Nibiru."

"Well, seems that Blue Sky made a deal with the enemy of her enemy. And now they're friends."

"Christ. So, you're saying that was Anunnaki tech that wiped out Gabriel and Uriel?"

He nodded. "And there's apparently a lot more of it on the way."

I groaned. "That's fucking perfect. We save the world only to have it turn into an Anunnaki war zone."

"Somebody say war?" asked Doc Kelly as she strolled through the door at that very moment. Standing behind us, she placed her hands on our shoulders and intently gazed at the picture on the bar for a long second or two. "Well, hello, Mr. Horseman. We've been waiting for your sorry ass."

And there was just something about the way she said it that made me think things were about to get interesting.

Typical.

~

The story continues in *Ride of the Horseman*. Read on for a sneak peek!

RIDE OF THE HORSEMAN
PROLOGUE

Everything changes.

Good, bad, or otherwise.

And much like death and taxes, change is one of the few guarantees in this crazy little thing called life. Or undead, pseudo-divine afterlife if you happen to find yourself in my particular situation.

At any rate, some folks embrace change. Others fear it. And yet others cling to the notion that change for the sake of change is nothing but a fool's errand.

Is it, though?

And who decides what's change for the sake of change, anyway?

Is there some random jackass out there who's the ultimate authority on this kind of stuff?

If so, they must not remember the eighties. I mean, hell, imagine if nothing changed since 1983, and we were all still running around with eighties hair and parachute pants listening to the goddamn Eurythmics. That's a terrible thought.

And just try to imagine a world with no internet.

Or binge-worthy TV shows.

Or online video clips about vengeful housecats and talking ferrets dressed like Elvis.

What would we do?

What would we watch?

What would we possibly have to talk about?

To that point, I dare say those kinds of changes for the sake of change were pretty damn necessary. Especially the Elvis ferrets. They're the best. You should really check them out.

Conversely, now imagine a world with celestial über beings floating about our friendly skies like brazen overlords and unnatural giants running up and down Main Street chugging beers. I'm guessing that's a change most folks could probably do without. But it's one that was coming anyway.

For the wheels of progress had already begun to turn, and despite the dissolution of the short-lived Eden Accords, there was no stopping the will of God. Man, angel, and nephilim alike would learn to coexist on the Earth. It was just a matter of time. And there was no amount of bloodshed or warmongering that would change it.

At least that's what we thought.

But we were wrong.

Perhaps even dead wrong.

In life, I was a soldier. An elite product of the U.S. military. Upon death, I became something else. No longer human but not quite an angel, I was conceived of mankind but no longer part of it. Something blessed and cursed with the power of God's wrath. A warrior of the light that existed in the shadows.

My name is Dean Robinson.

I am—to maintain the Balance.

For the time being, anyway.

RIDE OF THE HORSEMAN
CHAPTER 1

TRYING my absolute damnedest to keep pace with Doc Kelly, I burst out of the dark alley at unnatural speed and ran straight into some random dude wearing a cheap Santa suit. With a look of pure terror plastered on his face, the poor bastard careened backward, screaming bloody murder right up until he tripped over a plastic reindeer and faceplanted on the sidewalk. After that, he was pretty quiet.

Apparently, the blunt force of the blow knocked the wind out of him.

And I might've accidentally kneed him in the balls.

At least once.

Maybe twice.

Definitely not more than three or four times.

Jumping to my feet with an awkward smile on my face, the surrounding crowd of passersby collectively gasped as I helped the faux Saint Nick to his feet and muttered, "Sorry, pal. Merry Christmas?"

After he responded with nothing but a spirited hand gesture and a few choice expletives, the crowd gasped again at his Grinch-worthy behavior.

"Quit dicking around with the locals!" Doc's voice boomed from the Roostertech-infused communication device buried in my right ear. "We're losing him."

Looking up, I barely caught a glimpse of her petite frame sprinting through the late-night traffic before she ducked into the alley across the street. "Maybe if you slowed down a little bit—"

"Maybe if you kept up a little bit, we'd be done with this already!"

Making the mental note that fake Santa wasn't the only one acting a little Grinchy tonight, I bit my tongue and dashed across the street. Pulling up on Erin's flank, she motioned for me to stop as she peered into the darkness of the alley ahead of us. "What is it?" I whispered.

"He's here," she whispered back.

Squinting into the looming night, I struggled to see anything besides a few dumpsters lining the walls of the adjacent brick buildings. "You sure?"

"Yup. You smell that?"

I sniffed the air, and my nostrils were immediately assaulted by the familiar stench you'd expect to find in a downtown alleyway. "Piss?"

She groaned. "Cologne."

I sniffed again. "Not cologne. Unless it smells like piss and garbage with a lingering hint of ass."

Before she could say anything else on the matter, a hulking silhouette stood up from behind one of the dumpsters, and a deep, guttural voice shouted, "It's sandalwood body spray, douchebag!" And then the big bastard picked up the dumpster like it was made of cardboard and threw it at us before bounding into the darkness and out of sight. Typical.

Leaping out of the way of the three-ton metal box soaring towards us, Doc shook her head and glared at me.

I shrugged. "What?"

"We're here to help these people, Dean. Do you think maybe you could take it down a notch or two?"

"Wait, are you insinuating this is my fault?"

"No. I'm asking you to be more—"

"You think it's my fault they always run, don't you?"

She sighed. "How long have we been doing this for?"

"I don't know. A couple of months."

"Seven months."

"OK, and?"

"And every time you talk to them, they run."

"That's not true."

"It's totally true. You know it is. You frighten them. Like back at the docks, for example."

"No, no, no. I had that the situation completely under control."

"Did you?"

"Absolutely."

"Then why are we still chasing this guy through downtown Pensacola?"

"Because he decided to run."

"And you don't think you had anything to do with that?"

"Are you serious? I simply asked the big dope to come with us for his own safety."

"That's not what happened, Dean."

"That's exactly what happened, Doc."

"You pointed a shotgun at his balls and said, 'Come with me if you want to live' in your ridiculous Arnold Schwarzenegger accent."

I grinned. "Too much?"

She groaned for a second time as a chirp of static buzzed from our earpieces. "Ah, guys," came Charlie's cheerful voice after an awkward pause. "Don't mean to interrupt whatever it is you're doing right now, but Billy and I tracked the target to a warehouse a couple blocks north."

Doc tapped her earpiece. "Thanks, Charlie. At least somebody's on their game tonight. Lead the way."

"Follow the alley to the next intersection and take a hard left," he said, as the unmistakable sound of massive wings flapping through the night sky could be heard above the rooftops. I looked up just in time to see the muted silhouette of our resident she-dragon glide past.

Exchanging determined glances with Doc, we instinctively moved through the dank darkness until reaching a dimly lit street devoid of people. Hooking a left and staying to the shadows of the sidewalk, I caught another glimpse of Billy's massive frame as she and Charlie touched down on top of a sizable warehouse-like building a block or so in front of us. And within a second or two, she simply vanished. "How does she do that?" I asked.

Erin shrugged. "Do what?"

"Make herself invisible."

"She's a literal dragon. Her body's covered in indestructible scales. She can fly. And she breathes fire."

"Yeah, but—"

"Is the invisibility thing really that much more impressive?"

"Not when you say it like that," I muttered, as we broke into a cautious trot and closed the distance between the warehouse and us.

"Besides, she can only do it for short spurts."

"Well, that settles it. Consider me unimpressed."

Rolling her eyes, we pulled up to a loading dock with the words 'Bronze Cow Brewing' stenciled on the adjacent brick wall in bold, white lettering.

"He went in there," Charlie said, looking down at us from the rooftop. "Through the sliding doors."

Giving one of the massive metal doors a cautious tug only to find it unmovable, I shook my head. "Locked." Then I willed the gauntlets into being and instantly felt the otherworldly metal form over my hands and forearms. Curling my right hand into a tight fist, I was about to smash my way through the twelve-foot door when Erin said, "What are you doing?"

I grinned. "Unlocking the door."

"With your fists?"

"Yup."

"That'll just make him run again. And what if the rest of them are in there? Then we'll have four anakim on the loose in the city."

"And we're running out of time," Charlie added. "The Academy agents should be here anytime now according to the intel we got from Tony. We gotta get these folks out of here, guys."

I nodded. "OK, so what's the plan?"

"Well," Doc said, looking at the stenciled letters on the wall and pointing out the cleverly embedded glyphs. "It seems our large friends are hiding in the back of a nepher bar. So, why don't you go in the front and order a beer?"

"Not that I'm complaining, but how's me drinking a beer right now going to help matters?"

"Because hopefully seeing you inside will cause the anakim to sneak out the back where me and Charlie can reason with them."

"And if not?"

"Like I said, it's a nepher bar.

"So?"

"So, give the bartender one of Janser's coins. Tell them you're there to help."

"You think they'll believe me?"

She smirked. "Not a chance. And when they don't—"

"And when they don't," I grumbled, "the anakim will try and sneak out the back where you and Charlie can reason with them. Yeah, got it."

Vaulting off the roof of the three-story building like a supersized ninja, Charlie's eight-foot, flabby frame landed on the sidewalk next to us with uncanny agility. Wearing a bright blue Grateful Dead hoodie and matching sweat pants, our mutton chop-clad mini-giant had his shaggy blonde hair tied up in a man bun as he took post next to Doc. "Let's do this, guys," he said, tapping his regular-sized watch that looked absolutely ridiculous on his mammoth wrist. "Clock's ticking."

Nodding acknowledgement, I made my way to the side of the building and followed the alley until it dumped me out onto Palafox Street in the heart of Pensacola's historic downtown district. Bustling with holiday patrons drifting in and out of the various bars and restaurants, the entire street was lit up like a winter wonder-land. Endless strands of Christmas lights were draped over the trees, and oversized wreaths hung from every storefront. And even though it was mid-December and nearing midnight, everybody was wearing shorts and tee shirts as the temperature was a balmy seventy-eight degrees.

Making the mental note that I really wanted to live in a place where shorts and tee-shirts were standard winter attire at some point in my peculiar undead afterlife, I navigated the late-night crowd and stepped through the front door of the Bronze Cow Brew Pub. And damn, it was pretty sweet.

In keeping with the industrial warehouse façade, the rustic yet chic interior of the craft brewery was the perfect combination of function, comfort, and eclectic style. A massive wooden bar stretched the entire length of the warehouse floor, and enormous vats and fermentation tanks lined the walls on all sides. Scattered throughout the floor space were tables, couches, bean bags, and various games of all sizes and nature. The low drone of jazzy Christmas carols pumped through the speakers mounted high above in the exposed ceiling rafters as an impressive crowd of people sipped on pints of tasty craft beer under the soft glow of orange light.

Making my way toward an empty stool at the otherwise packed bar, I took notice of the sizable brick wall at the back of the building that separated the brew floor from where I imagined our friendly anakim pack was hiding out. Squeezing between a couple of heavily tattooed hipsters in skinny jeans and ugly Christmas sweaters, I sat at the bar and made eye contact with the bartender. She was young.

Or at least I thought so. To be fair, it was kind of hard to tell as she had a shaved head, no eyebrows, and piercings all over her face.

"Hey there," she said, in an amiable yet slightly condescending tone. "First time at the Cow, huh?"

I smiled. "What makes you say that?"

Glancing at my grizzled appearance and black Petulant Pig tee-shirt bearing the signature cartoon pig chugging a beer and catch-phrase 'Don't Cock-a-doodle, Bragh. Swig some Pig!' she reluctantly smiled back. "Just a guess."

Not sure whether to be offended or not, I turned my attention to the beer menu artfully scribbled on the wall behind the bar in various colors of chalk. "So, what's good here?"

"It's all good. What do you like?"

"How about an IPA?"

"We've got two IPAs on tap."

"What's the difference?"

"Well, the first one's a Session IPA that's been aged in a bourbon barrel with Jalapeño peppers and artichoke hearts for six months."

Not quite sure what to say to that, I simply grinned for an awkward second or two as I tried to figure out why somebody would do such a thing to beer. "And the other one?"

"The other one is my absolute faves. It's a Belgian IPA made with six distinct hop varieties." And just as I thought that sounded promising, she added, "But the best part is that it's brewed with beet juice instead of water."

"I'm sorry. Did you say beet juice? Like from beets?"

"Yeah, it's so good. The mouthfeel alone is—"

"I'll just have a water, please."

Muttering something to the effect of "douchebag," under her breath, she feigned a smile and scampered off to fetch my drink as static chirped from my earpiece. "Are you OK?" asked Doc.

After nonchalantly tapping my ear, I muttered, "Yeah, I'm fine. Why?"

"Because you just walked into a bar and ordered water. I feel like

303

we're going to be struck by lightning. Or it's about to start raining frogs. Or—"

"These people are monsters. What they do to beer is —unnatural."

She chuckled. "Still no movement out back. You see anything suspicious inside?"

And before I had the opportunity to answer, the bartender was back. Sliding a glass of water in front of me, she said, "Ten bucks."

"Ten bucks?" I scoffed. "For a friggin glass of water?"

She shrugged. "It's artesian."

"Meaning?"

"Meaning it costs ten bucks."

Digging around the pockets of my jeans for a couple seconds, I pulled out a ten-dollar bill and handed it to her. Then I carefully placed a crudely cut bronze coin on the bar. Old and tarnished, it was emblazoned with a series of overlapping Enochian glyphs arranged within the bold outline of a bear claw. And it immediately got the bartender's attention.

"Where did you get that?" she asked. Her tone was cold.

"From a friend."

"Friend, huh?" Her eyes flashed yellow, and I caught a faint glimpse of her aura. An aura that clearly wasn't human. "You do realize that coin bears the seal of—"

"Janser Berinhart. Queen of the Others. Yeah, I know."

She laughed. "Are you trying to tell me that you know Janser Berinhart? Bullshit."

"I do know her. Furry tits and all. And we're working together—"

"I don't believe you."

"Look, lady, believe what you want, but I know you're hiding some anakim in the back and—"

"You don't know shit, human."

"I know they're in trouble. And I can help them."

She backpedaled a step or two. "You're lying."

"Go ask my friends if you don't believe me. They're skulking about the loading docks in the back of your esteemed brewery."

"And who are they, exactly?"

"Well, there's a mini-giant named Charlie. He looks like fat Elvis but taller. And blonde. He's with a pint-sized badass named Erin. She's a doctor. And sort of my girlfriend. It's complicated. Oh, and her partner's on the roof. Her name's Billy. She's a dragon, so…"

"A dragon? Now you're just being a dick."

"I'm being serious."

Sizing me up for an awkward moment or two, she said, "I didn't get your name."

"It's Dean. Dean Robinson."

"I know that name," she muttered, as her yellow eyes danced with thought and she connected a series of dots. "You're with the Guild. You're a goddamn Deacon."

It was right about then when things got interesting.

And by interesting, I mean that the music came to a screeching halt, and everybody in the joint turned and glared at me with bad intentions.

Then, right on cue, four anakim of varying size between six and fifteen feet tall smashed their way through the brick wall in the back of the brewpub like it was made of paper. As the unsuspecting patrons scattered and ducked for cover amidst the chaos, the peculiar family of giants bound through the bar in a blur of motion before smashing their way through the front door and onto Palafox Street.

Making the mental note that the plan had now officially gone to shit, I shook my head and took a big gulp from my glass of hifalutin water. And wouldn't you know that it tasted like absolute shit.

Maybe I should've got that beet beer after all.

Typical.

RIDE OF THE HORSEMAN
CHAPTER 2

"WHAT THE HELL's happening in there?" Doc's voice barked from my earpiece.

Taking another labored gulp from my overpriced water, I placed the glass on the bar and rose to my feet amidst the calamity. "Things didn't quite go to plan."

"Meaning?"

"Meaning that our large friends just smashed their way through the front door instead of skulking out the back."

"Wait, what? Where are they now?"

Making my way to the gaping hole in the wall where the door used to be, I stepped out onto Palafox Street to find a frenetic gaggle of screaming people running around like their hair was on fire. "I'd say they're bar hopping their way through downtown Pensacola by the look of things."

"Goddammit! Which direction?"

"Southeast," I muttered, studying the trail of mangled cars and otherwise chaos. "Toward that park. The one by the bay we passed earlier tonight."

"OK, new plan. Get to the park. Hopefully, we can cut them off there. Let's move!"

Before I had the opportunity to reply, I felt as much as heard the swooshing sound of massive wings and looked up just as Billy launch from the rooftop with Erin and Charlie on her back. And right before her cloaking ability kicked in and she vanished from sight, the entire downtown block seemed to collectively piss themselves.

"Um," the bartender muttered as I turned to find her standing next to me. Still holding my ten dollars, she despondently gawked into the night sky while shaking her head. "Was that an actual—"

"Yeah," I grumbled. "Just like I told ya." And then I willed the cloak into being.

Its otherworldly power coursed through my body as it manifested in a spectral flash of white luminescence and billowed about my shoulders. Feeling the mental switch flip to the on position, I slowly pulled in a long, deliberate breath.

Cleared my mind.

Focused my thoughts.

Found the Balance — the perfect balance between wrath and clarity.

As the unfathomable power welled up in the deep recess of my soul, and the expected sensation of calmative awareness washed over me, I nodded at my awestruck bartender buddy. "Beer made from beets... You should be ashamed of yourself." Then I plucked my ten bucks from her hand and hauled ass across the street in pursuit of our supersized quarry.

With my adrenaline pumping on über overdrive and police sirens wailing away in the near distance, I sprinted down Palafox Street at unnatural speed. Weaving in and out of the amped-up crowd while doing my very best not to take out another Santa in the process, I hooked a hard right on Main and caught another glimpse of Billy a block or two in front of me. She was closing in on a dense patch of oak trees bordering Pensacola Bay which I knew from earlier in our misguided mission to be the William Bartram Memorial Park.

Reaching the quaint woodland just as Billy touched down and uncloaked herself, I joined Doc and Charlie. They had already slid down her mighty neck and were cautiously peering into the darkness, looking for any sign of the wayward anakim.

"It's OK, guys," Charlie called out, trying his best to sound endearing. "You can come out. My name's Charlie. And these are my friends. We're here to help—"

"Don't need help!" a deep, guttural voice bellowed from somewhere in the shadows of the trees. It was the same voice we'd heard in the alley. "Leave us. Now!"

"Can't do that," Doc said. "You and your family are in danger. The Academy knows you're here, and they're coming."

"You lie!"

"It's the truth," Charlie said. "Mortog and Janser Berinhart sent us."

The anakim groaned. "Wait, you know Mortog?"

"Of course. Nice guy."

"Mortog's a dickhead."

"OK, sure. He's a little rough around the edges, but he's looking out for you guys. Asked us to bring you to the Lowlands."

"The Lowlands? That place is a shithole."

"Yeah, it kind of is. But it's a safe shithole, right? And you don't have to stay there long. Just until the coast is clear."

"Not interested. We stay here!"

And as I stood there listening to perhaps the strangest negotiation that I'd ever been witness to, the faint whir of approaching helicopters echoed through the night sky like an ominous countdown timer.

I cleared my throat and took a couple steps toward the trees. "You hear that, big man? Those are CH-47 helicopters. At least three of them by the sound of it. And you know what they're bringing with them, right?"

He laughed a deep, booming laugh that made every hair on the back of my neck stand up. "Robot men don't scare us."

"They should. Because they won't stop coming until you're dead."

"What do you care? You're a Deacon! You hunt anakim like animals."

"No. I don't. Not anymore."

"Bullshit! You lie!"

Charlie pulled up next to me and put one of his meaty arms over my shoulder. "Dean here is my friend. And although he may look like an epic doucheball, he's telling the truth."

The anakim grunted. "You trust the Deacon?"

Charlie nodded. "Of course, I do. He saved my life."

"Wait, you serious?"

"Totally. And for his troubles, he got swallowed by a korrigan death bog in Nod."

"Whoa, for real?"

"Yup. And after he stopped peeing himself, he got captured by korrgians who were going to stick a can of beer in his ass and slow roast him over a bonfire."

He chuckled. "Never understood why korrigans are always shoving things in people's asses. It ain't right."

"It's really not! Anywho, my point is that my friends are good people, and we're here to help you. Please believe me."

As I stood there shaking my head, the snarky fifteen-foot bastard we'd been chasing around town for the past hour stepped out from the shadows and into view. Clad in a ridiculous outfit that looked like several burlap sacks were stitched together to create some makeshift clothing, he glared at us with his soulless black eyes. And slowly but surely, three smaller framed giants wearing similar sullied outfits took post on his flanks like lost puppies.

"I am Tarvos," the big bastard muttered. "Don't make me regret trusting you."

"We won't," Doc said, as her face curled into a warm smile and her brown eyes seemed to glow in the twilight. "Now, let's get the hell out of here, shall we?"

With the whirring getting louder by the literal second, I looked up to see several clusters of blinking lights and the silhouettes of Chinook helicopters a couple miles to the east. And, of course, dangling below them in the darkness were the twenty-foot, mechanized warriors we'd come to know as the Praetorian battle bots.

"I'll slow them down," Billy growled in her creepy dragon voice that made her Nordic accent sound that much goofier as she launched herself into the air with a mighty thrust of her wings. "Meet you guys back at the Quartermaster." And then she vanished into the night sky.

Making the mental note that those helicopter pilots were about to have a bad night, I tapped my earpiece. "Roy, you copy?"

"I'm here, mancho," the voice of Roy MacCawill answered. "You folks ready to get the hell out of Dodge?"

"Yes, please. And make it snappy. We're about to get some company of the big and metal variety."

"Roger that. Sending in the ass hat." Then, after a hiss of static where I swear I heard him chuckle, he muttered, "I mean asset. Sending in the asset."

And right on cue, a puff of purple smoke erupted from the center of the park and out stepped Five Finger George, our resident guitar god and interdimensional traveler. Fit with a wiry frame and wearing black leather pants, snakeskin boots, and a leopard print tee-shirt that was crudely cut into a tank top, he was glam rock incarnate. With his uncanny Paul Reed Smith electric guitar slung on his back, he ran a hand through his audacious faux hawk as he took off his mirrored aviator sunglasses and smiled at us. "Hey there, rockstars. Somebody call for a miracle?"

"We called for a ride, George," I grumbled. "Just like every other time."

"And a miracle?"

"No miracle."

"I'd like a miracle," Tarvos said, raising a mammoth hand.

George grinned. "Hell yeah! Can I interest you in some righteous rockstar skills, big fella?"

"How about some actual clothes? And some food for my boys?"

"Yeah, sorry. I don't do that kind of stuff. My miracles are kinda restricted to righteous rockstar skills." And when Tarvos replied with nothing but a couple grunts and a befuddled glare, George said, "Whoa, are you wearing sandalwood body spray? Smells fabulous!"

"On that note," Erin said, as the helicopters were now a mile out and making a determined beeline for us, "Everybody join hands. We need to leave. Now." As everyone followed suit, Erin turned to George. "We've got a train to catch."

"To the Depot then?" he asked.

She nodded. "To the Depot."

Nodding back, Five Finger reached into the pocket of his acid-washed jean jacket and pulled out his infamous Anunnaki-tech powered medallion before rubbing it a few times. And just like that, we were no longer standing in the park on the edge of downtown Pensacola, Florida.

We were standing in a long-abandoned subway tunnel underneath some undisclosed city that I assumed was somewhere in the continental United States. And although I'd been here several times over the past few months, I had no idea where it actually was. Nor would anybody tell me.

Lit only by a series of oil lamps haphazardly hanging from the graffiti-laden concrete arches looming above, the air was thick and stale and reeked of death. Any trace of subway tile lining the pitted walls had long been erased, and unlike where we just came from, it was cold. Unnaturally cold. As we all stood on the platform in silence for a long moment or two, the telltale clacking sound of an approaching train rang out from somewhere in the darkness of the tracks. Before I knew what the hell was happening, a dilapidated subway car pulled to a screeching halt right in front of us.

"Shit sticks!" Charlie shouted, jumping backward several feet and dodging the shower of sparks spraying through the air.

"Quit being such a pussy," jested a brawny, broad-shouldered woman with a thick mane of raven hair and stunning yellow eyes as she stepped out of the passenger car like she owned the joint. Wearing skintight pants made of tanned leather and an ornate animal skin vest that barely held her bulging breasts at bay, Janser Berinhart slapped Charlie on the shoulder. "You should be used to the ghost trains by now, baby man."

He grimaced. "Well, I'm not! They come out of nowhere. Every time!"

Grinning, she turned her attention to Tarvos and his litter of junior giants. "Welcome, welcome, my friends." Her voice was deep and rich and could easily be mistaken for that of man if not for its playful singsong nature that was clearly feminine. Albeit alpha feminine. "We are pleased by your company."

Tarvos nodded. His eyes, black like pools of oil, were fixated on Janser and the grotesque series of deep scars that ran clear across her chiseled face in the shape of harrowing claw marks. "Never thought I'd see the day when the Queen of the Others was working with the Guild."

"You haven't, big boy," she quipped. "The Guild is working with me. And don't let anyone tell you otherwise."

Getting a real kick out of that, his massive chest heaved up and down as he laughed. "Fair enough. And I hear Mortog's around here somewhere?"

"He's in the Lowlands with everyone else." Then she stepped aside and motioned for them to enter the subway car. "Charlie will show you the way. Oh, and best to hold onto something. The ride's a little rough." As the reluctant anakim and our resident mini-giant crammed inside, Janser shut the sliding door and tapped on it three times. Then she took a step or two backward as the infamous ghost train roared to life and rocketed down the tracks at breakneck speed before vanishing into the darkness of the tunnels.

"So," she said, turning to Doc. "Fun times in Pensacola, huh? Where's Billy?"

"She stayed behind to buy us a little time. The Academy helicopters were right on top of us when we left."

"Close call?"

"Yup. It shouldn't have been, though. Helping folks would be so much easier if they didn't try to run away from us every—single—time we showed up. Isn't that right, Dean?"

Figuring that was more of a rhetorical question, I just kind of shrugged and halfheartedly nodded.

Janser laughed. "Don't tell me he did the 'Come with me if you want to live' thing again?"

Doc groaned. "What do you think?"

"I think you should leave him at home next time."

"I think I just might."

"That's hurtful," I grumbled as George snickered.

"Speaking of home," Doc said. "We should be getting back to the Quartermaster. I need a stiff drink. And a hot shower."

"What an uncanny coincidence," Janser said with a seductive wink.

"What is?"

"I happen to have both of those things in my quarters. How about you accompany me back to the Lowlands, and we crack open a bottle of—"

"Hey!" I protested. "Knock it off."

"Knock what off?"

"Whatever it is you're doing."

"What's the matter, Dean Robinson? Jealous?"

"Of you? No."

She grinned. "You gotta realize that Erin's way out of your league, right?"

I grinned back. "You gotta realize you're a royal pain my balls, right?"

"Oh, don't get your panties in a wad, baby blue. I'm just kidding." And then she slapped my ass so hard it made me jump. "Besides, it's only a matter of time before she realizes I'm twice the man you are, anyway." Then she exchanged fist bumps with Doc as they both shared a hearty chuckle at my expense. Typical.

"Time to go," I muttered, turning to George. "You mind zapping us back to the QM?"

Before Five Finger could answer, Janser said, "Not so fast, Dean Robinson. Abernethy needs a word."

"Tell him I'll call him. We'll do lunch or something."

"Tell him yourself when we get to the Lowlands."

"No. No way. Not a chance. Just—no."

She shrugged. "What?"

"You know what. There's no way in hell I'm getting on one of those ghost trains again. They're friggin death traps. And besides, Doc and I have dinner plans—"

"See you later, Dean," Erin said as I looked up to find her and George waving at me. Without another word, they then vanished in a puff of purple smoke with a pair of grins on their faces.

So, there I was stranded in the apocalyptic train depot with no way out and an obnoxious Janser Berinhart smirking at me. Just as I was about to let loose with a series of heartfelt expletives, another ghost train pulled up to the platform in a torrent of hissing sparks and cacophonous rattles.

Awesome.

Sometimes I really hate my job.

ENJOYING RIDE OF THE HORSEMAN? Visit our website to get your copy now!

More From Steve Gilmore

Heaven's Dark Soldiers

Rise of the Giants

Wrath of the Fallen

Rage of the Heavens

Dawn of the After Days

Ride of the Horseman (Coming Soon)

Sign up for Steve's newsletter for updates on deals and new releases!

https://liquidmind.media/steve-gilmore-newsletter-sign-up-1

About the Author

A West Point graduate and former Army Ranger, Steve Gilmore hails from rural New England (the town of Acushnet, MA) and subsequently spent the good majority of his adult life in the southern US resulting from his time in the Army and ensuing misadventures in civilian life. After returning to Massachusetts for a spell, he again retreated to warmer climates and now resides in northern Florida with his beautiful wife, two amazing kiddos, and a yapping pair of slothful canines.

Visit **www.stevegilmore.net** for more information.